DARWIN'S TEARS

DARWIN'S TEARS

A Novel by

Michael Braverman

This is for Toots --
for her saintly patience
and infinite understanding.

1

Buddy Lee Garbrecht was on his way to get laid. As he moved down the dimly lit corridor, there was no haste to his gait, no adolescent smirk on his face or even a hint of boyish bounce to his step. This was his perk every Tuesday after lockdown, after Waldheim left for the night. Buddy Lee's arrangement with Bruno Waldheim, his supervisor, was mutually beneficial. On Tuesday nights, Waldheim would skip out on both his job and his wife to spend the night with his girlfriend up in Cochrane and Buddy Lee would clock him out in the morning. In exchange, Waldheim would approve dozens of phantom overtime hours every month for his young protégé.

For Buddy Lee, this Tuesday was no different. This was his day of the week. This was his time of the night. This was his kingdom, his domain, and they, all the so-called clients locked behind their steel reinforced windowless doors, all of them, man, woman and child alike, were his obedient and compliant subjects.

The thick clutch of keys clipped to his belt jingled like sleigh bells in rhythm with each step Buddy Lee Garbrecht took. His shiny black boots, with the Cat's Paw steel taps, picked up the rhythm as he strode across the yellowed asbestos tiles. Now he could feel the rhythm building within, the mood growing, the desire palpable and he knew exactly which room held his night's quarry. Buddy Lee had been thinking a lot about her all week – the new dark haired Jewish woman in C-2130. Levine. Sarah Levine.

On the outside, Buddy Lee had specific preferences in his sexual partners – big-boobed bottle blondes – but in here he was constrained to choose among the current population. In true

Darwinian fashion, his tastes conveninetly expanded to accommodate the circumstances. He was, after all, an equal-opportunity rapist.

A storm was gathering in the hills and Buddy Lee felt the thunder before he heard it. The subsonic frequency vibrated the loose wooden floorboards underfoot just before he heard the low moan rolling out of the west. And by the time Buddy Lee was returning from the locker room, clutching his three-pack of Lubed Featherlites Ribbed, the thunder was drawing closer and louder, sounding much like a hacking cough. Buddy Lee liked thunder. He especially liked the loud ass-slapping boomers, as he called them. He liked them because they masked the screams.

Dr. Sarah Beth Levine was thankful for the storm as well, but for vastly different reasons. Heavy rain would keep the dogs off her scent a little longer, giving her a slight but vital head start – that is, if she made it across the open field. She knew she had to work fast, before Buddy Lee came calling, and her only light source was the sparse shards of lightning that fleetingly licked the caged window above her head.

Sarah had planned for this night since she arrived three weeks ago. She knew her disappearance would have triggered a massive manhunt. They'd all be looking for her - the police, the FBI, her husband, Garland, the BIA and god knew who else. They would muster their forces and Sarah was absolutely convinced that they would find her – but would they find her in time? She couldn't take that risk. She had to get out. She had to expose The 610, shut it down and vigorously prosecute those responsible for the unspeakable acts of cruelty perpetrated within these old walls.

Lying awake at night, terrified, she replayed her mistake in her head over and over. It was a terrible, stupid, amateur mistake – and this was the price she was paying for her egregious error in judgment.

She rehashed the phone conversation she had with her friend and mentor, Dr. Abraham Spaulding. He had called and told her that several surgeons at his hospital had been approached by a young

Russian, Rudolf Capiloff, who intimated he had access to overstock pacemakers as well as transplantable organs from a reliable Eastern European source. Dr. Spaulding took it upon himself to meet with Capiloff and inspect his wares. Capiloff did, indeed, produce corneas and several pacemakers, which Spaulding immediately suspected were excised from fresh corpses. He alerted Sarah who arranged to meet Capiloff in Bethesda. Spaulding also told her that Capiloff may be driving a hearse – it was his day job vehicle. Consequently, when the hearse pulled up in front of her for their arranged meeting, she was not alarmed.

She checked her firearm in her purse and got out of her car. A man got out of the hearse to greet her. Except for the strange goggle-type glasses he was wearing, his expression seemed, to Sarah, relaxed and non-threatening. In the days that followed, she would come to know this man as Norman Starke. Starke had extended his hand to shake hers. In that same smooth movement, he pulled her toward him, spinning her off-balance and in the next split-second Sarah felt the prick of a hypodermic needle in her neck. Her breath caught, her knees buckled and Starke caught her before she fell.

She also vaguely remembered another man getting out of the hearse and moving toward them. He was much taller than Norman Starke and had a strange discoloration on his right hand resembling camouflage-like blotches of deep purples and browns that coiled around his fingers and ended abruptly at his wrist like a weathered glove. She heard them talking, but their words were unintelligible, garbled by the drugs. Sarah also vaguely remembered being lifted off the ground by Starke and the man with the discolored hand. Unable to speak or fight or resist in any way, they placed her in a bronze casket in the back of the hearse and closed the lid. Enveloped by the infinite blackness of the closed casket, Sarah's last conscious thought was that she had returned to the womb. And it felt good.

2

Dr. Nathaniel Garland fished around in his jacket pocket and dug out two ancient Maalox tablets. He blew the pocket fuzz off, popped them into his mouth and gave them a couple of perfunctory chews before choking down the chalky sludge. He knew it would take about ten minutes for the antacids to do their thing and he hoped the hearse wouldn't show before then.

There were four of them sweating in the black Crown Vic waiting for the hearse. Garland was accorded shotgun; Special Agent Carolyn Eccevarria was behind the wheel and that relegated Kessler and Dunbarton to the back.

Garland's stomach trumpeted loud gut sounds, announcing the arrival of the antacids. Carolyn Eccevarria shifted her gaze from the funeral home they were surveilling and glanced over at him.

"You okay?"

Garland nodded.

"Nerves?"

"Fajitas," he lied.

But he knew she was right. Nervous? Yeah. And with very good reason. Not too long ago Garland was an ordinary, overworked pediatrician. Now he was sitting in the stale air of a cramped Ford popping Maalox like M&Ms and carrying a Federal BIA badge.

Down the street, the mortuary doors swung open.

"Heads up. Party's coming out," Eccevarria said.

Mourners began filing out of the chapel doors, snapping open umbrellas like starburst fireworks against the downpour. They somberly followed the silver and bronze casket being wheeled out on a chrome gurney draped in purple velvet.

Dr. Eugene Kessler watched from the backseat with growing impatience. He made an exaggerated display of checking his watch and then slid his eyes to the portly lawyer sitting next to him. "I don't think he's showing," Kessler said. "What do you think, Nels?"

Nelson Dunbarton looked up from the case file. "I think it's too goddamned hot in here, that's what I think." He took a sip of his Starbucks double latte and went back to his file.

Garland wondered if he was the only one in the car who thought that Nelson Dunbarton had a peculiar odor. He noticed it the first time he met him. At first he thought it was something in Dunbarton's body chemistry that reacted with his soap or something. It took Garland a while to place the smell, but when he did, it was unmistakable. Feet. Nelson Dunbarton smelled like feet. Garland shook the thought and forced himself to concentrate on their business at hand. And that business was finding Sarah.

Dr. Sarah Levine had been missing without a trace for over three weeks and their investigation had come down to a tissue-thin arrest warrant for a Russian hearse driver who may or may not have pertinent information about her disappearance. Rudolf Capiloff, the hearse driver they were waiting for, was Garland's last lead. After this one, there was no place to go but backwards and retrace all of their previous steps. If Sarah was still alive – and their hopes for that dimmed with every passing day – having to retrace their steps would be an unconscionable waste of precious time.

A year earlier, when the Department of Health and Human Services established its pioneering Biomedical Investigations Agency as the criminal investigative arm of the CDC, Sarah Levine and Garland were recruited at nearly the same time. They went through training together, suffered the heat and hunger and humiliation of Quantico together and they received their gold Federal badges together. They were friends in the truest sense. And friends took care of friends.

Stuart Levine, her husband, had called Garland around 12:30 at night to report her missing. A day later, a full on police manhunt was set in motion and within twenty-four hours the search went national. As usual in these cases, Stuart was immediately considered a person of interest in his wife's disappearance by the local police, but that notion was quickly shelved for lack of a single crumb of credible evidence.

Then, like a sudden early frost, the leads went cold and Sarah's trail withered and died. Two days later Garland teamed with FBI Special Agent Carolyn Eccevarria. Together they scoured every one of Sarah's notes and files and phone records: home phone, cell phone, work phone, calling and cross-referencing every number on the list. And that ultimately brought them to a young Russian émigré named Rudolf Capiloff.

Now Rudolf Capiloff was late. And Garland's stomach-acid barometer was telling him something was wrong. He leaned forward and wiped the cloud of fog off the side window with his hand. The rain sounded like ping-pong balls as the fat drops bounced off the Crown Vic. Garland's stomach churned once more.

In the back, Dunbarton closed the case file and tapped it thoughtfully with his thick index finger. He exhaled, making a whistling sound through his gapped teeth. He was young, thirtyish, stout, with prematurely thinning hair that made him appear much older. Dunbarton finally said, "If this is all you've got on this guy then you've got nothing. Bupkies. There're too many pieces of the puzzle missing."

"That's why we're here, Nels," Garland said. "Try to squeeze Capiloff, get him to fill in the blanks."

"You're going to have to squeeze him like a month-old pimple. There's nothing here to link him to Levine's disappearance."

Down the street in front of them, pallbearers had lifted the casket from the chrome gurney and began to slide it into the maw of the waiting hearse.

Dunbarton settled back and said, "So what do you make of this biblical note in Levine's file?"

"What biblical note?"

"Right here." Dunbarton lifted the file to Garland's sightline and pointed at the notation. "This one: Animals. Ark." Dunbarton said them as two distinct words. "Nothing else is encrypted in her notes." Dunbarton's voice trailed off, as if he was thinking aloud. "Animals. Ark. Why would she code one reference?"

Eccevarria caught a glimpse of a gray vehicle in the rearview as it turned on to Burning Tree Road. The rain obscured most of her view, but it was impossible to mistake the big Cadillac stretch for anything other than a hearse.

"I think our boy's here," Eccevarria announced.

"About time," Kessler said as he pulled his gun from his holster and checked it. The gun was a 67-ounce .44 magnum Desert Eagle semi.

Dunbarton cast a dubious look at Kessler. "You really think you're going to need that cannon just to interview a kid?"

"It's called 'law enforcement', my friend. We're the law, this is the enforcement."

"Give me a fucking break, Kessler." Dunbarton said.

Garland watched the hearse approach in the side mirror. He glanced up the street to the funeral home where the mourners had just finished tucking the casket into their hearse.

"Let's wait until the funeral breaks up. Too many people around," he said.

Carolyn Eccevarria checked her own weapon, a double action rubber gripped .38 P Special, and glanced over to Garland.

"Firearm?"

"No."

"Goddamit, Garland, you're not giving flu shots to crusty nose kids anymore." She dug under the seat, pulled out her backup Glock and handed it to him. "And don't give me that doctors don't use guns bullshit. Get over it."

In the backseat, Kessler licked his lips nervously and said, "I say we take him as soon as he pulls in and opens the car door. We run the risk of losing him if he makes us."

"Christ," Dunbarton said, "four feds sitting in a black Crown Vic, steaming up the windows for over an hour and you think the entire state of Maryland hasn't made us already?"

"Once he's inside he's not going anywhere, Garland said.

He glanced down the street toward the mortuary. The chapel attendant had just slammed the rear door of the hearse and the mourners were beginning to disperse but there were at least fifteen to twenty people still milling near the hearse. In the side mirror, Garland saw the other hearse approaching fast and now he could definitely tell that Capiloff was driving. He could also see that Capiloff's eyes were focused on the mourners in front of the chapel. If Capiloff had made the Crown Vic, nothing in his face indicated it.

Then came the gunfire.

3

The first shot shattered the driver's side window of the hearse. An instant later, the reverberating boom of the shot vibrated through the Ford. The second shot drilled into the upper back of Capiloff's skull, shattering his left anterior parietal bone before tunneling through his brain, ricocheting through his occipital lobe and effectively splattering the upper third of his face across the Cadillac's dashboard and windshield.

Carolyn Eccevarria, her gun drawn, was the first one out of the car, yelling at Dunbarton to get down behind the seat and call for backup. In the same breath, Garland threw his door open and rolled out onto the rain-flooded street.

The crowd of mourners turned to the sound of the shots. That's when they saw Capiloff's hearse bearing down on them. Garland, seeing the same thing, took off on a full run after the hearse. He knew he was now an easy target and wondered what the bullet would feel like if, in fact, he felt it at all.

Kessler burst out of the Ford, raising his gun as he turned toward the low yellow brick building where he thought the sniper was hidden. "Where's it coming from?" he yelled to Eccevarria.

The shooter saw him first and fired. The shot caught Kessler in the left shoulder and the brute force of the heavy round knocked him off his feet and sent him skidding on his back across the slick pavement.

Eccevarria reacted instantly to the sniper's muzzle flash. Locating the shooter's position, she dropped to her knee and raised her gun with both hands. But she never got her gun completely up.

The sniper's next shot ripped into her neck, the frangible-point bullet easily tearing through her soft flesh. Eccevarria spun backwards and fell soundlessly next to Kessler, her life's blood rhythmically pumping out of her torn carotid artery.

Carolyn Eccevarria felt no pain. She was in shock, but somewhere deep in her fading consciousness, she knew with absolute certainty that her life was seeping away with every beat of her faltering heart.

4

It all played out in less than three seconds.

Like an errant missile, the two-and-a-half-ton stretch Cadillac slammed into the stunned crowd of mourners, carving through them before planting itself into the back of the standing hearse. One mortuary attendant and two elderly women, whose unfortunate timing had them standing on the street between the two hearses, were instantly crushed, their bones pulverized by the explosive collision of metal into metal. Other bodies were tumbled and tossed like stuffed toys into the street or dashed against the red brick wall of the mortuary. And for those not directly in the path of the hearse, the blizzard of glass and metal shrapnel exploding outward from the collision sliced through their soft flesh with the lethal efficiency of whirling Cuisinart blades.

The force of the impact knocked Garland backwards off his feet. The stinging tintinnabulation resounding in his ears deafened and disoriented him. When he was finally able to lift his head, he saw Eugene Kessler writhing behind him on the flooded street, clutching his shoulder a few feet from where Carolyn Eccevarria was lying lifelessly on her back.

Garland stumbled to his feet and staggered back toward Kessler and Eccevarria. He had neither fear nor wonder if the next bullet would strike him. It didn't matter; his goal was clear, to get back to Eccevarria and Kessler. Garland struggled to regain his balance, but his inner ears were still vibrating wildly and all he could hear was a loud, disorienting hiss. He had a deep shrapnel cut on his face that carved a jagged diagonal path from his left ear, across his upper cheek, to a point just beneath his eye. He didn't notice the pain or the swash of bright crimson blood on his face as he fought to reach his two wounded colleagues.

"Jesus god," Kessler screamed, "Jesus, damn, we're shot, we're shot. Son of a mother bitch…"

Kessler, obviously in shock, was conscious and talking – repetitively and incoherently – but talking. Carolyn Eccevarria was not.

Garland knew, of course, one of the hallmarks of shock was repetition of word sets and loss of sense of time and place. Garland had to bring Kessler back if he was going to be of any use helping Eccevarria.

"Gene, shutup! Right now. Stop it," Garland shouted at him.

Kessler stopped talking and fixed his gaze on Garland. It would take a few more seconds for him to comprehend Garland's admonition, but at least the words were beginning to shuffle themselves into some semblance of sense and order in his jumbled consciousness.

Garland had already shifted his full attention to Carolyn Eccevarria. Her body was lying near the middle of the street, perpendicular to the Ford. This particular stretch of Burning Tree Road was on a slight downward slope and Carolyn's body was acting as a dam for the rush of rainwater churning down the street. On his knees, Garland positioned himself at the right side of Carolyn's head, blocking the flow of water that was streaming over her face. He could hear the screams and moans and panicked cries of the other injured people down Burning Tree and part of him knew that many of them had a much better chance of survival than Eccevarria. But they were nameless strangers. Carolyn was not. His decision to treat her, hopeless as it was, and not help the others weighed on him, but he pushed the guilt aside and devoted himself to his fallen partner.

As he worked, he talked softly to Carolyn, his voice calm and reassuring. There was no way to know if she heard him or not, but he had often spoken this way to critical patients from his first day on the floor as a med student. And if it didn't help the patients, at least it calmed him.

Carolyn Eccevarria's eyes were open, but unfocused, and her dilated pupils were the size of manhole covers. Her face had taken on a grayish tinge and her lips were the faded blue of stone washed jeans. Bright cherry blood pumped in steady, rhythmical streams from the ragged tear in her neck. The blood that wasn't spewing out of her neck was dripping back into her, saturating her soft neck tissue. She had maybe thirty, forty seconds before she would bleed out, suffocate or drown in her own blood.

Garland turned her on her side, away from the flowing water and braced his knee against her back. He opened her mouth and turned her head face down as he stuck his fingers down her throat to clear her air passage. There was almost no blood and mucus to clear, indicative that the swelling tissue around her esophagus was suffocating her. Her deep choking gurgling sounds were getting softer. She was dying.

The back door of the Ford opened and Nelson Dunbarton's terrified face appeared.

"You hit?" Garland yelled at Dunbarton as soon as the door opened.

"No."

"Call 911, call, now."

"I did."

"Get out here. Help Kessler."

Crawling out of the back of the car, Dunbarton squirted along the flooded street on his belly to where Garland was working on Eccevarria. He had no way of knowing the shooter was long gone.

"Get over to Gene and put pressure on his wound. Use your shirt, whatever you have."

Turning back to Eccevarria, Garland dug his finger into the gaping wound in her neck. His fingers were cold and the warmth of the blood pumping directly from her heart would tell him exactly where the nick in the artery was. He found it and pressed on it hard, hoping to stem the fatal tide, but not squeezing off its entire flow. This was the artery that fed oxygen to her brain. He could only hope she wasn't oxygen deprived too long because, even in the unlikely event that he was able to save her, she would no doubt be brain dead.

If he could keep her alive another thirty seconds, maybe she'd have a chance. And maybe her brain would still be functioning.

In the distance behind them, he heard the advance of sirens.

Within three minutes, Carolyn Eccevarria was loaded into the first paramedic bus to arrive. Garland's index finger, painfully cramped and numbed, was still buried in her neck as the bus weaved through the rain-slicked streets to the hospital. By the time they rolled her into the ER, Carolyn Eccevarria's pulse was weak, but steady, and her respiration and blood pressure, although still critical, were gaining ground.

After Garland had handed Eccevarria off to the ER guys, a young resident guided Garland into an empty bay and cleaned the ragged wound on his face.

"Lot of people killed out there, huh?" the young resident said.

"Yeah."

"Must have been crazy, all the shooting."

"Yeah."

A year earlier, when the trauma of Daisy and Breezy lay heavy on him like a suffocating fog, Garland seriously contemplated the seductive peace of death. Now, after this slow dance with death on

Burning Tree Road, a dance so intimate he could feel it breathing hot and rancid in his ear, even now he was not frightened by the prospect of infinite nothingness as his permanent dance partner. Death was forever. He didn't care. Or so he had thought.

"You can use some stitches," the young doctor said.

"Just slap on a couple butterflies."

"It'll leave a scar."

"S'okay," Garland told him, "everything leaves scars."

5

The pungent smells, the hurried purpose, even the neutral mauve ambiance of the hospital felt reassuring to Garland.

In the small physicians' lounge, he washed his hands under the hottest water he could tolerate, inhaling the steam that curled up from the cool stainless steel sink and painted the mirror opaque. He scrubbed with pHisoHex, comforted by its distinctive aroma. As he rinsed, he watched with curious detachment as Carolyn Eccevarria's blood dripped from his hands and swirled in the white suds down the drain. In the linen room he found a fresh pair of scrubs and slipped into them. He then folded his leather CDC-BIA ID case into the top pocket of the powder blue shirt and moved out of the lounge into the belly of the hospital.

He rode the elevator to the third floor. Halfway down the corridor, Garland spotted the two very big FBI agents stationed at the double doors leading to the surgical suites. They were there to stand sentry for Carolyn Eccevarria. Garland had seen them both before during his training at Quantico and recognized them as Special Agents Gilroy Fitch and Avery Hollister.

Fitch, the larger of the two men, held up his palm like a traffic cop to stop Garland mid-stride. The agent's face softened with recognition as he glanced up from the ID to Garland's face.

"You did a helluva sweet job out there." Fitch said.

Garland shrugged modestly. "Any leads on the shooter?"

"Not yet, but we're taking this one to the house. We'll turn him."

Fitch and Hollister were among the new breed that came into the bureau after September 11th – young, smart, sophisticated, hipper than the old ham-fisted career guys – and they were intensely true believers. Garland figured them both to be surfers. Maybe it was their unruly, sandy hair or maybe just their cool. These guys had caches of both.

"I'm going to check on Eccevarria," Garland said, finding a gracious way to end the encounter, "I'll let you know her status as soon as I have something."

"Thanks, doc, appreciate it," Hollister said.

Garland swiveled and punched the red disk on the wall. The pneumatic doors to the surgical suites whooshed open like the gates of Oz and he stepped into pre-op. And then he stopped. The random noise in his brain was quieting and now it was as if he could hear his fragmented thoughts take hold.

He began walking again, sorting the facts as they fell into place: the shooting was not random, that was very clear to him now. And the shooter was professional, that seemed intuitively obvious, as well. Okay. Capiloff was the target. But why? Because, as Garland continued reasoning, Capiloff knew something important, something he may or may not have passed on to Sarah Levine. But whatever Capiloff knew, it was vital to someone that that information not be revealed – and it was worth killing the young Russian to keep it that way. What did not make sense to Garland was the next logical step: how did the shooter know the Feds were about to arrest Capiloff at that time and at that mortuary? If someone wanted Capiloff dead – and apparently they did – why not kill him someplace safe, someplace out of the way? He'd never be missed. Why take an enormous risk shooting him at a place and time where well armed, well-trained Federal officers could return fire?

Garland stopped again. Now it all became clear. The shooter didn't have the luxury of time to pick and choose his killing ground. It was last minute. Hurried. From the time Judge Lewin signed the warrant for Eccevarria until the time they parked the Crown Vic near the funeral home was what? Two hours? Three, tops? Which nudged him to the only logical conclusion – someone, or some persons, in one of the two agencies serving the warrant was most likely responsible for ordering the assassination. Someone in the FBI or the BIA wanted Rudolf Capiloff dead – maybe even one of the others sitting in the car with him. And, if all that was true, how safe was he? Somebody in the car or associated with one of them had called in the assassin. But who? Why?

As he entered the surgical suites, he wondered who would be next.

6

Carolyn Eccevarria died on the table.

By the time Garland had reached the O.R. window, she had stroked twice. Her heart and respiration went flatline and Dr. Gary Grody's surgical team dug deep into their bag of tricks and brought her back. Barely. When Eccevarria coded again – her second arrest in so many minutes – Grody's team flogged her relentlessly and heroically for another fifteen minutes. Finally, despite their best efforts, Grody pulled down his mask and called it. TOD – Time of Death, 3:18 pm.

Garland watched her through the window. Numb. Not a trace of emotion. A young surgical resident was allowed to practice suturing Eccevarria's neck while her skin was still pliant. Grody drifted out of the O.R. and approached Garland.

"She was already brain dead when they wheeled her in," Grody said as he stripped off his bloodied gloves and tossed them into the yellow hazardous material container.

"Yeah. I figured."

"Her body just caught up to her brain, that's all."

Garland found agents Fitch and Hollister still standing their watch and told them, simply and directly, that Carolyn Eccevarria didn't make it. Both agents nodded solemnly, their backs stiffening as they accepted the information. They tried, as men do, to accept the information without any display of outward emotion, but Fitch swallowed hard and his eyes moistened and Hollister held on to Garland's hand much longer than necessary.

Garland next got Eugene Kessler's room number from the desk and took the stairs up to the seventh floor. He spotted Nelson Dunbarton sitting on a chair outside Kessler's room. Dunbarton did not get up as Garland approached. He just lifted his head, his eyes meeting Garland's. His clothes were still wet and filthy from the ordeal and there was a pronounced odor of blood and vomit hugging him.

"How's she doing?" Dunbarton asked. His voice sounded as if even asking the question was a huge effort.

Garland looked at Dunbarton for a long beat, hoping his silence would answer the question for the lawyer. It didn't.

"Nate?" Dunbarton's eyebrows rose.

"She didn't make it, Nels. She died in surgery."

Dunbarton lost his breath in a burst as if he was hit in the gut. "Oh, no, oh, Christ," he said, now leaning forward and putting both hands to his head. "No, no, no," he said softly, more to himself and then, his head coming up, loudly spat, "Shit!" He took a deep breath and looked up at Garland. "I'm sorry, Nate."

"Yeah. Me, too. How're you doing?"

"I've had better days."

"Kessler?"

"They gave him some painkillers and he's been sleeping ever since they brought him up from surgery."

"You'll tell him when he wakes up?"

But Dunbarton wasn't listening. Garland followed his gaze down the hall and saw Haynes approaching. The Director's shoulders were thrust forward and his strides were long and heavy. This was a man with a mission.

"I have been looking all over hell and creation for you." Haynes' voice was deep and resonant and basted with the lilting remnants of his Southern upbringing. But under the lilt and ersatz Southern charm, he was seething and did very little to mask it. "You ever think of calling me when it hit the fan?"

Carter Haynes was a big man, four or five inches taller than Garland's six-foot-one, and he was built like a linebacker, which he was for Paul "Bear" Bryant's Alabama Crimson Tide, forty years earlier. There was no question that Carter Haynes had presence and that force of personality got in Garland's face, thrusting his thick forefinger like a baton and stopping just short of poking it into Garland's chest as he spoke. "What t'hell happened out there?"

Garland inhaled, released a long breath and shook his head. "I don't know."

"Well you'd better know real fast. Goddamn it. Seven people are dead, Nathaniel, seven. I'd say that's quite a prodigious body count for our first arrest, wouldn't you think? The agency's first real public operation and it blows up in our goddamn faces. You don't think the Secretary's thumbing through my CV right now wondering if she made the right decision handing me the reins? You don't think the President hasn't summoned her? You don't think the entire law enforcement community isn't laughing at us like we're a pack of rank amateurs?"

"It was an assassination."

"By who? For what?"

"I don't know, Carter. All I can tell you is the shooter was a pro, a marksman. He squeezed off four rounds, scored four hits in under ten seconds and vanished into the ether."

"Just like that."

"Just like that," Garland repeated. "If we're lucky, maybe there's some ballistics evidence, but I doubt it. He was too good."

Haynes' lips tightened into a laser straightedge. Although he was the head of what was arguably the most advanced biomedical enforcement agency in government, Haynes was not a medical doctor. He was, by education, a chemist; by training, a naval officer; and by vocation, a very astute and shrewd career politician. His appointment to the top position in the Department of Health and Human Services' newly inaugurated Biomedical Investigations Agency of the Centers for Disease Control was a political plum he had lobbied and politicked long and hard to obtain. And, Garland knew, he would protect his position with every political gift in his arsenal.

"They're assembling a press conference downstairs," Haynes finally said. "Reporters are rutting around down there like hungry hogs on horseshit and I'm not just talking about our locals. National press. Foreign press. Networks. Fitz is on his way over, the AG's coming down, as is our own esteemed Secretary. So I am going to appear like the ass end of a bad joke if all I can give 'em is a fancy foot shuffle and a 'sorry, folks, I just don't know what happened out there'."

"The truth is the truth, Carter, what the hell do you want me to say?"

Haynes stared at Garland for a full five seconds and then his face softened like a lump of cookie dough in a hot oven. He smiled. Paternally. Benevolently. Sympathetically. In politics, as in life, the hardest thing to fake is sincerity. Too much comes off as unctuous. Too little comes off as patronizing. Haynes owned the middle ground.

"Nathaniel," he began sincerely, "I don't know what t'hell was wrong with me just now. I am so genuinely sorry. In the heat of the moment, I completely lost sight of what is truly important here and that is the tragic loss of Carolyn Eccevarria. She was a good, decent, Christian girl, God rest her soul. Her death was a terrible loss. Terrible. Please accept my apology for being so insensitive just now. That is not my nature and I do apologize."

Garland accepted the older man's apology with a slight dip of his chin. He knew he was being manipulated by a master but was too exhausted to push the issue any further. Theirs was a strange relationship; not quite father-son, but still simultaneously affectionate and contentious. Carter Haynes was his mentor, his godfather, his rabbi. He had come through for Garland when he needed it most — for Daisy and Breezy — and for that alone Garland was forever grateful and indebted.

"What do you boys say we get ourselves a cup of coffee and chew on how we can best honor and dignify Carolyn's death at this press conference." The way Haynes said it, it wasn't a request.

"I'm not much for press conferences, Carter. I wouldn't be much help."

"Doesn't matter. You just stand up there with me and look sufficiently heroic and devastated."

And they both knew that he would.

7

The shrapnel cut on Garland's cheek was stinging like raw sin and the disorienting tintinnabulation in his inner ears, exacerbated by the noise of the press conference, had devolved into an annoying high pitched whine. He was physically, mentally and emotionally exhausted and all he really wanted to do was to get home and take the longest, hottest shower in recorded history. Excusing himself from Haynes, he went back to the ER Staff lounge to get his clothes and his cell and call Stuart Levine to come pick him up.

Garland's street clothes were still wet, but even so, they felt heavier than they should. And then he remembered. The gun. Eccevarria's backup. The gun she gave him. The gun he jammed in his jacket pocket as he ran down Burning Tree Road. Was that his souvenir of the day's work?

He fell heavily into one of the overstuffed, faded plaid armchairs in the far corner of the lounge and tried again to organize his thoughts – thoughts that continually came back to one nagging, burning, unanswered question: who called in the sniper? Obviously, he and Carolyn tracking down Rudolf Capiloff, as Sarah Levine had done earlier, irritated a major nerve somewhere. Sarah went missing for it and Eccevarria took a bullet for it. But what was "it?" And who was so threatened by their investigation that it became necessary to stop Capiloff dead before he could talk to Garland?

The moment Stuart Levine spotted Garland, he bounded over to the chair and pulled Garland up and hugged him like a long lost son. "Jesus Christ, Nate, Jesus Christ." Stuart kept saying it over and over until Garland had to physically break the embrace. "Your face, Jesus Christ, your face is all…"

"It's okay, Stu, I'm okay, I'm fine."

"Okay. You say so. Good," Stuart said it with emphasis, as if it was difficult for him to utter any word at all. "Good," he repeated.

They skirted out of the building and across the suspended concrete pedestrian bridge to the parking structure. Garland had lost track of time in the hospital and was surprised to see the last tangerine shards of daylight fighting to stay alive in the fading dusk and smog of D.C.

Stuart pressed the remote button on his key fob and a staccato horn burst located his silver Porsche Carrera among the herd of cars parked there. The Porsche fit Stuart. It was small, powerful and feisty, just like its owner.

To Garland, Sarah and Stuart always seemed like polar opposites. He an expensive, fastidious dresser, she a refugee from Wal-Mart. Stuart was an incredible financial whiz; Sarah couldn't balance ten-dollars in her checkbook. He had a lightening analytical mind; she was a deep thinker, a muller, a slow, unapologetic contemplator. But, then, she was almost always right.

Stuart Levine was definitely one of the smart ones. An astute fund manager, he rode the late 90's NASDAQ coaster up to its pinnacle and bailed to safety just before all the air farted out of the phony dot-com bubble. 'Pied Piper finance,' Stuart called it, 'never follow the greed,' he instructed Garland, 'let the greed follow you.'

Garland wasn't nearly as bad as Sarah Levine when it came to money, but he ran a close second. That's why he let Stuart handle all of his finances and investments. Of course, he and Daisy signed every check themselves, but with Stuart handling their money, Nathaniel and Daisy Garland became comfortably wealthy by anyone's standards. Then Daisy's paintings began selling and her aunt Marguerite died and willed her the Georgetown property plus millions in old stocks and insurance bonds and suddenly the money meter tracking the Garland's comfort level went off the charts.

Stuart and Garland rode the few blocks in silence to the Bread and Chocolate cafe on Pennsylvania. Stuart was, as always, lucky enough to find a parking space just outside the window. This was not a car he ever handed over to young acned valets.

Garland was surprised at how hungry he was. He ordered his usual peppered smoked salmon frittata, a toasted onion bagel and a really decent cup of Oolong tea. Stuart had a double espresso with his lox platter, as if he really needed an extra jolt of caffeine. As they ate, Garland filled him in on everything – their progress, or their lack thereof, in finding Sarah. Stuart listened and nodded, his face growing more despondent with each revelation.

"So we're back to square one," Stuart said. "Square fucking one."

"No. Not square one, but damn close to it." Garland forked a bite of frittata and gave his initial answer more thought. "We still have the mortuaries to comb."

"But with this Russian kid dead, you've got no link to the mortuary anymore. Shit. And besides, that mortuary's been so sanitized by now, you can eat off the embalming tables."

Garland nodded his agreement, choosing his words carefully for the next bombshell he was about to lay on his friend. "Look, Stu," he began slowly, "I'm going to recommend to Haynes that we turn the entire case over to the FBI."

"Good. More hands, more eyes. Good. S'bout time."

"No, what I'm saying is, I want to give it to them and take a backseat. Let them handle the whole thing. Sarah's case, too."

Stuart put his cup down and stared at Garland for a beat. "Are you shitting me? Why? What are you talking about, Nate? They'll fuck it up like they fuck up everything else."

"No, no. These guys are good. One of their own was just killed in the line of duty, they'll be swarming all over it anyhow. Stu, listen, the Fibbis are much better equipped to handle this than we are. They've got the personnel, the resources…"

"It's your exhaustion talking, Nate, not you. You can't let go now." Stuart was beginning to get angry. He took a sip of his espresso and then, swallowing hard to choke back the emotion that was welling in his chest, said, "It sickens me, Nate. I can't sleep. It's like I got a constant knot in my stomach. Can't keep food down anymore. When does the pain go away, Nate? When?"

"Never," Garland muttered, drawing his hands down his face, flinching when his fingers accidentally trailed over his wound. "I don't think it ever goes away."

The two men took long sips of their drinks, allowing a long, contemplative silence to hang there between them.

"People getting killed," Stuart finally mumbled. "What am I supposed to think about Sarah? What about her? You think Haynes really gives a shit about her? Or your friends at the Bureau? It's a job to them, Nate, just a paycheck. Sure, maybe some do it better than others, but it's still just a fucking job. I need you to keep at it, Nate, keep investigating, keep it alive. I trust you. I don't trust them." Stuart took a deep breath and let it out slowly. "I want to hire you. Let me pay you. Whatever it takes, whatever it costs, but I need you to help me find her. Please. That's all I want."

"Me too, Stu, me too."

"So you'll stay on it, right? You'll stay on her case for me."

Garland nodded his head slowly, not really agreeing, but not turning his friend down. "I'll do what I can. I promise."

8

When Sarah awoke from her drugged sleep she found herself in what looked to her like an antiquated infirmary. She was barely covered in a tissue thin hospital gown and her arms and legs were restrained by leather straps to an old chrome gurney. This was her terrifying introduction to The 610. Later, when she was fully conscious and wheeled to her cell, she realized it was some kind of bizarre medical facility. Not a hospital or clinic, not a lab, but more of a Daliesque warehouse for egregiously damaged bodies. It was also, she learned over time, reasonably safe during the day, but utterly depraved at night. Especially Tuesday nights. Buddy Lee rape nights.

Room C-2130, her cell for the last three weeks, was crammed with four steel frame beds. There were two other older women sharing her room, plus a teenage boy, probably sixteen or seventeen. All were constantly heavily sedated, but the boy, Calvin Burch, probably because of his youth, was occasionally responsive when his medication metabolized. Even before he arrived at The 610, Calvin had much more heart than wit, and Sarah immediately gravitated to the young boy's good and decent nature. She tried to teach him how to cheek his meds, but he failed far more often than he succeeded.

At night they were all strapped and locked to their bed frames. Calvin Burch was strapped face down on his thin mattress, his naked backside exposed to the chilly night air. He had a lumbar puncture and an exposed shunt that was being used, Sarah surmised, to harvest cerebrospinal fluid. From time to time, she was able to minister to his savaged spine, but only enough to give him some minimal relief without revealing to the staff that she was faking her own sedation.

Darwin's Tears

The two other women in the room, whom Sarah believed to be named Beatrice and Dalene, were so severely mentally handicapped they lacked the comprehension to even vaguely realize what was happening to them. Both were ambulatory during the day – even allowed out into the yard on nice days – but Sarah doubted they could tolerate their barbaric treatment much longer.

Early in her captivity, Sarah had learned to arch her wrists at lockdown so when the night restraints were fastened she could easily slip out of them. And that's exactly what she did now as she prepared for her escape.

Calvin was present and lucid enough this night to watch as Sarah slipped out of her restraints and slid under the bed. Woven through the steel springs on the underside of the frame were long strands of copper wire that she had stripped from behind the lathe wall in the abandoned barracks in the exercise yard. In the near total darkness of the cell, she worked quickly and methodically and mostly from memory, using the same methods she used to practice her procedures during her surgical rotation in med school. She closed her eyes and visualized and let her hands move from within.

Wrapping the long wire strands around her arm to keep them from snagging, she felt her way in the darkness between the beds and patted the wall until she found the two electrical panel cover plates. The multipurpose panels were antiquated versions of the type found in all hospitals, used to accommodate call buzzers, TV remotes, electrical outlets for lamps and light equipment, plus nozzles to regulate the flow of O_2 and CO_2. The 610, however, was so old, there was a second electrical wall panel to accommodate more demanding obsolete equipment, possibly fluoroscopes or even those behemoth iron lungs. This panel, Sarah guessed, was a 220-volt, 80-amp circuit. And the hell of it was, she had no idea if it was still connected to the facility's electrical grid or not. There was every probability it was taken off line long ago. There was no way to test it without blowing the circuit. Tonight would be its one and only test.

Having worked the cover panel screws loose over the last few nights, she quickly had the panel cover off and cautiously slid her finger down from the upper right corner. She probed very gingerly for the uppermost electrical wire she hoped would be the positive connection. This was critical surgery now. Even though the on-off switch was in the off position, if the panel was hot, which she was praying it was – a mistake could kill her.

Within seconds, she twisted the bare end of her purloined copper wire on to the existing positive terminal inside the panel and strung it along the wall to the iron doorknob of the cell. Attaching the second copper wire to the negative pole inside the panel was even riskier than the first if the circuit was hot, but Sarah had no choice. She closed her eyes and did it by feel. Making absolutely sure the two long copper wires did not touch each other, she inched it along the floor all the way to the door. There, she carefully attached this wire to the head of a loosened steel screw in the metal threshold at the door.

That's when she heard it: the distinct jangle of keys, Buddy Lee Garbrecht's keys, jingling and jangling in rhythm to the steel taps on his shiny black boots. She had seen him watching her intently in the yard since last Tuesday and she knew that she would definitely be his next victim. She also knew that that would never happen as long as she had a breath in her body.

Sarah's heartbeat reverberated in her ears as she emptied an I.V. bag of Ringers solution on the floor near the threshold and then opened the valve of a small oxygen canister and placed it on the floor next to the door. The escaping gas hissed like an angry snake.

In the corridor, Buddy Lee stopped at the door of room C-2130 and pulled the key ring from his belt. Unconsciously, he slicked his hair back and then smiled at the gesture, realizing its irrelevance. He reached to unlock the door and stopped, key poised at the lock. What's that sound? That hissing sound? Glancing down, he saw a tiny trail of the Ringers seeping out from under the door and meandering along the cracks in the worn tiles. Whatever it is, Buddy Lee thought, he wasn't about to clean it up. More often than not, the clients peed themselves most nights and he just left it for the day staff to deal with. The stench, though, he realized, certainly might impact his romantic interlude.

"Fuck it," Buddy Lee said out loud as he turned the key and twisted the doorknob of Room C-2130.

They were the last words he would ever utter.

He entered the room still holding the metal doorknob and planted his shiny black boots squarely into the puddle of Ringers. Sarah flicked the switch. There was a loud, instantaneous whip crack sound. The tiny room lit up with a brilliant blue flash of ionic light and the electrified orderly ignited like a flambé. A searing flash of lightening outside, accompanied by one of his favorite ass-slapping boomers, heralded Buddy Lee's arrival into hell. His body wobbled for a second then crumpled to the floor like a marionette. Tendrils of acrid smoke rose from his burned hand.

Sarah steadied herself. She was committed now. She had to act, there was no choice, no turning back. She had just killed a young man, murdered him, and whether it was justified or not was irrelevant. She had to seize control of her rising panic, to think – and think clearly. It was all so surreal. Now it was all animal instinct and adrenalin. And someplace, tucked deep within her reptilian backbrain, she knew her fear would fuel her survival.

Pushing herself to act, Sarah snatched the keys off of Buddy Lee's belt and moved across the room to unlock Calvin and the two women. Calvin was staring past her, mesmerized by Buddy Lee's lifeless body at the open door.

"Don't look at him, Calvin, look at me, listen to me, Calvin, listen to me."

"He's dead."

"Yes, he's dead." Sarah fumbled to find the right key on Buddy's ring. Her words came haltingly between short staccato breaths. "I'm going for help. Do you understand me?"

"Where's my sister?"

"I don't know. I haven't seen her."

"Is she okay?"

"Calvin, I don't…yes, yes…she's okay. Now listen to me. I'm taking your shunt out, but you have to lie still, don't move, okay?"

"I have to see Corinne. Where is she?"

"We'll find her. I'll bring back help. Now just lay still."

Sarah was across the tiny room now, unstrapping Beatrice and Dalene. She realized, at that moment, that she was no longer repulsed by their gruesome appearance. The transgenic engineering and stem cell experimentation she suspected had rendered both women hideously deformed. Beatrice had bone mass of a second skull growing from the upper half of the left side of her cranium. It oozed undifferentiated brain tissue, CSF and blood; the damage was irreversible. Dalene was only slightly more presentable with three distinct and perfectly formed additional ears growing on her head, two on the left, one on the right, one behind the other. Her hair could cover the extra ears, but not the gaping hole beneath her chin where a bizarre lipless mouth was beginning to take shape. Teeth were growing down from her jawbone that aggravated the newly formed tissue of the nascent mouth and kept her in a perpetual state of acute, unmitigated pain.

"Sarah," Calvin whispered, "Don't go."

Sarah finished unstrapping Dalene and hurried back to Calvin's bed. Even in the dim light she could see the mist gathering in his eyes. "I'm going to find Corinne," she lied, "I promise, I'll be back."

9

Brilliant flashes of lightning cracked like a mule whip across the sky as Sarah cautiously eased open the storm cellar doors and looked across the south field. Hugger Wood, the forest that offered her freedom, was at the far end of the field, beyond the concertina razor wire fence. Now, it was completely obscured by the torrential rain. Even in the erratic, stroboscopic lightening of the storm, Sarah could not make out a single tree in the stands of the sycamores and cottonwoods surrounding The 610.

Easing out of the storm cellar into the wicked rain, Sarah knew the downpour would cover her escape, that is, if the accompanying hypothermia didn't kill her.

She took off at a run.

Inside, the night janitress, an elderly Creole woman, smelled Buddy Lee's burned flesh before she found his body. Her scream reverberated down the empty corridor, startling awake many of the clients who mindlessly joined in a chorus of involuntary sympathy screams.

An hour later, the men were already gathering in the field. Directed by Norman Starke, the head of security for The 610, a dozen local mountain men, some with hunting rifles and shotguns and others with barking, agitated dogs, criss-crossed the south field. Swords of white light from their powerful flashlights slashed through the black rain as they walked. They moved in a loose, random configuration toward the distant fence.

A young man, tall and lanky, no older than Buddy Lee, climbed out of the storm cellar and approached Starke.

"She t'ain't in there nowhere, 'as fer sure," the boy confirmed.

"Keep looking," Starke said, his voice quietly modulated as always. "Take the other boys and search every inch of the camp; every room of every building and every shed and barracks, you understand?"

"Yessir, Mr. Starke."

The boy hesitated, shifting nervously on the balls of his feet, not quite sure how to address the bigger dilemma perplexing him. Starke was instantly irritated by the boy's hesitancy.

"What the hell you waiting for, boy? Get moving."

"Yessir, Mr. Starke," the boy stammered, "but wha' 'bout t'other one? You need I be a'lookin' fer her, too?"

"What other one?" Starke barked so suddenly the boy involuntarily stumbled backwards.

"I dunno. All's I hear is tha' Miss Russell, she's a'sayin' one a'them young girls from C-ward is a'gone missin', too, but she don't know when."

"Damn," Starke spat. "God damn it." He looked across the field as he spoke to the boy. "Find them both. Now."

The boy took off at a run back toward the main building and Starke turned to join the other men in the field. As he did, ribbons of water streamed off his worn gray Stetson and cascaded down the back of his slicker. Starke was not a tall man, but what he lacked in stature he more than made up for in pit bull intimidation. People feared him. Maybe it was his unusual eyewear – tube-like half-inch thick smoked welders' goggles fastened by a small enamel clasp at the back of his head. The glasses alone intimidated many and Starke always used it to his advantage.

Darwin's Tears

The mountain men had found the trench burrowed beneath the fence and signaled Starke with their lights. His boots made garbled sucking sounds in the soft Arkansas mud as he moved across the field to where they had congregated. He momentarily thought about the fresh first-growth Bordeaux he had just uncorked and decanted when the call came in. It was wasted now. It would be vinegar by the time he got home.

They had an escape once before, but from the Fayetteville facility, before they moved the operation here. The escapee was a bull of a man named Enos Hostettler who literally dragged three orderlies out the door with him and disappeared into hills. But that was different. Hostettler would be written off as insane, but not Dr. Sarah Levine.

The other one, the young girl escapee was, in all likelihood, dead in the woods, but the doctor was obviously smart and clever and resilient. If she made it through the woods all the way to Mountain Home, damage control would be difficult, if not impossible. One call from her and the Feds would swoop in and seize The 610 before the locals even had their breakfast.

The dogs at the fence were circling and whimpering as Starke knelt in the soft, saturated mud and examined the trench. What struck him first was the absence of mounds of red clay and dirt either behind or on either side of the trench. This told him that the trench was not clawed out in the rain, it was dug over time and skillfully hidden beneath the dead foliage strewn nearby. It was obviously the same passage that the girl, Corinne Burch, had used for her escape. Starke wondered if Levine and Burch had planned and executed the escape in concert or did one just profit from the other's labor. No matter now. They were both gone.

Ferris Semple, the elder statesman of the local group, read Starke's mind before the question was asked. "Ain't gonna git any of 'em goin' in dere, ya know. Only a damn fool go in dem woods at night."

"Two hundred dollars a man," Starke said, "cash, right now."

"T'ain't the money, Mr. Starke," Semple assured him, glancing into the black belly of the forest. "Dey ain't goin' in dere no how, 'as fer sure."

Starke knew that for these men, the immobilizing fear of superstition held more sway than any amount of money could allay. Hugger Wood at night was one of those superstitious places. None of the locals would ever go in there in the dark. Ever.

"Bring your boys back at sunrise," Starke said.

"Two hunred a man?" Semple pressed.

"Two hundred if you bring 'em both back alive. A hundred if they're dead. Fifty for your boys' time and trouble if they come up empty."

And as Starke sloshed back to the main building, his boots sucking through the soft Arkansas mud of the south field, he contemplated the very difficult and uncomfortable call he would now have to make to the Director.

And then he would pay a social call on Bruno Waldheim.

10

When she could no longer tolerate the piercing stitch in her side, Sarah stopped running and stood hunched over, hands on her knees, sucking deeply of the saturated air as she fought to catch her breath. The sounds of the dogs had receded, but Sarah knew that was no reason to quit pushing. She wasn't, as the expression goes, out of the woods yet. She knew they would continue to hunt her down because she knew their secrets, secrets worth killing for. Hadn't she killed? She had to press on, despite the pain and the skin-numbing cold and her unrelenting fear. She had to press on.

A branch snapped behind her and Sarah whirled to the sound, all animal instinct now, hands raised chest high, fingers curled forward, claw like, a primal defensive posture. Infused with a new rush of adrenalin, her senses intensified, eyes and ears straining to pierce the blackness of the woods and the obfuscation of the storm. Frozen in concentration, she saw and heard nothing.

But they saw her. Two rabbits had picked up her scent and were studying her curiously from the protection of their dry, leafy warren. Moments later they were joined by several others. But these rabbits were different. They were as big as dogs and each was, in some way, as repulsively deformed as the victims of The 610. One had two additional eyes on its face; another had a human ear and a human mouth implanted gruesomely on its neck; another had a partial human eye on its back. But the most grotesque among them had the vestiges of a second, stunted human head seemingly grafted to its own head.

The usually soft-spoken Sweetwater Creek, a meandering tributary from Bull Shoals Lake, was swollen like an aneurysm where

Sarah had reached it a few minutes later. It flowed with a ferocity she hadn't expected and, rising perilously above its banks, it was now far too wide and moving too fast to cross. She'd have to move downstream and find a narrows. She prayed it wasn't too far; her strength and stamina were diminishing and both Mountain Home and the highway were on the other side of the angry river. Sarah gathered her strength and began moving downstream as fast as the pain in her side would allow.

From a distance, the rabbits followed.

If she couldn't see the rabbits, then there was certainly no way for Sarah to have seen the snake. Almost fully submerged, anchored to a banyan root with the stream rushing past its flat spade head, the twenty foot long reticulated python flicked its sensitive tongue in her direction. In the heat sensing pits along its lips, the snake gathered all of the information it needed to know about her. And it liked what it sensed. Although pythons were not indigenous to Arkansas – or any other Southern state, for that matter – this one seemed perfectly at home in the damp woods. As Sarah made her way downstream, the python followed in the water at a safe distance.

Within ten minutes of trudging downstream along the mud soaked bank, she was exhausted. She desperately wanted to sleep, to find a relatively dry spot beneath the heavy foliage of the banyans and sycamores and just curl up and sleep. But that luxury was impossible and she knew it. For a moment, though, she would allow herself to sit and rest, to regroup, to reorganize…to think.

Moving up from the bank, she found some semblance of shelter beneath the wide leaves of a tight stand of catalpas. Rain still pelted down, but the arboreal umbrella these trees provided diffused the bigger drops that would otherwise fall on her like heavy water balloons. She closed her eyes, promising herself that it was just for a minute or two.

Her stalkers were soundless. Camouflaged and hidden behind dark trees and well-nourished ground fauna, the rabbits watched her as they spread out now into what could only be described as an intelligent attack formation.

The reticulated python, still unseen and undetected, continued shadowing her from the rushing water.

A twig snapped with a resounding crack and Sarah was instantly on her feet again, crouching down and squinting through the cruel storm. Seeing and hearing nothing, she cursed herself for taking even a moment's rest, then turned to move back down to the swollen stream. That's when she saw the rabbit.

It was sitting casually on its haunches five yards from her, but blocking the stream bank. Even with its saturated fur slicked down, it was as large as a rottweiler and looked just as vicious. The grotesque, fully formed human mouth and ear that grew on its neck was not as disconcerting to Sarah as the rabbit's eyes; they were as cold as the rain and they never left her. With her eyes locked on the rabbit's, Sarah slowly knelt and groped the ground for a potential weapon – a branch, a rock – anything her fingers could find. As she did, out of the corner of her eye, she saw the second rabbit. It was directly to her left and, like the first, it was huge and grotesquely deformed.

She knew what they were – escapees like her. They were the original transgenic test animals, the creatures used in the early experimental trials. And like Beatrice and Dalene and so many of the others inside, they were the failures, the mutants, the pathetic losers upon whose forsaken souls success would ultimately be achieved. Sarah knew that no one expected any of these animals to survive, much less breed and prosper in the woods and bogs surrounding The 610. But here they were, very much alive – and stalking her.

Sarah never saw or heard the other two rabbits – they attacked stealthily from behind. With surprising speed, agility and coordination, they came at her from three sides: two at her legs to bring her down, one at her ribs, one at her throat. Sarah's screams were drowned quickly in the storm, not even rousing the chickadees and thrashers roosting in the branches above. She fought ferociously,

41

fighting them off, blood now trickling from her neck and side. The two rabbits gnawing at her legs finally brought her down. Sarah kicked out violently, sending one of the rabbits tumbling backwards and yelping in pain.

From the stream, the reticulated python watched the battle with its tongue. And when the scent of Sarah's blood warmed its palate and incited its appetite, it charged out of the rushing water, running up the riverbank on eight legs, mouth open, fangs bared. Although some of the python's legs were withered vestigial stumps, the others were long and scaly and powerful, vaguely similar to those of a Komodo Dragon, complete with lethal, razor-like claws. The huge legged snake attacked the closest rabbit, instantly snapping its neck in its hinged mouth. Another of the rabbits, valiantly defending its turf, tried to attack the snake, but the python's tail whipped around like a saw blade and severed the rabbit in half.

Sarah had never known such terror in her life. Bleeding from her neck, arms and chest, gulping frantically for every breath, she clawed her way toward the stream, dragging her nearly severed leg behind her. In the brief but furious melee, the python had completely annihilated the rabbits without contest. It then turned its attention to Sarah, tasting the air for the sweet perfume of her blood. In a heartbeat, the serpent picked up her scent...and began walking slowly – almost nonchalantly – toward her.

Sitting tightly curled on a branch halfway up a thick, leafy Sycamore, Corinne Burch, bit her lip hard to keep from crying out as she listened to the slaughter playing out beneath her. She could see nothing, but the grisly sounds and the hideous shrieking terror in Sarah Levine's screams were horrifying enough. Whatever guilt the young girl felt by not trying to help the older woman fend off her attackers faded in the pragmatic umbra of her own self-preservation. With the rabbits slaughtered and the python otherwise engaged, Corinne Burch exploited the opportunity to cross the stream to relative safety.

11

Fighting the current, the torrential rain and her advancing hypothermia, Corinne Burch made it safely to the other side of the creek. Less than three hundred yards from where she landed on the opposite bank, Norman Starke's '96 Chevy Caprice fishtailed out of the main compound and paralleled the creek to Horner's Bridge. The Chevy's wipers were no match for the deluge and Starke had to lean far forward in his seat, hunched over the steering wheel, squinting through his thick goggles just to barely see the road. There were no lights and very few reflective markers on the mountainous rural roads between the Bull Shoals compound and Cochrane, but Starke had complete confidence in himself and his vehicle. His Caprice was equipped with the full police package, including the 5.7 LT1 V-8 engine and Go Rhino Interceptor push bumpers welded to the front of the car like an angry bowsprit. The car was often confused for an unmarked police cruiser, even by many of the state troopers, which was exactly his intent. Yet, despite the difficulty of the drive and the brutal conditions outside, Starke was remarkably sanguine. He punched the Black Eyed Peas on the CD and cranked the volume as he turned off Route 62 to pickup highway 201 south toward Little Creek.

The phone call he reluctantly made to his employer, the call he had dreaded, went far better than Norman Starke could have predicted. The Director, as he liked to be called, was surprisingly calm and analytical regarding the two escapees. He agreed with Starke that the likelihood of either of the two women surviving the night in the infested woods was next to nil. Still, he authorized the ten thousand dollar expenditure Starke requested to hire the Clementine brothers out of Jonesboro as the lead trackers to find them in the morning. Among the locals, the reputation of the Clementine brothers was legendary. Mountain lore had it that the brothers could find pig spit in a horse trough. Starke assured the Director that between the Clementines and Ferris Semple's mountain men, they would absolutely find the two women – or whatever was left of them. The Director also gave his blessing to Starke to deal with Bruno Waldheim any way he saw fit.

Waldheim's abandonment of his post every Tuesday night and his allowing the simpleton Buddy Lee Garbrecht to rape his way through the wards was inexcusable. The moment Buddy Lee fried at the hands of Sarah Levine, Waldheim's cover was blown and his scam exposed. Now the only thing Waldheim had to trade for his personal safety was confidential information about The 610. And that was an unacceptable position for Norman Starke and his employers. "Do what you will," the Director told Starke and that was exactly what he was going to do.

The surprisingly positive nature of the call left Norman Starke in much better spirits than he anticipated, especially in light of the escapes. In fact, as he turned off State Highway 201 onto the back roads of Cochrane, he had decided to reward himself later by uncorking his last bottle of '87 Médoc Bordeaux when he returned home. But first, of course, there was the little bit of unpleasantness that he had to visit upon Bruno Waldheim. For Norman Starke, it was always business before pleasure, even when the business was pleasure.

Cochrane was located in the north rising hills of the Ozark National Forest. It was a typical small Southern town, catering mostly to trout and bass fishermen and motorhome tourists. As Starke expected, Brenda Jo Peabody's house was easy to find among the small old cabins and clapboards off of Foothill Road, especially with Bruno Waldheim's big red Ford pickup parked so prominently in the driveway. This told Starke that Brenda Jo did not care what the neighbors knew or thought, which further meant that she was probably not married or involved with a boyfriend. Or she could be a pro, that was always a possibility. Either way, Starke knew this was a good sign. It meant no enraged husband or jealous boyfriend to deal with before or after. It would be short and sweet. And his wine was waiting.

It was true what the Director had told him about sensory compensation. He realized soon after he initially lost his sight that his senses of smell, hearing, touch and taste improved dramatically. In his blindness, he found that food had never tasted so good. And good, expensive wine was like foreplay on his palate and sex on his tongue. This from a cheeseburger and beer guy. Not too many years ago he would have ridiculed pretentious wine connoisseurs; now he was one, but, he liked to think, without the pretension.

There were no more than a half dozen homes on Brenda Jo's street, all set far back on their large lots, all with long driveways shadowed in stands of old Ozark Chinkapin and white ash and Basswood trees. Behind most of the houses were weathered out buildings – mostly tool sheds, barns, potting sheds, coops and animal pens – and behind those, well tended truck gardens. Every house on the block had a big truck garden, with rows of beans and collards and cabbage ready for the picking. Brenda Jo Peabody's house was no exception.

Starke pulled up and parked on the paved road above her driveway. Even in the heavy rain there was no need to risk leaving tire tracks on the driveway's soft gravel. He was, as his employers knew, a consummate professional who took pride in his work, attending to the tiniest details like having changed both license plates on the Caprice to phony Missouri plates before he left Bull Shoals.

Starke killed the Caprice's engine and headlights and let his eyes adjust to the darkness. Other than the muted light coming from the shaded and curtained windows of Brenda Jo's house and some scattered yellow dots escaping from the other nearby houses, all was dark. Starke scanned the street. Not a soul was out. Bruno Waldheim's pickup and an old Dodge were the only vehicles in the driveway. The narrow rear window ledge of the Dodge was lined with tiny stuffed toys, the cheap type given away with kids' meals at fast food restaurants. The Dodge was, no doubt, Brenda Jo's car. With no other vehicles in the driveway and none parked on the street, Starke reasoned that she lived alone or with an older parent or child, although she probably wouldn't be entertaining Bruno if that were the case. It didn't matter, though, it was nothing he couldn't handle.

Satisfied with the security of the venue, Starke checked the gun in his pocket. It was a Smith & Wesson 22 LR Airlite. The .22 was a very small caliber gun that Starke chose specifically for this encounter. It was light, only 13-ounces, and not very loud, even with the slightly friskier LR ammo. But what was particularly appealing to Starke about the .22 was that it was not necessarily lethal. This allowed him the freedom to fire all eight rounds into Waldheim over an extended period of time giving the old fart the opportunity to feel each one of the bullets tear into his flesh and burrow into his bones and organs before he expired. And, of course, being no fool, he kept his backup .45 tucked in his belt under his jacket. If necessary, the .45 could blow a bowling ball through an elephant's head.

Starke reached into the glove box and pulled out three pairs of surgical booties. He slipped the first pair over his shoes. He would replace these wet booties for a dry pair after he entered the house and use the third pair to return to the car. Second, his gloves. Not rubber or latex since he knew latex could still leave thermal prints or powder residues – he'd never make that amateur mistake. Rather, Starke pulled on his old favorites, a pair of well-worn snug black kid leather gloves that were as soft as a buttered baby butt.

Starke knew that none of this would have been necessary if Bruno Waldheim had just stayed put, kept his pants on and did his job. Even with the two escapes on his watch, the repercussions from Starke would have been far less severe. A few bumps and bruises, maybe he'd be pissing blood for a day or two, a reminder to shape up, that's all. But now he was a major liability to the project and a genuine security risk – and unfortunately for Bruno Waldheim, a completely unnecessary risk.

12

Not surprisingly, Starke did not need his lock kit to open Brenda Jo's back door. It was unlocked – as so many rural homes are – and he quietly let himself into the tiny mudroom. He changed his booties, placing the wet ones in a plastic bag in his pocket, and then cradled the .22 in his gloved hand as he moved silently into the kitchen.

His sense of the small house was that the mudroom led to the kitchen, which it did, and that room, in turn, flowed into a connecting dining and living room. To the rear were two bedrooms and one shared bath. There was, of course, a basement below and storage attic above, but he wouldn't think they would be in either of those two spaces. It was a small house, devoid of little secret hiding places. It was a house with no escape.

Starke moved slowly and noiselessly into the kitchen and stopped only when he heard a strange sound like a rubber band snapping on cardboard. He couldn't place the sound. Each time the rubber band snapped, he heard what could only be described as a muffled grunt and a woman's soft voice, her words hissy and unintelligible. Could be the TV in the back bedroom or living room, Starke thought, and he squeezed the rubber combat grip on the .22 just a little tighter as he carefully moved along the kitchen wall toward what he suspected would be the dining area. He flattened himself against the wall separating the kitchen from the dining area and, raising the gun, took a deep breath, held it and slowly peered around the doorjamb into the dining area.

In an instant, Starke saw and processed all that he had to know and immediately realized that the gods of such matters had smiled upon him. He pulled his head back, lowered the gun and released his breath. He took a second to collect himself, then, gun held at his side, he brazenly walked into the dining room.

The rubber-band sound was louder now as Brenda Jo vigorously slapped the end of the short leather riding crop across Bruno Waldheim's naked lumpy mashed-potato ass. Occupied, as she was in her erotic exercise, she didn't see Starke approach until he was practically next to her as she cocked her arm back for another crack at Waldheim. Starke startled her so that the crop flew out of her hand and her mouth sprang open to scream. But no sound came.

Starke raised his gun. "Don't scream. Don't say a word. Don't move."

Brenda Jo froze, but couldn't stop the involuntary trembling that erupted deep in her belly and quickly wracked her entire body. She squeezed her legs together so tightly to keep from peeing on the floor that she nearly fell over.

Starke heard her struggling for breath so that she was literally wheezing like a squeeze toy. "Take it easy, relax," Starke told her in a calming voice. "Don't give me a reason to hurt you and you'll be fine."

Bruno Waldheim, on the other hand, couldn't fall over if he wanted to. His arms were trapped in a bondage device and suspended high above his head. His wrists were firmly secured in tight leather cuffs attached to the opposite ends of a wide metal spreader bar, the ends of which were linked by thin braided steel cables. The cables went up and through an industrial turnbuckle attached to screw eye mounted in the highest point of the arch between the dining room and the living room. Together, the steel cables and the spreader bar formed a thin triangle, not unlike a trapeze. Waldheim's thick ankles were also cuffed to the opposite ends of a second thick steel bar, spreading his legs so wide that he resembled a rotund version of Da Vinci's famous drawing, "Vitruvian Man".

Waldheim's back was to Starke and Brenda Jo, but at the sound of Starke's unmistakable voice, Waldheim screamed – a scream completely muffled by the fat red ball gag fastened into his opened mouth by a thick latex strap that encircled his head. He twisted his body and pulled and shook violently against his restraints, but the cables and bars held firmly, exactly as they were designed to do. Starke noted that the bondage contraption was homemade, probably in Waldheim's own workshop, and was not a bad job at all.

"Bruno," Starke said to Waldheim's back, his voice mockingly parental, "stop making such a fuss. We're just going to have a little conversation."

Brenda Jo squeaked loudly and her hands went up to cover her breasts. Starke had barely noticed the couple's playwear. Brenda Jo was, Starke guessed, in her late thirties. She was round, but not fat, and still had nice definition to her legs. She was wearing a black corset or bustier, Starke didn't really know what they were called, with garters that hung down from the bottom of the garment and were fastened to black fishnet stockings. Her bare breasts hung over the top of the corset like half filled rice sacks with two wide brown sink stoppers for nipples.

Starke jerked his chin to Brenda Jo as he saw her hands move to her chest. "S'okay, darlin'. Cover 'em up. And put your underwear on."

Brenda Jo quickly turned her back and tucked her breasts into the bra top of the corset. She still couldn't stop shaking as she knelt to the floor, found her panties crumbled in a ball on the carpet, stepped into them and pulled them on.

Bruno Waldheim continued to fight and pull against his restraints. Starke noticed that the hair on Waldheim's back was long enough to mow and was now glistening with the rancid sweat of fear. He was naked except for a cheap, black, mail-order garterbelt that required an elastic extension sewn in the back to accommodate his substantial waist. A slight beer belly draped over the front of the garterbelt like a fleshy waterfall. Below his buttocks, the elastic garters, which were stretched to their limits, supported old-fashioned sheer black nylon stockings, the kind with seams that ran all the way up from the heels. His thick thighs protruding from the tight stocking tops and his chunky buttocks made his backside look like two overstuffed vanilla ice cream cones. Red welts, the size of postage stamps, courtesy of the riding crop, littered his butt like candy sprinkles on the white cones.

Starke knew this pathetic scene was strictly amateur. To him, there was absolutely nothing even remotely erotic about this tableau. He was there on business.

"What's your name, darlin'?" Starke directed his question to the woman's back as she was stepping into her panties.

"Brenda Jo Peabody." She could barely squeak the words out.

"You have a cell phone, Brenda Jo?"

"Yessir," she said, her voice barely audible, "I rightly do."

"Where is it?"

"In m'bag, in m'bedroom, sir." Her voice quavered.

"Where are the other phones in the house?"

"One in the bedroom an' t'other in that kitchen yonder, sir."

"Who else lives here? In this house?"

"Nobody. Jus' me."

"Are you expecting anyone else tonight? Any other callers?

"Oh, no, sir. No."

Starke knew from the brief interview that this woman would pose no problems for him. She would be cooperative and compliant and do what she was told. "What I want you to do, Brenda Jo, is go fetch your cell phone and bring it to me. If that phone is not in my hand in fifteen seconds, I will have to kill you. Do you understand?"

"Yessir, I do."

"Good. Now go get it for me."

Brenda Jo didn't have to be told twice. She skirted past Starke and raced toward the bedroom. Starke then moved to Waldheim, grabbed the upper spreader bar near his cuffed wrist and, even with Waldheim resisting, pulled him around like a side of beef on a butcher's caddy. The turnbuckle groaned under the weight, but held firm.

Waldheim was gasping, his chest heaving. His face was candy-apple red, his eyes the size of satellite dishes. Foamy saliva was dripping from the corners of his gagged mouth and sweat was avalanching down his chest and cascading over his lumpy belly. In a misguided nod to eroticism, Waldheim's entire pubic region was shaved and the waning moon flesh of his pubis contrasted sharply with the black garterbelt. The terror of the moment had, as nature intended, traveled protectively to his groin, shrinking his genitalia so that his small, flaccid penis trying to hide atop his shriveled scrotum looked like a small cochleated snail.

"You really fucked up this time, Bruno." Starke's voice was steady and casual, without threat or anger.

Waldheim's frantic eyes lit on Starke's goggle-like glasses and stayed with him, hoping that he made eye contact through the thick lenses. He nodded vigorously, taking the cooperative approach to his situation.

"Here, sir, my…m'phone." Brenda Jo was back, holding the cell at its very tip, hand shaking, extending it to Starke.

"Thank you, darlin'," he said, accepting the phone in his gloved hand. Then to Waldheim, added, "This is one sweet girl, isn't she, Bruno?" He then turned back to her and said, "Brenda Jo, is that your Dodge I saw in the driveway?"

"It surely is, yessir," she answered dutifully.

"Does it run good?"

"Yessir. Jus' had it lubed an' the tires rotated 'bout a week a'fore."

"Good. Maintenance is very important." He paused and glanced down at her legs. "Now what I want you to do is give me one of your stockings, one you're wearing."

She stared at him; the request wasn't registering. "My stockin'?"

"Uh-huh."

"Which a'one?"

"I don't care. Doesn't matter. You choose."

Waldheim's eyes moved back and forth between Starke to Brenda Jo like one of those big-eyed pink plastic cat wall clocks. She unclasped the garters on her left leg, rolled the fishnet down her to her ankle and handed it to Starke.

"Thank you," he nodded, casually shaking the stocking out to its full length as he continued talking to her. "Brenda Jo, you have any friends or relatives outside of Cochrane?"

"Like kin?"

"Right. Kin."

"Jus' m'sister...an' her husband, they up to Arkana."

"That's just on the other side of the hill, isn't it?"

"Yessir."

"Good. So what I want you to do now is go pack a bag, one bag, Brenda Jo, pack some underwear and clothes, lipsticks and such, you know, makeup, whatever you'll be needing for a few days and you're going to pay them a visit."

"Right now?"

"Right now. You have two minutes to get back out here with that bag. And if you close that door or I hear you touch that phone or hear a window open in there, I will have to come in there and kill you. Am I clear?"

"Yessir. Can I change m'clothes?"

"No. I want you to keep wearing just what you're wearing."

Brenda Jo nodded and dashed past Starke toward the bedroom. Flicking the stocking out once more, Starke moved toward Waldheim and then stepped behind him. Waldheim tried to twist his body around to face Starke, but couldn't purchase the leverage.

"That's a really nice girl you've got here, Bruno. You really don't deserve a girl like her." Starke slipped one end of the stocking around Bruno's neck and let it hang there like a scarf for a few seconds, letting Waldheim feel it against his skin, letting the reality set in.

Waldheim's entire body trembled and his cries and screams of protestation were completely nullified by the gag. He started swinging and twisting his arms and legs against the restraints.

Starke picked up the other end of the stocking and, twisting both ends in his hands, began tightening the impromptu garrote around Waldheim's neck. "Since I like her, Bruno, I'm going to help you out. Did you ever hear of Victorian Viagra?"

Waldheim was now gasping and flailing. A ragged gurgling sound crept up from deep in his chest.

Starke twisted the stocking tighter, working hard now to keep Waldheim's violent gyrations from loosening his grip. "Victorian Viagra is a strange artifact of asphyxia. A bonus, you might say.

Consider this my gift to you. Look down, Bruno. Check it out. See how hard your sorry dick is getting? I am giving you an erection to die for." Starke grunted and twisted the stocking with a sudden jerk, snapping Waldheim's windpipe.

Waldheim went limp. His penis did not.

Starke stepped back, leaving the stocking in place around Bruno's neck. He was sweating from his exertion but it didn't bother him. Grabbing the upper spreader bar, he pulled Waldheim's body around so that his back was once again facing the dining room, away from them. Brenda Jo came out of the bedroom carrying an old grey Samsonite suitcase with a broken chrome clasp. She had also put on a thin white chenille robe over her corset and had slipped on a pair of garden clogs. She barely had a moment to glimpse Waldheim's back before Starke grabbed her elbow and pushed her toward the kitchen.

As they neared the mudroom door, Starke placed Brenda Jo's cell phone on the Formica counter and he changed his booties before going back outside.

The rain pelted them as Starke gave Brenda Jo very specific directions over the hill to State 201 North to Arkana. He warned that he would be following her closely to see exactly where she was going. He also cautioned her to drive slowly and carefully, especially along the top of the hill around Grady's Point.

"How long I need t'be up to m'sister's place?"

"Not long. A day or two, that's all."

"What 'bout Bruno, sir?" Brenda Jo asked nervously as she glanced back at the house.

"He'll be fine," Starke assured her. "He's just going to hang around your place a little while longer."

Brenda Jo put her suitcase on the back seat of the Dodge and slid behind the wheel. Starke politely closed the car door for her and then walked carefully along the edge of driveway to the street where his Chevy was parked. Brenda Jo could have taken off if she wanted to, could have escaped – but Starke knew she wouldn't. Even if she did, how could she go to the police? Dressed like a whore, hastily packed suitcase in her car, married boyfriend strangled with her own stocking hanging in a bondage contraption in her own house, even a simple woman like Brenda Jo Peabody knew the convenient "mysterious intruder" story would never fly. Instead, she did exactly what Starke had instructed her to do, as he knew she would.

The two cars caravanned up Foothill Road and twisted up the hill toward Route 201. As Starke had warned, driving in this blinding storm was particularly treacherous and Brenda Jo took the turns slowly and cautiously. Along the top of the hill, near Grady's Point, Starke eased up on the gas slightly and allowed Brenda Jo to pull ahead fifty, sixty feet. Then, gripping the wheel tighter, he accelerated, smoothly, evenly, so as not to fishtail on the slick asphalt. The Caprice nimbly gained speed and momentum, effortlessly catching up to the Dodge. As soon as Starke saw Brenda Jo begin to turn into the second sharp switchback, he tapped the accelerator and the Caprice's Go Rhino Interceptor push bumpers smashed hard into Brenda Jo's left rear bumper – a chase technique police call the Pitt Maneuver – that sent the Dodge skidding to the left. Brenda Jo, panicked, stood on her brakes and twisted the steering wheel hard to the right, raising her car's left tires off the road. The car skidded another thirty feet on two wheels before becoming airborne and launching itself through the guardrail into the rocky ravine below. It bounced off of two granite outcroppings before rolling to stop against an old ash. It was not a survivable accident.

Starke slowed, but didn't stop. He pressed the CD button on the sound system and listened to the rest of the Black Eyed Peas. He was anxious to get home where a hot shower and a fine bottle of '87 Médoc Bordeaux were waiting for him.

13

Some men are born of the sea. They have the innate ability to read the faint nuances in the currents of the ocean and taste the capricious moods of her winds. Other men are born of the land. Possessing an amazing and mysterious preternatural sense, they can hear the whispers of woods and become one with the secret rhythms of nature. The Clementine brothers, Warren and Darren, were just such men. Although they modestly referred to themselves as simply trackers, they were renowned to be the best in Arkansas and possibly the entire South.

Norman Starke had hired the Clementine brothers to track two "clients". Warren and Darren did not have to be told it was a no-questions-asked mercenary assignment. For this service they charged $10,000 per week, one-week minimum. Starke hired them for the minimum, believing that some semblance of the remains of both Sarah Levine and Corinne Burch would be found in the woods within hours.

At first light, Starke and the Clementines slogged across the muddy south field of The 610 so the brothers could personally examine the trench under the concertina fence through which the two women went AWOL.

Although the storm had moved on, Starke still wore his wide Stetson, a light L.L. Bean Gore-Tex rain jacket and Gore-Tex Knife Edge Trail Boots. His Smith & Wesson .45 was now holstered at his hip and he carried a 12-gauge Winchester Supreme Select shotgun cradled in the crook of his right elbow. The Clementines both wore 12-pocket Ranger Vests over old t-shirts, older jeans and still older army issue jungle boots. The shell loops on their vests were empty and Starke could not tell if they were armed or not, but suspected they were.

As they slogged through the rice-paddy mud, Starke handed Darren and Warren Clementine photos of both Sarah and Corinne. The brothers barely glanced at them and folded them into their pockets. Across the field, the brothers saw that Ferris Semple and his rag-tag mountain crew were already gathered at the fence, armed like revolutionaries, their hunting dogs yelping and straining at their leashes.

Warren jutted his chin toward Semple and the mountain men. "Small woman an' a young 'un…don't make sense you need a army and all that firepower you got yourself here jus' to bring 'em in."

"It's not for them, the patients," Starke bristled. "There're some pretty nasty critters in these woods. Those boys are armed just to protect themselves and pick up a few bucks in bounties if they get a chance."

Uh-huh." The Clementines said in unison.

"Meaning no disrespect to your fine boys here, Mr. Starke, but Darren and me find it's a whole sight quicker trackin' jus' ourselves," Warren said politely.

Before Starke could respond, Darren Clementine clarified, "All them extra boots and dogs stomping through the brush might be a tad more hindrance than help, if you see our meaning."

Starke did. He didn't argue. He knew he would get his money's worth with the Clementine brothers, but he wasn't about to let them go at it alone, not knowing what they might stumble across. "Right," he nodded, "but I'll be coming with you."

Darren and Warren just shrugged at each other in a "whatever" gesture and continued walking. Warren said, "Suit yourself."

As they approached, the mountain men parted as if their huddle was cleaved by an invisible axe. Ferris Semple stepped forward to introduce himself and his men and shake Warren's hand; even celebrity trackers had their fans.

"They burrowed out right here?" Darren asked. He kneeled at the point where Starke indicated Sarah Levine and Corinne had made their escapes through the fence.

"Yeah." Starke said.

Darren shook his head, obviously peeved.

"We filled in the trench last night," Starke explained, ignoring Darren's displeasure, "make sure none of the other guests left without permission."

"Uh-huh," the brothers said in unison. "Les' do it."

There was no gate in the concertina fence, no direct access into Hugger Wood along the entire south side of the compound. When they appeared on the opposite side of the fence forty minutes later, Semple and the other men were still waiting there, eager to watch how the Clementines worked.

Warren and Darren both looked down to where the trench had been and "uh-huhed" quietly to each other. Starke looked from one brother to the other like he was watching a tennis match. After a few minutes, Warren finally spoke.

"The young 'un, the girl come out first," he said. "Maybe two, three hours a'for the grown woman. The girl's wearin' shoes a good sight bigger'n her feet."

There were murmurs of appreciation from the Semple group.

"How do you know that?" Starke asked, impressed, but still trying to ascertain if he was getting sandbagged.

Darren said, "Ground's awful soft from the rain. Girl's heels dig a whole lot deeper than the toe even when she's a'runnin'. Front of the shoes kinda bend up, meanin' there's no weight in them."

"The woman's track is on top of her's, meaning she came after." Warren added, answering the remainder of Starke's question. "Tracks are deeper, woman bein' a tad heavier'n the girl."

Semple's assemblage on the other side of the fence nodded and mumbled their agreement with the Clementine brothers.

From where Starke and the Clementines were standing at the fence, there were 180 points on the compass, any one of which the women could have chosen to follow, yet simultaneously, Warren and Darren turned and looked south-southeast. "This way," Darren said.

The Clementine brothers moved through the woods unlike any trackers Starke had ever seen. Once they had picked up the visual scent, they moved quickly, Darren pointing here, Warren pointing there, communicating silently, the brothers reading each other's subtle signals. Starke, whose goggle-glasses kept fogging over, had a hard time keeping up with them. Within twenty minutes they found the first rabbit carcass at the base of the Sycamore that Corinne Burch had climbed for refuge.

Breathing heavily, Starke nervously watched a very curious Warren Clementine examine the partial remains of the eviscerated rabbits while Darren plucked a long strand of blonde hair from the Sycamore's bark. Warren's gaze moved slightly beyond the remainder of a rabbit's severed haunch. Scavenger rodents and birds – the forest's industrious janitors – had already feasted on the flesh of the dead rabbits before they began to decay. Hordes of insects would move in later for the final mop-up, leaving only a few scattered bones as calcified monuments to their existence. Starke scanned the broken carcasses, looking for the bizarre physical anomalies he knew these rabbits possessed.

"Darren." Warren waved his brother over. "Damndest thing I ever seen."

Darren joined his brother and looked where he was pointing. For the first time, he kneeled close to the soft ground to get a better look. The red Arkansas clay beneath the carpet of dead flora had taken on a deep purple hue where the rabbits exsanguinated. The blood, saturated into the ground, mixed with the natural decay of the fauna offered up a pungent, rancid smell of iron and death that affected Starke far more than the Clementines.

"What t'hell is that?" Darren asked.

"Dead rabbit," Starke injected preemptively as his right hand moved almost imperceptivity toward his holstered .45. The last thing Starke needed was these two inquisitive mountain hicks raising questions about the mutated animals in these woods.

"Yep, right 'bout that," Warren said. "Biggest fuckin' rabbit I ever seen, but that ain't what I'm talkin' 'bout here."

Warren and Darren stared at the ground and slowly raised their heads simultaneously, looking off toward the bank of the creek.

"What is it?" Starke asked. "What do you see?"

"Komodo?" Warren asked Darren, ignoring Starke.

"Yep. Could be."

"Nile monitor, maybe?"

"Yep. Could be." Darren replied. "Damn that's weird."

"Too weird." Warren confirmed. "Can't be Komodos or monitors 'round here. A'sides that, that reptile's got too many legs."

"What t'hell are you boys talking about?" Starke was getting edgy, second guessing himself about hiring the Clementines in the first place, worried now they might discover much more than they should.

"There's some big fuckin' lizard type reptile 'round here close by. Can't explain it." Warren said to Starke as he stood up. "A big fucker, uh-huh."

"What about the two women?" Starke asked, some tight nerves playing on his voice as he tried to get them back on track.

"The girl scooted up this Sycamore," Darren said. "T'older woman din't. Then there's this fracas t'ween the reptile an' these here big-ass rabbits. The girl comes down the tree after the fracas, when the rabbits are stone dead and she heads yonder." He pointed toward the creek.

"Uh-huh," Warren confirmed. "She come down the tree after the woman and the lizard move on." Then looking back at Starke he explained further, "Blood was already soakin' the ground when she walked through it with her big shoes."

"So where the hell are they?" Starke was getting worried now.

After very briefly studying the muddy ground, the Clementines took off, picking up their pace as they followed a trail invisible to Starke. Warren pointed to the creek; Darren nodded and said "uh-huh." He pointed forty-five degrees the other way, into the fat of the woods and Warren grunted, "uh-huh." Starke had to trot to keep up. The indiscernible path they followed took them to the edge of Sweetwater creek; it had returned to its gentle, good-natured flow now that the rains had moved on. Warren pointed across the creek and they both "uh-huhed".

"So where the hell are they?" Starke asked.

"Gone."

"Gone?" The little color Starke had drained from his face.

"Yep." Darren Clementine nodded. "But not together. They went which a-way and t'other."

Starke rubbed a hand over his face. "You can find them, right? For ten grand you had better fuckin' find them."

"Well, sir, lemme explain. We don't rightly 'preciate you bein' so rude. It's not a'tall necessary. Second, you touch the butt a' your sidearm again and we will have to confiscate it."

Starke straightened.

"Like I was sayin', we reckon the older woman is gone, meanin' we're thinkin' the reptile – or whatever t'hell it is – did her in. She was a'runnin' over there," he went on, pointing up the bank, "then she took a tumble there and the lizard or whatever got to her. After that, the lizard thing kinda jus' drug her – see these here skids from her legs? Drug her right into the creek."

"What about the girl? Starke asked, knowing the answer.

"Gone." Darren nodded. "But she's gone gone."

"She cross the creek?"

"Sure as shoot looks that way. She did it las' night when the water's runnin' high. Coulda made it across, coulda been swept downstream a might."

"But if she did make it across, it's only a few miles to the highway," Starke said, realizing the situation just went from bad to worse.

"That'd be true. When the rain stopped, she'd be able to hear it – traffic an' the semi's. Noise would guide her right to it, uh-huh."

"Shit." Starke hissed. "What are the odds we can still find her out there?"

"Lil girl, scared and dirty, wetter'n a shaggy dog in a pond, wearin' them too big shoes…nah, t'wouldn't be nothin' findin' her out there." Then, pausing for effect, added, "'Course, it'll cost you extra."

14

2:35 am and Garland, as usual, was still staring at his bedroom ceiling, unable to turn off the chaotic brain-noise pinballing through his head. But now, in addition to the usual noise of Daisy and Breezy and Sarah, a new noise had entered the fray, the noise of Carolyn Eccevarria. The 50mg of diphenhydramine he took three hours earlier barely provoked a decent drowse and he was now considering an injection of the good stuff, knowing it would mess him up for the next two or three days. He lay there, watching the shadow theatre of the swaying elm branches outside his Georgetown window playing out on his ceiling, trying to convince himself that the shot was worth it. He needed sleep. He wanted sleep. He craved sleep. But he was afraid of sleep.

A day after the shooting, Garland went back to Simmonds and Sons Mortuary on Burning Tree with carloads of Feds, but Stuart was right. The mortuary's holding company – Turner/Eterna, Inc. – had immediately gone into hygiene hyperdrive and the company was so clean it was damn near antiseptic.

Garland also attended two very different funerals after the shooting – Carolyn Eccevarria's and Rudolf Capiloff's.

Where Carolyn Eccevarria's Catholic funeral was quiet, dignified and reserved, Rudolf Capiloff's Russian Orthodox funeral was an emotional celebration and religious spectacle. Garland could barely hear the service over the siren-like wailing of the chorus of babushkas. In a strange way, he liked the emotional outpouring of this funeral – it was raw and unpretentious and somehow viscerally satisfying.

Capiloff came from a big family, but of all of his brothers and sisters, only his older sister, Golina, spoke English well enough and was willing to talk to Garland. He learned from Golina that Rudolf had been driving for Simmonds and Sons for just slightly over a year. His job was simply to drive the hearse at funerals and occasionally transport bodies from one funeral home to another if one of the homes in the chain was jammed up with too much business and needed some help. Capiloff, however, was not paid by the local Simmonds and Sons, but rather by the parent holding company, Turner/Eterna; Golina knew because she would deposit her brother's checks for him. At the time he was killed, Rudolf was transporting a body from one of the chain's Roanoke funeral homes. From that far away, Garland had asked? Sometimes even farther, Golina had told him. Memphis, Atlanta, other places just as far. But it was okay. Rudolf loved to drive, loved to see the country, see America. Garland asked Golina if her brother had ever mentioned the name Dr. Sarah Levine, but she couldn't remember.

3:15am and Garland was on the verge of treating himself to the injection when his eyes finally closed. And then, of course, the phone rang. More asleep than awake now, he scooped it out of the cradle before the ring echoed out.

"Dr. Garland?" The accented voice said.

"Speaking. Who's this?"

"Dr. Mulum, Mohammed. Sorry for waking you, doctor."

"S'okay," Garland said. "What do you need?"

"It's a bit unusual. We got a call from Fairfax. It went up the ladder at CDC and down your ladder at BIA from Carter Haynes himself. He says even though you're not on tonight, he was hoping you could take the call, do the prelim on this one, check it out, you know, the usual drill."

"Haynes? He say why me?"

"Uh-huh. He said he needed a pediatrician on this one."

"Where is it? The call?"

"Not far. FRH." Mulum was now referring to Fairfax Regional Hospital.

"You don't happen to know what the case is?" Garland asked, knowing from experience that ninety-nine percent of their middle-of-the-night emergency calls were usually from overworked ER docs who were having trouble identifying uncommon, but not unheard of pathogens.

"Not a clue," Mulum responded. "All I can tell you is that the initial call came from a shrink, a Dr. Hobbs. I'm guessing he's the one who requested a pediatrician."

Garland took the address and contact information from Mulum, thanked him and was on the road within fifteen minutes. Anything was better than sleep.

15

The young Hispanic orderly, whose ID tag simply read, 'Horacio', unlocked the solid metal core door and pulled it open for the two doctors. Dr. Anson Hobbs vaguely gestured Garland to enter ahead of him and they stepped into the long, wide corridor of the secure psychiatric wing of Fairfax Regional Hospital. The psychiatric floor was, as expected, under-funded and in the oldest wing of the hospital, but Hobbs ran a clean, tight ship and Garland liked that about him.

"Deputies found her wandering up in Essex," Hobbs said, keeping his voice low. "She was completely disoriented and incoherent. ER docs tell me she was physically and sexually abused over an extended period and they're quite sure by more than one person."

"How bad?"

"Savagely." Hobbs said. "Perineum is torn up, apparently from the insertion of large, rough objects. Did a full rape kit. Put her gown and shoes in with it. When you examine her you'll see the hand imprints all over her thighs and arms. She was probably held down, you know, restrained, by some pretty strong hands. Working hands."

This was not a description Garland had not heard before. Like most doctors, he had a visceral abhorrence of abuse, especially abuse of children and the elderly – those most vulnerable and least able to protect themselves. Garland nodded and looked over at Hobbs and read his expression. "There's more?"

"I'm afraid so," he said. "She also sustained multiple injuries, fractures and contusions, including several broken ribs consistent with a hard fall of some kind, maybe from a window, down a flight of metal or concrete stairs…something like that." His left hand made small, delicate circles in the air as he spoke. "On this floor, I don't usually get them like this."

"Did your people pull the prints they found on her?"

"Yes, although admittedly we're really not equipped for forensics. I can't vouch for the results."

Garland liked this man. He figured him to be late fifties, early sixties, but Garland always had difficulty guessing the ages of older African-Americans. Hobbs, he noted, was well groomed, soft-spoken, and, most appreciated by Garland, self-effacing and unpretentious. In Garland's dealings with psychiatrists that was unusual, especially this high up the politico-medico dog-eat-doctor food chain.

"No I.D. on her?" Garland knew his question was rhetorical since Hobbs referred to her only as "she", but he felt compelled to ask.

"All she had when she was picked up was a generic hospital gown – no underwear – and running shoes. No hospital tags, markings or bracelet. Strange thing, though, the shoes aren't even hers – look like men's shoes, probably two or three sizes too big for her."

"Missing persons?" Garland asked.

"None her age reported in the last seventy-two hours, but the deputies are checking the lists of missing and exploited children." Hobbs looked at Garland and shrugged sadly. "It's a very long list."

"Yeah. I know."

As the orderly unlocked the door to the girl's room, Hobbs adjusted his seamless bifocals and reread Garland's card still in his hand, "'Nathaniel Garland, M.D., Ph.D., Special Agent, United States Department of Health and Human Services, Centers For Disease

Control and Prevention, Biomedical Investigations Agency'." He looked over the top of his glasses at Garland. "I've read Russian novels shorter than your title."

Garland smiled.

They stepped back as the orderly opened the door to her room and Hobbs, once again, gestured Garland to enter first. "One last caution," Hobbs hesitated, touching Garland's elbow, looking for the right words, "the, uh...oddity... uh...anomaly or whatever you want to call it is quite shocking. Be prepared."

The room they entered was monastically small and smelled of antiseptic and urine. A single south facing window with a generous view of the park was insulted by heavy chain link over the glass on the inside and thick steel bars hugging the sash on the outside. The fixed-height Fowler bed was bolted to the floor, the mattress securely anchored to the bed frame; there was nothing in the room to hurt with or be hurt by. The girl on the bed was drifting in and out of consciousness. There were large, nasty purple bruises and ragged contusions all over her face and her head was lightly bandaged.

Neither Hobbs nor Garland had any way of knowing that the young girl they were treating, Corinne Burch, had suffered no bruises or contusions when she escaped from The 610 through Sarah's trench. She had no injuries when she made it through the horrific infestation of Hugger Wood and none when she crossed the churning water of Sweetwater Creek. Her life threatening injuries occurred only after she reached what she thought would be the safety of good, decent, Christian people on the other side of the highway. She was wrong.

As the young orderly hung back near the door, Garland and Hobbs approached the bed, Garland took his stethoscope out of his jacket pocket and draped it over his neck.

It was immediately obvious to Garland that this young girl was abused in a most horrific and unspeakable manner. "How old you think? Thirteen? Fourteen?" Garland threw the comment over his shoulder to Hobbs.

"That would be my guess."

Garland took his penlight from his breast pocket, gently opened each of the girl's eyes and brushed the soft beam of light over her pupils. He made a mental note of their unusually uneven dilation.

"We obviously didn't want to medicate too much," Hobbs volunteered as if reading Garland's mind, "but I would like to get her into surgery as soon as possible."

Garland nodded slightly in acknowledgement. He then gently turned the girl's head to one side and carefully pushed back her long, gnarled and matted hair. Then, working slowly, he eased the bandages up on her forehead. And there they were, just as Hobbs reported – located just below the hairline on the upper right third of her face: another pair of perfectly shaped and formed eyes. Garland could barely conceal his astonishment. "Jesus Christ," he whispered, not realizing his words floated easily in the still air of the small room.

"My words exactly," Hobbs said.

Turning back to the girl, intrigued and curious, he gently touched her closed eyelids. "Skin is soft and responsive," he reported to Hobbs, neither expecting nor receiving a response. Then, sticking his penlight in his mouth, Garland used both of his index fingers to slowly pry open the first eyelid. "Left...uh, what do we call it? Ancillary eye, supernumerary eye – I guess, left superfluous eye – has no pupil, cornea is a bluish gray mass of nonspecific tissue. I'm sure it's non-functional." He lowered her eyelid, turned her head slightly and again very gently pried open her right eyelid. The eye beneath that lid was absolutely perfect: a moist white sclera, a clear, transparent cornea, crystal blue iris and a responsive pupil that reacted quickly, spontaneously and appropriately to the crossing beam of the penlight. Garland was amazed and fascinated.

He turned his head to speak to Hobbs and in that split second, the girl's normal, indigenous eyes sprang open, her pupils were demonically dilated and as black as puddles on asphalt. Her deafening scream was barely out of her mouth as both of her hands lunged upwards and grabbed the ends of Garland's stethoscope dangling down from around his collar. In the next breath she had the stethoscope twisted around his neck, choking him, pulling him down as she pulled herself up. Garland somehow resisted his reflexive instinct to punch her and instead tried to loosen the grip of her fingers on the garrote. But the girl was surprisingly strong, twisting the rubber tube harder, screaming in the universal language of primal terror. Horacio, the orderly, was across the room in three leaping strides. He and Hobbs wrestled the girl to her back on the bed and pulled and twisted her fingers until she finally released the stethoscope. Garland, clutching his throat and gasping for air, stumbled backwards, falling against the wall and bouncing to his knees. Hard.

Despite the jarring shock to his spine and neck, Garland quickly scrambled to his feet to help subdue the girl, but saw his help wasn't needed. With Hobbs and Horacio gently but firmly restraining her, the girl mercifully fell back into the comfort and protection of her semi-conscious state.

Ignoring the dull pain in his knees and back, Garland moved to the bed and studied the girl for several long seconds before speaking to Hobbs.

"I'd feel much more comfortable if she was in our facility," Garland said, "And I'll need the complete rape kit and all the fingerprint evidence."

"Of course," Hobbs said.

In less than half an hour the young girl was sedated, secured to a gurney and wheeled into a waiting red and white EMS bus. Hobbs accompanied her in the back. Garland instructed Horacio to drive the eighty-five miles to BIA's medical facility at the speed limit, no code-3 lights and sirens, nothing to draw attention.

Garland slid into his own car, a pristine classic green Jaguar XJS V12 convertible. He bought it years ago, at Daisy's urging, when they were barely scraping enough money together to pay the rent. It was his reward, she insisted for completing, with honors, his nearly ten brutal years of medical education.

"Don't worry," she said, "the money will come. And besides, it's just money, not like it's anything important." The Jaguar was Garland's one and only capitulation to conspicuous indulgence.

He turned the key in the ignition as he watched the ambulance begin to roll. He put the Jaguar into gear and followed it out of the parking lot.

Parked at the far end of the lot, concealed in a blind between a AAA Plumbing truck and an old lived-in Astrovan, the Clementine brothers sat patiently in their blue Ford Explorer sipping cocoa from a Thermos. As the EMS bus and the Jaguar glided out on to 31st Street, Warren Clementine jotted down Garland's license plate number. Darren Clementine retrieved his cell to call Norman Starke. He then put the Explorer in gear and pulled out after them.

16

The long drive to BIA headquarters gave Garland time to absorb the impact of the young girl's startling condition. Not just the horrendous damage to her body and the appalling brutality inflicted upon her, that in itself was unspeakably cruel, but it also gave him time to ponder the possible – or impossible – pathogenesis of the young girl's superfluous eyes. In his nearly twenty years in medicine he had never encountered anything like it. Of course, he had certainly seen his share of polydactyl cases – extra fingers and/or toes on newborns. And during his pediatric practice he had even been called in several times on consults where babies had been born with conjoined organs or redundant partial limbs resulting from non-formed siblings. But he had never encountered an anatomical incongruity like this: a patient with four eyes, three of which were seemingly functional.

On his first day of rounds as a young med student, Garland learned the axiom that stays with every doctor through his or her entire career: if it looks like a duck, walks like a duck and quacks like a duck, it's probably a duck. And the corollary Occam's razor: if you hear hoof beats, think horses, not zebras. In short, look for the simplest explanation first.

The duck in this case, the simplest, most reasonable and most logical explanation was that the young girl was simply born with her unfortunate anomaly. So why, Garland wondered, was he having such a difficult time accepting the obvious? Was it just the sideshow freakishness of it? Was it what he imagined the young girl's life must have been like growing up with such a bizarre medical condition? Maybe her life wasn't hellish if she had loving, caring parents. Surely she had seen specialists, there would be extensive medical records, there would be medical literature documenting her case. Yet he still came back to one unanswered question: what was this young girl doing roaming the back roads of Fairfax dressed in nothing more than a hospital gown and someone else's shoes?

When the ambulance swung on to I-270 and headed north toward Frederick, Maryland, Garland speed dialed Grover Wheeler, the agency's chief of medicine, to prepare Con-Con 1 for their new patient.

Con-Con 1 – Contamination Containment 1 – was the first of four bio-safety levels at Fed-Med. It was specifically designed for patients with unidentifiable pathologies, the assumption being there may be an unknown and potentially dangerous contagion involved in the patient's disease process.

Garland led the EMS bus down the transition off the interstate as it picked up Route 15 north. A few minutes later they were passing the sprawling grounds of Fort Detrick, home to the USAMRIID – U.S. Army Medical Research Institute of Infectious Diseases. As lofty and impressive as the name was, everyone knew USAMRIID's real purpose – the collection, analysis, design and manufacture of America's offensive and defensive Chemical and Biological Warfare weapons. Twenty-five minutes farther north on Route 15, was Fort Isenmann, Fort Detrick's smaller, poorer cousin, unceremoniously abandoned after the Soviet breakup. Years later, after the 9/11 massacre, Isenmann was reopened and ceded to the Department of Health and Human Services and renovated for use as BIA headquarters.

At the time of its closure, Ft. Isenmann was a very nasty place that did very nasty work – work that was deemed even too hot for USAMRIID. Headed by its 23-year-old wunderkind director, Dr. Christian van der Veldt, a brilliant molecular geneticist, Ft. Isenmann scientists created germs of such virulence and devised diabolical delivery schemes of such deadly magnitude, their kill capability extended into the billions. Even at the height of the cold war, when the most hawkish of the Defense Department's leadership was openly advocating the judicious use of tactical nuclear weapons, whispers of the deployment of Doctor V's germs was considered to be even beyond their bounds of bloodlust. The outrageously lethal pathogens of van der Veldt's creation – genetically altered and enhanced viruses – were ultimately frozen in time and still resided in cryogenic chambers deep within the bowels of the Fort.

Bolted to the rough red brick pedestal at entrance was a large, polished brass plaque that read: "Fort Horace T. Isenmann, United States Department of Health and Human Services, Centers For Disease Control and Prevention, Advanced Research & Biomedical Investigations Agency". That was the facility's official name, but in Washington and Atlanta it was simply referred to as Fed-Med.

At the security gate entrance, Garland swiped his ID across the card reader and the first of two steel arms rose effortlessly, like a youthful erection, to allow him to roll forward to the second arm. As the car crossed the imbedded sensor, the first arm swung down, effectively trapping the Jag between the two barriers. Automated digital cameras photographed the Jag's license plates and when a match was made between Garland's ID and the plates, the second arm rose allowing the Jag access into the Fed-Med compound. Garland had phoned ahead to security to get a gate pass for the ambulance.

As he waited for the EMS bus's authorization to enter, Grover Wheeler opened Garland's passenger door and hopped in. As a six-foot-four, two hundred twenty pound, lean, muscular African-American man, Wheeler could easily be mistaken for a professional athlete – maybe a wide receiver or a defensive back, but in truth, Grover Wheeler couldn't catch a ball if he had six hands with Velcro on every finger.

"What do you have in the box?" Wheeler said.

"A kid, runaway maybe, I don't know. Beat-up, raped, sodomized, god knows what else. She's a mess. Vitals are like a rollercoaster."

Wheeler was confused. "Then why the hell did you transport? She was already in Fairfax, they could've handled this."

"No, not this, Grove." Garland stuck his arm out the window and signaled the ambulance to follow him around the parking lot to the patient receiving entrance.

"Not what?" Wheeler's voice took on that slow, low tone of suspicion.

"Okay. Here it is. She has three eyes. Technically, four, but as best as I can tell, only three are functional."

"What the hell are you talking about, Nate?"

"I'm talking about a messed up kid with four eyes on her face."

Wheeler stared at him, trying to decide if Garland was just yanking him. It wouldn't have been the first time. "You're serious," he finally said. It was a statement, not a question.

Within minutes, the young girl was being processed into Con-Con 1. Under Wheeler's careful and compassionate direction, the intake team worked quickly, quietly, efficiently and professionally. If they were shocked or repulsed by the girl's anomaly, they certainly didn't or wouldn't show it.

There were only two other patients being treated in Con-Con 1 at the moment: a woman with a mutated West Nile virus and an older man with a stubborn, unresponsive case of group A streptococci necrotizing fasciitis – flesh eating bacteria.

"How long do you think it'll take?"

"I don't know. She's so beat up, god knows what they're going to find internally. She needs the GYN surgery first, that's for sure, and then the orthos have all those bones to set and a load of reconstruction work. I think we're looking at ten to twelve hours. If you're thinking of talking to her, that's probably not going to happen until tomorrow some time and even that depends on her pain management."

Garland nodded. "The sooner I can talk to her…" He let the sentence trail off, and then said, "So what do you think? The pathogenesis of her eyes?"

"Definitely not surgical," Wheeler said. "Those eyes weren't implanted, if that's what you're thinking."

"You're sure?

"There's no healing bone mass, no orbital cellulites, tissue's pliant, not a trace of scarring. Yeah, I'm sure. Damnedest thing I've ever seen."

"Could be a genetic birth anomaly," Garland offered.

"Could be." Wheeler agreed."Possibly a radiation effect of some type?"

"One isolated case? I don't think so. I would expect there would have to be more exposure if it was radiation." Wheeler countered.

"Yeah, you're probably right."

They walked toward the elevators, mulling in silence. It was Garland who spoke first. "Alright, look, don't get all over me, but, uh, what do you think about the possibility of spontaneous organogenesis?"

Wheeler shot a dubious look at his friend. "Like she's sitting home one night eating chips and dip, watching Oprah and suddenly she's got two more eyes on her face? Come on, Nate, you know organs and limbs form in utero."

"I'm looking for another answer."

"Maybe there isn't another answer."

"Yeah, well, there is. Somehow somebody did this to her."

"Let's not jump from the absurd to the ridiculous," Wheeler cautioned. "We'll do it by the numbers, see where it takes us."

"She was wearing this hospital gown when the deputies found her, Grove," Garland said, "where do you think it's going to take us?"

"Wait for the genetics, okay? We'll know soon enough."

Wheeler was Nathaniel Garland's yin. His calming influence. His voice of reason when the noise and chaos in Garland's head got too loud. He was his friend and confessor and Garland trusted Wheeler as much as he could trust anyone.

"We'll have the complete genetics profile in two, three days. We'll have all our answers then."

Garland nodded. "Sorry. I'm just a little tired and cranky."

"Trust me, Nate, you're cranky even when you're not tired. And the shooting on Burning Tree didn't help."

"Call me the minute she's out of surgery." Garland started to leave, then stopped and turned back to Wheeler. "You notice her mouth, Grove?"

"What about it?"

"The way it turns up at the corners. Doesn't it kind of remind you of Daisy?"

Wheeler took a short breath, wondering how far this was going to go. "I don't know," he shrugged, "I wasn't married to her, Nate, you were. You see Daisy in this girl?"

"No, just the mouth thing."

17

In the morning, Garland found Arleta Farleigh changing into her lab coat in the main forensic lab's utility room. As usual, her dull brown hair was piled high on her head like a rodent's nest and held in place by what looked like red chopsticks. Vanity was definitely not her sin. In the plus column, Arleta Farleigh held two Ph.D.s, one in chemistry, one in biology, and, say what you would about Arleta, there was no one on the floor who was smarter or who knew her way around a forensics lab better than she.

Garland decided on the direct approach.

"I'm not here yet, Garland," Arleta cut him off before he spoke. "Haven't had my coffee yet. Come back later."

So much for the direct approach.

"We've got an emergency situation."

Arleta took a sip of coffee and dipped her eyes to the rape kit and green evidence bags in Garland's hands. "You have something there for me? What are we talking about here? The kid downstairs with four eyes?"

What surprised Garland most at that moment was that he wasn't surprised that she knew. Probably everybody in the building already knew. Hell, probably everyone in the compound knew. There were very few secrets at Fed-Med.

"You know about her?" He felt compelled to ask anyway.

"Hell, yes, who doesn't?" Arleta Farleigh's face sponged into a cynical don't-be-so-naïve expression. "When can I see her? Four eyes. I want to take some tissue samples."

"Dr. Wheeler already took some. I've got them right here."

"Do I look like I'd trust Wheeler's technique?" She took another sip of coffee and looked at him over the rim of the cup. "All right, let's have it. This one's going to be good."

Garland handed her everything.

"That's all she had when they found her. A hospital gown and sneakers which are obviously not her own."

"I'll do what I can. Call you when I've got something."

"These are all we have to go on. We've got to squeeze everything we can out of them."

"Are you telling me my business? I said, I'll let you know after they've been processed."

"I need something else, too." Garland waited for Arleta's arched eyebrow to recede to its resting position on her face. He pulled a photo Corinne Burch out of his pocket and handed it to her. "I need your guys to check every hospital, clinic, and inpatient care institution in a hundred mile radius of Fairfax, see if any of them are missing a patient."

"Jesus Henry Christ," Arleta exploded, "you know how many facilities you're talking about? Huh? That's practically the entire Eastern seaboard."

"Yeah, so let's get all the techs, all the assistants upstairs, everyone we can working the phones. And put her photo out over the national missing persons' wire and the National Center for Missing and Exploited Children. This kid is missing from somebody somewhere, let's find out who and where."

Arleta stared at Garland for several long seconds and then said, "Hey, Garland, you really got a set of stones, you know that?"

"So they tell me," Garland answered, leaving, not knowing whether to be flattered or repulsed by Arleta's compliment.

In the elevator, Garland swiped his ID key across the security sensor and pressed CC-1. The Fed-Med elevators may be the only lifts in the world where as the numbers go up, the car goes down. L-1, where he entered the elevator, was actually the ground floor. CC-1 was belowground, one floor down; CC-2 was two floors down, etcetera. The elevator went as low as CC-5, each floor designating a higher level of security and biohazard contamination-containment: hence, Con-Con.

Garland found Wheeler observing the girl's surgery. When they made eye contact through the glass, Garland held his wrist up and tapped his watch; in response, Wheeler held up three fingers. Garland nodded, then pressed the small white button below the window frame.

"Why so long?" Garland said to the window.

Wheeler's voice came back through the hidden speaker above the glass. "Complications." The Rolling Stones' Brown Sugar was wailing in the background behind his voice; it was the surgeon's music of choice.

"It's a mother," Celeste Reynolds, the surgeon, said.

"Is there anything you need?" Garland asked. "Anything I can do to help?"

"Nada. We're good here." Wheeler said. "We'll have her out by four."

"Five," Reynolds corrected.

"I'm on my cell if…if anything comes up, don't wait."

Garland took the elevator back up to IAS – Investigations Administration Support, two floors above the forensics lab. Off the elevator was a large bullpen, not unlike the gopher farm in Dilbert cartoons. A dozen or so glass-fronted offices for BIA investigators like Garland surrounded the bullpen. His personal office, all 120-square feet of it, was furnished totally government issue. But unlike the other investigators, he had added no personal touches, no art or posters or tzotskies anywhere in the office. Books and medical journals were neatly piled everywhere; case folders were stacked on the corners of his steel desk like pylons; the center of the desk was dominated by his laptop. There was only one exception to Garland's minimalism: a butt ugly Chinese pump-top electric teapot with a god-awful green and gold floral design around the base. But it served its purpose admirably, not just heating water, but keeping it at a constant near boil as decent tea required. He steeped a cup of Barnesbeg Estate Darjeeling.

Garland was going to begin researching the medical literature for other cases of supernumerary eyes. He knew he would have to dig into all the current genetic research – a huge, tedious job and he quickly realized that at that moment he had neither the patience nor the fortitude to begin such an intensive project. He reached for his phone and called the FBI switchboard at Hoover.

18

Garland took I-270 south to the Muddy Branch exit in Gaithersburg and easily found the Starbucks that Fitch and Hollister had suggested. It was halfway between the Bureau in D.C. and Fed-Med in Frederick. They were waiting for him in the small parking area. Garland got into the backseat of their Ford and Fitch greeted him with a venti cup of Tazo Awake tea.

"So you got something for us, doc?" Hollister asked.

"Nothing but nagging questions. You? Anything?"

"Stone cold, dude."

"What about ballistics?" Garland asked

"The lab's still on it." Fitch said. "Frangible points. Fragments of the slugs that hit Eccevarria and Kessler were apparently washed away in the rain. Nothing solid was recovered from the scene. Not a thing. The round that lit up Capiloff was probably fused to the metal of the cars in the collision. Metal lab's combing through it now."

"So you guys are nowhere on the shooter."

"Not exactly nowhere. The shooter took four shots, made four hits, all moving targets. His primary was obviously Capiloff, who he nailed dead-center in the head after first blowing out his side window. W   e think Eccevarria and Kessler took fire to disarm and disable, not to kill."

"One shot, one kill," Garland said, mimicking the well-known motto.

"That's our guess, too." Fitch said. "Our boy is Sniper School trained."

"We have a team at Benning right now," Hollister continued, "digging around at Sniper School, but the Army's being real dicks about their classified shit."

Garland took another sip of tea. "What about the casket? What was in it? The one in Capiloff's hearse. Did your guys check it out?"

Fitch and Hollister looked at each other. "Somebody must have," Fitch said. Then to Garland, "You know something we don't?"

"No. But there's something bothering me I just can't put my finger on. Capiloff worked for the mortuary. He had information or something for Sarah Levine. She goes to meet him, poof, she vanishes. We, I'm talking now about Eccevarria, Kessler, Dunbarton and myself, we go to interview Capiloff but we really didn't have anything substantial to go on. Capiloff comes cruising down the street in his shiny hearse and gets his head blown off. Somebody knew we were going to interview him."

The implications didn't have to be spelled out. Both Fitch and Hollister nodded their understanding.

"Okay, so where you going with this?"

"Piecing together Sarah's files, we know she was investigating trafficking in pacemakers and body parts. Pacemakers are only removed if the body's going to be cremated – they have a habit of blowing up in the ovens. What we mined out of Sarah's notes was she suspected that the mortuary chain had been systematically harvesting generators from the bodies they received. And if they're harvesting generators, they're probably harvesting everything else they can, too – gold and silver dental appliances, mechanical valves, corneas, false eyes, dentures, bones, veins, skin and any other body part that's saleable."

"Billion dollar business," Hollister said. "Fucking ghouls."

"Look, you guys are better at this than me. I was thinking you get the warrant and we hit the funeral home together, get the paperwork on that casket."

Hollister drew a hand across his chin. "Gil and I aren't point on this one. The D. D. assigned a squad higher up the food chain. What we're sharing with you is classified Bureau information, not firsthand intel. But since it's about Eccevarria, you know, we're all giving and getting everything we can develop."

"I'm open to back channel," Garland said, floating what he knew to be a risky proposition for the two agents.

Neither Fitch nor Hollister answered immediately. Then Fitch finally said, "Quiet and informal."

"Totally." Garland said. "Look, what if I talked to Haynes? He's probably got some juice with your boss. You know how these big wheels turn."

Fitch puffed out his cheeks, held his breath for a moment and exhaled in a rush. "Not a good idea, Doc."

"Why not?"

"Because your boss is under investigation."

Garland was momentarily stunned. "Jesus, for what?"

"Don't know."

"Justice is your department, for chrissakes, and you're telling me you don't know why your own department is investigating Haynes?"

"It's a big fucking department. We don't know what goes on in the AG's office any more than we know what goes on in any other DOJ office. We only know what we're told."

Garland's eyes shifted from Fitch to Hollister. "Is there any way you can find out? I mean, who's investigating Haynes for what?"

"Yeah," Hollister said. "We'll poke around. And if you get anything…"

"I'll call you." Garland said.

"One other thing, Doc," Fitch said. "Watch your six."

Garland looked to Hollister for a translation. "Your six, Doc, your back. Watch your back."

19

When Garland got back to Fed-Med, Wheeler brought him up to speed on the girl's surgery and prognosis. There was more damage than they had initially suspected, including a hairline fracture of her jaw.

"Kopelson wire it?" Garland asked.

"No," Wheeler answered, "pinned it. But she's still not going to be able to talk for a while. Besides, I think we should keep her sedated as long as we safely can. Her pain has to be excruciating; makes no sense to wake her into it."

"How long you think?"

"Twenty-four to forty-eight, depending on her vitals. Then we'll get her up and introduce some effective pain management."

"Grove, I need five minutes with her awake and cogent. Just a short window before you start the drip."

"She's your patient, Nate, but personally I'd let her sleep 'til Christmas."

Garland knew Wheeler was right. If the girl were his daughter, he'd do everything in his power to keep her pain at bay.

They turned into the I.C. and saw Carter Haynes and Nelson Dunbarton staring through the glass at the young girl. The girl, just out of surgery, was back in her bay, attended by a Navy surgical nurse. A clutch of wires and tubes rose like wild vines from the girl's broken body, the vines connected to an array of LCD monitors clustered in the wall above her head. An oxygen cannulae directed fresh breath into her nostrils.

"I didn't realize she was just a pup," Haynes said without bothering to turn his head from the window.

"We're guessing thirteen, maybe fourteen," Garland said.

"Jesus, poor kid," Dunbarton concurred softly.

"Will she make it?" Haynes let the question float like an infield popup.

"She tolerated the surgery very well," Wheeler said. "Vitals are good. She's malnourished, but still young and strong. I'd say her prognosis is very good for full recovery."

"Good," Haynes nodded. "And the superfluous eyes? Ya have any thoughts 'bout their origin?" Haynes allowed his accent to seep through and he pronounced the word 'origin' as 'ah'rigin'.

"No. Not yet."

"So the eyes could be natural. An unfortunate birth defect?"

Wheeler's gaze shifted to Garland; a subtle movement not lost on Haynes.

"I take it that you may suspect more than the hand of god involved in this poor child's disfigurement."

"Truth, Carter, we really don't know. You want my personal opinion? I don't think she was born that way. But I have no scientific evidence yet to back up my suspicions."

"What suspicions?" Dunbarton raised his eyebrows. "What t'hell are you guys talking about? If she wasn't born that way, then what?" Dunbarton let the question hang, looking from Wheeler to Garland. "C'mon. What is it?"

"Transgenic engineering," Garland said.

"Bull. Shit." Haynes grunted. "Don't tell me you concur, Dr. Wheeler?"

"There's no way of knowing until all the lab results are in. Transgenic engineering is just one possibility among many others."

Dunbarton, still confused, looked to Haynes. "Sorry, I'm a lawyer, not a doctor, would somebody mind?"

"Gene altering, Nels," Wheeler said. "Could happen naturally, through chemical or radiation exposure or some other pollutant or," Wheeler paused, not believing what he was about to say, "or it could be biomedically engineered."

"You're kidding me, right?" Dunbarton shook his head. "You're saying somebody could have altered this girl's genes so she'd grow extra eyes? What're you guys, out of your fucking minds?"

"With the fresh lines of embryonic stem cells now available and the right genetic roadmap it's theoretically possible, that's all we're suggesting."

"Theoretically." Haynes snorted derisively, then, focusing on Garland, said, "Do you know Jason Beck?"

"The ophthalmologist? Only by reputation. I hear he's pretty good."

"Dr. Wheeler?" Haynes turned his attention to the bigger man.

"Don't know him personally, but from what I hear on the street his clinic is almost on par with UCLA's Jules Stein Institute."

"Better than the Stein Institute, so my sources tell me. But at that level, it's a spittin' contest, right? Regardless, he'll be here in the morning, take a look at the girl, give us his informed opinion."

"Excuse me? Carter, that's not the way it works."

"What do you mean that's not the way it works?"

"She's my patient. I'm the attending. And based on the medical needs of my patient, I decide who, if and when a consult is even necessary."

"Maybe in your world, son, not mine. Last time I looked I'm still head of this Agency and I will do what I damn well please to protect its integrity."

Garland felt the juices begin to bubble in his gut. He was about to respond when Wheeler laid his hand firmly on Garland's arm, stopping him from erupting.

"No. That's totally unacceptable." Garland made no attempt to mask his anger.

"Hey," Haynes shot back, "you don't like my peaches? Don't shake my tree. Beck and his assistant'll be here in the mornin'. You jus' make damn sure they feel welcome, ya hear?"

20

There are distinct advantages to chronic insomnia. For Nathaniel Garland it was the ability to stay awake all night and watch over the young girl. It allowed him to check her vitals often and to stroke her hand and speak to her through her deep drug-induced sleep. He spoke to her as if he was speaking to his own daughter and that gave him – and hopefully her – some comfort.

Con-Con 1 was in night mode with the lights at half staff and only a skeleton crew at service. Garland liked this time of night there. It was quiet. Peaceful. Restful. He glanced through the I.C. bay window and saw Maria, the night duty nurse, leaning back in her chair, feet up on the desk, ankles crossed, reading the Spanish edition of People Magazine. He checked the girl's vitals one more time, held her hand for several more seconds, then went back to the bedside chair and his laptop.

Driven tirelessly by Breezy's illness, Garland came to know his way around the biomedical research websites better than most. He searched specifically for case studies of supernumerary organs, particularly eyes. He also wanted to get some background on Dr. Jason Beck, Haynes' consult whom he would meet in a few hours.

Garland started his search at the NCBI PubMed site, a central clearing house for general medical and genetic research. On his first query, the amount of information returned from the database was staggering. Worldwide, there were thousands of articles, reports and experimental proposals all keyed to transgenic research. Garland took some notes and then, in succession, went to the OMIM site, the GeneCards site and finally Merck Medicus.

Garland's search soon began to take on some semblance of order. By culling through the abstracts, he had narrowed his search to less than a hundred recent articles on vascular tissue engineering, hematopoietic stem cells engineered in bone marrow, genetic osteoblast manipulation and genetic techniques of macular regeneration. The last article held particular interest for Garland — one of the study's authors was Dr. Jason Beck.

Surprisingly, Garland could not locate any reports, research articles or even anecdotal material on transgenically engineered eyes. There were pockets of researchers, including Jason Beck, who were experimenting with optic nerve regeneration, engineered cranial bone growth, muscle, tissue and vascular cell manufacturing — all tangentially related to the young girl's supernumerary eyes, but nothing specifically that would indicate how they developed. He was reluctantly coming to the conclusion that Grover Wheeler was right: there was a tragic genetic mistake in utero and the girl was simply born with four eyes. So why, Garland wondered, was it not reported in a journal somewhere or investigated by any noted scientists? How could such a unique phenomenon be missed or, worse, ignored?

Garland knew biomedical research required big money, large teams and shared authorship and credit on most published papers. Biomedical research is big business. From initial grant writing to final patent approval, billions of dollars are at stake and the fortunes and reputations of universities and international conglomerates often hang in the balance. Knowing this intimately from his recent undercover work at Jensen-Dillard Pharmaceuticals, he catalogued all of the relevant articles and began the tedious task of cross-checking all of the papers' many authors.

He found that Jason Beck appeared as co-author of five significant studies all dealing with macular regeneration and the genetically engineered repair of optic nerves. The studies were certainly germane to the young girl's condition, but none could be directly linked to transgenically engineered eyes. Garland also noticed that several of Beck's more recent papers were co-authored by what he assumed was a biotech company, Evin Co. VIXI. Garland continued cross-checking and quickly found eleven other papers also co-authored by Evin Co. Vixi, all with the notation "CVDV". The Evin papers, all extremely scholarly – and many being the research work of Dr. Erno Pniak – were only tangentially related to the girl: bone and cell tissue manufacture, vascular growth, nerve sequences, again, germane, but no cigar. Garland made a note to call Erno Pniak. The footnote showed him to be the chief orthopedist at Walter Reed Army Medical Center.

Although the primary researchers differed, the one co-author listed on all the studies held Garland's attention. Evin Company. What the hell are the Roman numerals VIXI and CVDV? Is the first fifteen or seventeen? And CVDV, is it 610? What the hell do those numbers mean? Garland whispered the words aloud to himself as if hearing them would trigger some memory or association. It didn't. He wondered, of course, who and what the Evin Company was. He clicked over to NASDAQ and found no listing for them; same for the NYSE, the OTC and the major foreign markets. It seemed clear to Garland that Evin was probably a privately held company – there were hundreds of small, privately owned biotech companies playing the genome sweepstakes and Garland made a mental note to have Stuart check them out for him.

He had been searching nearly three and a half hours and had realized an hour earlier that his bladder was about to burst. Damn tea. He got up, leaned over the young girl and whispered, "I'll be back in a few minutes. Maria's right outside the bay, so if you need anything, she'll be right there for you."

In the Con-Con 1 men's restroom, Garland enjoyed a satisfying pee, then scrubbed his hands and face and brushed the fur out of his mouth with his shaving kit toothbrush.

Leaving the restroom, Garland was struck by the thought that maybe the girl wasn't American. If she was foreign and perhaps born in an obscure village or town, then maybe the anomalous birth defect wouldn't have been reported. Maybe it would have been kept secret out of shame or superstition.

Coming around the hub, Garland did not immediately see Maria at her station. But he did notice that the privacy curtains had been pulled closed across the girl's window. That's odd. Did Maria close them? Did something happen? Was something wrong? He walked faster and turned into the girl's bay.

A figure was leaning over the girl. A man. He was wearing scrubs, but they were a much darker green than the normal Con-Con color. Garland moved into the room, running directly toward the man, grabbing him by the shoulder. "Who are you?" Garland's voice was louder than he expected.

The man, startled, whipped his head around and looked directly at Garland. He was wearing what Garland thought to be welder's goggles, incredibly thick smoky lenses with a leather strap that clasped behind his head. The man was Norman Starke. In his right he deftly palmed a hypodermic needle. Garland pushed past Starke to get to the girl on the bed. The first thing he noticed was that the thick gauze cap had been pushed up on her forehead.

"What the hell are you doing here?" Garland quickly moved toward the security alarm button above the bed and slapped it hard. Muffled sirens whooped and excited security strobes immediately flashed throughout the building.

Garland never saw Starke's hand come up. When he did turn, it was too late. Starke plunged the palmed hypodermic into his exposed neck. Garland yelped and his arm came up reflexively, his elbow catching Starke squarely in the jaw. Starke's head snapped back, but he kept his balance.

That was more than Garland could do. Whatever was in the syringe electrified his nerves. His knees buckled and he fell, bouncing off the edge of the bed just before the darkness enveloped him – and then the world went black.

21

Somewhere, hidden deep among the wild ganglia in the less traveled canyons of his backbrain, Garland knew it was the drugs that kept him submerged in the heavy slumber. On one level, he fought to rouse himself, to push through the smothering taffy of his induced sleep. But on another level, a more inviting place, he felt an enveloping peacefulness he didn't want to leave.

Daisy was curled up in the crook of his shoulder, her wheatfield hair splashed across his chest like summer. They were floating in a white tiled room. Peaceful. Serene. Timeless. Garland's senses were alive. And with Daisy snuggled up against him, the feeling went beyond ecstasy to pure rapture. It was perfect. It was bliss.

"It's the drugs," Daisy whispered, but she wasn't really speaking.

"I know," Garland answered, and he, too, wasn't really speaking."

"Sweetie, you have to get up."

"No. I'm not leaving you again."

"Our little girl needs you. You have to get up, Nathaniel – get up now."

The voice was different now. Unsettling. It wasn't Daisy's sweet, lyrical voice, it was harsh and discordant and grating.

"Get up," the voice demanded. "Nate, wake up. Wake up."

Garland glanced down at Daisy. But it wasn't her curled up against his shoulder. It was Wheeler. "Get your ass up, now, come on, get up, wake up."

Garland's eyes fluttered open. His lids weighed a ton each and they fell shut again like slamming doors.

"No, no," Wheeler said, "Nate, open your eyes, come on, up, up, let's go."

Garland slowly raised his lids and light poured into his eyes like a shower of needles. Consciousness returned slowly. The realization dawned that he was in a Fowler bed in the small infirmary on Con-Con 1. Voices were now filtering through, but Garland didn't immediately recognize them.

"Get him up," he heard.

"Let's get him hydrated," came from a second voice, a woman's voice.

Garland fought to bring the room into focus. He tried to speak but his words slurred and what little saliva he had in his Mojave mouth was drooling out of the corner. He tried to lift his head; it weighed as much as a small Chevy and somebody, the Navy nurse, he thought, helped ease it back down to the pillow.

Then, slowly, the veil began lifting in Garland's head and images of the intruder, the goggles, the hypodermic, the attack, the little girl in Con-Con 1 all came flooding in at once. Garland forced himself up into a wobbly sitting position and blinked at Wheeler, clearing the haze from his eyes. The nurse, the voice he heard earlier, steadied him and handed him a paper cup of water.

"Welcome back." Wheeler smiled.

Garland moved his mouth to speak, but the words wouldn't come out. The nurse put the cup of water to his lips and he slurped some down. He tried to speak again but the only word he was able to utter sounded like "girl".

"She's fine, I mean, in relative terms," Wheeler assured him. "Whatever that guy was up to, you stopped him before he could do anything to her. You took the juice meant for her — it was a combo platter: Demerol and a monoamine oxidase compound. If he had gotten it into her line, with the amount of D already in her system, she would've O.D.'d or died of liver failure two, three days from now — and nothing would've turned up at autopsy."

Garland nodded his two-ton head, letting Wheeler know he understood. "We...we...should..." Garland mumbled and then his words faltered again.

Wheeler knew exactly where he was going. "Yeah, yeah, it's done. We moved her down to Con 2; armed security, 24/7. She's safe."

Again Garland barely nodded, but the corners of his mouth rose slightly in the semblance of a smile. "How...how long was...was...I...?"

"Let's just say it was probably the best sleep you've had in years. It's almost 9:00 am."

The door opened and a mountain of a man wearing a blue blazer and khakis filled the entire open doorframe. He was Pender. He had a first name — Marvin , Melvin, Mervin, something like that, but everyone just called him Pender. Pender was head of security for Fed-Med. Military through and through and aggrandized by rumors of Delta Force action in both Afghanistan and Iraq. Pender did nothing to dispel the rumors and he neither confirmed nor denied anything about his past. Pender took his job very, very seriously, culturing the notion of active terrorist paranoia in extremis.

And last night he failed. An intruder got in past Pender's security apparatus and apparently attempted to kill one of Fed-Med's helpless charges. Heads will roll.

"How much longer?" Pender asked from the doorway.

"He's conscious now," Wheeler said., "Half hour until he's cogent, another thirty minutes to have him on his feet, a few hours to completely metabolize."

"Get him to my facility in fifteen minutes." And Pender was gone as stealthily as he arrived.

The security building across the Fed-Med compound was filled with electronic surveillance equipment. Its banks of monitors resembled a NASA launch facility. Pender was waiting with two uniformed security officers when Garland and Wheeler finally arrived.

"Do you know of anyone who might want to harm your patient?" Pender directed the question to both Wheeler and Garland, looking from one to the other.

"No," Wheeler answered for both of them.

"Dr. Garland?"

"No." Garland repeated. "How'd he get in, Pender?"

"I'm getting to that."

It was precisely that kind of authoritative bullshit that set Garland's teeth on edge. He motioned Garland and Wheeler to a console and indicated the screen.

"Here's your bad guy. See if there's anything you recognize about him. His size, clothes, hat, car, anything, you got that?"

Wheeler looked at Garland. Had Pender really said 'bad guy'?

Pender punched a button on the console. The monitor immediately displayed an exterior view of the Fed-Med compound's Columbia Road entrance and security gates. In the lower right hand corner, the image was dated and time-stamped: 3:18 AM. On screen, a nondescript car pulled up to the security gate entrance. It was a Ford Taurus or Toyota Something – hard to tell in the relative darkness at that distance.

"You recognize the car?" Pender asked.

Both Wheeler and Garland shook their heads.

"You mind speaking out loud for the record?"

"You recording in here?" Garland asked, both surprised and suspicious.

"The car? You recognize it?" Pender asked again, completely ignoring Garland's question.

"No." Both Wheeler and Garland answered in unison.

"Just asking. We believe it's a stolen vehicle. We've got the local authorities checking it out. Keep watching."

On the screen, the driver of the car lowered the window and swiped his ID across the sensor and the first of the two steel railroad-crossing-gate type arms rose up. The man was wearing a hat, not a baseball cap, more like a wide-brimmed Stetson that completely shielded his face from the cameras.

"Recognize anything about him now?"

Again, Wheeler and Garland answered 'no'.

The car rolled forward to the second security arm. As the car crossed the sensor, the first arm swung down, trapping the car between the arms. Automated cameras flashed as they photographed the car's license plates. When a match was made between the man's ID and the car plates, the second arm rose allowing the car into the Fed-Med parking lot.

"He's one of us," Wheeler whispered, amazed by what he was seeing.

The rest of the disk, which ran about three and a half minutes, showed the man entering the building wearing green scrubs, getting in the elevator, sliding his ID in the elevator card reader and pressing the Con-Con 1 button. On Con-Con 1, it carried the man's activity all the way through his attack on Maria, the night nurse.

"Maria?" Garland remembered, guilty at not having asked about her earlier.

"We found her behind the desk." Pender said.

"How is she?"

"Dead." Pender said flatly. "He used a garrote, probably piano wire. We didn't think it was necessary to show you the homicide here."

Garland, stunned, could only nod. Wheeler patted his back in support. The security tape continued, showing the man taking the syringe out of his pocket, approaching the girl in the I.C. bay bed, his surprise by Garland and the attack that followed. Garland also saw how his inadvertent elbow to the man's chin staggered him and forced his retreat without ever harming the girl.

Without taking his eyes off the screen, Garland said, "That guy knew where every single camera was. He knows the security procedures. He didn't show his face once, just an occasional glimpse of those goggles he was wearing."

"He's one of us," Wheeler said again.

"There's nothing about him you recognize, Doctor?"

"No." Garland turned when he suddenly realized that Pender knew more than he was volunteering. "You know who he is, don't you? Who? Who is it?"

Pender shrugged. "All I can tell you, doctor, is who he isn't. He was able to enter the fort and get past security because the license plates on his vehicle and the ID he used to breech are registered to Dr. Sarah Levine."

22

"You think Sarah's still alive?" Wheeler was helping Garland cross the expansive Fed-Med parking lot from Pender's office.

Garland shrugged. His knees were still weak, but at least the fog in his head was lifting and it seemed that he could think clearly now, or, at least better than he could walk.

"I mean, if the guy had Sarah's ID and license plates, it stands to reason he's got her and her car, too, right?"

"Maybe. I don't know, Grove."

"C'mon, don't mess with me, Nate. Sarah's disappearance wasn't just a, you know, a carjacking or a mugging or something like that. It had a purpose. That's why I think she's still alive somewhere."

As much as he wanted to believe that Sarah was still alive, Garland knew now that her life or death was at the pleasure of this psychopath who had no fear or compunction about entering a tightly guarded government facility for the purpose of murdering a comatose child. If Sarah was still alive, it would only be because this man needed her alive.

"Nate, you think this was the same guy who gunned down Eccevarria and the hearse driver? Once you start connecting the dots, it seems pretty obvious, doesn't it?"

"I don't think we have enough dots yet."

"You going to tell Stu?"

"I haven't decided. The last thing I want to do is get his hopes up."

"Yeah."

"We've got to wake the girl. I know it's going to be sheer hell for her, but we've got to talk to her."

"She's the missing dot, isn't she? Sarah and our little girl are somehow connected, right?"

"It's quacking like a duck, Grove."

They walked on in silence, Garland letting the puzzle pieces snap together in his head. And they fit together beautifully.

"The intruder knew all of the security procedures of the fort," he said, "knew where every camera was inside and out, knew where the girl was. He had to be a Fed-Med insider or working for someone on the inside. Maybe the same insider who knew the exact time and place we were arresting Rudolf Capiloff. The same person who knew the exact time and place Sarah was meeting Capiloff the night she disappeared. Yeah, it's a duck, Grove, a fucking duck."

"Damn," Wheeler said. His cell warbled and he answered it. He listened for two seconds and responded, "Okay, thanks. Tell them we're on our way, be there in thirty seconds." He clicked off and in the same motion said to Garland, "Beck's waiting at security in the lobby."

"Wonderful," Garland said.

23

Jason Beck was clipping a plastic Visitor ID badge to his lapel when Garland and Wheeler met him at the security desk. Accompanying Beck was a much younger, slender woman whose face was partially hidden behind large, fashionable sunglasses. Her thick hair was as black as a pirate's heart and pulled back into a severe bun. That, plus her high cheekbones and the distinctive shape of her face, spoke to an obvious Asian heritage. The usual courtesies were exchanged and Beck introduced the woman as Dr. Polly Collier, his assistant.

Beck's handshake was firm and confident, his banter came easy, his small talk pertinent. Polly Collier's handshake, however, was nothing short of imperious as she extended her arm slightly and briefly touched her fingertips to Garland's and then to Wheeler's. She didn't smile and the only word she uttered to either of them was a simple, soft-spoken "Hello." Collier's hands and fingers, Garland noted, were long, tapered and delicate to the point of feeling fragile in their brief touch. Surgeon's hands, Garland thought. And the thin, unobtrusive gold wedding band on her left hand also did not elude his notice.

Still feeling a little buzzed from the drugs, Garland fell back and let Wheeler lead the schmoozing waltz to the elevators. He played the perfect host, making sure to include Collier in his explanations. She nodded politely and appropriately, but never said a word. They stopped momentarily at the gallery on the foyer's east wall and, under the framed portraits of the President and Vice President, Wheeler pointed out the formal photographs of the Secretary of Health and Human Services, her Under Secretary, the director of CDC and eventually worked his way down to Carter Haynes, the first Director of the BIA.

"I don't see your portraits up here, gentlemen," Beck smiled.

"You couldn't pay me enough to kiss that much ass," Garland said and was immediately sorry that he had opened his mouth.

"And who is this?" Polly Collier stopped and pointed to a formal, but somewhat faded photograph of a young man, probably only twenty-three or twenty-four, swimming in a lab coat much too large for his frail frame.

"He was the original director of the Fort when it had a more nefarious purpose." Wheeler said.

"Christian van der Veldt," Beck nodded. "Who doesn't know Chris?"

'Chris'. Give me a fucking break, Garland thought as they moved en masse to the elevator. Garland found the duo fascinating. Polly Collier, he guessed, couldn't be more than thirty-two, tops. Her tailored designer linen skirt suit was tasteful and expensive and she wore it with a combed eggshell silk blouse beneath the slightly flared jacket. Her low brown and white heels were simple, but sensible, and perfectly complemented the raw earth tones of her suit. This was a woman who knew fashion and wasn't afraid of it. Guessing she was five-eight or nine, Garland reasoned that she could have easily been a fashion model. Maybe she was in her life before medicine. And if he had one more criticism, it was that she wore much too much makeup, especially this early in the day.

As they turned into the elevator vestibule, Garland had already concluded that Jason Beck was the perfect Episcopalian: mid-40's, tall, patrician, meticulous haircut with just the right dusting of gray at his temples. His jacket was custom tailored, his shirt monogrammed on the French cuff, his shoes were butter-soft Italian loafers, his body sculpted, no doubt, by a personal trainer named

Hugo or something like that. If Haynes had called Central Casting for an archetype, they couldn't have done better than Jason Beck and his exotic assistant. Garland guessed that he was a five-handicap golfer, an aggressive but gracious tennis player and sailed 10-meter boats competitively in his spare time. He probably knew who won the last America's Cup and he bought futures of first growth Bordeaux. As Garland knew well, the Jason Becks of the world ran the world. They are a type. A breed. A look. They are the genetic ubermensch who wind the clock that makes the world tick.

In the elevator, Wheeler said, "Our patient was moved down to Con-2 this morning so – and I apologize for the inconvenience – you'll have to take a full body disinfectant shower before entering the floor and a decontamination shower before leaving. It's hell on your skin but, you know, policy."

"Sure. Whatever." Beck said amiably.

Polly Collier didn't respond at all. And Garland found that fascinating.

24

Polly Collier's long hair was still damp from the disinfectant shower and was now pulled back in a thick, lustrous ponytail. She had washed off her makeup and Garland noticed a rosy discoloration on her left cheek that crept up to just beneath her eye and also a darker discoloration on the right side of her chin. Both bruises were previously covered by her artfully applied makeup. And without her large sunglasses to hide behind, Garland was struck by her extraordinary eyes. Collier's eyes were startling in their stark beauty. Her pupils seemed to float like oil spills in an intensely radiant sea of green foam irises. And now those turquoise eyes were playing over Garland. Her pupils, black and liquid as her thick graphite hair, ratcheted open a few notches and pulled him into focus. Garland stared back, finding it difficult to break his gaze.

There were two security guards stationed at the girl's bay, both dressed innocuously in scrubs like everyone else and would have passed for orderlies except for the UZI submachine guns they held in both hands. Polly Collier stopped, apprehensive to see the armed guards. She looked to Wheeler.

"We had a little incident earlier."

Beck nodded perfunctorily, not pursuing a conversation as he became engrossed in the girl's chart. He scrolled down the screen. "No name, no age?"

"No," Garland said, "we haven't been able to talk to her yet."

"No relatives, next of kin, no one looking for her?"

"Hard to believe, isn't it?" Garland said. "A deformed little girl no one seems to have missed. It's a hell of a commentary on us, isn't it?"

Garland thought he detected Collier nodding slightly in agreement, but when he looked at her, she was expressionless and made no effort to meet his eyes again.

Gretchen Holder, the Navy nurse, joined them and they entered the girl's bay. She was still in her coma-like state, but looked peacefully asleep. The CV line that ran from her chest to the monitors on the wall behind her showed that her heartbeat, respiration and O2 saturation were barely within normal limits. Her Demerol drip had been cut back to the least possible dosage to still maintain an analgesic effect. At best, Demerol can only be administered for three days. The drug has a very bad habit of producing normeperidine in the body, a nasty byproduct that could quickly reach lethal toxicity levels.

Beck gloved quickly and stepped up to the girl's bed. Barely touching her closed eyelids, his fingers glided over them, transmitting reams of information to him. Beck looked to Gretchen. "If you'd be so kind…"

Gretchen carefully cut away the bandages with her round-tip Metzenbaum scissors and exposed all of the girl's eyes.

As he had every time, Garland was startled to see the additional pair of eyes on the girl's forehead – not shocked or repulsed, just startled. He glanced across to Beck and Collier to gauge their reactions.

Collier's reaction, Garland noted, seemed totally in character: her body initially stiffened, her head cocked and her eyebrows arched as if they were jerked up by fishing line. But it was Beck's reaction that held Garland's attention. His face remained completely expressionless as he stared at the girl's eyes for a full five seconds. Then Garland saw his brow furrow and his eyes involuntarily narrow as if a sudden dark anger had seized him.

"Incredible," Beck finally said, but said in such a way that told Garland he wasn't referring just to the eyes, per se.

"You've seen this before?"

"Oh, no, uh-uh," Beck answered a little too forcefully and again let his fingers glide over the girl's upper lids, feeling every nuance of skin and bone.

"You know, I've read your papers on optic nerve regeneration, Dr. Beck. I thought maybe in your research you encountered something like this before."

"You read my papers?" Beck said, flattered, allowing a smile to show it.

"Those that I could find online that I thought were germane. It's out of my field, but from what I could tell, your papers contained some extraordinary work."

"Yes, they did. Thank you," Beck nodded, extremely pleased with Garland's recognition.

Collier opened the ophthalmic kit and handed Beck the shiny, stainless steel ophthalmoscope. As Garland had done days earlier with Hobbs, Beck pried open the girl's left supernumerary eyelid and studied the unformed mass of bluish-gray tissue with the ophthalmoscope. He closed the lid and lifted her right supernumerary eyelid. Her eye beneath that lid was, as Garland knew, perfect.

"Amazing," Beck said as he hovered over her face with the ophthalmoscope. He clicked the scope to increase its magnification, then straightened up, stepped back and handed the ophthalmoscope to Collier. They traded places and she leaned over the girl to examine the eyes herself.

"Amazing," Beck repeated. "You read about these rare cases of natal supernumerary organs in some obscure text, but to actually get an opportunity to see them up close and personal."

"So you think she was born this way?" Garland asked, not hiding his skepticism.

"That would be my preliminary opinion, yes. I don't mean this unkindly but, to me, this kid's anomaly is just a freak of nature."

"Dr. Beck," Wheeler asked, casting a look toward Garland, "what are your thoughts about adolescent onset spontaneous organogenesis?"

"You mean like the growth of breasts and sexual development as an anomaly of her puberty? I wouldn't think so. I've never heard of an organogenesis case involving sensory organs. I've seen several cases of teeth and hair growing on internal organs — pancreas, kidneys — but eyes? Never. What are her hormone levels?"

"Normal," Wheeler said.

Beck shrugged, resting his case.

"If you'll excuse me, doctor," Garland said, "I don't believe she was born with these eyes."

"Oh?" The rise in pitch of Beck's voice was an unmistakable signal that his expertise was being questioned.

"What else could it possibly be?" Collier said. It was a statement, not a question, said to defend her mentor.

"Well, that's what I was hoping you could tell us," Garland said.

"I just did."

"Yes, I know, but…" Garland pointed to the skin around the girl's eyelids, "the soft tissue here," he indicated, "it's a slightly different color and texture than her other facial skin. It looks sunburned. Pink, like a baby's skin, no wrinkles, no ostensible previous sun damage. I'm not a dermatologist, but to me it indicates that this is new skin."

Beck and Collier both glanced down at the comatose girl.

"What are you suggesting?" Beck was now curious, but non-threatening.

"This is going to sound crazy," Garland said, "but I think these eyes were somehow genetically induced."

"I see," Beck humored him. "How? By what or whom?"

"Good questions. I don't know." Garland rubbed his cheek thoughtfully and felt the stubble. He realized he hadn't shaved in two days. "Transgenic engineering," he continued, "with the right genetic codes and clean lines of embryonic stem cells —hey, there're a lot of people working on it. Theoretically, it's very possible."

"I believe the operative word here is 'theoretical'." Beck's tone was patronizing, but Garland ignored it. "My institute is focused on genetically engineering very specific optic nerves. It has taken us years, using the brightest teams of molecular geneticists to accomplish even the small successes you read in my papers. For what you're suggesting, you'd have to program embryonic stem cells to replicate incredibly precise tissues, nerves, bone, skin, vascular pathways, muscle...c'mon, doctor, just determining the specific coding for one of those proteins would be monumental. Getting the codes right for all of them? You're looking at genetic combinations and permutations that are in the hundreds of billions."

Without being asked, Collier opened the ophthalmic kit and handed Beck a small bottle of eye drops. He opened the girl's left normal eyelid and squeezed a tiny drop of the phenylepherine into the corner of her eye to dilate her pupil.

"But theoretically...?" Wheeler pressed.

"Theoretically, if my aunt had balls she'd be my uncle."

Who could dispute that? Case closed, Beck turned his attention back to the girl, opening her right normal eyelid to squeeze in a drop of phenylepherine. As he was handing the tiny bottle back to Collier, the girl suddenly opened her left eye. Garland immediately noticed that her pupil, which should have begun dilating, was constricting.

Despite the narcotic I.V. dripping into her veins, all three of the girl's functional eyes sprang open in wide-eyed terror. They danced demonically from Beck to Wheeler to Garland to Collier. The girl's mouth opened, she wanted to scream but could only force anguished, gasping sounds out of her throat.

Garland reached for her hand. "It's okay, shhhhh, it's okay," his voice was soft and reassuring as he drew his fingertips gently across her forehead.

Then it happened. The convulsion wracked the girl's body like a whipsaw.

Collier jerked backwards, her hands flew open and she dropped the bottle of phenylepherine. It smashed on the tile floor into a starburst of crunchy shards. Collier's eyes flashed fearfully at Garland, as if she had committed a major atrocity.

"Christ," Wheeler yelled, "she's coding."

With the girl's second convulsion, all of the CV monitor alarms shrieked at once. The code blue alarm sounded out of every speaker on Con-Con 2.

Techs started running around the hub and began pouring into the girl's bay. Gretchen raced around the bed to the crash cart and fired it up. Her practiced hand automatically hit the start button on the large sweep-hand clock on the wall above the girl's bed. Each loud tick of the clock robbed the girl of another second of life.

Garland squeezed the girl's hand harder. "It's okay, it's okay," he kept repeating to her, "you're okay. Hang in, hang in…"

The girl's fright filled eyes begged Garland to make it stop, make the excruciating pain go away. Garland knew that look intimately. He lived with that look from his own daughter, lived with it longer than any father should be forced to endure.

Another convulsion electrified the girl's frail body; it was so intense it nearly snapped her spine.

Collier leaned across the girl to help. She and Garland restrained her so Wheeler could work on her, checking for obstructions in her throat.

Gretchen hit three switches on the stainless steel panel above Beck's shoulder and a huge bank of wall mounted LCD screens and monitoring instruments lit up like Broadway.

On the CV monitor, the girl's heart rate was accelerating, her respiration was failing, weak and labored…and then it stopped.

Beck stepped back and let the others work her.

"Trache tube," Wheeler shouted at Gretchen.

"I've got it," Collier told him.

"Grove, she's going tachy," Garland yelled.

"Get that goddamned tube in," Wheeler said, then, barely turning his head to Gretchen, "defrib – bolus epinephrine…"

Gretchen jabbed the bolus directly into the girl's thigh.

"Epinephrine in."

"Damn it, get her tubed."

Collier was struggling with it. "Her throat's swollen shut. Give me a knife."

Gretchen slapped a scalpel kit in Collier's thin hand. She pulled the Swann Morton scalpel from the plastic pouch and made a quick, decisive incision in the girl's trachea. There was no pain; there was very little blood. Within three seconds she had the tube in the girl's throat and began bagging her, forcing air into her lungs.

"O2 at 100%," Wheeler snapped.

Garland's eyes swept the monitors. "Still reading the tachycardia. Respiration negligible. Fever spiking, one-zero-seven. Pressure falling, eighty over fifty… forty-five…forty…"

"Cardiac needle," Wheeler yelled.

Gretchen slapped the eight-inch needle into his hand and he one-timed it directly into the girl's heart.

"C'mon," Garland pleaded to the girl, "c'mon, hang on, fight, come on, goddammit, GODDAMMIT FIGHT."

"Nate, numbers."

Again Garland swept the monitors. "Blood gases erratic. O2 saturation down to fourteen percent."

"Mark, one minute thirty," Gretchen shouted to the group.

"Jesus," Garland's eyes were glued to the LCD screens. "Grove, look."

On the middle screen was a highly magnified view of the girl's blood cells in her carotid artery. The cell walls were bursting open, releasing their oxygen molecules into the arteries.

Garland was astounded. "What is that? What the hell's going on?"

"Major cytotoxicity," Wheeler said, "and I mean major."

Beck stepped forward and stared at the screens incredulously. "T-cells? They're T-cells."

"They're chewing up the erythrocytes like fast food," Wheeler said, "I've never seen anything like this before."

"We've got to transfuse," Garland shouted.

"Mark – two minutes." Gretchen announced loudly.

"There's not enough time to transfuse."

"Oh, c'mon, no, no...she's going flat across the board," Garland said. "Ventilator?"

"It's not going to help, Nate, look at her cells, she's being eaten up alive from the inside."

"Grove, come on..."

"What? What the hell do you want me to do?"

One by one, all of the screens and monitoring instruments began falling flat like a row of dominoes going down.

"I can crack her," Collier said.

"Mark – two thirty." Gretchen's voice could barely be heard above the sound of the flat-line monitors.

Wheeler shook his head to Collier.

Collier nodded her response and stepped back from the bed. Her bootie covered shoes crunched on the broken bottle glass on the floor. She looked across the bed, over the dead girl to Garland who was still holding and squeezing her hand. Their eyes met for a fraction of a second, but long enough for Garland to read her pain. A defeated silence fell over them as they waited for the official pronouncement.

"Nate," Wheeler's voice was barely a whisper, "you're the attending."

Garland barely nodded. He took a short breath and exhaled loudly. "Call it."

Gretchen slapped the stop button on the sweep-hand clock above the young girl's head and checked her watch. "T.O.D.," she said softly, "eleven-forty-one a.m."

113

25

When the President leaves his house, traffic in D.C. moves like fat globules through clogged arteries. And when the DHS terrorist threat level is elevated and the President is out dialing for dollars, motorcading from one fundraiser to another, traffic in D.C. grinds to a crippled crawl. That was the Gordian traffic knot Garland encountered the moment he hit the Beltway.

After the young girl died, Garland had decided to cancel his dinner plans with Stuart, but Grover persuaded him to go. It wasn't like he hadn't witnessed the deaths of many very sick children over the years in his pediatric practice, but this one was profoundly painful. The girl died nameless, without family or friend or loved one to comfort her in her passing. And unless they could identify her, her autopsied remains would be sent to the morgue and held for a year before her anonymous and unceremonious disposal.

Stuart was at the bar working his second apple martini when Garland arrived forty-five minutes late at Le Petit Pinot. Garland apologized, cursed the President and the traffic and ordered a glass of Beaujolais. He figured he would probably go through a full bottle by the end of the night, but decided to start slowly with one glass. Within minutes, Andres showed them to the table he held open for them by the window and Garland and Stuart moved out of the bar and into the cherry wood and crisp linen dining room.

Garland didn't particularly like Le Petit Pinot. He found French food heavy at night and Pinot's food saucier than most. But the ambiance was lovely, the wine list righteous and the location close enough to walk home if he got too drunk to drive. Their original group – Stuart and Sarah, Garland and Daisy, Grover and Wendy –

ate at Le Petit Pinot regularly because they all knew how much Stuart preferred its large, attached parking lot where he could self-park his precious car.

Garland and Stuart small-talked over the dill bread and spicy, dairy-free asparagus soup and Garland finally ordered a bottle of California Cabernet when the endive and radicchio salad was served. Surprisingly, Stuart decided to share the wine with him which assuaged Garland's guilt of possibly draining the entire bottle himself. When the entrées were served – Garland had the spit roasted chicken, Stuart the crusted sea bass – Garland carefully revealed the events of the last several days to his friend. When he told about the intruder using Sarah's ID, Stuart dropped his fork.

"Are you fucking kidding me, Nate?" he asked rhetorically, catching his breath. "Jesus fucking Christ – she could be alive. Holy shit, Nate, Sarah could still be alive. Right? This dickwad got her someplace. He's holding her or something. Right? I mean, this has got to be a great fucking sign, right?"

"We have some leads now. They're thin, but they're real."

"What? What do you have?"

"The shooting on Burning Tree, that bizarre intruder last night, Sarah's ID and license plates, they're all tied together somehow. Once the autopsy of the girl is completed and we get the forensics on her gown and shoes, we might have something concrete to go on."

"Might have. Christ. Might have."

"Okay, it's not much. But it's something."

Andres approached the table, all teeth and smiles and thick French accent. "May I interest you gentlemens in dessert perhaps? Coffees? Aperitifs?"

Both Stuart and Garland declined. "Not tonight, Andres, thanks," Stuart said. "Just the check please."

Garland waited for Andres to retreat, then reached into his pocket and pulled out a folded piece of paper. "You ever hear of this company?"

He slid the paper to Stuart who read it aloud. "Evin Co.?" His eyes slid upward from the paper as he attempted to pull the information out of his memory. "No, never heard of them. What do they do?"

"It's probably a biotech company. I don't know exactly what area they specialize in. I was hoping you could tell me. I couldn't find a listing."

"So it's not a public company then." He glanced down at the notation on the paper again. "What's all this other gibberish next to it, the CVDV VIXI?"

Garland shrugged. "It was listed after the company's name in a couple medical journals. The Roman numerals could be 15 or 17 and 610. I don't know what they mean."

"Lemme look into it," Stuart said, folding the paper into his pocket. "You think this company's hot? They're on to a major breakthrough or something? Let me tell you, biotech is what's happening, my friend."

Andres dropped the puffy faux leather Amex check folder in the middle of the table and Stuart grabbed it first.

"Hey, it's my turn," Garland said and meant it.

"You get the next one." As he reached for his wallet his cell phone vibrated in his pocket. Stuart clicked the phone and tossed his credit card on the folder without looking at the amount. The plastic had barely hit the folder as Andres swooped by and scooped it up.

Garland only heard Stuart's hushed side of the conversation, something to do with the Nikkei Dow in Tokyo and one of Stuart's clients losing his shirt. Stuart tried to calm the caller and told him to stay at his phone, Stuart would return to his office and check things out. He clicked off. Pissed. Then, getting up abruptly, he said, "Nate, do me a favor, will you? Sign the check for me. This asshole's going to jump out of a window if I don't take care of something right this fucking minute. Hang on to my card. I'm sorry, man, this sucks."

"Don't worry about it. Call me when you're through."

Stuart took off and a sudden movement across the room attracted Garland's glance. A man was helping a woman up from her chair by her elbow. But what snared Garland's attention was that the man wasn't so much helping her as pulling her up harshly and then physically steering her past several tables with a firm grip on her arm. At the end of the row, he yanked her to the right and they moved toward Garland's table. Garland saw the woman's face – it was Dr. Polly Collier. She was wearing the same clothes, her hair was pulled back in the same severe bun and even her makeup was thickly applied as when he first met her that morning. Garland and Collier locked eyes for a flash and then she quickly looked away, obviously very embarrassed.

Garland rose from his chair just as Collier and the man reached the table and effectively blocked them from passing. "Dr. Collier," he said, loud enough for other diners to hear. "Nice to see you again."

"Dr. Garland," she replied softly, head dipped, eyes quickly averted.

The man still gripped her arm tightly. He was obviously pissed at the sudden interruption and his face telegraphed his displeasure.

Garland ignored him. "I never really got a chance to thank you for all of your help this morning."

"No need," she said. Then, realizing her social obligation, Collier was forced to introduce the man holding her arm. "This is my husband," she said, "Brendan Collier." Then to her husband, who had yet to change his dour expression, "Dr. Nathaniel Garland."

117

Collier had no choice but to remove his hand from his wife's arm long enough to shake Garland's. "Yes, yes, very nice," he said in a high British accent, not even trying to fake pleasantness. "If you will excuse us," he said looking pointedly at Garland who was still blocking his path.

"Of course." Garland feigned a polite smile and stepped back. "Have a nice night."

He watched as Collier once again grabbed his wife's arm and pulled her toward the bar and the exit. And Garland now knew why Dr. Polly Collier wore large dark glasses and so much makeup.

26

The night sky was as clear as an epiphany and a buttery Ritz cracker moon hung low in the horizon but Garland didn't notice the rarity of the evening as he came out of Le Petite Pinot, lost in thought. Ambling toward the parking lot, he contemplated the young girl's death. It continued to baffle him. The surgery went well. She was stable. Growing stronger. So what caused her blood cells to burst like over-inflated balloons? He had never seen it before, never read about it in any texts, never heard of it at any of the myriad of medical conferences he attended.

He ransomed his Jag's keys from the bored valet and entered the short narrow alleyway into Pinot's adjacent parking lot. The lot was filled. There were four long rows of expensive cars and SUVs, each neatly parked in two aisles.

As Garland reached his car he heard a scuffle. It came from the next aisle and sounded like a dull thud with a lingering echo, like a fastball hitting a catcher's mitt. Then he heard the shoes scraping followed by an aborted yelp and then a second, louder thud and a high-pitched squeal. It sounded like someone kicking a small dog. Angered by the thought, Garland squeezed into the next aisle through the space between his car and a bloated black Hummer.

He saw Polly and Brendan Collier at the far end of the next aisle. She was on the ground in an oily puddle leaning against a car in a half-sitting-half-hunched position. Her hose was torn and a thin ribbon of blood trickled down from her scraped knee. She supported her body on her right arm while her left hand cradled her face. Brendan Collier was leaning over her, a stiff finger jabbing the air angrily in front of her. Garland could hear the low guttural hissing of his words, but not make out what he was saying. Tears streaked Polly Collier's makeup, but she was not crying.

"Hey!" Garland said as he walked toward them. Not getting any response, he moved faster and yelled again, this time much louder.

Brendan Collier straightened up and turned to confront him. Garland glanced down at Polly and she quickly averted her eyes. He looked back at Brendan.

"What's going on?"

Brendan flicked an unconvincing smile. "A mindless accident, that's all."

"Sorry to hear that." Garland responded, just as unconvincingly. "Dr. Collier?"

"It's nothing, I…I just tripped, I fell. I'm okay. Thank you." Her voice was reed thin, as if speaking any louder would crack it.

"Here, let me help you." Garland extended his hand and took a step forward but Brendan immediately shifted his position to block him.

"She said she's fine, mate, this is none of your concern." Brendan's voice was low and steady, like the guttural hum a dog makes before flashing its teeth.

Garland pulled his leather badge case from his pocket and flashed his gold. "Federal officer. I'm making it my concern."

"I don't give a rat's balls who or what you are, shitwit. I have diplomatic immunity, so just take your tin and bugger off."

"Mr. Collier, let's not make this any uglier than it already is," Garland's tone was conciliatory, his palms turned up.

"I've given you proper warning, now piss off."

"Please step aside, Mr. Collier, this isn't necessary." And Garland once again tried to move around Brendan to get to Polly.

Brendan got right in his face, his teeth clenched. "You don't listen very well, do you, boyo?"

Garland pointedly ignored him and stepped the other way. He reached down for Polly and Brendan's arm came up as he leaned forward to push Garland's shoulder back. Garland spun, grabbed his wrist, twisted it hard with both his hands and pulled up and forward. Brendan flew over Garland's hip, landing hard on his back, his head bouncing off of the asphalt, his breath squeezed from his lungs like a bellows. Hand-to-hand training at Quantico had served Garland well. As Brendan lay groaning, Garland stepped around his prone body and reached down for Polly.

"Come on, I'll take you out of here," he said it as a statement.

"No, please, just go, you don't know…you'll make it worse."

"Excuse me, are you saying there's a worse than this?" He let those words sink in and then smiled and shrugged boyishly. "Come on." He reached for her hand. As he did, he saw her eyes dart suddenly over his shoulder.

On the wet ground next to Polly, Garland saw Brendan's reflection as the enraged Brit lunged at him. Garland lowered his shoulder, brought his elbow up and snapped his body around, twisting it like a taut rubber band and driving his elbow like a piston deep into Brendan's fleshy groin. Brendan instantly lost what little breath he had left, expelling it all in a choked groan as he doubled over. As his head came down, Garland thrust his right fist straight up and caught him squarely beneath his chin. Brendan's head snapped back like a Pez dispenser and they all heard the sickening crunch of bone and teeth shattering. He collapsed on his back, gasping for air. Blood drained from the corners of his mouth, carrying bits of broken teeth in the syrupy flow.

Garland kneeled down next to him. Brendan was in excruciating pain and trying desperately to catch his breath. Garland lowered himself so the older man could hear him and he said, very distinctly, "You touch this woman again or hurt her in any way, you'll be sorry you were ever born."

Brendan, choking back blood, summoned what voice he could and rasped, "Are you threatening me?"

"You're goddamned right I am."

Polly Collier was stunned. She scrambled to her feet and stood protected behind Garland. She didn't know what to do. She didn't know what to say. Didn't know what to feel. Garland rose to his feet and Polly moved around him and bent down to her husband to examine his jaw. Still lying flat on the damp pavement, Brendan's arm arced like a catapult and knocked her over.

"Don't come near me, you miserable cunt."

Garland reacted instantly and in one motion was down with his knee firmly wedged on Brendan's neck, pressing more and more of his weight against his windpipe. "You don't listen, do you, asshole?"

Brendan's eyes bulged. He gasped. His hands tried to push Garland off. He slapped at his knee, but Garland caught his flailing arms and held them as he pressed down even harder.

"Give me a reason not to fucking kill you right here and now." Garland was shaking as adrenalin flooded his veins.

Polly scrambled to her feet and rushed to Garland. She grabbed his arm. "No, please, stop, don't...don't do this, please, Dr. Garland, no..."

Garland yielded to her coaxing. He stood up and Brendan's hands immediately went to his insulted throat. Polly Collier stood rocking, both arms clutched her body as she hovered over her husband. She was trembling.

"Get out of my sight, you bloody sow bitch," Brendan spat from the ground, "go rot in hell."

Garland guided her away with gentle pressure on her shoulder. "You can make a life changing decision here, Dr. Collier. You can stay or walk away. It's your choice."

And Dr. Polly Collier nodded almost imperceptibly.

27

With a comforting arm around her shoulder, Garland guided Polly toward his car. Brendan had pulled himself up on a Mercedes and was coughing out incoherent invectives at their backs. Garland urged Polly to ignore him. She was trembling, but Garland couldn't bring himself to hold her any closer or any tighter.

"I'll get you to the hospital, take a look at your face," he said.

"No," she said, her voice barely audible. "Thank you. I'll take care of it myself." Then, allowing an ironic smile, said, "I've had enough practice."

"Do you have family or friends you can stay with?"

"No. Not close by." They took a few more steps and she said, "It's okay. I'll stay at my office or at a hotel tonight."

Garland stopped her. "Dr. Collier...it's not just for tonight."

Polly stared straight ahead, understanding. All of the nasty, ugly implications of this final encounter were now sinking in.

Garland spotted his car in the next aisle. The black Hummer was still parked next to it, hogging the narrow space. He indicated they'd have to squeeze between his car and the SUV to open the door and Polly held back, allowing him to go first. Garland took a step forward, but without his support, Polly's injured knee buckled. Squealing, she fell against his back as she started to go down. Garland instantly twisted to catch her, dropping to one knee to break her fall.

In that same instant, a .50-caliber round exploded into the driver's window of the Hummer, precisely where Garland's head was a nanosecond earlier. Garland flattened himself on top of Polly, taking the brunt of the glass showering down on them. And even before the sound of the first shot reached them, the second shot ripped into the Hummer's door, barely inches above them, shredding the metal as if it was paper.

Still covering Polly with his body, he rolled her under the Hummer and pushed her hard against the rear axel. Simultaneously, a burst of .50-cals drilled a line of holes in the asphalt like a punch-press and flattened the Hummer's two left tires. Polly screamed, covering her face as a spray of black asphalt shrapnel cut into them. Again, Garland grabbed her and pulled her protectively against his chest. Her heart was racing like a hummingbird's, but so was his and as he clutched her, he couldn't distinguish between the two.

The shooting stopped and within a second or two Garland heard the unmistakable thwapping roar of helicopters approaching from three directions. Did the shooter miscalculate? Did he forget? Did he not even know? When the President is on the move, he does not move alone. An army of agents marches with him and the sky swarms with airborne security.

Garland released his grip on Polly to look out in the direction of the shooter. He could see a UH-60L Blackhawk helicopter and a Sikorsky MH-60K gunship converging on the buildings directly across from the parking lot. Blinding sunguns from two of the helicopters illuminated the three story greystones across the street. Army and Secret Service sharpshooters stood braced outside on the skids of the Blackhawk, their Bushmaster AR-15 automatic rifles trained on the rooftop of the southernmost building where the muzzle flashes originated.

Garland turned his face close to hers. "Stay here. Do not move. No matter what happens, stay here. I'm coming back for you."

Too frightened to speak, her eyes blinked and she shook her head in hard staccato movements.

Garland snatched a breath and squirted out from under the far side of the Hummer and rolled until he pinned himself against his own car. He drew no fire from the sniper. He heard a third helicopter closing in from the south. He stole another breath and, before he could think about the risk, ran a wild zig-zag pattern to the low parking lot wall. Still no fire. And from this angle, the shooter couldn't touch him. Hunched over, he sprinted along the wall toward the alley that led to the front of the restaurant, gauging his exposure to the shooter at less than two seconds to cross the open distance from the wall to the alley. He ran for it and again he drew no fire.

The alley was completely shielded from the shooter by a three story commercial building. Garland used the safety of the enclosure to catch his breath. He had no way of knowing if this was the same shooter as on Burning Tree. He had no way of knowing if this was a random act or if he or Polly was the target. What he did know was that he would have to get to the shooter to find out.

He ran to the mouth of the alley. For some insane reason, traffic on the street was still moving in both directions. But the pedestrians, caught in the open when the shooting began, huddled against buildings, pressed themselves into door wells, squatted against parked cars, none of which offered any protection.

And then the shooting started again. The shock wave of the ear numbing noise reverberated down the canyon between the buildings. People started screaming. The shooter on the roof of the greystone had found cover in the air conditioning compressor array and stupidly decided to take on the choppers. The shooter was good, hitting the closest Blackhawk in the canopy with his .50-cal. The boys on the skids returned automatic fire, but the Blackhawk had to retreat.

Garland, panting now, steeled himself and made his move. Holding his badge high above his head, he dodged the traffic like an aging running back as he plowed full bore across the street and flattened himself against the shooter's building. Screeching police sirens signaled their advance. Four unmarked cars slid to the curb,

126

finally blocking traffic in both directions. Still waving his badge, Garland skirted the building looking for the shooter's way up to the roof. In the back alley he found the lowered fire escape and began scrambling up. Men in suits with big guns drawn were chasing after him. Garland assumed they were Metro police and Secret Service. His job was to make sure the shooter was taken alive. If it was the same guy – and all indications suggested that it was – he was Garland's best and probably last lead to Sarah.

The shooter, wearing what Garland thought to be an urban Ghillie suit, knew he was trapped. What must have gone through his mind when he realized he was about to be done in by a political fundraiser? But if he was going, he was going to take some heavy metal with him and took on the armored MH-60K gunship mano a mano. The shooter peppered the chopper with round after round of .50 caliber heat, but this gunship didn't back down like the Blackhawks.

The entire building was shaking from the deafening roar of the turbojet and the sucking vortex thwaps of the chopper's rotor. As Garland climbed to the roof, loose, razor sharp cement chips and thick clouds of dust assailed his eyes. His face felt as if it was being sandblasted. The shrapnel cut on his cheek was stinging as if a saw blade was ripping through it. The Secret Service guy under him on the ladder tugged Garland's pant leg and signaled him with a jutting thumb to move up or get out of the way.

Pulling himself up hand-over-hand, Garland made it to the top cornice. The brilliance of the chopper's sungun momentarily blinded him, but he squeezed his eyes shut and rolled over the cornice on to the sharp graveled roof.

The shooter's attention was concentrated totally on the chopper. He kept firing hollow-tipped .50-caliber rounds and several penetrated the gunship's frame, but the ship still didn't back down. Then, as Garland watched, with a deafening surge of power, the chopper suddenly swung wide in a pivoting arc and from its own nose-mounted .50-cal machineguns sprayed a wide swath of ear-shattering death in a double X-pattern across the shooter's position.

It was no contest. The shooter died instantly. His body cavity was filled with so many bullets he could have been a bean bag.

Again, holding his badge high above his head for the chopper pilot to see, Garland raced across the roof to the shooter's position. Secret Service guys and now Metro police were right behind him, but Garland was the first to reach the body.

The shooter's face and upper torso were obliterated. The top of his skull and an ear were the only recognizable parts left to his head. His face was completely gone. He was floating in his own blood, the last of which was draining from a dozen holes in his neck and upper body. The first Secret Service agent stopped a few feet away, his gun out and pointed at Garland.

"Let's see it," he yelled.

Garland held up his badge case and the agent leaned in to read the ID.

"What the hell are you doing on this one?" He yelled over the roar of the chopper's turbojet.

"I think this guy might be the Burning Tree shooter," Garland yelled back.

The other agents and cops moved in around a perimeter. An agent waved off the helicopter and the noise receded like thunder moving out across flat plains.

"I needed this guy alive."

"Sorry, dude. Had to be what had to be." The agent squatted down on the other side of the body. "So you don't think this was a random psycho?"

"No."

"You know who his target may have been?"

There was something odd about the shooter's left hand that caught Garland's eye. He lifted the dead man's hand and examined it while he talked to the agent. "I think it may have been me," he said.

Garland continued to study the dead man's hand. It was variegated with blotches of pink, brown and yellow skin that gradually tapered off at his wrist, giving his hand the appearance of wearing a glove. The overall effect resembled a camouflage pattern but it was definitely not a tattoo. The fingers were odd, too. It almost appeared as if his ring finger and middle finger had switched places.

"What's that on his hand?" The agent asked. "Acid burns? A tattoo or something?"

"No. I don't think so. It almost looks natural." Garland lifted the man's right hand. It looked completely normal. "You on a wire?" Garland asked the agent.

"Yeah."

"See if you can get a couple local Fibs down here. Names are Fitch and Hollister?"

The agent stood and turned away and Garland dropped the shooter's normal hand and picked up his variegated hand to reexamine it. He was messing with critical crime scene evidence, but he didn't care. Once this body left the roof, he'd probably never see it again. He shifted his back to the Secret Service guy and dipped the fingers of shooter's strange hand into the blood pooled at his side. Then, wiping off the plastic insert covering his ID in his badge case, Garland pressed a set of the shooter's fingerprints on the insert. He flipped the plastic and took a hasty set of prints from the dead sniper's other hand. There was no way Garland was going to be denied this killer's identity.

28

They were in Garland's spacious kitchen – Fitch on the phone, scribbling notes, Hollister rooting a beer out of the Sub Zero refrigerator and Garland at the long slate counter making a pot of Jasmine Oolong tea.

Neither Fitch nor Hollister would ever have pegged Garland to live in a home this luxurious on arguably the most upscale street in Georgetown. They knew about his V-12 Jaguar, of course, but they just assumed Garland was a classic car nut. Ironically, now they respected him even more knowing that he had all this and still busted his balls for a puny government paycheck.

Fitch hung up the phone, scribbled one last note and looked at the other two men. "They're taking him to Dover," he said, referring to the National Mortuary and pathology lab at Dover Air Force Base across the bay in Delaware.

"Any chance I can get in on the autopsy?"

"No way. T-boys have it nailed down."

"Why Secret Service and not your guys?"

"Don't know, yet," Fitch said. "So what was that hand thing all about? You seriously think it's connected to the girl with the eyes?"

"I don't know. It may not be. But when I see two very weird physical anomalies back to back, I have a hard time buying coincidence. Wait – I've got something for you."

Garland left the kitchen and returned carrying a Ziploc bag by its corner. In the bag was the small plastic insert from his ID case. He gave the bag to Fitch who raised it up to the light and looked at its contents curiously.

"What is it? Prints? Looks bloody."

"The shooter's."

"Sweet." Hollister whistled appreciatively. "Nice work, doc."

"I'll bet anything you get a 100% match at Benning."

Garland walked them to the door. Outside, their black Crown Vic was parked at the curb with its FBI tagged visor down and the dash mount light clearly visible to ward off the local parking police.

"You need some help with the lady?" Fitch asked, sincerely concerned. "Domestic shit can be a bitch. We've got safe houses all over town, put her on ice for you, keep an eye on her."

"I'll ask her again, but I think she wants to do it her way, whatever that is."

"Let us know. And watch your six, doc. Whoever put that shooter on you isn't going to give up just because his first guy got popped."

"I know. I'll be careful." And Garland meant it.

They shook hands and Hollister said, matter-of-factly, "By the way, your boss, Haynes. Our guys are looking at him very hard for money laundering."

"Money laundering? Why the hell money laundering?"

"Go figure," Fitch said. "But when we know, you'll know."

29

Garland filled an ice pack, grabbed two mugs off the wooden spindle on the counter, scooped up the pot of the freshly brewed Oolong and carried it upstairs to his study on the second floor. Polly Collier was exactly where he had left her, curled up on the sofa, wrapped in the colorful wool afghan. The telephone was on the arm of the sofa within her reach.

"I've got hot and cold," Garland said, entering the study. "Ice for the bruises and tea for the soul."

Polly pushed herself up into a sitting position as Garland put the teapot and mugs down on the low table. She sniffed the air. Closed her eyes. The corners of her mouth lifted slightly into the semblance of a smile. "Oolong?" she asked.

"Yeah. I didn't know if you like it or not, but I thought I'd give it a shot." Garland poured the tea carefully into the mugs so as not to rouse the loose tea leaves on the bottom of the pot.

"Smells wonderful. Formosa?"

"Of course." Garland was impressed she could distinguish the different aromatic nuances inherent in Oolong. "How did you know?"

"In case you haven't noticed, I'm Chinese."

"I did happen to notice."

She accepted the tea mug in both hands; a respectful Chinese custom.

"So you worked in China? I'm not psychic. The plaque on your wall from Beijing University. You lectured?"

"Four months. They sent me over to do some pediatric work during the H1N1 epidemic. I liked it there. I hope to go back some day as a tourist."

"So you speak Mandarin?" Polly was more fascinated than curious.

"Not much."

"Say something."

"What? Come on. No. I can't."

"No, really, I'd love to hear your accent."

Garland looked away, so as not to be too embarrassed, then looked back at Polly and said, "Zǎo ān, nǐ hǎo ma," meaning, 'hello, how are you'?

"Wǒ hǎo, nǐ, xié xié" Polly answered, meaning, 'I am well, thank you'. Then she said, "You have a very nice accent. A good ear."

"Xié xié," Garland thanked her, "and you've just heard the extent of my Chinese vocabulary."

"I think you're just being modest, Dr. Garland."

"Qǐng, wǒ xìng Nate or Nathaniel," he said with a perfect Mandarin accent.

"Okay. Nathaniel, then. And please call me Polly." She sipped some tea. "It's really Pu Li. Tzhang Pu Li," she said, putting her last name first in the customary formal manner. "In preschool they just changed Pu Li to Polly and it stuck ever since. My mother hates it."

Silence. So much for small talk.

They allowed the long silence to join them in the room as they each sipped their tea. Garland remembered and gave her the fresh ice pack.

"Put this on your face. It'll keep the swelling down."

She held the ice gingerly to her cheek and said, "That man shooting at us, the sniper, it wasn't a random act, was it? He wasn't trying to kill us — I don't mean 'us' per se, it was you. He was trying to kill you."

"Yeah. Probably."

"Why?"

"He apparently didn't like me."

"Nathaniel, it's nothing to joke about."

"I think I'm getting very close to something. I just don't know what it is." He moved back to the stuffed armchair. "The ice," he reminded her.

Polly dutifully held the ice pack to her swollen cheek. "Is it about the young girl who died this morning?"

"I don't know. Maybe. Probably. Yes." Garland took another sip of tea and said, "Why did Beck get so angry when he saw the girl's eyes?"

Polly shrugged and shook her head. She peeled off the afghan and put the ice bag down on the side table. Garland saw that the cut on her knee had clotted into an ugly mess. She seemed so vulnerable.

"I think," she said, "because he thought somebody beat him to it."

Garland looked at her, his expression asked her to clarify.

"I've only been Beck's associate for a few months. My husband's in the Foreign Service so we move from place to place a lot." She paused as another reality of her past life fluttered up. She had to take a deep breath to keep her emotions in check. "Sorry."

"That's okay." Garland's sincerity was as comforting as his words.

"As he said, Jason is doing some amazing work in optic nerve regeneration. That's what attracted me to his clinic. He had some incredibly promising results in restoring limited vision to select patients with severe nerve damage. I mean, really promising results. In the beginning, growing optic nerve fiber from a patient's spinal stem cells wasn't showing much promise, but then he got several clean lines of cells and that's all he needed. For me it meant the opportunity to surgically implant the new fibers. It was a procedure I was developing with him to bypass damaged nerves with the home grown fibers."

"That's incredible," Garland said and meant it.

"God, yes," she said, "totally incredible. What we'll be able to do for so many types of blindness is…it's just awesome."

For the first time since Garland had met her, Polly Collier was truly animated. Beneath the hard-shell exterior defensiveness she had carefully cultured was a woman who was extremely passionate about her work and had the talent and skills necessary to attract a mentor of Jason Beck's caliber.

"But if you were already doing this procedure, what did you mean he may have thought somebody beat him to it?"

"It's not just nerve fiber he's engineering, he's also working on lenses, corneas, differentiated eye tissue – the whole package."

"You're telling me he's growing eyes in Petri dishes?

"No, not quite, well, not yet, anyway," Polly smiled. It was the first spontaneous smile she allowed Garland. "As he said, it's still all theoretical. What held him back was that he had been waiting years for the clean embryonic lines.

"So Beck saw his work in the little girl? Realized someone else was pursuing the same line of research. That's what pissed him off?"

"You know, it just doesn't seem possible. Jason Beck is the acknowledged frontrunner in the field. He's one of maybe a half dozen researchers in the entire world to bring optic nerve regeneration this far. Everyone else is building on his work, not the other way around." Polly paused, lifted her eyes to Garland. "And do you mind if I ask you a similar question?"

He nodded.

"Why are you so angry?"

"I didn't know I was."

"Believe me, you are. I saw it immediately when I first met you. I saw it when Jason was examining the girl. And the look on your face in the car park. You could have killed Brendan. Maybe would have if I wasn't there."

"I was in control," he said defensively.

"No, you weren't." She paused, realizing. "Sorry. That was way out of line, wasn't it?"

"No. Not at all."

Polly's foot fished for her shoe on the floor next to the sofa and slipped into it. "Look, uh, the hotels in town are all booked. If you could take me out to my office, I'd really appreciate it. I've got a change of clothes and a sofa and…"

"My offer's still good. I have a perfectly serviceable private guest room, complete with indoor plumbing and running water."

"That's very generous, but I don't want to impose any more than I already have."

"It's no imposition."

136

"Will it be alright with your wife?"

"My wife passed away almost two years ago," Garland answered, forcing a polite smile.

"Oh. God. I'm sorry. I...I feel like such an idiot."

"Please. There's no way you could have known. Don't worry about it."

"But your house looks like, you know, a woman lives here – a family. The art, the kids' drawings. It's in every room I've seen."

"I've kept it pretty much the same as when she and Breezy were alive. Never really had the time or inclination to...," Garland fished for the right word. Couldn't find it. Instead said, "Change it."

"Breezy?"

"My daughter. Her real name was Meg. Megan."

"She's dead, too." Polly said it so softly, as a statement, not a question.

Garland nodded, "Yes, she is."

30

Garland showed Polly the guestroom which Daisy had decorated in an early Ralph Lauren style. He got her towels from the guest linen closet and showed her where the soaps and shampoos and other sundries were stored in the antique corner cabinet. From the guest closet he offered her a choice of several freshly laundered thick chenille bathrobes. "We used to have a lot of guests." Garland said it almost apologetically. "Oh, you'll need clothes."

Garland guided her down the hallway to the master bedroom and opened Daisy's closet and antique wardrobe. All of Daisy's clothes and shoes were neatly displayed, undisturbed since she last touched them.

"The stuff on this side she had never worn. Tags are still in them. She was a little shorter than you, but I'm guessing you're pretty much the same size."

"Nathaniel, no, thank you, I couldn't."

"It's not going to freak me or anything."

"Why don't we do this in the morning, okay?"

"Sure." Garland said. "One last thing: the house is totally alarmed. There are sensors on the stairs and everywhere else, so if for whatever reason you have to go downstairs, just let me know. Don't be shy about waking me, if you have to."

Polly nodded. They looked at each other uncomfortably for too long as if they were each looking for something more to say to keep the moment alive. Neither came up with anything.

"Well," Garland finally said, "good night. Sleep well."

But neither of them could sleep, much less sleep well. For Garland it was the usual noise in his head which he couldn't turn off. And when his head noise finally did subside, the sound of Polly took its place. She was crying. Sobbing. It was the sound of her realization that her life was in ruins, that she had vested in the wrong man, an abusive bully whom she now knew she would have to shed. It was a major failing that was physically, emotionally and spiritually painful – and the sound of her anguish floated down the hallway to Garland.

At one point, he had gone down the hall and to knock on her door and ask if she needed anything, if he could somehow offer her some small comfort. He would suggest they not try to sleep, that instead they go downstairs and have some tea and talk. But with his hand curled in a loose fist, poised over the door to gently knock, he didn't. He couldn't.

The soft knock on his door came an hour later. His eyes were closed, breaths drawing deeper. He thought he had dreamt the sound, but she tapped again and Garland sat up and flushed the near sleep from his eyes.

"Nathaniel?" Her voice was barely audible through the door.

"I'm up. C'mon in."

Polly opened the door wide enough to poke her head in. Garland, who slept shirtless in Façonnable cotton boxers, pulled himself up and twisted to turn on the bedside lamp. He immediately saw that her eyes were red-rimmed and swollen and with the nasty facial bruises she acquired from Brendan, Polly looked like she had just gone ten minutes in a cage match.

"I'm sorry," she whispered, fearing her voice would crack if she spoke at normal volume.

"Don't be. Please. Come in."

She was barefoot and wrapped tightly in the white robe. "I really hate to bother you, but, now you're going to think I'm weird or something."

"No."

"I, uh, I really don't want to be alone right now," she hesitated, pointed, "would it be alright if I...your sofa here...I won't disturb you, promise, I just..." Polly sighed and shook her head. Embarrassed. "Oh, god, sorry, sorry, sorry. Please try very hard to ignore this moment, now that I've made a complete and total ass of myself." She pulled her head back to close the door.

"Polly." The door opened again and she stepped into the room. "It's really okay," he said and peeled back the other side of the bedcovers as an invitation.

Polly hesitated only momentarily, then pulled her robe tighter around her body and moved very quickly to the bed as if hesitating would sap the last of her waning courage. She climbed in and immediately turned away from him. Garland pulled the bedcovers over her, up to her neck, like tucking in a child, and then he, too, turned away and switched off the lamp.

He lied on his back, both of his hands under his head, then closed his eyes and let the darkness settle over them like an extra blanket. He was careful not to let his legs accidentally touch hers and, consequently, couldn't be as relaxed as sleep normally required. They both embraced their own thoughts for at least ten minutes before Polly spoke. She was still faced away from him and her voice was barely a whisper.

"You never asked me why I stayed with Brendan."

Garland hesitated. He knew the answer – it's almost always the same, tied to issues of low self esteem and lack of self worth, almost always a malignant gift from overbearing, fault-finding, you're-never-good-enough, impossible to please parents. Garland knew this, but instead he said, "You're a very smart woman – I'm sure you had your good reasons."

"He wasn't always abusive."

"I don't doubt that."

"In fact, he has many fine qualities."

"You wouldn't have married him if he didn't."

"You're right, that's what I'm saying."

"But you didn't marry him to be his personal punching bag, either."

"That's why you think I'm such an idiot for staying with him."

"No, no, no, that's not what I think at all. Look, I don't know you. I don't know what personal demons haunt you. The only thing I do know is that we're all us just walking wounded anyhow, so who am I to judge? Who is anyone to judge?"

31

The bed rippled gently like a summer lake as Polly turned to face Garland. He was still on his back and she spoke to him after her face had settled comfortably into the pillow, her hands tucked underneath. "Nathaniel, what happened to your family?"

Garland took a breath and the bedcovers rose and fell with his sound. Polly could see his face, see his chest rise. He spoke without looking at her. "Breezy had ALL," he said in doctor speak, meaning acute lymphoblastic leukemia. "She was just turning seven."

"God, I'm so sorry. I thought ALL has an extremely high remission rate."

"Yeah. 80%-90% when it's diagnosed early, as it was in her case, but she had a mother of a resistant pathology." Garland turned his head to look at her. He noticed that the welt just beneath her left eye, Brendan's departing gift in the parking lot, had turned a deep maroon at the center.

"Go on," she said softly.

"None of the standard protocols worked. Every work up indicated they should have. Breezy was the bravest person I've ever known. God damn, she was incredible. When she had the lumbar puncture she didn't even wince. Not one word of complaint during all her chemo regimens. I called in everyone I knew. A couple fantastic guys from med school, real heavyweights now at Sloan-Kettering, flew in and took over her protocols, systemic and intrathecal chemo, total body radiation. And you know what? It was just like Kryptonite to her. All she got was sicker and weaker."

142

Polly raised her head to look at him and then rested it in her hand, supported by her elbow. "I'm sorry. You don't have to say anymore. It was so uncool for me to even ask."

"No, it's okay. I – truthfully, I don't think I've ever really talked about it with anyone. Not like this anyhow. It's okay." And, in truth, Garland didn't know what now compelled him to tell this woman, this relative stranger, details of his most intimate experience. Maybe it was the fact that she was a stranger. Or maybe because she was a doctor who could understand the intricacies of the protocols. Or maybe, just maybe, because they were both so utterly damaged – blindsided – by bitterly altered lives.

After a few long moments of silence, Polly asked, "How did your wife handle all of this?"

"She didn't. She couldn't." His voice once again took on a calm, detached, almost clinical tone and his eyes fixated on the undulating tree shadows on the ceiling. "Breezy was her life. Everything Breezy suffered Daisy suffered tenfold. I think what was particularly difficult for all of us was that I wasn't just an internist, I was a pediatrician. And now I was absolutely powerless, totally impotent against this monster. More than anything, I think Daisy felt betrayed by that. In her mind, which was so beautiful and fragile to begin with, in her mind she was doing the right thing. Breezy's suffering was intolerable to her, she needed to cure her, make her well and happy again, end her suffering, stop the pain. My medicine wasn't working; she believed hers would. She really believed that."

Polly was confused now. Her hand came out from under the covers and her fingertips found Garland's arm. "I don't know what you mean," she said softly.

"I'm sorry. I was getting ahead of myself." He paused, sorting his thoughts, choosing his words. "We took Breezy home. We spent a day, the three of us, putting the room together upstairs next to Daisy's studio. Breezy picked the colors, the furniture, everything. She had her mother's artistic sensibilities. She was really a remarkable

143

kid." Garland paused. Regrouped. "I took leave from my practice so I could stay home and do whatever I could for my girls. But Breezy just kept slipping away and taking Daisy with her. I had gone out for groceries. Errands, you know, the usual, cleaners, gas station, bank. It was a Tuesday morning. A beautiful day."

Garland stopped talking. Polly tensed. Her fingertips remained touching his arm; she needed the physical connection to his pain as much as he appreciated the anchor of her touch.

"I found them both in this bathtub. She was holding Breezy against her chest. She had used a single edged razor blade from her studio to open the veins on both their wrists. She had tied her left wrist to Breezy's right. She was trying to transfuse her with her own blood. By the time I reached them, Breezy had already bled out. Daisy was still alive. Barely. I did what I could to stop her bleeding..." Garland's voice trailed off. "There wasn't enough time to wait for an ambulance, so I carried them both downstairs, still tied together at their wrists. I got them into the car and drove like a maniac – I don't remember exactly how – I got them to the ER in two minutes, maybe less, but – Daisy died in the car. We couldn't resuscitate. She died tethered to her baby. It was a Tuesday morning."

Polly wanted to say something comforting, but could not form the words. She didn't think she had any tears left, but she did and they rolled down her cheeks to the corners of her mouth. She wiped them away with the back of her free hand. When she could finally speak, she said simply, "I am so sorry."

"The M.E. officially listed their deaths as murder-suicide, but that wasn't it, that couldn't be it, I just...I couldn't accept that. It happened so goddamned fast – our last best hope for Breezy was a chemo cocktail of Altron-Alpha Interferon and stem cell RT. The stem cell replacement was showing some positive results, but the Altron wasn't doing a goddamned thing. We doubled the dose. We knew it would be excruciating, but if it could save Breezy's life...? We had to do it. But Nothing changed. No reaction. I couldn't understand it. No one on the team could. It didn't make sense, those lymphocytes kept marching on. Just marching on. I went over and over every procedure, every protocol, every option, every drug. But by the time I found the answer, it was too late. My girls were gone."

32

Garland had fallen asleep on his back, something he rarely did, and when he woke he had to extricate himself from Polly's arm sprawled across his chest and her face nestled against his shoulder. The feel of Polly lying next to him was surprisingly not all that unpleasant. He slid out of bed silently, careful not to disturb her, and was showered and dressed by the time her eyes fluttered open.

"I put up some coffee."

It was the most neutral statement he could make to this sleepy woman in his bed without embarrassing either one of them.

"It's in the kitchen. Beans weren't that fresh, so I can't vouch for the flavor."

"Thank you."

He fished his favorite old brown worsted-wool jacket out of the closet and slipped into it.

"Etta will be here in an hour or so. Housekeeper. Comes every morning after she drops her kids off at school. I left her a note downstairs, let her know you were up here."

Polly stretched feline-like under the blankets and made one of those it-feels-so-good stretching sounds and yawns. She had slept uncharacteristically soundly and actually felt pretty good, but the loud, unfeminine morning groan still embarrassed her.

"Ooo. Sorry. Good morning."

Garland smiled. "I wrote my cell and office numbers on the pad in the guest room for you. You're more than welcome to stay here, but if you have to go out, go to work, whatever, I left Daisy's car keys next to my numbers. It's in the garage. The Volvo. The garage door clicker's on the visor. I don't think there's much gas in it, so…" his hand made a slight waving gesture in the air.

"Thank you. That's very generous."

"Not to get too personal, but is your bank account, your credit cards and all that stuff in your name, your husband's or both?"

Polly had to think about it for a few seconds, running a mental inventory. "Both. I think."

"Then consider them all closed or cancelled. As far as he's concerned, it's not over and he's still going to try to regain as much control over you as he possibly can, including making or keeping you financially dependent."

"No. I make much more than he does."

"It's not the amount. It's the control. That's his schtick." Garland turned to her. "Polly, your husband is not going to just let you go. He's invested in control over you. He's really pissed now. Injured. Humiliated. You didn't come home last night. No doubt he checked and found you didn't go to the places you usually go. He's going to be prowling, spoiling for a fight. It can get very ugly."

"Get very ugly? It is very ugly." Polly was surprised that she was able to talk about Brendan and her victimization so freely with someone she barely knew. It was, for her, a unique and somehow liberating experience.

"All I'm saying is be careful," Garland said. "He's probably going to show up at your work. Make sure you're not alone with him anywhere."

"I know. I do. I mean, know not be alone with him when he's like this." Polly touched her face, gently rubbed the remnants of sleep from her eyes and felt the bruise above her cheekbone around her eye. It hurt like hell.

Garland noticed her wince. He looked at her face and, aside from the horrible bruising, the brilliant luminescence of her turquoise eyes were startling in the hazy morning light.

"I am a licensed doctor. I could take a look at your eye before I go?"

"I am a licensed doctor, too," she smiled back at him as she pulled back the covers and swung her feet out of bed. "Does it look as bad as I think it looks?" Her fingers passed gingerly over her bruised eye.

"Let's just say it's not pretty."

"Yes, I'm sure you're right." Still wrapped in the chenille robe in which she fell asleep, Polly sat on the edge of the bed and looked at Garland, trying to figure out the missing piece. And then it came to her. Beneath the veneer of his anger she could detect genuine warmth. Compassion. Empathy. And, most important, he really was non-judgmental. He let her be her without a grain of prejudice. She watched him move toward the door. He had a thought, stopped and turned back to her.

"If you're thinking of going home to get some of your stuff, don't go alone. I'll go with you later or I'll have some very large men escort you if I can't make it."

"Thanks. Nathaniel, I certainly appreciate everything but I truly don't want to impose or in any way be a burden."

"You're not." And he was out the bedroom door, trotting down the stairs before she could respond.

Polly listened as his footsteps faded and then she flopped back down on the pillow. This man, this wounded pediatrician may have given her enough courage to finally deal with Brendan.

33

Before leaving his house, Garland brewed a quick cup of tea and called Grover Wheeler to get an update on the young girl's autopsy. Wheeler was excited as soon as he heard Garland's voice.

"You're all over the news this morning"

"What news?"

"What do you mean 'what news'? All the network morning shows, CNN, MSNBC, the Post, the Times. Turn on your TV, man, the news choppers caught everything. You on the roof. The guy getting blasted. Everything. Why didn't you call me back, I left you a dozen voicemails? Stu did, too."

"I'm sorry. I didn't check. Tell me about the autopsy."

"Vic just got here a little while ago," Wheeler said, referring to Mass General's Victor Brotman. "Haynes sent the chopper to pick him up. Can you believe that? You sure you don't want to stand in? We'll wait for you."

"No. Go ahead."

Garland had no desire to witness the girl's autopsy. He was still too emotionally attached to her to watch her deconstruction and knew that when Vic sectioned that part of her head, he would be called down to pathology so he could see the optic wiring for himself. And as for determining cause of death, nobody did it better than Vic Brotman.

Garland cautiously opened the interior door of the garage. Even with a sophisticated alarm system, if he – they – could stroll

149

through security at Fed-Med as if it was cheesecloth, then getting in and out of his Georgetown garage undetected would be cake.

Before he got in his car Garland walked around it, inspecting it for any signs of tampering. Satisfied, he clicked open the exterior garage door and as it rumbled up on its aluminum tracks he made a quick visual sweep of the rooftops across from his house. He then checked the street in both directions before pulling out into the morning traffic. He wasn't paranoid, he was frightened. And the most frightening part was that he had no idea what he had stumbled into or who or what had shot at him the night before. He kept the Jaguar's rag top up and continuously checked his mirrors as he worked his way out of the city. He waited until he was rolling safely on 270 and then called Fitch and Hollister.

"I think we made a positive match on the shooter's prints you gave us."

"That's great news."

"Bad news is," Hollister broke in, "Gil and I are out of the loop. The results went right upstairs, we got frozen out."

"So you have no idea if it's the same shooter who killed Eccevarria or not or if he's Army sniper or not?"

"Yeah. Army sniper grad, that much we were able to glean from the coffee talk," Fitch confirmed.

"…and my getting into Dover for the shooter's autopsy?"

"Not going to happen, doc, not a chance."

Garland took in all of the non-information he was just given and thanked them for at least trying to keep him in the loop. He wanted to believe that Fitch and Hollister honestly didn't know the answers because the investigation really was being conducted on a higher level. Or Fitch and Hollister were playing him.

"Doc, we're just as frustrated as you. Eccevarria was one of ours, so whatever is going on with this investigation is the shits. We thought we had something with the prints, but it was snaked out of our hands. We don't know what the fifth floor is doing with this one. But you've got my word, if Gil or I turn something, we'll deal you in. We're asking you do the same with us."

"Sure, why wouldn't I?"

"No reason. Cool. Okay. Thanks, doc. Just watch your six."

As Garland clicked off, he was reminded of med school and one Dr. Martin Pincus. Pincus was the biggest prick he had ever met. He was a humorless, supercilious, constipated physician whose greatest joy and pleasure in the world was tormenting med students – Garland, more than most. Pincus's reputation was such that behind his back, students and staff alike at the hospital referred to him as Dr. Bohica, a med school acronym for "Bend Over, Here It Comes Again."

During clinical rounds, Pincus would pimp every one of his students mercilessly – pimping, in med school jargon, meant posing difficult questions to students for the sole purpose of embarrassing and humiliating them in front of their patients, superiors and classmates. It was supposed to be a Socratic teaching method when, in fact, it was sadistic bullshit. However, it was because of Dr. Pincus that Garland learned the true value of a "didja tube".

As an intern, Garland often drew blood from patients and ordered lab work as a normal part of the diagnostic process. Since lab tests were expensive and time consuming, it was customary to order tests just for the suspected pathology rather than order scattershot tests for everything imaginable. But this was Pincus Country. Bohicaville. So, to cover his ass, every time Garland drew a patient's blood for workup, he would draw two tubes rather than one and pocket the second tube, the "didja tube". Invariably during rounds, Pincus would pimp Garland and scrutinize the patient's chart for the tests Garland had ordered. Then Pincus would screw up his face and growl 'didja test for this, didja test for that, didja test for the other thing?' and Garland would one-up him and say 'we're just waiting for the labs'. Pincus, who didn't like to be one-upped, would grunt and move on to pimp another frightened student and Garland would take the "didja tube" in his pocket down to the lab and have it tested for whatever Pincus mentioned.

The lesson of the "didja tube" was never lost on Garland. That's why he had made a backup copy of the shooter's fingerprints before he gave them to the two agents the night before. And as he pushed the Jag to its 85-mph cruising altitude north on I-270, he realized that he had absolutely no compunctions about not telling Fitch and Hollister about his "didja-prints".

34

"How's the shoulder, Gene?" Garland asked as he walked into Eugene Kessler's office and saw his colleague's arm vacationing in a sling.

"Look who's here," Kessler chuckled, "Matt Fucking Damon, running across rooftops, unarmed, chasing those bad guys – Jesus Homer Christ, Nate, what the hell were you thinking?"

"I don't know, Gene. Seemed like a good idea at the time."

"Oh yeah," Kessler replied, "one of those good ideas, right up there with sticking your face in a lawnmower." Another chuckle and Kessler's expression morphed into deadly seriousness. "He was our boy, wasn't he?"

"Yeah. I'm pretty sure."

"Damn, now I'll never be able to get a piece of him." And as a sudden afterthought, added, "And Carolyn, too, I mean, mostly for her. So, we ID him yet? Army sniper, right? You can smell those maniacs a mile away."

"Treasury and Justice usurped us on that one. Took the body to Dover, won't let us in."

"Why the hell not?"

Garland shrugged, took a step back and quietly closed Kessler's office door. Kessler's eyes shifted warily from the door to Garland. "Gene, I need a favor."

"Is it about the shooter?"

Garland nodded and reached into his pocket and pulled out the "didja prints" he had folded in a plastic bag. He handed the bag to Kessler. "Shooter's prints. Both hands."

Kessler let out a low whistle.

"Can you run 'em down for me? Not here. Outside."

"Bet your sweet ass. I'll have 'em out over CJIS by this afternoon." Kessler said, referring to the national criminal justice information system.

"And is there any way you can get into the DOD system?"

"Not from here, we're locked out," Kessler said, lowering his voice to a conspiratorial whisper. But I've got friends at DOD. Good friends. They owe me. No one's going to know. If the shooter was Army sniper, we'll know it."

"Good. Thanks. You've got my cell, right? Call me as soon as you get a match, okay?" Garland turned and reached for the door.

"Nate. Wait." Kessler got up and moved toward Garland. "Maybe you can do something for me, too." Garland's open expression encouraged him to continue. "You know that little prick is going to steal my promotion, don't you?"

"Which 'little prick' are we talking about here, Gene?" Garland was genuinely baffled by where this was going.

"Dunbarton. Who else? Everyone knows I'm in line for Deputy Director, right? Am I right? And that little cocksucker has his head so far up Haynes' ass he can see daylight every time Haynes opens his mouth. It's my promotion, Nate, and Nelson is sucking it right out from under me."

"I didn't know."

"Yeah, well…I'm telling you straight up. Look, Haynes is your man. Your mentor. Your patron. He's in your pocket. It's no secret, everybody knows what he did for you to help you stick it to Jensen-Dillard."

Garland didn't know "everybody" knew. He was surprised. He had always thought – assumed – his foray into Jensen-Dillard Pharmaceuticals was confidential.

"All I can say, Gene, is that Haynes was a good friend when I needed one."

"Right," Kessler said. "That's why all I'm asking is that you put in a good word for me with him. A word from you. That's all I need."

"I'm not exactly in his good graces right now."

"Bullshit. The man loves you like his long lost son."

"Okay, look, when the timing's right, I'll talk to him for you. That's the best I can promise."

"And that's all I'm asking. Thanks, Nate, I owe you. And I'll have those prints matched before you know it."

Garland moved to the door. Before he opened it, he turned back to Kessler and said, "Gene, are you taking anything for the pain in your shoulder?"

"You kidding me?" Kessler smiled, "I am so buzzed I can play Chopin with my teeth."

35

Dr. Victor Brotman pressed down on the anterior lobe of the young girl's exposed brain and positioned the wand shaped camera above the cranial nerve. "Take a look. See where the CN III enters the lateral wall of cavernous sinus?"

Although Brotman was short and bald, save for a fringe of wild grey feathers that haloed the back of his head from ear to ear, he had one of those slow roasted, deep baritone speaking voices that dripped of authority and credibility. He also had the added benefit of being one of the top pathologists in the business.

With all eyes on the plasma screen positioned above the autopsy table, Brotman pressed on. "See the "Y" juncture here? From the normal eye to the right supernumerary eye? Okay, that's all new. This tissue here and the nerve bundle. See it? But over here, there's no optic nerve at all on the left supernumerary."

Both Garland and Wheeler were stunned by Brotman's show-and-tell. It was Wheeler who voiced what they were both thinking. "Are you sure, Vic? What you're saying is this girl was blind?"

"Blind as a bat. Probably from birth. But if we introduce an electrical impulse on the new nerve bundle, I have absolutely no doubt we'll get a significant pupil response."

"Wait a second, when I initially examined her at Fairfax, both of her normal eyes and the right supernumerary responded. I know she saw the light I flashed and I swear we made eye contact."

"Amazing grace," Wheeler said. "Was blind but now I see."

"You're sure, Vic?

The older pathologist nodded as he retracted the camera and released his grip on her frontal lobe. "Ninety-nine percent sure. I'll make it a hundred percent after I section the nerves." He used the back of his gloved hand to push his half-lens magnifying glasses up his nose. "You see it all the time in CN III palsy. It's aberrant regeneration. Very normal in most cases. But, and this is the big but fellas', it only happens on the diseased eye and this girl presents with absolutely no scarring."

"So she definitely wasn't born with the extra eyes," Garland said. "Then how?"

"It's a bitch alright," Brotman said as he moved to the sink and stripped off his gloves. "Tell you the truth, I ran through all the same possibilities you fellas did. Thought maybe some kind of LeSeur Syndrome, or a radiation mechanism, or menarche instigated genetic program, or maybe even some new kick ass toxic pollutant somewhere. But at the end of the day none of those scenarios felt right. And then I found the cellular anomaly and I, for one, believe we're on to something here."

Brotman replaced the girl's calvarium – the sawed off top of her skull – back over her exposed brain and covered her body with a plastic drape. The three men then moved across the hall to the other side of the suite where the scanning electron microscope was housed in a small anteroom. That's where Nelson Dunbarton, out of breath, caught up with them. Garland literally smelled him coming. Feet. He still smelled like feet.

"Haynes wants to see you."

"Tell him I'll be up in a few minutes."

They all kept walking. Dunbarton had to move quickly to keep up.

"He said now. He wants to see you right now. Something about a diplomat at the British Embassy?"

"Catch you inside," Wheeler said as he hustled Brotman into microscopy.

"I'll be right in." Then, turning to Dunbarton, Garland said, "Nels, not now."

"Why do you have to be so difficult about these things? You know Haynes is that close to shit-canning you."

"This is more important. Just tell him I'll be up as soon as I can."

Dunbarton glanced at the microscopy room door. "That was Brotman, wasn't it? You guys discover something in the autopsy?"

Garland couldn't tell if Dunbarton was genuinely interested or just looking for a scoop to report back to Haynes. "We don't know yet," he said.

"Mind if I sit in?"

"Sure. Why the hell not."

The SEM room was kept much cooler than even the pathology lab to keep the electron microscope from overheating. The instrument was on a metal counter and consisted of a small electronics console with a white, tube-like apparatus rising like a periscope from a rectangular shoebox size specimen container. Two large flat panel plasma screens stood side by side next to the console on the counter.

Wheeler tapped the keyboard and two cellular images appeared on the plasma screens.

"Alright, you tell me, what do you make of this, Nate? The left screen was sectioned from her normal eyes, the right screen from her right superfluous eye."

Garland slowly scanned both screens up and back, allowing his eyes to adjust to the images. And then he saw it. He leaned in closer to the screens, not quite believing what he was seeing. Both Wheeler and Brotman looked at him to gauge his reaction.

"Holy shit."

"Pretty astounding, isn't it?" Brotman spoke first.

"What? What do you see?" Dunbarton asked.

"Give me the 23rd," Garland said to Wheeler.

Wheeler used both joysticks and navigated across the cellular image until he located the 23rd chromosome in the cell.

"Damn," Garland said. "That's unbelievable."

"What?" Dunbarton asked. "What is it?"

"A 'Y' chromosome," Wheeler said, "the 23rd chromosome. The sex chromosome."

"Didn't I tell you?" Brotman smiled to Garland. "Pretty astounding, am I right?"

Garland leaned back from the screens but didn't take his eyes off the images. He was processing what he saw, but it didn't make sense to him. "They're haploids. That's not possible."

"Believe it, my friend. You're seeing it, so it is possible."

"What?" Dunbarton said. "What do you guys see there?"

You remember your high school biology?" Wheeler said. "Chromosomes come in pairs, right? And the 23rd chromosome is the sex chromosome. XX is female, XY is male. Paired chromosomes are called diploids. Unpaired or single chromosomes are haploids. What you're looking at here shouldn't exist in a young girl. These cells – her cells – contain male haploids."

"So maybe she's really a boy."

"This girl had no gender confusion diseases," Wheeler said.

159

"Nate?" Brotman's pudgy hand swept toward the screens, gesturing for his colleague's opinion.

"What I'm looking at here doesn't occur in nature. It's absolutely man made. Not a doubt in my mind it's a transgenic mutation. Totally fabricated, genetically engineered." Garland looked from Brotman to Wheeler. "This girl was messed with, Grove, I mean really messed with. Somebody did a real grisly number on her."

"I concur," Brotman nodded. "But whoever did it would have had to instigate it at the germ cell level. They'd need a matching male gamete to accomplish a genetic mutation like hers."

"Germ cells from a natural brother or her father?"

"The father for sure, the brother if the match was close enough. But they'd have to be willing donors," Brotman cautioned. "The cells would have to be extracted from their spine."

"Wait, just hang on a minute," Dunbarton cut in. "Are you saying you can take somebody's cells, mess around with 'em, and from those cells make eyes grow on somebody else's head?"

"That's exactly what we're saying, if the DNA is a close enough match. It's basic recombinant engineering. Her eyes came from male cells. Haploids don't lie. The beauty of it is, she was blind, so the donor would have to be sighted."

"If what you're suggesting is true," Dunbarton said, "you're talking about an unforgivable crime against god and nature."

"Against god and nature, hardly, Nels. But against this little girl, I couldn't agree with you more."

"All I'm saying is man was created in god's image and we do not tamper with his work."

"Really, Nels? Tell me, exactly which man was created in his image? Black man? White man? Neanderthal man? Cro-Magnon

160

man? Homo erectus man? Homo habilis man? Which is the right image? Which is the right man?"

"You know exactly what I'm talking about."

"No. I don't. And neither do you, so just let's drop it."

The room fell into an embarrassed silence until Brotman continued where he had left off. "But, of course, the same therapy that may have given her blind eyes sight was exactly what killed her."

"How'd she die?" Dunbarton asked, composing himself.

Wheeler turned back to the keyboard and reduced the magnification on the screens. The new images that appeared showed streams of dark colored cells being surrounded by nearly clear cells. It looked like a helicopter's view of rush hour traffic on an expressway.

"T-cells, killer T-cells," Wheeler explained it simply for Dunbarton's benefit. "Lymphocytes. Those are the clear ones. White blood cells. The dark ones are erythrocytes, red blood cells. T-cells are cytotoxic, they kill bad cells and infected cells. They're the body's immuno-army. And these T-cells you see here, they got confused by the haploids. They called in the troops, all the killer T-cell reserves and they just started killing every red blood cell in her body. No red cells, no oxygen. Her body dies."

The phone on the console rang and Wheeler answered it. He listened for a moment and then handed the phone to Garland. "For you."

"Garland." He held the phone to his ear for a few seconds and his face darkened with concern. "Listen, Polly, listen to me, you find the biggest cop you can and glue yourself to him, understand? Stay right there. I can be there in forty-five minutes."

He hung up and looked at the three men. "Jason Beck," he said. "He's dead."

36

The Jason Beck Eye Institute was spitting distance from the Johns Hopkins hospital complex in Baltimore and it took Garland forty minutes longer to get there than he planned. Inside the modern I.M. Pei designed structure, Garland trotted up three flights of stairs to the exquisitely decorated executive office floor where a female cop steered him down the plush carpeted corridor to the last office. Two techs from the medical examiner's crew – the stretcher fetchers, as they were known – were waiting for the M.E. and the homicide detectives to finish their preliminary before they would be allowed to remove Beck's body.

The first thing Garland noticed at the door was the engraved name on the polished brass nameplate: Dr. Polly Collier. This was her office. Not Beck's. He stepped into what was obviously a secretary's outer office. The room was in shambles – drawers emptied, furniture overturned, lamps broken. The floor was littered, but most prominently with Jason Beck's body. He lay across the open door, between the outer office and Polly's sanctum, his legs in the inner office and his head and torso in the entry.

Beck had been shot in the head at fairly close range by what Garland surmised to be a medium caliber handgun. Pieces of his skull, clumps of hair and significant blood spatter insulted the beige Berber carpet all the way to the desk. Beck's casual Bruno Magli loafers rested inches away from his feet as if he had been shot out of his shoes. He had obviously been attacked in the inner office and fell into the door, banging it open as he died. From the door, Garland could see that the inner office was tossed and ransacked as well.

"Who you?" The disembodied voice was inquisitive, not hostile, and belonged to Det. Sgt. Devon Chambers, kneeling behind the inner office door.

Garland raised his badge to the door. "Garland, BIA."

Chambers got up and walked around the door to get a better look at Garland. He was in his early forties, about five-ten, slight build, African-American. He was also well dressed, on a cop's salary, wore stylish frameless glasses and carried himself confidently.

"Where's Dr. Collier?" Garland asked.

"Down the hall," Chambers replied as he jotted down Garland's name, badge number and particulars in his notebook. Then, without looking up, said, "Lou," to the cop at the door, "you want to bring Dr. Collier back down here." Then, back to Garland, said, "Feds have a particular interest in this crime, do you?"

"Possibly. What've you got so far?"

"One dead eye doc and another one scared out of her skin." Chambers offered Garland a wry smile. "What've you got so far?"

"It might be connected to several cases we're working."

"Uh huh. And which cases might those be?"

"Wish I could help you, Sergeant."

"It's gonna be one of those, huh? Should of known. It always worries me when the Feds show up on scene before my lieutenant."

"I'll cover with your brass," Garland said. He considered his options for a moment and then said, "Here's what I can give you. Your victim and his associate, Dr. Collier, were both at Fed-Med yesterday morning consulting on one of my medical cases. Last night, a shooter up on a roof in Georgetown…"

"That was you," Chambers cut him off. "That's where I saw you. The news."

"Not just me. Dr. Collier was there, too. Shooter fired at both of us."

"This is her office, so you're thinking she was the intended target?"

Garland shrugged. "Initially, I thought I was the target, but now…"

"Let me save you some guesswork. She was. We've got two intruders on the security disk. Entered through the back delivery door at 5:50 this morning. Came up the fire stairs. Broke into her office and waited right inside here for her to show up."

"You've got them on security?" Garland contained his excitement.

"Two men. White. One about five-six or seven, the other close to six-feet. Both wearing coat jackets, slacks, collared shirts, no ties. And no faces. They turned away or covered up at every camera."

"The shorter of the two, were you able to see if he was wearing goggle type glasses, almost like welder's goggles, you know, leather strap around the back of his head?"

"No. Didn't see anything like that. But like I said, they covered their faces or turned away. Maybe when the images are enhanced…" Chambers cocked his head and looked directly at Garland. "Who is goggle guy? What's his connection? You think he'd be after Dr. Collier?"

"How'd you know they were waiting for her?" Garland asked, deflecting Chambers' questions.

"Cameras followed them out of the building at 8:05. That's just about the time the doc here got popped. He had the misfortune of walking in on them. You're not going to answer me, are you?"

"What were they looking for?"

"Nothing. They weren't looking for anything."

"You seem pretty positive."

"Dudes were waiting in here for over two hours. They tossed the office after they shot the doc. Blood is under all the stuff on the floor, not on top of it. If they were looking for something in particular, they had plenty of time to find it and boogie."

"And Doctor Collier is sure nothing is missing?"

"No, I'm not sure," Polly said, entering with the other cop. "I haven't taken an inventory, but I don't keep anything important here. Certainly nothing worth stealing or killing Jason for."

Garland was surprised by how relieved he was to see her and yet those same emotions made him suddenly uncomfortable. He tried a reassuring smile and said, "Are you okay?" He knew it sounded dumb the minute he said it.

Polly nodded. She was wearing her oversized sunglasses again, hiding her face, and Garland immediately noticed her clothes were the same as she had on the night before. Polly had obviously decided against borrowing any of Daisy's. Garland felt somehow pleased by that gesture, but didn't know why.

"Detective, do you think the M.E. can remove Dr. Beck or, at the very least, cover him?" she said softly.

"We're almost through here." Then, motioning to her face said, "Do you always wear sunglasses indoors?"

"I have sensitive eyes."

"And I have this strange quirk, doctor, I like to look people in the eye when I speak to them. You mind?"

Polly reached up, removed her sunglasses and looked directly at Chambers. Her reddened eyes were sunken beneath puffy circles dark as licorice. The bruises on her cheek and beneath her eye were now a deep purple ringed with a pale yellow border, like an oil spill on a beach. It didn't take an expert to read the bruises and from

Chambers' complete lack of expression it was apparent he had seen similar bruises many times in his career.

"Is that better, detective?"

"Please understand I'm just doing my job."

"Yes, of course," her tone was just a hair shy of sarcasm. "You might like to know I finally reached his wife," Polly went on. "She was in Boston visiting their daughter. I gave her your name and number." She put her sunglasses back on.

"Dr. Collier, I'm sorry to have to put you through this, but I'm going to need your help here."

"I don't know what more I can add to what I already told you."

"Dr. Garland said you may have been the intended target of the sniper last night."

"I didn't say that."

Polly shook her head. "Why? Why would someone want to kill me?"

"You tell me." Chambers shrugged. "They failed last night, so they tried again this morning."

"Last night's shooter is dead," Garland said. "So you're suggesting there's an active conspiracy to kill her? One hit man fails, bring in another? My investigation has nothing to do with her. She and Dr. Beck were brought in by Director Haynes to examine my patient's eyes. Nothing more. They came, they saw, they did, they left. End of story."

"You've got to give me something to run with, Garland. I've got a murder here that was up close and in your face. If Dr. Collier was the intended target…"

"That would only be because of me. I may have inadvertently put her in harm's way."

"Uh-huh. So that brings us full circle, doesn't it, doctor? And you're not even going to give me an inch, are you?"

"I can't, detective. But I will as soon as I can."

"Yeah. Right. I'll hold my breath."

37

Garland shifted his eyes nervously across the Jag's mirrors. They had been driving a full fifteen minutes in silence before Polly finally spoke, her voice drained flat and completely devoid of emotion.

"They didn't have to kill him. What did Jason do to deserve that? If they were after me..."

"Do you have any idea who 'they' might be?"

"No."

Garland glanced over to her. "Were you or Beck working on anything else that might be considered unconventional?"

"No. Yes. I mean, we're doing – we were doing – some very unique work. I told you about it last night. But there's nothing illegal or unethical or anything like that if that's what you're implying. We adhere to every N.I.H. guideline and protocol. Before Jason published his last paper, the work was thoroughly peer reviewed." She tilted her head to Garland. "You think Jason was killed because of the research we were doing?"

Garland shrugged, checked his mirrors again. "Were you using male haploids in your research?"

"Haploids? For what purpose? No, of course not, we use diploids, active stem cells, like everyone else. Why are you asking that?"

"At autopsy we found male haploids in the girl's optic nerves.

168

"What? Please. That's absolutely ridiculous. How could that possibly be?"

"The girl was blind from birth. Someone had transgenically engineered her cells with male haploids from a sighted male relative. And it worked. She could see."

"No, c'mon, that's insane. No one can do that yet. It's not possible. Besides, what about the rejection factors?"

"That's what killed her."

"Oh my god. Really? And you think Jason had something to do with this line of research?"

"He's the man, world's leading authority. You said so yourself."

"No, uh-uh, it still doesn't make sense. We've got a half-dozen research assistants. Anyone of them would have raised issues with haploids. What would be the purpose? Uh-uh, Jason's murder had nothing to do with our research." Polly gave it another moment's thought and added, "Those men were there to kill me. The detective said that they were waiting for me in my office and Jason walked in on them."

"Or it was made to look that way. That wouldn't have been difficult to do."

Garland checked his mirrors again. Although they were on the interstate, traffic was moderate and Garland had noticed that a silver Mercedes, staying four cars behind in the right lane, had been following the Jag for at least five miles. Garland could not make out the driver.

"Look, we both know research is ridiculously competitive. So many of the top players have paper thin egos, they're easily threatened. Financial stakes are astronomical. C'mon, think, Polly, did you make enemies?"

"You really give me a lot more credit than I deserve. Did I hurt someone? Offend somebody? Do something so awful? I honestly can't think of a thing why someone would want to kill me."

Garland noticed that she curled her tongue between her lips in the Mandarin habit when she pronounced the 'L' in 'lot' and the double 'L's' in 'kill'. He had noticed it the night before and was completely charmed by this innocuous gesture.

"You're sure," he said, "no enemies?"

"Give me a break, I'm a research ophthalmologist, not some wild-eyed mad scientist. The most heated professional disagreement I've ever had in the last six months was with my malpractice insurance company when they raised my premium 200%. Bastards." She drew in a long breath, blew it out and said softly, "I know he sometimes appeared pompous, but Jason was a good decent man. He had a wonderful, loving family and was an incredibly gifted doctor. What did he do…what did any of us do to deserve that?"

Garland checked his mirrors as he listened to Polly. The silver Mercedes was still four car lengths back. It could be nothing, just a driver zoning out, lazily following the car in front. Could be completely innocent. Maybe not. He told Polly to hold on and he lay a little more foot on the accelerator. The Jag squirted out from behind the SUV Garland was following and sprinted into the left lane. He kept his foot on the gas and the Jag's needle crept from 75 to 80 to 85. Another quick check of the rearview mirror and Garland saw the Mercedes swing into the left lane behind him. He pressed harder and the Jaguar bolted in response, the speedometer now moving past 90.

Polly looked at Garland and saw his concentration, his eyes flashing from the road to the car's mirrors. "What is it?" she asked, concerned but not frightened.

"Maybe nothing. Slide down. Keep your head below the headrest."

Now she was frightened. She slid way down in her seat and braced her body against it.

Garland pushed the Jag over 100. The silver Mercedes kept pace. 110. He tried to make out the driver of the Mercedes but it was too far back. The license plates were impossible to make out. There was traffic in all lanes in front of him and there were several slower vehicles in the right lane. If he moved up behind the traffic in front of him he would be forced into the fast lanes and risked the possibility of getting trapped there, so he slowed and paced himself with the traffic in the right lane – a yellow Hertz Rent-A-Truck and a small white Toyota. The Toyota was practically climbing up the yellow truck's ass.

The Monrovia exit ramp was 200 yards ahead. Garland tapped the brakes and the truck in the right lane blew past him. The Mercedes was forced to brake hard but stayed in control. In the right lane, there was barely spitting room between the Hertz truck and the white Toyota, but Garland still slid sharply into the right lane and surgically inserted the Jaguar between the two vehicles, timing it perfectly to hit the Monrovia exit ramp in the same motion. The Jaguar's tires screeched in angry protest, but gripped the road tenaciously as Garland struggled to rein the car in on the sharp ramp curve. The Mercedes didn't have a chance. It was trapped on the interstate, sewn in by the yellow truck and the Toyota. If it was following them, it was following no more.

38

Garland skidded the Jag to a stop at the end of the off ramp. He looked over to Polly scrunched down in her seat, terrified. She was trembling. He pulled off to the side of the road and waited until he caught his breath before he spoke.

"You okay?"

"You mean aside from being chased by a maniac on the interstate? Aside from my mentor being murdered or my leaving my husband last night? Sure, I'm fine, I'm absolutely fine." She flicked at a stray tear on her bruised cheek. "I'm sorry, I'm sorry. I get a little edgy and sarcastic when I'm nervous or scared and right now I am off the charts on both."

Garland nodded his understanding.

"What is happening? For godssake, Nathaniel, what is happening? When did I completely lose control of my life? He's dead. Murdered. These things don't happen, they just don't happen." She brushed away another tear. "Without Jason, our work at the Institute is over. Oh, god, I can't believe I'm so self-centered. He's the one who's dead."

"Hey, you have every right to be frightened and confused. If it's any consolation, I am, too." He looked around and checked his mirrors. "It's not safe to stay here. Are you okay enough for me to drive?"

Polly nodded.

He put the Jag in gear and took alternate local roads to Fed-Med rather than risk getting back on the interstate. Twenty minutes later, they passed through the security gates and Garland parked in his reserved space. He turned off the ignition and they sat in silence for several long beats. It could have been very uncomfortable, but somehow it wasn't.

"This is my fault, I'm sorry," Garland said, "believe me, it was never my intention to get you involved."

Polly turned in the leather seat to face him and took off her sunglasses. Her molten cobalt eyes surveyed his face and then locked on his eyes. "Nathaniel, I appreciate everything you've done for me, I really do, but I'm not your responsibility and you have nothing to apologize for.

Maybe it was true, but those were not the kinds of guilt-free thoughts Garland would allow himself. And it was definitely not what he was thinking at that moment. What he was thinking just then was how much he wanted to kiss her. But even kissing her did not fully describe his thought or his desire. He wanted more, he wanted to wade into the turquoise seas of her eyes, bask in their brilliance and assimilate the quiddity of their color. Of course, he didn't act on his impulse. He couldn't. He wouldn't. He would never betray her trust. Or Daisy's.

39

Wheeler extended his condolences to Polly as the three of them walked through the Con-Con 1 hub to the elevators. Wheeler then got them up to speed on the girl's autopsy. The final serology and toxicology tests would be completed soon but the results will no doubt confirm everything they suspected.

"I still can't wrap my head around the whole thing." Polly said. "How could she have been blind from birth and then die sighted, so young? It's just not right, not fair."

"Sighted and nameless," Wheeler said.

"She didn't fall out of the sky," Garland said. "She's missing from somewhere. From somebody. We start by canvassing every school for blind kids in the tri-state area right now."

"I work with practically all of them," Polly said, "and I'm networked into hundreds more. If she attended any one of them…"

"You sure you don't mind?" Garland asked.

"No, it's – no, it'll take my mind off of – please. I'd like to help."

"Okay. Thanks. What do you need – I mean, besides a computer and phone?"

"I need to borrow some scrubs and get out of these clothes. And if it's not too much trouble, I'm dying for a cup of coffee?"

"How about a quick lunch?" Wheeler offered. "Nate?"

"No, thanks, not before an encounter with Arleta."

In the tiny glass enclosed evidence room at the far end of the Fed-Med forensics lab, Arleta Farleigh had the entire contents of the young girl's rape kit spread out across the table, each item secured in an individually tagged plastic evidence bag. Everything was neatly and legally labeled. Through the clear plastic bags, Garland could see where 1-inch squares of fabric had been cut from several places on the hospital gown for chemical analysis and comparative DNA testing. The oversize shoes that the girl was wearing when she was found were in separate bags and they, too, had pieces of material carefully cut out. To the side of the table, a half dozen translucent DNA charts were fanned like playing cards. Arleta was a monumental pain in the ass, Garland's thought, but man, she is good.

He clipped the top DNA plate up on the light box. "Where's this from?"

Arleta squinted at the notation she had written on the bottom of the plate. "Left shoe. And you mind not screwing around with the order I've got it laid out."

He picked up the plastic evidence bag containing the gown.

"Jesus Christ, Garland, you weren't even listening." She took the package from him and pulled out the girl's hospital gown. "It's a standard off the shelf 50-50 cotton-poly. There's a pharmacopoeia of organic stains all over it, so we know it was definitely used in a medical environment – a clinic or hospital or some other health services venue. No laundry marks, no distinguishing characteristics. We traced the weave pattern to a company named GeoTex, Georgia-Textile. They supply the fabric to hundreds of garment manufacturers in the southeast, from Texas to Florida. Seven of 'em manufacture and distribute hospital and surgical garments and we're waiting for their customer lists which is like pulling fucking hen's teeth."

"DNA?" Garland asked.

"Hers and four others." Arleta stated matter-of-factly. "We've got statistically perfect matches to the anal and vaginal swabs they took at Fairfax."

Garland absorbed the confirmation that the young girl was raped and sodomized by four different men. "Anything come up on CODIS or VICAP?" he asked, referring to the FBI's national DNA and violent criminal databases.

"No, but that doesn't mean the donors didn't have priors, it just means their DNA markers haven't been entered yet, that is, if they were ever arrested."

"So there's nothing on the gown to get us closer to her ID?"

"Not so fast, Garland." She cocked her head and produced a self-satisfied smirk. "We've still got the algae."

"What algae?"

"On the gown. Same as on the shoes." Arleta folded the gown back into the plastic evidence bag and reached for the shoes. "They were submerged. The gown. The shoes. Under water. A river, stream, creek, maybe a stream fed lake."

"Can you be more specific?"

"Green," she said flatly. "Green algae means fresh water as opposed to blue-green which is usually saltwater. This particular algae's Spirogyra. And chlorophyta. Which, this time of year is usually Southern. But the phosphate content moves it west. So originally I was thinking southwestern Tennessee, but then the shoes..." her sentence drifted off as she pulled one of the girl's shoes out of its plastic evidence bag. "You see the ridges here?" she said pointing to the sole. "It's 101 stuff. You pull the gunk out of the ridges and crevices in the crepe sole — the deeper the gunk, the older it is. You spread it out and process it in order. Problem with these shoes is that they were underwater. I'm guessing a river or a stream that runs through a forest or woods or something. In the shoe gunk I found these." Arleta handed Garland a small glassine evidence envelope that was inside the shoe bag.

Garland held the glassine envelope up to the light and studied it. "These look like pine needles."

"Lodged in the mud in the shoe crevices. Bald cypress, loblolly and short leaf – they're southern yellow pines, except, of course, for the bald cypress."

"And they grow where?"

"Southern Missouri and Arkansas." Arleta said it as if any idiot should know.

Garland processed the information she had just thrown at him. "Fresh water algae, southern Missouri, Arkansas…"

"For Christ's sake, Garland," Arleta huffed as she ran out of patience, "Bull Shoals Lake. The White River. Arkansas. What the hell's the matter with you?"

"You're saying she was in or near Bull Shoals."

"I'm not saying. Her shoes are saying."

"But the police found her in Virginia. Nothing in the shoes to locate her between Arkansas and Virginia?"

"You've got to figure she didn't walk from Bull Shoals to Fairfax, right? She had a ride. Car, truck, bus, something. Maybe she drove. Maybe somebody she knew gave her a lift, maybe she thumbed."

"Or maybe she was kidnapped. Go back to the shoes. They've got to tell us how a little girl traveled eight hundred and fifty miles, dressed the way she was, probably soaked through to the skin and nobody helped her or reported it."

"Had to be somebody she knew," Arleta ventured.

"Four men raped her, beat her and left her for dead. I doubt if she knew them. If she did, they would have killed her to keep her from identifying them. My guess is they were strangers. Probably some men who picked her up on the road. Hunters or fishermen maybe. Maybe at a gas station, truck stop, rest stop someplace. Had to be rural. Otherwise she would have flagged down a police officer or the highway patrol or something."

"Or maybe she was too scared." Arleta offered, getting into it now. "I mean, she was probably running away from her family."

"Why would you jump to that conclusion?"

"Because the shoes belonged to her father or brother."

That stopped Garland cold. "What are you talking about?"

"We're running the analysis again, but the DNA tests from inside the shoes came up with hers and probably the shoes' owner. Key markers were nearly identical to hers. But male. Brother or father. Who knows."

"You're sure?" Garland said. "The shoes belonged to her brother or father?"

"If I was sure would I be running the analysis again? I'll let you know when it's confirmed. If I had to bet, though, I'd say the shoes belonged to a brother."

"Arleta, were there enough markers to indicate they could be twins?"

"You know as well as I do fraternal twins don't share the same DNA."

"But they're close."

"No closer than any other siblings. I just get a sense from the key markers that they're male and female and definitely related, that's all."

178

And that's all Garland needed to cement his suspicions. The male haploids. Her father or brother were the most likely donors, the brother particularly because the shoes were a young style, not an older man's style and worn at the tips and heels. An active boy's shoes. Was he a willing donor, Garland wondered? An active participant in a grotesque genetic experiment? Maybe. Maybe not. But Garland now knew – knew it deep in his gut – that if he could find the girl's brother and or her father, it would all fall into place.

"Specifics, Arleta, I need a specific location. Maybe some protozoan material, localized bacterium, something, anything you can dredge up to get me closer."

"See what I can do, Garland, but I'm not a magician."

"Yeah, but you're the best, Arleta, you're the best."

"Fuckin'-A. You got that right."

40

Sitting across from Polly in the executive cafeteria, Grover Wheeler shook his head incredulously and forked another bite of salad into his mouth. "Nate actually told you about Daisy and Breezy? The whole story?"

Polly shrugged. "I think so."

"Damn, I am…impressed. He never talks about it. Ever."

"There was one part that confused me, though. He said that by the time he found the answer, it was too late. What did he mean? What answer?"

Wheeler smiled. "Let's take a walk," he said.

Despite the bright sunshine, a cool breeze sliding off the Catoctin Mountains rippled across the parking lot as Wheeler and Polly walked back to Con-Con.

"Nate told you how they died?"

"Yes. She, his wife, cut their wrists. She was delusional and thought she could transfuse her daughter."

"No. That was only the result, that's not what killed Breezy. Truth was, none of us could understand why the chemo wasn't working. Especially Nate. He guessed it had to be the interferon, so he took a dozen different types and doses to Carter Haynes' lab when he was over at CDC and had his team analyze them. The results of the tests were conclusive: his daughter's drugs had one-quarter the necessary interleukin to make the drug effective. It was diluted four to one, that's why it had no effect at the recommended dosage."

"What? How's that possible?"

"That's what we all wanted to know." Wheeler said. "But Nate, God, Nate couldn't stop beating himself up over it. Still is. Why he waited so long to test the drugs. If he had known earlier, a few months, even a few weeks earlier…"

"But he had no way of knowing. Pharmaceuticals are all…" Polly stopped. A dawn of recognition altered her expression. Her mind raced ahead to gather the fragments of fact that she already owned. "Oh my God," she said, "that was him. I know this story," her tone rose in recognition. "I read about it. The interferon. It was the one manufactured by Jensen-Dillard Pharmaceuticals, right? That was him, Nathaniel, wasn't it?"

"Yep."

"It made all the papers. There was a feature article in JAMA," she said, referring to the Journal of the American Medical Association, "he put JDP out of business."

"If you ask Nate, he didn't. The courts did."

"Something to do with mislabeling the drug, if I remember. No, it was more. It was a big scandal, right, price-fixing or something like that?"

"Something like that," Wheeler acknowledged. "Jensen-Dillard was secretly manufacturing several tiers of their interferon. One for the American market and diluted versions for foreign markets, so it could be sold much cheaper in Asia and Africa. The difference was in the dosing. Even though the foreign drug was much cheaper, the dosage requirement was five times higher, so, in effect, they were skirting the law and getting the American price for their product. What happened with Breezy's medicine was that some poor dumb schmuck on the line made a mistake and put American labels on the foreign product."

"Did you ever find out how many other kids were affected?"

"We know of sixty-six. There were probably a lot more. Nate discovered that Jensen-Dillard management was already compiling a list of the affected patients when he borrowed their documents. Breezy was on that list."

"Borrowed? What do you mean? How did he 'borrow' their documents?"

"He went to work for them." Wheeler said. "With the help of some very good friends in some very high places – like Carter Haynes – he created a fictitious CV and JDP hired him. He went to work early and stayed late and just combed through every file he could find in their interferon division. The paper trail was like a corporate cancer spreading all the way to the top. All the way to Herbert Harrison Jensen, his very self."

"So he knew? He knew what his company was doing?"

"Jensen more than knew. It was his idea, his business plan. He told Nate everything."

"Come on, why would he tell him that? If I remember, the settlement was in the billions. It put JDP out of business, so why would Jensen make an admission of guilt like that? It would expose him to all kinds of additional criminal charges."

Wheeler shrugged. "I don't know the details. You'll have to ask Nate yourself. All I know is that somehow he met with Jensen and persuaded him to hold a conference call with the Attorney General, the FDA, FBI, IRS, SEC... whole damn D.C. alphabet soup. Jensen spilled his guts. Admitted his complicity and voluntarily turned over all of the company's records and documents to the Feds."

"Why would he do that? These guys have buildings full of lawyers."

"As I said, I don't know."

"If I remember, it didn't even go to trial. Jensen-Dillard settled. Cost them billions. That's what put them out of business."

"Right. But Nate still had a problem with that. It drove him nuts. Of the billions that JDP had to pay, none of that money was coming out of Jensen's pocket. Somehow – and don't ask me how, I don't know – before Jensen went to prison, Nate negotiated a personal settlement with him, persuaded him to give up his golden parachute, his pension, all his options and all the other hidden compensation packages that these guys finagle to bilk their stockholders."

"Are you saying he coughed it all up, just like that?"

"Amazing, isn't it? Nate took the money and gave every cent of it to this dinky hospital in West Virginia to build a pediatric cancer center, but don't tell him I told you."

"Why West Virginia?"

"It's in the town where Daisy grew up."

They trotted up the steps to Con-Con and Wheeler opened the door.

"Did Jensen have a family?" Polly asked.

"He was married, I know that," Wheeler said. "And if I'm not mistaken, I think he had a daughter, too, just about Breezy's age."

41

Garland leaned in over Eugene Kessler's shoulder to get a better look at the images on his computer screen. They were two fingerprints, each side appropriately labeled 'left index' and 'right index'. The magnification gave them a Rorschach appearance, but the loops, arches and whorls, indigenous to all fingerprints, were remarkably clear. Kessler was actually chortling and Garland knew his colleague's wacky behavior was due, in large part, to the robust pain killers he was still popping.

"I swear, Nate, when Elise told me, I just about peed my pants. She never saw anything like it."

"Gene, I haven't a clue what I'm looking at here or what you're talking about."

"These are the prints you gave me this morning, cowboy. I scanned 'em and emailed 'em over to my friend at Hoover just like I said I would."

"Okay. Now tell me what's so funny about them."

"I swear to god, Nate, you're going to squirt your knickers when I tell you."

"I'll try to control myself."

"All right, look, I don't know much about the finer points of fingerprintology either, but you got them from the shooter, right? I mean, right there on the roof, you took fresh prints, right?"

"Right."

"So look over here," he said pointing with his pen, "the left index finger, see where the center has a sort of bull's-eye circular pattern, see? Here? It's called a whorl among fingerprint cognoscenti. Now look at the right index finger. Notice anything strange?"

Garland leaned in closer and studied the image. "No whorl in the center."

"Give that man a fucking cigar. And you know why there's no whorl in the center? Because this shitcake's prints don't match each other. How's that for a slap upside the old melon?"

Garland straightened up, ready to strangle his colleague. "Gene, that doesn't mean a goddamned thing. All fingerprints are different. That's why we take a set of ten. They're all different."

"I see you're still dubious, my friend. Just trust me on this one. The fingerprints on your boy's right hand don't match the fingerprints on his left hand. You don't find that bizarre? Only the right hand prints are classified. DOD. My contact couldn't dent that armor and she wasn't about to take on the Pentagon. But the shooter's left hand came up big on IAFIS." Kessler referenced the FBI's Integrated Automated Fingerprint Identification System. He slid some papers across the desk to Garland. "My friend emailed her sheet. The non-classified prints belong to one Donald Mottz Polachek of Joliet, Illinois."

Garland scooped them up and quickly scanned the few pages.

"So what do you think, Nate?" Kessler said, all serious now. "This the guy who shot me? This the guy who killed Carolyn? This the guy on the roof who tried to take you out?"

"I don't know. Did you read his sheet? He was arrested a couple times for petty crimes. That's when they took his prints. Stealing a tractor for a joyride doesn't seem like the seeds of a professional assassin. Also says he was in the army, two year hitch, so he's definitely not a career man. And no mention of Ft. Benning or sniper school, but he did spend some time at Ft. Bragg. Special operations school is there."

"Special ops - those guys are crazy fuckers. Hey, maybe they surgically changed his fingerprints on his left hand, you know, for some of special ops voodoo bullshit thing."

Garland folded the papers into his pocket. "Great work, Gene, thanks."

"Do me one and keep me in the loop, will you? This one's personal."

"You got it." Then, almost as an afterthought, said, "Gene, you happen to have an extra sidearm you could loan me for a while?"

Kessler stared at Garland for a beat, then swiveled in his chair, slid open the bottom drawer of his desk and pulled out a dark plastic case. He popped it open, withdrew his agency standard issue Glock 18, which he never used, and slid it across the desk. Garland picked it up and popped the clip to check it.

"This isn't your kind of play, Nate. Do you know what you're doing? What you're getting into?"

"No. Not really. Thanks for everything, Gene." And he jammed the gun in his pocket and left to go back to his own office.

42

Garland plopped into the chair in his tiny office and idly patted the jagged tear on his face. What Kessler had unknowingly suggested was that the shooter's hands apparently belonged to two different people. As if the dead assassin had a Frankensteinian hand.

Yes, Garland had seen his left hand and, yes, its strange variegated coloring was unusual. But it couldn't possibly be somebody else's hand. Garland had studied it briefly on the roof and knew then and there that it was not surgically attached. Or was it and, in his excitement, had he missed the scarring under the camouflage patterned skin? A cadaver's hand maybe? Could it be? Was such a surgery even possible? No way. Then why the secrecy, Garland wondered? Why was the shooter whisked away? Why were his fingerprints and his military file immediately classified? What were the FBI and Treasury and the Pentagon covering up? Was that man up on the roof really Donald Mottz Polachek of Joliet, Illinois? Or was Kessler's FBI contact, Elise Whomever, running their game on him, too?

Garland got up and paced to the other side of his desk, continuing his internal dialog, reexamining each unanswered question. He was eager to connect the dots, but the dots kept moving and shifting. A bigger question soon flushed the others aside: how was this shooter – if he was, in fact, Polachek – related to Sarah Levine and the carnage on Burning Tree Road? How was he related to the man with the goggles who obviously had access to Sarah's license plates? Why did Polachek try to kill him last night? What information does he now have – that he doesn't even know he has – that would make him a prime target for assassination? Or was Polly really the target last night and this morning? And the bigger question, the mother of all questions still dangling out there like bear bait — who tipped the shooter to the Capiloff search warrant they were serving on Burning Tree Road?

Garland reached for the phone and called the Joliet, Illinois PD. He was bounced from person to person until a Lt. Kathleen Quigby was able to provide all the information Garland requested. Lt. Quigby was personable and cooperative and did her best to help Garland pinpoint the current Joliet whereabouts of Donald Mottz Polachek. He had neither a local address or phone number under that name, but Lt. Quigby did find nine Polachek residences in both the listed and unlisted directories. She gave Garland all the phone numbers, told him she would check with the local courts, the Sheriff's office and the Will County Clerk's office. Garland thanked her, plugged in his ugly teapot, opened his laptop and went to work.

Seven calls and forty-five minutes later, growing ever more frustrated, Garland placed a call to number eight on Quigby's list, Mrs. Margaret Polachek.

"Hello?" The voice on the other end was cheerful despite having that flat, nasal Midwestern tone.

"Mrs. Margaret Polachek?"

"Yes. Who's this?"

"Mrs. Polachek, I'm Dr. Nathaniel Garland with the BIA at the Department of Health in Washington."

"Yes. I can see your area code right here on my caller I.D. How can I help you? Dr. Garland, is it?"

"Yes. Mrs. Polachek, I'm calling in reference to your husband. Could you tell me if he's home right now."

"Is this some kind of joke, sir?" Her voice was cold now. *"My husband's been passed now nearly fourteen years."*

Garland sighed. Another dead end, he thought, no pun intended. *"No, ma'am, it's not a joke and I do apologize for disturbing you. I'm actually looking for a Mr. Donald Polachek, would he by any chance be a relation?"*

"Donnie? He's my son."

"Donald Mottz Polachek?" Garland's interest meter rose, but he kept his voice steady and professional.

"Yes. Mottz is my maiden name."

"Do you know where your son is right now?"

"Uh-huh. Out of town."

Garland heard her voice catch.

"Oh, good God, did something happen to Donnie? Something awful?"

"I don't know, Mrs. Polachek, that's what we're trying to determine. Have you had any recent calls or conversations about him with the Department of Defense or the FBI?"

"No. Nobody's called me about anything."

"Mrs. Polachek, is Donald in the army?"

"Not anymore. No. No, he's not. Oh, dear God, please don't tell me he got hurt."

Garland listened with uninvited compassion to the voice of a worried mother. Probably a loving, even doting mother, a mother who loved her child as fiercely and intensely as Daisy loved Breezy. And yet Margaret Polachek was most likely the mother of a murderer. Would she feel differently about her son if she knew he was a sniper? A paid assassin? That he, in fact, tried to kill Garland? He brushed the thought aside and asked:

"Do you know if Donald received special military training at Ft. Benning in Georgia?"

189

"No, he didn't. He wasn't at Ft. Benning. He was at Ft. Bragg in North Carolina. Beautiful out there, isn't it? I mean, compared to how flat it is here and all." Then she quickly added, *"Dr. Garland, could I please ask you what this is in regards to?"*

"Yes, ma'am, I'm investigating a hand injury. Did Donald ever have a serious hand injury?"

"No. Ah, yes, yes, yes, now I see your confusion."

"I beg your pardon?"

"Your confusion, doctor. Donald didn't have the hand injury. It was his brother, Ronald. His twin brother. They always confuse people. Ronnie had the injury. He was the one at Ft. Benning. Made corporal, you know."

Garland could feel his heart race. He knew his blood pressure had just jumped twenty points. *"Mrs. Polachek, could you describe Ronald's injury to me?"*

"It was horrible. Heartbreaking, I swear. I saw it when I visited him in the hospital. You know the army hospital right there in Washington..."

"Walter Reed?"

"Yes. Of course, Walter Reed. Was almost two years ago. Had the best doctors and nurses, they took such good care of him. Wait, wait, let me think now, doctor's name...maybe you know him, you're both being doctors in Washington, ummm...it was like he had missing letters in his name."

"That's okay, Mrs. Polachek. Ronald's injury..."

"Pniak. That's it. Erno Pniak. Major Pniak. He tried so hard to save Ronnie's hand, but he just couldn't do it. They had to amputate."

"His left hand."

"Yes and thank God he's right handed."

Pniak. Pniak. Erno Pniak. Garland recognized the name but couldn't place it. He shouldered the phone against his ear, tapped some keys on his laptop and logged on to NCBI PubMed as he continued his conversation with Mrs. Polachek.

"Could you please tell me what happened?"

"It was one of those freak accidents, but aren't they all freak accidents? I mean, he was in Afghanistan and Iraq and all those horrible places and never got so much as a scratch on him. Then back home at Ft. Benning, sitting on his porch cleaning his rifle, they said a magazine exploded in his hand. He doesn't remember a thing about it, but I could tell you it was horrible."

"And you're sure his hand was amputated?"

"Oh, yes, yes, absolutely. What was left of it. I flew in for the surgery. So did Donnie. We stayed with him all week."

Garland found the computer notes he had written to himself and leaned into the screen. "Erno Pniak, Dr. Mjr. USArmy. Co-author 5 journal articles w/Evin Co. VIXI - CVDV / same co-author as Beck. Pniak research: bone & cell tissue synthesis, vascular growth, nerve sequences / cross X w/Beck – see abstracts".

"Mrs. Polachek, please forgive this question, but, did you ever see your son's left arm without dressings after the surgery?

"Excuse me? I'm not sure I know what your mean?"

"I'm sorry. Ronald's arm. The end of it where his hand would be. Did you ever see it without bandages?

"You mean the stump?"

"Yes." Garland leaned back and let his subconscious do the heavy lifting. He was talking with a woman in Joliet, Illinois, the mother of a sniper school graduate whose hand was operated on by a doctor whose research was funded by the same company that funded Jason's Beck work. What were the odds? Garland knew it was a duck. A slam duck.

Margaret Polachek breathed into the phone and made soft clicking sounds with her tongue as she thought about Garland's question. *"Now that you mention it, doctor, I don't think I do recall seeing it without bandages."*

"What about now? Have you seen it recently?"

"No. Ronnie's been in rehab all year. I haven't seen him in a while. The rehab doctor asked me not to, you know, it upsets him and all. Talk to him a lot, though. Talked to him just a few days ago."

"You call him often?"

"No, uh, usually he calls me."

"So you wouldn't have his number then?"

"Oh, no, sure do. Got it right off the caller I.D. If you just give me a minute here..."

Garland heard some pages being turned, as if Margaret Polachek was thumbing through an address book.

"Ah, here it is..." and she dictated a number in the 479 area code, then added, *"If you do see him, I mean you are trying to locate him, right? When you see Ronnie, would you tell him to please call his mom? Tell him I miss him?"*

"Yes, ma'am, if I find him, I certainly will. And thank you so much for all your help."

43

Garland immediately punched another line on his phone and 411'd the number for Walter Reed Army Medical Center. It took three minutes to work through the voice system to orthopedics.

"This is Dr. Nathaniel Garland, BIA, for Maj. Pniak."

"Sorry, doctor, he's not here."

"Could you please tell me when he'll be back?"

"I have no idea. Maj. Pniak's been transferred."

"Really? When?"

"Almost a year ago."

"Could you tell me where he's been transferred to? This is quite urgent."

"Sorry. Wish I could. Don't know." The voice paused. *"Wait, let me see if Maj. Ogilvie knows. He replaced Pniak as Chief."*

Click. Hold. And Garland was subjected to an insipid slow paced piano version of Elton John's *Benny and the Jets.*

Click. The voice was back. *"Sorry, doctor, the Major doesn't know. He thinks maybe the U.S. hospital in Landstuhl."*

"Germany?"

"Unless they moved it." She paused again. *"Is there anything Maj. Ogilvie can help you with?"*

"No, thanks. If you do find out where he was transferred, could you give me a call? I'm at Fed-Med."

"Gotcha. If I do, I will."

Garland slid his notes from Margaret Polachek in front of him and punched in the number she had given him. It was a long shot, to be sure, but long shots do come in. Garland waited, tapping his desk. One, two and on the third ring someone picked up.

"V.A., how may I direct your call?" It was a man's voice, soft, with a Southern lilt.

"Excuse me," Garland said, *"which V.A. is this?"*

"V.A. Hospital in Fayetteville."

"Arkansas?"

"Yessir. How may I direct your call?"

"Maj. Erno Pniak, please."

"One moment please," the man's voice sang, *"I'll try his office."*

Garland's back stiffened in his chair. This wasn't a long shot. It was a duck. *"Wait,"* Garland suddenly blurted out. *"Could you please tell me how far you are from Bull Shoals Lake?"*

"Why I surely can. I'd say was 'bout a hundred miles as the crow flies."

"Thank you."

"You still want Maj. Pniak?"

"Yes. Thank you."

"One moment, please, and you have yourself a nice day." Click.

Click. *"Maj. Pniak's office, this is Sgt. Williger."* The voice was young. Male. Polite and efficient.

"Hello, Sergeant, Dr. Nathaniel Garland for Maj. Pniak."

"Major's due in surgery now, doctor, can I tell him what it's about?"

"I'm calling from HHS in D.C."

194

"Yessir, one second, please."

Click. Hold. Click. *"Pniak, here. Garland is it?"*

"Yes."

"I'm running late. How can I help you doctor?"

Garland's heart rate jumped, but he kept his voice steady. *"I'm calling about one of your patient's, Major, a Cpl. Ronald Polachek, a sniper school graduate out of Ft. Benning. I believe you operated on him at Reed."*

"Yes. That's correct."

Garland's heartometer revved higher. *"Major, did you amputate Cpl. Polachek's left hand?"*

"Yes." His tone became impatient. *"What is this in regards to?"*

"I believe Cpl. Polachek may have been killed last night. I'm just trying to verify it was him."

"Killed? Killed how?"

"By the Secret Service. Shot. He had barricaded himself on a rooftop in Georgetown and was using his sniper training to shoot at innocent civilians."

"Oh, Jesus."

"Major, your research papers dealing with bone and cell tissue synthesis, vascular growth, nerve sequences, I see your research partner was the Evin Co. Seventeen CVDV…"

"Who?"

"The Evin Company Seventeen CVDV?"

"What the hell are you talking about, doctor? Wait. Do you mean Evinco Vixi?" Pniak said it as two distinct words, not a company, not a number and ignored the CVDV.

"Yes." Garland lied as he scribbled notes on his pad next to the phone. *"Could you please tell me how I can reach them?"*

There was a long silence. Garland could hear Pniak breathing.

"Major?"

"Where are you really calling from?" Pniak asked. His tone was nervous now, maybe even frightened.

"I'm a special agent with the BIA of the CDC."

"Oh, Jesus…"

"Major? I need some information from you. Will you be…"

"I've got to go. Sorry, I'm late for surgery."

"Can we talk later, after your…"

"Goodbye, doctor."

Click.

Garland held the dead phone in his hand for several seconds before hanging up. He realized the one question he didn't ask was about Sarah Levine. It was not a big leap from Pniak to Sarah. The how and why were still missing and the connective tissue was vague, but somehow – Garland knew deep in his gut – somehow Sarah's disappearance would trace back to Pniak.

While it was still fresh in his mind, Garland turned to his laptop Googled *"Evinco Vixi"*. He was just told by Pniak that it was not a company and not a number, so it had to be either a name or a code or a cipher of some kind. But Google came up blank: *"your search 'evinco vixi' did not match any documents"*. Garland narrowed the search to just *"Vixi"* and Google cooperated with over a hundred responses. At the top of the list was the Victor Hugo poem, *"Veni, Vidi, Vixi"*.

"Latin," Garland whispered out loud to himself, "it's Latin."

He opened the Google Translate app and typed in "Evinco Vixi". The translation appeared almost instantaneously: *evinco* – to conquer, subjugate, defeat. *Vixi* – to live, be alive. Garland stared at

196

the results on his screen. What was the loose translation - "Conquer to live" "Defeat to live"? Conquer what? Defeat who? Yes, of course. Garland smiled, of course. Conquer sickness and injury and aging and death will be defeated. It was cryptic, but accurate. Someone, some entity, some organization or corporation or financial interest or even a government auspices was funding specific biomedical research under the obscure banner of "*Evinco Vixi*" – conquer death.

Jason Beck's research was funded by Evinco Vixi.

Major Erno Pniak's research was funded by Evinco Vixi.

How many others? Garland went to his PubMed notes. Eleven. Eleven other doctors and researchers shared publication credit with Evinco Vixi. Nine of them, in fact, worked at major universities. Someone in that group had the answers. And Garland knew he had to find them. Unless they got to him first.

44

Garland packed his laptop, gathered his handwritten notes and shoved them into the side pouch of the soft Tumi shoulder bag that Daisy had bought him for his thirtieth birthday. He carefully packed copies of all the files and photographs relating to Sarah and the girl and zipped them into the Tumi as well. He unplugged the teapot, then quickly checked the desk, floor and wastebasket for any indicial trash he may have discarded. His goal was to get off the floor before Haynes or Dunbarton stumbled in and found him there.

He located Wheeler and Polly in the utility kitchen where they had set up shop. At a rear table, Polly was on the phone, quickly jotting notes as Wheeler stood expectantly at the FAX machine. The machine chimed and automatically picked up the incoming call.

"Liz," Polly said into the phone, "it's coming through. Give us a few seconds to verify."

"Verify what?" Garland asked as he entered.

"We think we've got an ID on our girl."

Garland reached the FAX machine in three strides. A scratchy black-and-white photo was just clearing the machines platen, jerking up line by impatient line. Polly got up and moved to Garland's side, the phone still at her ear. The three doctors watched the photo emerge, finding its way from the FAX machine at Kelsey School For The Visually Impaired in Lady Lake, Florida to the FAX machine in the Con-Con 1 utility kitchen at Fed-Med in Frederick, Maryland. Within ten seconds, enough of the girl's grainy photo emerged to confirm that she was, indeed, their young victim.

198

"That's her," Wheeler said.

"Yeah, that's her."

"That's her, Liz, absolutely, no doubt," Polly spoke into the phone. "Can you tell us her name?" Polly went back to the table and reached for her pen. "Corinne. Corinne...Burch. Right. Got it."

Garland and Wheeler stared at the facsimile photo. What struck them both instantly was that she looked like a normal, smiling, healthy fourteen year old girl with two eyes – and *just* two eyes. Garland stepped to Polly at the table.

"Can I talk to her?"

"Liz? Dr. Garland would like to speak to you." She handed Garland the phone. "Liz McConnell. Director of the Kelsey School in Florida."

Garland took the phone. *"Ms. McConnell...Nathaniel Garland. Do you mind if I ask you a few questions about Corinne...?"*

They talked for nearly twenty minutes. Wheeler and Polly listened to his side of the conversation. Garland found Liz McConnell, the school administrator, to be charming, forthcoming, eager to cooperate and now, very worried.

Corinne Burch, just a few months past her fourteenth birthday, was a ward of the Florida Department of Children and Families. Her father was an unknown, her mother in prison. Corinne's sketchy medical records indicated that she was probably blind from birth – a gift from her crack smoking mother – and she had an older brother, Calvin, sixteen. There were no other living relatives noted in her file. Calvin was sighted and they lived together in foster care near the school. He and his sister were apparently very close and he brought her to school every morning.

"The source of the haploids?" Wheeler suggested.

199

"Probably. Since there's no father in the picture or other brothers."

What Garland now knew was that it was most likely Calvin's shoes Corinne was wearing when she was found. Which meant that they were together in Bull Shoals. Which also raised the possibility that Calvin may still be there. But where is there? And it still didn't answer the question of how Corinne, wearing her brother's shoes, got from Bull Shoals, Arkansas to Fairfax, Virginia.

Liz McConnell explained that in late January, Corinne failed to show up for school with her brother. Her teacher waited a day and then called her foster parents. The foster parents, Willy and Flora Burton, told them that CFS – Children and Family Services – had picked up the children over the weekend. The reason for their removal, given the Burtons, was that there was an opening at a better facility to treat Corinne, although Liz McConnell was hard pressed to know of a better or more appropriate facility in Florida than hers. She gave Garland the Burtons' phone number and told him she would do whatever she could from her end to help locate Calvin Burch. Garland thanked Liz profusely, hung up and then immediately dialed Willy and Flora Burton.

Flora Burton picked up on the fourth ring. She had a pleasant voice and seemed totally unruffled by the loud sounds of several children playing in the background. Garland pictured the home to be small, but tidy, much like he imagined Flora Burton to be.

Corinne, she told him, was a wonderful child, shy and reclusive, yet very intelligent and extremely capable despite her blindness. They had no trouble with her at all. The Burtons generally foster only special needs children, but took in Corinne's brother, Calvin, because she and her husband didn't believe in separating siblings. Calvin was initially kind of aggressive, like most sixteen year old boys, but he was also totally protective of his sister and looked after her with such devotion and attention, it actually freed the Burtons to spend more time with the other children in their charge.

Flora Burton remembered distinctly when DCF came to pick up Corinne and Calvin. It was this past January. On a Sunday. Children come and go all the time through their home, so transferring the Burch kids was expected. But it usually never happened on a Sunday. It's always during the week, so the proper papers could be filed. For some unknown reason, though, DCF wanted to move them on a Sunday. And then she added:

"I suppose that's why Bette didn't come for 'em. Bette Baker. She's our usual social worker. Comes 'round at least twice a month, but I've never yet seen her on a Sunday."

"Did she ever tell you why it had to be that Sunday?"

"No. Afraid not. When I called her Monday morning, they told me she quit. You know there are all these state and DCF investigations going on and all. Guess she just had enough and retired."

"Did you know the social worker who came for Corinne and Calvin?"

"Nope, but he was a nice enough man. Very nice, very polite. And all the papers were in order, Lord knows we've seen enough of 'em. But since it was a Sunday and all, well, obviously we couldn't call the office or anything."

"Do you have copies of the paperwork, Mrs. Burton?"

"Oh, yes, of course."

"Do you suppose you could FAX or email copies to me?"

"Yes, of course, but don't expect I can do it till tomorrow. Have to go down to the library to FAX."

"Thank you. And you say you didn't know the social worker who came for them?"

"That's correct, doctor. But there's so many of them, you know, and they do tend to come and go. Like I said, he was very polite, very professional. Ah, here they are...Corrine's and Calvin's release."

"Could you please tell me the social worker's name?"

"*Well it's a copy I have here, you know, one those pink carbonless forms they use…hmmmm…signature's a kind of blur, very hard to read. Nope. Can't make it out. But I do remember his name was something like Clark or Stark or something like that.*"

"*Clark or Stark? Is that a first name or last name?*"

"*Last name. Darn, can't recollect…*"

"*That's okay, Mrs. Burton, we'll call DCF and get the information. Thank you so much for your time, do appreciate it.*"

"*Well I do certainly hope those children are just fine. Especially Corinne, she is special. I think maybe that's why the social worker was extra kind to her, you know, both of them having vision disabilities.*"

"*Excuse me?*"

"*The social worker. He said he understood blindness. I mean, he was darn near blind himself.*"

"*He said that?*"

"*Oh, no, not directly. But you could tell. His glasses were so thick you could barely see his eyes behind them. In fact, they weren't like normal glasses at all, you know, they were more like…how do you say…?*"

"*Goggles?*"

"*Yes. Exactly. They were like thick goggles.*"

45

Garland hung up and noticed Polly's thoughtful expression. "What?" he said.

"Nothing. Okay. I'm not sure, but the name – Clark - Stark – the goggles, it sounds familiar."

"How?"

"I think that's the name Pasha made those lenses for. One of Jason's private patients. I never see them. They're his. I mean – was his. Look, it's only a vague memory at best, but I'm pretty sure that's who Pasha Sharrev made the lenses for – he's our chief optician. Pasha mentioned making a ridiculous pair of sports glasses for this patient. It was maybe six months before I joined Beck."

"Why ridiculous?"

"Once the glass was ground, the prescription had to be nearly a half-inch thick but the patient wanted the lenses in sports glasses?"

"Sports glasses as in goggles?"

"Yeah. They have an elastic band or leather strap that stretches around or clips behind the head to hold them in place. Professional skiers, basketball players – lots of athletes order them. But never patients with that profound an acuity differential. That's why I remember. Pasha joked that this guy was legally blind and probably couldn't even see the field, much less play the game."

"See if you can get Pasha on the phone."

As Polly dialed Pasha Sharrev, Garland got on the phone with Florida's DCF. Within two minutes, Polly learned that because of the tragedy of Jason Beck's murder, the optical lab was closed and Pasha sent home for the day. It took Garland just a few minutes longer to find out that the Florida DCF had no social workers named either Clark or Stark in Lake County, Florida and there was no custodial transfer ever issued for either Corinne or Calvin Burch. As far as DCF was concerned, both children were still safely in the custodial care of Willy and Flora Burton.

46

Grover Wheeler saw him first. He glanced up and there was Carter Haynes filling the doorframe of the Con-Con utility kitchen.

Haynes strode into the room, acknowledging Garland and Wheeler with barely a nod while extending his catcher's mitt sized hand to Polly. "Dr. Collier, I presume? Carter Haynes."

Polly lifted her hand, offering Haynes her slender fingertips. "My pleasure, Dr. Haynes."

"I apologize for not being able to make your acquaintance earlier. And I am especially sorry to be meetin' you under such tragic circumstances. Jason was a friend. And let me just tell you, it sickened me when I heard the news. Please accept my deepest sympathies and pass on my sincerest condolences to his family."

"Thank you, I will."

Garland watched the exchange and marveled at Haynes' inspired aptitude for saying just the right things in just the right way. It was the politician's gift which he had meticulously honed over the course of his career. Watching Haynes work her like soft clay, Garland suppressed a smile as he heard Daisy's voice in his head reminding him, once again, to at least *try* to play well with others.

"With my apologies, Dr. Collier, Grover, I need to speak to Nathaniel in private for a moment."

Wheeler and Polly quickly gathered their things.

"It was good to meet you, Dr. Haynes," Polly said.

"The pleasure was all mine, doctor. And I am truly lookin' forward to seein' you again at happier times."

"We'll meet you at the car, Nate." Wheeler said. And they were gone.

Haynes moved to the coffee urn and plucked a Styrofoam cup off the wobbly tower. "Going somewhere?"

"Taking Dr. Collier back to the Institute."

"I see. And how long did you think you could avoid me?"

"Avoid you? What are you talking about, Carter?"

"My mama did many peculiar things, Nathaniel, but the one thing she didn't do was raise a jackass for a son." Haynes sipped the coffee and made a face. "God, this stuff is awful." He fixed his eyes on Garland. "Now tell me what t'hell's going on with the Brits. Their senior Embassy staff have been all over the Secretary like Baptists on a sinner – and they're gunnin' for your hide, boy."

"I had a little run-in with one of their diplomats last night. He wasn't very diplomatic."

"Well now you had better cut that diplomat's wife loose before this little incident finds its way 'cross town. If the White House gets involved, you're sorry white ass will be out on the street. She's a fine lookin' lady but she's not worth your career. Or mine. You un'erstand me?"

Garland studied him. He knew Haynes didn't search him out just to talk about Collier.

"Where d'ya say you goin'?"

"Beck Institute."

"And here I thought maybe you'd be goin' a tad farther. Like Arkansas."

"For what?"

"Oh, for chrissakes, Nathaniel, never bullshit a bullshitter. What t'hell kind of idiot you take me for? You think I don't read the reports comin' 'cross my desk? I read what Arleta found in the girl's rape kit. I know she traced it back to Bull Shoals. And then I got Nelson, annoying little toady that he is, buzzing all around me with that haploid shit. And son, I wouldn't know a haploid from Kelsey's nuts. So why don't you just have yourself a seat there and tell me what the hell is going on in my department."

"First I need some straight answers, Carter."

"You need answers from me?"

"Yeah. I want to know who was responsible for bringing in the sniper that killed Carolyn Eccevarria?"

"I surely wish I knew."

"It wasn't me, it wasn't Kessler, it sure as hell wasn't Carolyn, so who does that leave?"

"I'll tell you who. Ever'body in the Bureau who Eccevarria had to deal with and ever'body in Judge Lewin's court who processed the warrant, and the registrar of documents and the fucking carpool mechanics and a thousand other people. And just what the hell are you implying, son?"

"Tell me why you skipped over the docs on call and chose me to go to Fairfax for the girl that night?" Garland intentionally didn't use Corinne's name.

"Because you're the only pediatrician on my staff, that's why. Who'd you expect me to send? Kessler? I want to know right now what t'hell you're driving at?"

"Why'd you bring in Beck against my protests?"

"Because he's the best damned eye surgeon on the entire east coast. We needed the best, I brought in the best."

"He was experimenting in optic nerve regeneration. It's what killed the girl."

"You're telling me Beck's connected to this?" Haynes reacted genuinely surprised. If he was faking it, Garland couldn't tell.

"Yes."

"How?"

"I don't know yet."

"Then find out. Get your ass to Arkansas and find out."

Haynes' voice rose, but it was in frustration, not anger, a difference Garland was able to discern. And then Garland saw it. Fear. It was subtle. Unintentional. Facial. He knew now that Haynes was revealing far less than he knew. He also knew that Haynes knew. He changed the subject and said, "What about the shooter who like to take your head off? They identify him?"

"Not yet," Garland lied. He couldn't trust Haynes completely yet. Then he said, "Carter, you okay? Are you in any trouble?"

"'Course not. What makes you think that?"

Garland shrugged innocently.

"I'm gettin' some heat from above, that's all there's to it."

"Okay. That's all I wanted to know." Garland studied Haynes' face a moment and then added, "Carter, you were there for me when I needed it. You took a huge risk you didn't have to take. I can't ever repay what you did, but I can still…"

Haynes cut him off. "You just do your job as I know you will and you will get my tail out of the fire with the boys in the home office."

"That's it?"

"That's all she wrote." Haynes took a breath. "I got authorization for you to use one of the department planes. It'll be fueled and ready by 8:00 pm. Don't disappoint, son."

Haynes squeezed Garland's arm and moved past him towards the door.

"Carter…"

Haynes stopped.

"The FBI is investigating you. They're trying to make a case."

Haynes nodded, turned and continued walking out of the kitchen. "I know. It's Washington, son. Ever'body's investigatin' ever'body else." He stopped at the door and turned back. "Dump Collier. All she can give you is a bushel of grief, son. DS is looking for her. So is Metro. She's of no value to us. Dump her."

47

"Yo, Garland, wait up...hang on..."

Wheeler, Garland and Polly were halfway across the parking lot when they heard Arleta Farleigh's voice. They looked back and Arleta was rumbling toward them, running as if she was holding a Christmas tree between her knees.

"Garland, goddamn it, wait up...Jesus fucking Christ, didn't you hear me?" Arleta was out of breath when she finally caught up to them. She thrust a handful of papers at Garland. "Here. I found it. Amebiasis. Amebiasis. Fucking amebiasis." She was panting.

"This is fantastic. Thank you."

Polly and Wheeler looked at each other quizzically. Both were completely lost.

"They're parasites," Garland said by way of explanation.

"Goddamn right they're parasites. Protozoan parasites. They infect snakes. Wildly contagious disease...if you're a snake. And these little fuckers are like on steroids. The ones I found were still alive."

"Where'd you find it?"

"Mud from your victim's shoelaces."

"Were you able to localize it?"

"I called Fish and Game. There's a big die-off and they don't know why. Black Racer's, Prairie Kings, Plainbellies...the whole gamut of indigenous snakes. The outbreak is localized to the southeastern part of Bull Shoals."

"Great work, Arleta, really, I owe you on this one."

"Fucking-A you owe me." She looked past Garland to Wheeler and Polly. Not getting any congratulatory response from either one of them, she looked back at Garland. "These two dipshits don't know what the fuck we're talking about, do they? Twenty four years of med school between them and…ah, what the fuck." And with that she turned and headed back towards the lab.

"What was that all about?" Wheeler asked.

"Corinne Burch. We know where she ended up, now we know where she came from."

Garland drove, Polly rode shotgun and Grover Wheeler somehow managed to accordion his six-foot-four frame into the elfin back seat of the Jag. They were heading back to the Jason Beck Eye Institute to plumb Pasha Sharrev's files. Grover Wheeler was along for added muscle – a role that really freaked him – and to pick up Daisy's car which Polly and Garland had left at the institute.

The drive was tense. All three of them nervously scanned the road, scrutinized every onramp and overpass and checked every car in their vicinity. The silver Mercedes never materialized. It wasn't until they got to the Institute's parking lot that Garland realized it would have been far better, tactically, for Grover to drive, Polly to be scrunched down in the back and he ride shotgun. This cop business did not come naturally to him.

Pasha Sharrev's optical lab was downstairs, relegated to the first basement. Nuts-and-bolts labs never have the same panache as outpatient surgeries and luxury examination suites. As expected, Sharrev's optical lab was dark and the door locked. He looked over to Wheeler.

"Not me, dude." Wheeler said.

"Hold the macho," Polly said, "there's a key in Jason's desk."

211

When they finally entered, Wheeler said, "Looks just like a LensCrafters,"

"It is just like a LensCrafters," Polly said.

"Alright, let's check the drawers and cabinets over there," Garland said, "I'll check the files in the office."

Within ten minutes they had collected sixty-one possibilities, all patients with variations on the names Clark, Stark, Mark, Parke. They split up the files.

Wheeler started thumbing through his stack. "What exactly am I looking for? I've got Clark, then Clarke with an 'e', Stark, Starke with an 'e'."

"Toss out all the obvious female names." Garland said.

Then Polly added, "Should be a prescription card stapled inside the front of each folder. Check the prescription boxes. Look for sphere numbers in the plus or minus 5.00 range. Next to those numbers are cylinder and axis designations. Cylinder should be in the range of plus or minus 1.00 to 2.00. That's some serious blindness. Also look for a notation for sports lenses."

"I think this is it." Garland waved a file card at them.

Polly took the card from him and scanned the notation. "Starke. N. Starke. Looks like he tried to grind the lenses in Lexan, but they were too thick, so he went to special shatterproof glass. God, those glasses have to weigh a ton."

"Maybe that's why he put them in wraparound goggles? That would be the only way he could keep them on." Garland said.

"And the billing code is weird." Polly noted. "No amount, no insurance, no guarantor address, nothing. Just the notation 'CVDV'. Roman numeral, I guess?"

Garland shook his head. "Yeah. It's got something to do with Evinco Vixi."

They both looked at him.

"It's Latin. Roughly translates to 'defeat death' – I'm pretty sure Evinco Vixi is a privately funded biomedical research outfit." His eyes snared Polly's. The coruscating iridescence of her turquoise eyes made him pause momentarily. "Evinco Vixi, whatever it is, probably financed a lot of Beck's research. For all we know it paid your salary."

"You're saying Jason was part of this?" Polly shook her head in disbelief. "I don't accept that. It can't be."

"Then what's he doing with Starke's prescription in his private patient file?"

"And you think Starke is the guy who juiced you? Wheeler said. "He's the guy who came into Con-Con to kill Corinne?" Then, realizing the full implication, said, "the guy with Sarah's license plates?" Wheeler took the card from Polly and studied it, cocking his head as he read the address: FayArk, VA - Where the hell is Fayark, Virginia?"

Garland took the card and read the address notation. He nodded. "It's not Fayark. It's Fayetteville, Arkansas. The "VA" is the VA hospital there."

48

Polly went upstairs to retrieve the change of clothes she had stored in her office. Garland and Wheeler walked outside and ambled toward the Jaguar.

Wheeler said, "I talked to Wendy. We'd be more than happy to have Dr. Collier stay with us for as long as she needs."

"That's very generous, Grove, but it's not going to work. It puts you guys in too much danger."

"It's okay. We discussed that."

"C'mon. If someone's trying to kill her, there's no way you can stop them. Besides, you've got kids. Forget it."

"So where's she going to go?"

"Some Bureau guys are going to put her in a safe house. Then we'll figure it out."

Polly came out of the Institute empty-handed, still wearing the scrubs. Even with the oversized sunglasses obscuring most of her face, both men could easily see in her halfhearted walk and her slumped shoulders how despondent she was. She told them that the crime scene technicians needed a few more hours and wouldn't let her in until they were through. She shrugged. And both Wheeler and Garland knew she was utterly lost. No husband. No home. No clothes. No job. No money. No place to go.

The reality had finally hit her. Hard. Very hard.

Wheeler drove Daisy's car back to Fed-Med. Garland and Polly headed west on I-70 and then Garland turned off the Interstate and headed south on 29. Polly had not said a word since they left the Beck Institute and Garland's attention was fragmented between his concern for her and his need to scrutinize the road for whatever may be lurking. If they were being followed, the silver Mercedes never showed itself. Garland hoped that Wheeler didn't inadvertently attract the wrong attention. He called him on his cell to check.

It wasn't until Garland turned off on Little Patuxent Parkway in Columbia that Polly turned her head from the window and looked at him. "Where are we going?"

"I don't know about you, but I'm getting awfully tired of those scrubs."

The corners of Polly's mouth turned up slightly, Mona Lisa-like, and Garland volleyed back his hundred-megawatt grin.

The Mall was practically empty and he had no trouble finding a space near the Nordstrom's entrance. He got out first, scanned the parking lot and, when he knew it was safe, opened the door for her.

"This is a loan," she said, "just a loan."

"Of course."

"I'll make this really quick."

"I was hoping you'd say that."

"Nathaniel. Xiè xiè," she said in Mandarin – thank you.

"Bù kèqi. Don't mention it. All I ask is that you stay close, okay?"

They started in cosmetics and flew through the store like Wile E. Coyote and the Roadrunner. From sportswear to outerwear, Polly had a keen eye for what looked good on her yet would be comfortable and functional. She knew her designers, brands and sizes and did not try on a single garment. Her modus vivendi, at the

215

moment, was speed and efficiency. She reasoned she could always return whatever didn't fit properly. Shoes, however, required a stop for fitting. They bought three pair – Addidas, low heels and casuals. Shopping bags were quickly filled and Garland muled them from department to department. Lingerie, or intimate apparel, as the department sign read, was last. Here again Polly knew exactly what she needed and what she liked. Garland marveled that her hand seemed to naturally gravitate to the more expensive designer labels. He marveled, also, at how utterly unlike shopping with Daisy this experience was – Daisy, the queen of comfort, aficionado of loose sweatpants and baggy t-shirts.

The shopping spree was hardly joyful, but neither was it somber and Polly did manage an unconscious smile from time to time. Bras, panties, pj's, socks and stockings filled yet another shopping bag. Done. She had her essentials.

It was at the checkout kiosk that Garland first caught sight of the two men.

A mirrored security camera pod, like a reflective half basketball, clung to the low ceiling just behind the kiosk. It was positioned to spy on the cashiers, but it's convex shape allowed for a view of half the department. The men were hanging back near the escalators – one tall, the other much shorter, both in suit coats, no ties, exactly as Chambers described them from the security tape. Both were working very hard to appear casual and nonchalant, a difficult task for two men to pull off in a lingerie department. Shuffling next to the bra displays, they stood out like nipples in January.

As Garland signed the credit card reader, he said in a low voice to Polly, without looking at her, "There's a blue nightgown or something hanging behind you. I want you to act cheerful and take it to the fitting room."

"What?" She seemed amused. "That? You're kidding."

Garland's face hardened. "Xiàn-zài," he practically hissed the word, a command meaning – now.

Polly got it. The color drained from her face. She forced a smile and said too loudly, "I'm going to try this on."

She plucked it off the rack and headed directly to the fitting room behind the kiosk. She had to dodge a short Hispanic man who was pushing a box-laden dolly out of the rear stock room to the right of the fitting rooms. Garland handed his credit card back to the pudgy grey haired clerk.

"We're going to take that gown, too."

"Maybe we should wait to see if it fits."

"That's okay. It will." He waited for the clerk to swipe his card and when she handed it back to him, Garland leaned in, subtly opened his badge case and whispered, "I'm a Federal officer. Please call security. Now. Don't look. Listen. Ma'am. Look at me. Pick up the phone and press the security code. Ma'am, now. There are two men by the escalators..."

"Yes..." She could barely get the word out.

"Are you calling security?"

"Yes."

"Okay. I'm going to the fitting room. Ma'am, don't look at them. Listen to me. The men are known terrorists. Call upstairs, let them know we need the police. Do you understand me? Call. Now. Right now."

The frightened clerk shook her head so hard Garland could hear her teeth rattle. She could barely speak into the phone.

Garland made a large gesture of signing his new receipt, putting his ID case in his pocket and picking up the shopping bags. He forced a big smile to the clerk and said loudly, "Thank you very much. Have a nice day." Garland realized his acting was just as abysmal as Polly's.

Now came the hard part. He intentionally turned his back to the two men — whom in his mind he was now calling Frick and Frack. Gripping the shopping bags, he walked slowly, casually toward the fitting rooms, then turned into the narrow vestibule and moved along its line of louver doors.

"Polly."

"In here."

"C'mon."

A louver door opened. Polly's face registered enough fear for both of them. "It is them? The men who killed Jason? They're after me, right? They want to kill me?"

"Let's not hang around to find out."

They heard the loud commotion in the lingerie department. Voices raised. Shouting. Store security personnel had obviously converged on Frick and Frack.

"With me. Through here. Stay close."

They pushed into the storeroom and moved quickly through the racks of clothes and shelves of merchandise until they found the wide doors leading to the loading dock. Garland, still ridiculously clutching all the shopping bags, pushed the doors open and an explosion of deafening alarm bells clanged in protest. It didn't matter. They were out. And didn't look back.

49

Frick and Frack slammed out of the store and hit the parking lot at a full run. Simultaneously, Garland's green Jaguar fishtailed out of the mall onto Little Patuxent. The two men heard the Jag before they saw it, but when they looked up, they knew they could still catch it. Their silver Mercedes was parked just a few yards away, maddeningly close to where the Jag was parked just minutes earlier.

Frick, the shorter of the two, jumped in behind the wheel. Frack charged around the back of the car and literally hopped in as Frick geared into reverse and stomped the accelerator. It was only Frack's athletic agility that saved him from being flattened by the open passenger door.

They had made a tactical mistake. Underestimated Garland. Now they were made, their faces recorded by Nordstrom's security cameras. The store's security personnel were clearly no match for them physically, but they had really, royally, fucked up. Now they had to clean things up. Fast.

In their frenzy to get in their car and chase down the green Jaguar, neither of them felt a need to look on the floor of the back seat. That's where Garland was hunched on his back, holding Kessler's gun in both hands straight up. If either of them had looked in the back, he would have fired – that he knew.

Garland felt the Mercedes accelerate and skid to the left. He had braced himself against the bottom of the rear seat to keep from being jostled by any of the car's sudden movements. A hard turn to the right, immediately followed by tire-screeching acceleration told him that Frick had pulled out of the mall and was pushing hard to catch up to the Jag. Polly, he hoped, had followed his instructions, waiting at the lip of the parking area until she saw the two men and then lure them after her. Garland had given her his cell and told her to call Detective Chambers and then Fitch and Hollister. She was then to drive directly to Garland's house and wait for him.

It was more than risky, it was stupid, but separating from Polly and taking on Frick and Frack was the only way he thought he could protect her and find out who these men were and what they wanted. He knew he wouldn't be able to take them into custody without serious backup, and even then he would probably never get the truth out of them. This was his solution. And, if nothing else, he felt it would give Polly time and distance – two allies that would keep her safe. For now.

Garland's pulse was surging in his temples. There was so much adrenalin coursing through him that he was literally shaking. He waited another fifteen seconds, rallying his courage while trying to gauge where they were on the boulevard. Surprising even himself, he suddenly sprang up and rammed the barrel of the gun against Frick's, the driver's, head.

"Pull over! Pull over!" Garland screamed the words and heard them as if someone else was screaming them.

Frick, utterly startled, momentarily lost control of the wheel.

Frack instantly twisted in his seat and his right hand went to the holster under the breast pocket of his jacket. It never made it there. Using all the torque he could muster from his position, Garland backhanded the side of his gun into Frack's head. The blow caught Frack just above his left ear, but with enough force to hammer his head into the passenger window. It bounced back and Garland hit him again. Frack screamed. His hands flew up to his head and blood was already trickling through his fingers.

"Pull over pull over pull over," Garland yelled again.

Frick didn't know what to do. Frack still couldn't catch his breath.

"Pull the fuck over." And Garland fired a shot into the instrument cluster, narrowly missing Frick's hand on the wheel. The cluster exploded in a kaleidoscope of plastic splinters and wadding and metal. The sound of the shot inside the tight confines of the car deafened all three of them, but it was particularly painful for Frack. Thick pungent curls of sulfur and cordite from the discharge hung like a suffocating blanket in the air.

"Easy mate, easy, squeezing over, squeezing over now."

They were screaming over each other's words now, all trying to stay just this side of panic.

"You, hands on the dash where I can see 'em. Now NOW NOW."

"M'ears...m'ears..."

"NOW. Hands."

Frack didn't move fast enough. Garland cocked the gun. That motivated him. Frack's hands lunged for the dash in front of him.

"There. There. There. My hands, boy, my hands."

Garland could feel the car slowing, moving to the right.

"Stop the car! Stop it. Hands on the wheel."

Garland slid to his left so he could better see Frick's hands. Frack was leaning forward. Garland pressed the barrel of the gun against the back of Frack's seat.

"Stop the car."

"Traffic."

"Cut 'em off."

Frick hesitated.

Garland's hand swept left and he fired again, obliterating the burled walnut center console. A thousand spears of the splintered wood tore into Frick's right side, tearing into his neck and face, ripping through the fabric of his jacket and pants. Frick screamed and jammed on the brakes.

The Mercedes stopped cold. Cars traveling near them squealed and shrieked, braking hard to avoid a collision. Garland pushed the gun into Frack's seat back.

"Who are you." Garland asked. He was breathing hard.

No answer. Frick and Frack did not look at each other. Cold. Stoic. Trained.

Garland cocked the gun. The sound was as ominous as it was unmistakable.

"I'm going to ask you one more time, then I'm going to fire. Can you feel where I'm holding this gun? Your upper spine. T-5, T-6, somewhere around there. So when I shoot you, it won't kill you. It'll severe your spinal column and make you a quad. Paralyzed for the rest of your miserable fucking life. Pissing through a tube, shitting in a bag. Mate."

"We're only looking to retrieve Mr. Collier's wife for him." Frick squeaked the words out through clenched teeth. Blood was rolling down his face and neck, soaking his clothes. The wood fragments had obviously found comfortable lodging in his flesh.

"You work for Collier?"

"Fer the bloody embassy, ya fuckwit."

The advancing police sirens signaled the conversation was almost over. Garland needed more. "S.I.S.?

Neither answered. That confirmed it for Garland.

"Simple, see? 'Is wife goes home and Bob's your uncle."

"All this for that?"

"You broke my fuckin' skull…"

"You killed Jason Beck for that?"

"Nothin' personal, you understand."

"You killed him because some demented asshole is pissed at his wife?"

Cops swarming now, surrounding the Mercedes. Nervous young officers with guns drawn. Garland heard them, saw them out the window. He could still barely catch his breath. His hands were shaking, especially the hand holding Kessler's gun. He was fighting an urge. An irresistible impulse. It was overwhelming him. Rational thought abandoned him. Primal ire reigned. His whole body was trembling now as he desperately wanted to squeeze the trigger of the gun. His finger tightened around it. His teeth clenched so hard he thought they would crack.

Frick barely turned his head. His eyes slid to Garland. He could see the strain in his face and the sweat on his forehead. The police were advancing, but not fast enough.

"No, no. Dunnut shoot, boy, don't fuckin' shoot."

Frick raised his hands above his head, pressing his palms against the roof of the car so the cops could clearly see them. Frack quickly did the same.

"Wha' the fuck…wha' the…" Frack squeezed his eyes shut, waiting for the bullet that would surely shatter his spine.

Garland's breath was staggered, sounding like a handsaw on soft wood. All the anger he had banked, all of the rage and fury he buried and suppressed for Daisy's and Breezy's death, all of it was now electrifying his finger on the trigger of Eugene Kessler's gun.

Cops, crouched behind the open doors of their patrol cars, were yelling orders through bullhorns. More sirens and screeching tires and the thunderous sucking thwack-thwack of helicopters shook the Mercedes.

For reasons he could not understand, Garland's eyes became moist as he lowered the gun and put it in his pocket. He wiped the tears away with his fingertip.

"You tell Collier he's going to pay dearly for Beck."

And Garland pressed his badge against the rear window and slowly opened the door, raising his hands high above his head as he displayed his badge.

50

Detective Sergeant Devon Chambers drove Garland back to Georgetown. There was absolutely no doubt in Chambers' mind that Frick and Frack – real names Colin MacDonough and Bobby Steele – were the men responsible for killing Jason Beck. The murder weapon was found in Bobby's ankle holster and ballistics would positively confirm it was the gun used in the homicide. Both Colin and Bobby were contractors for British S.I.S., Secret Intelligence Service – the equivalent of the CIA – but both were carrying diplomatic passports at the time of their arrests.

"Don't tell me they're going to walk." Garland said.

"Hey, man, what can I say? They both have diplomatic immunity."

"There's no D.I. for murder."

"No, but there are other precedents. We nailed a Russian diplomat a couple years ago for vehicular man. He skipped on appeal and we couldn't extradite." Chambers glanced over to Garland as he drove.

"Turn here." Garland pointed to the left. "I should have held court in the car when I had my chance."

"That's not you, man," Chambers said. "We're a couple of throwback Joe Palookas. Remember him? From the old comic books? Everybody'd be fighting real dirty and Joe Palooka would stand there, square jaw and that never-messed-up blond hair, he'd just stand there getting the crap beat out of him with two-by-fours by these jamokes with brass knuckles. But old Joe wouldn't fight dirty, he'd just take it. And they'd leave him for dead, all bloodied and black-and-blue, but good ol' Joe would pick himself up and, by the end of the comic, he'd win."

"And your point is…?"

"We still have to look at ourselves in the mirror when we're shaving."

Garland vaguely pointed down the street. "Behind the Crown Vic. That's me over there."

Fitch and Hollister were standing in front of Garland's house with Polly. Garland's green Jag was parked on the other side.

"Fibbis." Chambers said flatly.

"They're both stand up guys. You want to grab some dinner with us?"

"Some other time. My boy's got a game tonight. Told him I'd be there."

Garland nodded and extended his hand. "Thanks for the help and the lift."

"Any time. And thanks for the collar."

"Any time." Garland opened the door and started to get out of the car. "I don't want to disillusion you, Chambers, but somebody should tell you – you don't have a square jaw and I just can't see you as a blond."

If this were the movies, Polly would have run to Garland as soon as he stepped out of Chambers' car. But here, now, what was she going to do? Hug him? Throw her arms around his neck? Tell him how incredibly relieved she was that he's okay and came home in one piece and the bad guys are in jail? Instead, she held back by his door, rubbing her fingertip against her lips as she tried to work through a confusing tangle of conflicting, contradictory emotions.

Fitch and Hollister came toward Garland. They did not look happy.

"What's wrong?" Garland said. No 'hello', no greeting.

"We pooched the screw, dude, we can't take her."

"What? I'm going out of town tonight."

"We're sorry. It sucks. I know we promised, but it's coming from the top. She's hands off."

"Does she know?"

"No. Not yet."

Garland took a deep breath and exhaled loudly. He garaged the Jag and they regrouped in the kitchen. Polly made green tea while Avery Hollister grabbed a beer from the fridge.

"Your hubby's working the A-list, doc," Fitch said, directing his words to Polly, but said loud enough to include Garland. "He filed an M.P. with the locals."

"What's that?" she asked.

"Missing persons. He obviously knew where you were, but filing got the big wheels rolling. Diplomat's wife missing, you know the drill. That brings in Treasury and State. Like I said, the big guns. DS jumped on it immediately."

"DS?"

"Sorry," Fitch said. "Diplomatic Security."

Hollister jumped in. "We told our DD what was going down – our Deputy Director – we told him where you were, tried to smooth some of those ruffled feathers, but the truth is, no offense, your husband's being a real dick."

"There's news."

"What we're saying, ma'am, our DD won't authorize safe house protection."

"What if I give you some juice to go back with? Garland asked.

"Like what?"

"Like the shooter who killed Eccevarria. That should make your boss do the happy dance."

Hollister and Fitch stared at him, stunned, not knowing if he was jerking them or not.

"That's where I'm going tonight. To confirm it."

"You're leaving?" Polly looked up from the tea.

"Yes."

"How long have you known? The shooter, I mean?" It was Hollister asking.

"Got it this afternoon."

"Who is he?"

"Was. He's dead. Cpl. Ronald Polachek of Joliet, Illinois. Sniper School. Benning. I'll bet even the Director doesn't have that information. And the DOD's never going to cough it up. Never."

"How'd you get it?" Fitch was very impressed.

"I called his mother in Joliet."

"No shit."

"You want her number?"

"An Army sniper takes out one of ours? Why?"

"No. An Army trained sniper," Garland corrected. "His service was over on a disability. So what do you say? Go make your DD a hero and buy this lady some protection while I'm gone."

"If it was only that easy…shit, she's too hot right now. Way hot. The AG will have his ass." Hollister ran his hand over his close-cropped hair. "Alright, look, I've got some friends at Langley, maybe we can…"

"Friends and maybes don't cut it."

Polly slammed the teapot down on the stovetop, hissed an "excuse me" and hustled out of the kitchen.

Hollister put down his beer. "Damn," he said for all of them.

"What time you leaving?" Fitch asked.

"Wheels up at 8:00 pm."

"We'll see what we can do."

51

He found Polly in the second floor study. She was hanging up the phone, slamming it, really. Angry. Defiant. Holding herself together by sheer will and obstinacy. "How is it possible there's not one hotel room available in this town?"

"I'm sorry," Garland said, "I should have said something."

"You don't have to explain anything to me and you certainly don't have to apologize. You'd think there'd be one goddamn room available."

Garland looked at her, searching for the right words, unable to say the things he'd like to say, unable to tell her the things she wanted to hear.

"Please, just take me home or…or…loan me cab fare."

"You can't go home."

"I have a home. I have to go."

"Don't you see what he's doing?"

"Don't you see what I'm doing? I'm getting people killed. What did Jason have to do with this? What right did he have to send those thugs to kill Jason? You think there aren't two more where those men came from? And two more after them? Take me home. Please. I'm not going to have more blood on my hands."

"The blood's not on your hands, it's on his. Do you understand that? His. Not yours. You didn't kill Beck. He did."

"He should have killed me instead."

"You go home and that's exactly what he'll do. Bastard's messing with your head, Polly, listen to yourself. Every time he hits you. Hurts you. Humiliates you, you blame yourself. You've got to stop it right now. You're too smart, you're too good, you're too – too valuable a person to let his sick perversions control you. You did not kill Jason Beck. As tragic as it was, you are not responsible for his death. He is. Brendan. Your husband."

Polly's eyes clouded, but she willed herself not to cry, refusing to humiliate herself again. She took a step back and perched on the arm of the overstuffed sofa. Without lifting her head she looked up at Garland, her exquisite eyes were moist and mesmerizing. He would tell her, much later, that her eyes were not just blue – they were the Zen of being the color blue, much like great music and art resonate in the soul as the Zen of being art.

"I cannot do nothing," she whispered. "I'm a doctor, a surgeon, a wife, a person."

Garland held her eyes, cursing himself. Why couldn't he speak? Why couldn't he tell her what he was feeling? A word, a touch, a gesture, some small comfort, that's all she was asking. Something. Anything to affirm her self-worth. Why couldn't he do it?

And then he saw it, as clear as a winter night's air. It would be a betrayal, that's what it would be, a betrayal of Daisy. As if giving any part of himself to anyone else would be taking it from her, diminishing their wholeness, obfuscating the clarity of her memory. He was apart from her, but not separate. Alone, yet bound to her. And this other woman was unknowingly clutching and tugging on the same emotional strands as his tie to Daisy.

"Take me home, Nathaniel. Please."

Their eyes were still joined. Neither blinked.

"No," he finally said, "no."

He took a step forward to where she was half-sitting on the arm of the sofa and put his arms gently around her head and drew her face to his chest. She closed her eyes and he closed his and he held her just like that. Polly put her arms around his hips and clutched him tighter. They stayed that way for a long time. And then Garland bent down and kissed the top of her head. Her thick black hair still smelled of his shampoo.

"You can come with me. If you don't want to come, you can stay here. In the house. Lock yourself in, I'll give you the alarm codes and hire some good private security. You'll be safe."

"Which do you want me to do?"

"Whatever makes you most comfortable."

"That wasn't my question."

"I should be back in a day or two. Three at the most."

"That still doesn't answer my question."

"What I want is not necessarily in the best..." He stopped himself. "The truth is, I would feel better knowing you were safe with me."

Polly pulled back and looked up at him. "How smart is that?"

"Who said anything about smart?

52

Garland went to the garage and retrieved the Nordstrom shopping bags they had hurriedly thrown in the back of the Jaguar. Before they started packing, they ordered in Chinese food. Polly's idea. And when the lanky Caucasian deliveryman came to the door, Garland gave him fifty bucks with his left hand while he clutched Kessler's gun behind his back in his right hand.

At the kitchen table, he uncorked a six-year-old Pouilly Fuissé that he was saving, but couldn't remember for what occasion. Polly made Oolong tea and they drank both the tea and the wine with their meal of cold Singapore rice noodles, vegetable dumplings, chicken in black bean sauce and tea smoked duck. They ate it Chinese family style, from large serving plates into small hand-painted rice bowls filled with sticky bigh-fan – white rice.

During their rushed dinner, Garland realized that he was once again charmed by the way Polly's tongue curled on "L" words, such as "lau-jou" – a very spicy chili dipping sauce. Polly was delighted that he had lau-jou in his fridge, yet somehow she expected it.

Clearing the dishes, their conversation widened to include art and literature and music. Of course Polly played the piano, she laughed. What self-respecting Chinese-American girl didn't? Always two Chopin pieces and a Bach memorized for their first recitals. Hadn't he seen The Joy Luck Club? But she refused to play for him that night. The piano hadn't been touched since Daisy's death. And Garland, once again, felt the hole in his heart where Daisy once lived.

He missed her. Not just their love, that had settled into a relaxed natural comfort, but mostly he missed the intimacy of their friendship. They were for so many years each other's best friend. They could confide anything and everything in one another. No subject was forbidden. No emotion prohibited. Unabashed affection was the bud of their friendship. Sex was the flower. Breezy was the bouquet.

And perhaps it was his need to talk, to share, to connect with someone who understood his estrangement that encouraged him for the first time to open himself, even if only slightly, to Polly.

Garland rinsed the dishes for the dishwasher and Polly put the leftovers in the refrigerator. That's where she found the insulin, on the middle shelf behind some tubes of yogurt. The small white box of Humulin L was still sealed, but the 'use by' date stamped and embossed on the bottom flap was recent. Polly knew insulin should be stored no longer than three or four months. This supply was relatively fresh. From the sink, he watched her study the insulin box and when she put it back on the shelf and turned, she realized he had watched her. He didn't have diabetes. They both knew what the insulin was for.

The phone rang and Garland picked it up in the kitchen. It was Stuart, finally returning his call.

"Nate, it's me. What time you leaving?"

"How'd you…?"

"Grove told me. You got a line on Sarah, right? Grove said you had a really hot lead. What've you got?"

"I don't know yet. Stu, you know how it goes, it's probably nothing."

"Fuck. I thought you had something real. Damn it, Grove had me all pumped. I thought…I thought…oh, fuck it."

"I'm sorry, Stu."

"Yeah. Okay. So what time you going?"

"Plane's out of Reagan at 8:00."

"Pick you up 7:15. I've got some papers for you to sign before you go."

"Can it wait?"

"No. I'm trading through Hong Kong."

"Okay. 7:15. Stu, there's two of us going, so we'll take my car, okay?"

"Sure, whatever – see you in a few."

Garland and Polly packed in the upstairs bedroom. He opened the antique French Regence armoire but had forgotten about its screechy left door. He cringed at the grating sound and then rummaged through a drawer in the armoire and found his Glock neatly wrapped in its black nylon vertical shoulder holster. Polly stopped packing to watch him as Garland slid his arm through the holster loop and pulled the webbed strap around his back and clipped it to the side buckle. She could tell by the way he twice turned it inside out and continued to adjust it that he was not accustomed to wearing it. She found it oddly endearing.

When he settled into a relatively comfortable position for the holster, he went back to the armoire, opened another drawer and dug out a second gun – Carolyn Eccevarria's .38 P Special which he had placed back in its small clip-on leather holster. He turned and offered it to Polly. She refused it with a shake of her head.

"If you don't want to take it for yourself, take it for me."

"I can't. I'm sorry. I don't know anything about guns."

Garland understood. He jammed the gun in his pocket, turned to the armoire one more time and from the bottom drawer retrieved a large manila envelope. Daisy referred to the envelope as their "secret pig" – a grown up piggy bank. It was their stash of emergency cash, probably around ten thousand dollars. Without counting it, he split the stack in two, putting half in his pocket and handing the other half to Polly.

"Here. In case we get separated or, you know, an emergency or something."

She hesitated. He smiled.

"Take it. I'll put it on your tab."

"Promise?"

"Sure."

"I'm serious. I mean it."

"So noted."

The polite front door chime ended any further discussion. From the bedroom, after checking the closed-circuit security camera, Garland buzzed Stuart Levine into the foyer. He then wrestled their luggage downstairs, left it in the foyer and met Stuart in the kitchen. He could tell that all of the air was out of Stuart's balloon.

"I gotta stop getting excited over every scrap, don't I?" Stuart said as he pawed through the refrigerator.

"Why?" Garland answered. "It's called 'hope'."

"Yeah, well I'm just about out." He opened the carton of Singapore noodles. "This stuff fresh?"

"Delivered an hour ago."

Stuart scooped up several of the cartons and brought them to the counter. He put them down and then opened his thin Prada briefcase and pulled out a handful of documents. "You want to read this stuff over? Shit's all boilerplate. The H.K. bonds."

"You read it?"

"Course. We're gonna clear about 200-thou on these pups."

Garland opened his jacket to reach for his pen.

"Nice piece," Stuart nodded to the holstered Glock under Garland's jacket. "Somebody finally knocked some sense into you, so now you're carrying, huh?" Stuart opened the drawer, pulled out a fork and plunged into the noodles. "Fucking Grover. Got me all excited."

"Stu, it wasn't his fault. He shouldn't have said anything."

Stuart was about to answer when Polly appeared at the kitchen entry. She was wearing casual tan slacks and an off-white blousy top from their Nordstrom's adventure. "Excuse me for interrupting," she said standing at the entry. "Nathaniel, do you have a small bag or something for my sundries and makeup?"

"Sure. Polly, this is Stu, Stuart Levine, Sarah's husband. Stu, this is Polly," then, for some reason, felt the need to add, "Dr. Collier," as if that would clarify everything.

Stuart's fork stopped halfway to his mouth. "Hey."

"Hello."

"Nate didn't tell me. You his new partner?"

"No, I'm not with BIA; I'm an ophthalmologist."

"Didn't tell me that, either. Jeez, what happened to you?" Stuart was eyeing her face. "You got some nasty bruises there," he said with all the subtlety of a nose tackle.

"Car accident," Polly said without hesitation.

Stuart forked some more noodles into his mouth. "Nice to meet you."

And Polly self-consciously touched her face as she turned and left the kitchen.

53

They made it to Reagan in fifteen minutes, circumventing the terminal traffic by going through general aviation. Garland's badge greased them through security and Stuart helped Garland wheel the luggage across the tarmac to the waiting CDC plane.

"So what's with you and the doc here? Jesus, what a looker she'll be when her face clears up."

"It's strictly professional."

"The way she looked at you, you fuckin' kidding me?"

"No, I'm serious. Nothing's happened, nothing's going to happen."

"Okay, you say." Stuart smiled, then grabbed Garland and gave him a back slapping hug. "You just watch your ass out there, man, okay? You need anything, anything at all, you give me a call. I'm serious, Nate, you find anything on Sarah, any fucking scrap, anything, call me, okay?"

"I will, Stu."

At 8:11pm the CDC Cessna Citation X lifted off runway 19 and made a long looping bank as it sliced skyward to its cruising altitude. Drake Field, the airport that serviced Fayetteville, Arkansas was two hours and 940 miles away. Garland and Polly settled in for the flight. They were the only passengers in the eight-seat cabin. This particular Cessna was configured with two seats per row and they sat across a narrow aisle from one another. Twenty minutes after takeoff, when the jet leveled off at 37,000 feet, Garland closed his eyes.

He saw their faces behind his closed lids – his mother, Daisy, Breezy, Sarah, Eccevarria, Corinne – women who had touched his life and he theirs. Garland was not the least bit superstitious. He was a staunch atheist and purchased no credence whatsoever in anything even remotely supernatural. So why, he wondered, why could he not shake the ridiculous notion that to the women in his life he held dear, his touch was the kiss of death? And that's why, when he opened his eyes and glanced across the aisle and saw Polly, he believed he had made a terrible mistake.

As the plane settled into its cruising altitude groove, Garland reached under his seat, pulled out his Tumi bag and withdrew a blue folder filled with evidentiary photos and files. Polly glanced at him, but didn't say anything. Thirty minutes into the flight, she again looked across the aisle and had a quizzical look on her face.

Garland glanced up at her from the files. "Tzo mei toe," he grinned. *Tzo mei toe*, which rhymes with tomato, is an untranslatable Mandarin idiom. Loosely, it means 'furrowed brow', referring to someone's confused and/or worried facial expression, accompanied by wavy lines on the person's forehead.

"Tzo mei toe?" she smiled back. It tickled her that he would use such a uniquely Chinese expression. She shrugged, embarrassed, then leaned across the aisle and said, in the most charming, naïve way, "Tell me again why we're going to Arkansas?"

For the next hour Garland explained everything. He gave her the highlights and mile markers of his investigation, beginning with Sarah's disappearance, through the shooting on Burning Tree, the assassination of Rudolf Capiloff and the sniper murder of Carolyn Eccevarria. He talked about his first encounter with Corinne Burch at Fairfax Hospital, his accidental foiling of the attempt on Corinne's life and how possibly Starke, if it was Starke, used Sarah's license plates to enter Fed-Med. He brought her through the sniper on the roof trying to kill them in Le Petit Pinot's parking lot. He told her how he identified the shooter, how he located Dr. Emil Pniak in

239

Fayetteville, everything. He told her everything he knew. And he felt remarkably comfortable doing so.

Polly listened intently, nodding an "uh-huh" every so often, interrupting occasionally to ask pertinent questions or seek clarifications. Garland could tell by her responses that she was getting it, analyzing the information as it was fed to her and just as quickly assimilating it. "A quick study," his father would have said. Garland had seen her work as a surgeon when they were flogging Corinne in Con-Con, trying to keep the dying girl alive. He had noticed then that she wasted no motion and was just as precise in thought as action. She was, as his father would have also said, "smart as a whip."

Polly looked away for a moment, stared out the window as she thought through the implications, then turned back to Garland and said, "How good a pathologist is Victor Brotman?"

"The best. Thorough. Careful. Methodical. Not to mention brilliant."

"And he was sure Corinne Burch was blind from birth?"

"I saw the vestigial nerve bundles myself."

Polly shook her head. "No. It's not possible. Jason Beck was the acknowledged world authority on macular regeneration. He was the tip of the spear. I know, Nathaniel, I worked with the man side-by-side for months. I would know if there was a breakthrough anywhere in the world, by anyone in the field. I know them all, I would have known."

"Look, I saw the girl's supernumerary optic juncture. Saw the haploids. Saw it all with my own two eyes. It's the truth, Polly, Corinne Burch's eyes were transgenically engineered."

"How could that be? This is my line of research. That's why I joined Beck. And I'm telling you we're two years away from animal trials. At least five to ten years away from human clinical trials — and now you're telling me someone has already completed the trials?"

"No, not completed. Bypassed. I believe that's why Corinne and her brother were abducted from Florida. I think the Polachek twins either volunteered or were used without their knowledge. And logic tells me there must be a hell of a lot more victims where they came from." Garland paused, letting it sink in, then continued, "Evinco Vixi was partially financing Beck's research. He had to know, had to be part of it."

Polly looked at Garland and he could see the tide of sadness rise in her eyes. "I must be the stupidest person walking the face of the earth. How could I not have known? It's my life's work, Nathaniel, now it's what? Totally negated? Worthless?"

"No. Just the opposite." Without thinking, Garland reached over touched her arm reassuringly. "What killed Corinne was the same stem cell therapy that gave her sight. Vic Brotman is absolutely positive. She died of cytotoxicity. If the Army and Secret Service didn't kill Polachek on the roof, he probably would have died within days or weeks of the same pathology that killed Corinne."

Polly sighed, closed her eyes and nodded slowly. "Maybe. So what do you expect from Pniak? The keys to the kingdom?"

"Expect? I've given up on expectations long ago. But he knows all about *Evinco Vixi* – knows who's running it, who's financing his research, who's benefiting – just as Beck knew. And now I want to know what he knows about Sarah, about Corinne, maybe even her brother. One way or the other, he's going to give me Sarah. And Starke."

"You think he abducted her? Sarah, I mean."

"Yeah. I'm sure it was Starke, just as he abducted Corinne and her brother, so he's no stranger to kidnapping. And he also had access to Sarah's license plates, so he has her car someplace. My gut feeling is Pniak is a big part of this and he knows where they both are. As far as I'm concerned, it's not a big leap from Pniak to Sarah. Ronald Polachek was Pniak's patient. Polachek had to know or be told or ordered to kill Capiloff and Capiloff is a direct link to Sarah."

"And you think because Pniak did the surgery, he's calling the shots here?" Polly said it as if she was trying the thought on for size.

"Uh-uh. No. But Army sniper, Army surgeon – there has to be some connective tissue there. I don't know what. But something."

"Jesus," Polly said as she analyzed the implications, "you think the Army's behind this?"

Garland raised his shoulders and shook his head. "I have no idea. I just *know* this is much bigger than Pniak or Starke. Someone, some group, some organization or corporation or major financial interest or maybe even a government auspices – like the Army or DOD – some entity is funding specific biomedical research under the obscure banner of "*Evinco Vixi*".

Now Polly touched Garland's arm with her long tapered fingers. By not moving, he allowed her hand to linger on his arm. He noticed, peripherally, she was no longer wearing her ring. "Let me ask you something," she said. "If Pniak cut you off on the phone, what makes you think he'll talk to you now?"

"I'm a Federal officer, "Garland smiled. "I've got the full authority of the United States government behind me."

"And he's a Major. He's got the United States Army behind him."

Polly withdrew her hand from his arm and settled back into her seat. Even in the dim cabin of the Cessna, Garland could make out her LEMS – lateral eye movements – so he knew she was thinking, analyzing, digesting. He admired the way her thought processes worked. Clean. Linear. Analytical. She was, after all, a scientist and was approaching Garland's investigation from that perspective.

Polly took a sip of her bottled water and said, "Who knew Dr. Levine was going to meet Capiloff the night she disappeared?"

"I don't know. She didn't tell me, so I don't know whom she might have told – if anybody. There're dozens of us in the field. We all investigate independently. I mean, like now, aside from Haynes and Grover, I didn't specifically tell anyone where I was going or what I plan to do in Fayetteville."

"But someone has to coordinate. Someone has to make assignments, review the reports, the legal stuff. Somebody signed for this plane we're in. The car we're going to use, hotel, food. Stuff. People have to know things. All of you have fat paper trails following you everywhere."

"Yeah. We've got our pencil necks just like every other DC bureaucracy."

"But everything filters to some executive. Administrator. You know what I mean. Somebody in charge."

"Sure. Haynes, ultimately. Much of the day-to-day stuff goes through Nelson Dunbarton."

"They have assistants? Secretaries? Support staffs?"

"Where are you going with this?"

"It just seems logical to me that Dr. Levine's abduction had to be an inside job."

Garland leaned forward to look at her and chuckled. "Inside job?"

"Well just think about it. Someone in your agency had to know who and what she was investigating the night she went out to meet Capiloff. And what about Starke? How could he have known about Fed-Med's security procedures and where every security camera was? Someone on the inside had to tell him."

"You're right," Garland nodded and felt no need to elaborate that he had already carefully considered that scenario and the irrefutable logic kept sending him back to Haynes. But he knew – *he knew* – that logic had to be flawed. Carter Haynes certainly had his faults and eccentricities, but ordering abductions and murders of his own personnel were not among them. Even the notion that the FBI was investigating Haynes for money laundering was inconceivable to Garland. The truth, Garland was convinced, lay someplace else. The truth lay with Maj. Erno Pniak.

54

The car waiting for them on the tarmac of Fayetteville's Drake Field was a black Ford Expedition. The young woman who had supplied the car was Dr. Shamala Patel, a graduate research assistant from the CDC's Fayetteville office.

Since it was just getting on its feet, the BIA, still relied heavily on its parent department's other agencies, bureaus, administrations, and commissions for ground support. Obviously, as a lowly CDC assistant, Dr. Patel drew the short straw and had to hustle out to the airport to meet them with a company car.

Garland loaded their luggage and slammed the hatch door closed. That's when Polly noticed the license plate – a white U.S. Government plate. There was also a large 'U.S. Department of Health and Human Services, Centers for Disease Control' sticker on the back window.

"Well that's subtle," she said pointing to the license plate, "very convenient for undercover work."

Undercover work. Garland smiled in spite of himself.

Dr. Shamala Patel was courteous, if not gracious, and made their ten-minute drive from the airport to the University of Arkansas campus pleasant enough. The CDC's field office and Dr. Patel's own car were both on campus and she asked to be dropped off at the main entrance on 6th and Razorback. She gave Garland very simple directions up College Avenue to the Radisson Hotel downtown, and, more importantly, to the VA Hospital several blocks further north.

Although it was nearing 10:00 pm local time, Garland wanted to check out the VA hospital first on the off chance that Maj. Erno Pniak was still at work.

"I could drop you off at the hotel if you're tired," Garland said as they drove up College Avenue.

"No, s'okay," Polly said, "although I could use a restroom."

"VA's five minutes from here. Or are we talking gas station?"

"VA's fine if it's that close." She leaned back in her seat and stared out the window. Without looking at Garland she said, "Brendan would never let me go."

Garland glanced at her quickly, then his eyes returned to the road. "Divorce?"

"No. Pee. It was like a perverted game with him." She spoke without looking at him. "I'd say I have to go and he'd say, okay, and then just ignore what I said until I had to tell him again. And then he'd say he'd find a gas station or something, but he never would. The more uncomfortable I got, the more he enjoyed it. I'd say, please, Brendan, I really have to go, now, please, pull in someplace, and he'd just keep going. A few times I even threatened to jump out of the car if he didn't stop. I even opened the door once as he was driving and he just went faster. Just sped up. Twice...twice I actually peed myself. Sitting right there in our car, through my clothes, down my legs...I soaked the car seat. He thought it was the funniest thing he ever saw."

Garland wanted to respond with what he was feeling, wanted to tell her what a sick, demented asshole Brendan was, but held back only because he didn't want to appear self-serving. Instead, he said, "Real charmer, isn't he?"

Shamala's directions were perfect and Garland easily found the Fayetteville VA Medical Center. It was a small, stark white facility set back from the street in a broad, tranquil park-like setting. The adjoining parking lot was nearly empty and Garland maneuvered the big Expedition into a space clearly marked 'compact'. Looking around at the odd assortment of cars still parked there, he knew instinctively that Erno Pniak's car wasn't among them.

In the hospital's small foyer, a young military security guard with close-cropped hair directed Polly to the ladies' room while Garland approached the night desk and asked the gray-haired civilian clerk about Pniak. The woman checked the computer and then called upstairs to confirm that Maj. Pniak was, in fact, gone for the night.

"Do you have his home address and phone number in there?" Garland asked nodding toward the computer.

"I'm afraid I cannot divulge that information," the night desk lady said with a thick but pleasant drawl.

Garland reached into his pocket and produced his badge. "I can appreciate that, ma'am, but this is a Federal matter of some urgency."

The woman took Garland's leather badge case and lowered her reading glasses from where they were perched high on her forehead. She studied the badge and Garland's photo ID card. "Hmmmmm. I don't know…"

Polly joined him at the desk, which is probably why Garland did not raise his ire. Speaking softly and distinctly he said, "Ma'am, please, I need Maj. Pniak's home address and phone number and I do need it now."

"But…"

"No, buts, ma'am. Just write it down for me, please."

"You understand, I'm not supposed to…"

"I do appreciate that very much, ma'am, and I know you're just doing your job, but if I have to file a report that says you were uncooperative with a Federal officer, I don't see how that is going to have a good outcome for you and I don't believe either of us wants that now, do we?"

The woman's eyes slid from Garland to Polly and then back to Garland again. "No, sir," and she indignantly handed him his case, slid her glasses back up and clicked the keyboard. A moment later the printer hummed and she handed Garland the information he had requested.

"Thank you very much for your cooperation, ma'am. Good night."

When Garland and Polly were walking back across the parking lot to the Expedition, Polly said, "You were really restraining yourself with her, weren't you?"

"It was that noticeable?"

"Oh, yeah," she said as she climbed into the Expedition.

And as Garland moved around to the driver's side, he thought to himself again *how many times had Daisy told him to play well with others?*

55

Erno Pniak's home – a year-around cabin, really – was located out of the city not far from White River. It was more difficult to find than Garland anticipated and, in the Ozark darkness, he managed to get lost several times before Polly convinced him to shelve his ego, stop at a 7-Eleven and buy a local map.

The map helped immensely.

Polly saw the flashing lights first as Garland turned off the main road and headed up the hill towards Pniak's address. There were a half dozen law enforcement vehicles in and around the Pniak driveway – Fayetteville Police, Arkansas State Police and Washington County Sheriff's cars.

"This doesn't look good," Garland said rhetorically as he stopped the Expedition a hundred feet from the house.

He and Polly got out of the car and walked toward the house. Garland folded his badge case into his jacket pocket to display the gold shield. An anxious State Police officer, much younger, taller and wider than Garland, stepped forward from the long driveway to vet them before they reached the property.

"Evening, officer," Garland said as they approached. "Is this the Pniak home?"

"Sir," the young cop responded curtly as he squinted at Garland's badge.

"Special Agent Nathaniel Garland." He extended his hand to the young man who was surprised at first, but then shook it politely.

Garland didn't feel it was necessary to explain Polly. He'd let the young officer assume she was a BIA agent as well. "Maj. Pniak's?" Garland repeated, jutting his chin toward the house.

"Yessir."

"What happened here?"

"Not here, sir, up t'gorge."

"An accident?"

"A'ppears so."

"Oh, no. Is the Major alright?"

"No sir. A'ppears he was a fatality."

"Forensics guys are sure it was him? You had a positive ID?"

"Yessir, not a doubt. Was Pniak, for sure."

Polly gripped Garland's arm, an involuntary gesture not lost on the young officer. He turned his head to his lapel and spoke into his radio, invoking the words 'Federal agent' to motivate his superior. Within a minute, several ranking officers ambled out of the house to make Garland's acquaintance. The most senior of the pack was a large barrel-shaped man who introduced himself as Captain T.X. 'my friends call me Tex' Abernathy of the Arkansas State Police. His first order of business was to ascertain Garland's legitimacy and the Fed's interest in their small local incident.

"It's a case we want to close the books on," Garland said. "Dr. Pniak operated on a soldier, recently deceased, who may have been involved in a series of fatal shootings in the Washington area."

"That sniper fella?" Abernathy asked. Then seizing Garland's hesitancy, added, "We do get the cable TV and the occasional Time Magazine out here."

"Yes, the sniper case." He was impressed by Abernathy's astuteness and decided not to lie more than he had to.

"Whatcha say your name is?"

"Special Agent Garland, Dr. Nathaniel Garland. This is Dr. Polly Collier."

"Abernathy," the older captain said, holding out his beefy hand, "T.X., but most ever'one calls me Tex." Abernathy glanced over his shoulder then nudged Garland and Polly away from the driveway. "Les' take us a saunter, ya mind?"

"Damn, I don't believe this," Garland muttered loudly in frustration. "I spoke to Maj. Pniak this morning. This morning."

When they were out of earshot, Abernathy said, "Why they havin' you science folks investigatin' down here rather than the Fibbis?"

"Actually, my former partner was FBI. We think the sniper that Pniak operated on was the shooter who killed her."

"Killed her? Awfully sorry, didn't know, truly sorry t'hear tha'."

"We just came down to tie up some loose ends about the boy's surgery. What can you tell us about the accident, Captain? Multi-car? Single car? Where was it? What happened?"

"Tex. Please." The older man drew two sausage fingers across his bushy moustache and gave his response some thought as they continued walking. "Happened up in the hills, jus' a few miles east a'here. Road curved, Pniak's car didn't. Went over the side and took a header three hun'red feet into the gorge. Damn if he didn't take out the whole guard rail with him."

"Was it raining, the road slippery? Fall asleep at the wheel? What?"

Abernathy stopped to light a cigarette. As he bent over the flame of the Zippo cradled in the bowl of his hands, his eyes danced from Garland to Polly. "Was gonna ask if you mind if I smoked, but you both bein' doctors and all – road up there was dry as a dusty doormat," Abernathy continued, exhaling a jet of blue smoke. "Truth is, we think he had some help goin' over."

"What do you mean? How?"

"We got our forensic AIS team headin' up from Little Rock right now, but the broken tail lights and braking skid patterns indicate t'me and t'other fellas that he was hit from behind – shoved and pushed, if you know what I mean."

"So you believe it was intentional?" Polly asked.

"Sure do, doctor. Fact, we got us a witness. Trucker comin' 'round the curve t'other way maybe two, three seconds after Pniak's car go over. Sees a patrol car, he says, big ol' Chevy with push bumpers. Missouri tags. 'Cept Missouri don't have Chevy cruisers, 'specially down here."

"Did your witness see the driver's face? Get a description?

"No. Fact is, didn't really strike him 'bout the patrol car till he came 'round and saw the busted guardrail. So my question to you, doctors, is who wanted to kill Pniak?"

"If I knew that – damn , I can't believe this."

"Dr. Collier?"

Polly shook her head.

"Well maybe ya can enlighten me as to 'zactly wha' you Washington folks wanted with him?"

"Like we said, Tex, just tying up some loose ends."

"Uh-huh. 'Zactly wha' kinda loose ends you come a thousand mile t'tie up?"

"The kind that don't make sense. I'm not trying to be evasive, but we're kind of lost ourselves. As I said, Pniak was an orthopedist who operated on the man we believe to be a sniper responsible for multiple killings, including my partner. What we wanted to learn from Pniak was, very simply, the medical procedure he used to heal the sniper's hand."

"Musta been one helluva operation t'bring you folks all the way here t'interview him." Abernathy dropped his cigarette butt to the street and ground it under his heel. "A'ppears somebody didn't want him talkin' t'ya."

Garland sighed. "Or it could be totally unrelated. Even an accident."

"Uh-huh."

Garland and Polly realized that Abernathy had walked them back to the Expedition. They stopped at the passenger door.

"You have a card, Tex?" Garland asked.

"Uh-huh." Abernathy reached for his wallet.

"Here's mine. If I get anything at all, I will let you know. I would very much appreciate if you did the same."

"Deal." He opened the car door for Polly.

"Captain Abernathy," she said, "does Dr. Pniak have a family here?"

"Yes, he does, ma'am. Wife an' three little ones. They're inside." His head motioned to the house. He closed the heavy Expedition door for Polly, then, looking at them added, "Y'all have a good night now."

And Tex Abernathy strode back to his waiting troops in the driveway.

56

They had connecting rooms on an upper floor of Fayetteville's downtown Radisson. For security, Garland insisted the doors between their rooms remain open. While Polly showered, Garland placed Eccevarria's gun on the nightstand next to her bed. He would be firm she keep it close while they slept in their separate rooms.

Polly came out of her steamy bathroom wrapped in a white terry bath sheet with her hair turbaned up in a smaller towel and stood at Garland's door. He could never figure out how women were able to do that with their hair — for him it was one of life's great mysteries.

"They knew you were coming to see Pniak, right?" she said, obviously having thought about it in the shower, "so they killed him?".

"Yes." He answered without looking up from his laptop. Garland could now smell the aroma of Polly's subtle vanilla coconut bath soaps waft over him. He glanced up. "Let me show you something."

Clutching the bath sheet tighter around herself, she glided into his room and moved over to the tiny desk where Garland was working. He swiveled his laptop so she could see the graphic on the screen. It was a Google Earth map of the southeastern United States. There were red dots situated over a half dozen cities forming a crescent shape from Baltimore to St. Louis, dipping as far south as Tallahassee, Florida and creeping back up through Atlanta, Georgia.

"What are the dots?" she asked.

"Cities, biotechs and institutions cited in research papers co-authored by Evinco Vixi. Nine of the eleven are home to a major research university and or medical school. In Tallahassee you've got Florida State University, Atlanta, Emory, St. Louis, Clayton, Washington University, Little Rock, University of Arkansas College of Medicine. This one's you, Beck Institute, in Baltimore. See? All nice and contained is the same geographic area."

"But Pniak was here in Fayetteville. There's no medical school or biotech that I know of here."

"But there is a VA Hospital. He was transferred here very abruptly from Walter Reed. How many major med schools and research hospitals are within a hundred mile radius of Reed? Including GWU, Mass General, Harvard, Johns Hopkins and a dozen more?"

"You're reaching."

"Am I? Then why are all Evinco Vixi research papers coming from the same general area? It doesn't feel random. What's the pattern here?"

"I don't know. But the forensic evidence showed that Corinne Burch came from the Bull Shoals area, that's over a hundred miles from here and not even close to any medical research facility. So how does that fit into your pattern?"

"Just because I can't see it doesn't mean it doesn't fit. There's a pattern. There's a logic. I know it."

Polly pondered it for a moment. "Maybe it's related to 610?" Is there any relationship on the map to that number?"

"What 610?"

"You said all of the papers were co-authored by Evinco Vixi 610."

"No. I said 'Evinco Vixi CVDV'."

"Isn't that 610 in Roman numerals? Evinco Vixi is Latin, so doesn't it makes sense CVDV is a Roman numeral?"

"Of course," he said, more to himself. Garland really liked the way Polly thought, admired her process.

Polly straightened up. "I'm going to bed." She turned and moved toward her room, leaving her scent behind like a wave retreating from a sandy beach, then she stopped at the door and looked back. "Those dots, those Evinco Vixi research partners – what are you planning to do?"

"Warn them," he said.

"About what?"

Garland shook his head. "I don't know. Pniak. Beck. Warn them."

"And if they're all in it together somehow," she floated the idea as a trial balloon, "if it is some kind of bizarre conspiracy, aren't you tipping them off about how close you are to them?"

Yes. He really liked the way her mind worked.

57

Even on the thin carpeting, Garland heard Polly's bare feet padding to the open connecting doors. He was on his back, eyes closed, unable to sleep. He heard her pause at the doors, heard her light breaths as she listened to his, gauging whether or not he was asleep.

"I'm up," Garland said.

"I have to ask you something."

He sat up and reached for the bedside lamp. "I'm turning on the light." Polly averted her eyes.

When Garland's eyes adjusted and he racked her into focus, he saw that she was wearing one of the pink sleeping T-shirts they bought at Nordstrom's. It was a loose-fitting long cotton V-neck that, because of her height, only reached mid-thigh.

She was nervous, hesitant and finally said, "I know this is crazy, but just, please indulge me, okay? I have to know." She paused nervously, then said "What were you thinking when you kissed my head in your study? Do you remember? What were you thinking?" Then having second thoughts about even bringing it up, said, "I'm sorry, that was a stupid, presumptuous question. I know. Okay. Goodnight. Sorry. Sorry." She turned to return to her room.

"No, it's okay," Garland said. He waited for her to turn back. "To tell you the truth, I was thinking how good your hair smelled. You know, clean, like freshly shampooed."

"Clean."

"Yeah."

"That's it? That's all? Clean."

A life's course is steered by a multitude of choices. Some are subtle, others innocuous, most are mindless and routine. Then there are those choices that grab the tiller and, intentionally or not, steer lives into uncharted turbulent waters. When Polly said 'that's it? that's all?', Garland could easily have said 'yes, that's all' and that would have been the end of it. But he hesitated and her finely tuned feminine radar locked in on his hesitation. She cocked her head ever so slightly to coax his verbal response and that's when he said, "No, that's not all." It was a choice. And Garland knew it was the wrong choice the moment he uttered it. With a simple 'no' he could have put the whole thing to rest, fought back his attraction to her and got on with his life. Instead he chose to head into uncharted turbulent waters.

"So, uh, were you thinking anything else?" Her voice was tenuous.

Again he hesitated.

Polly unconsciously wrapped her arms around herself. "Please don't let me stand here and make a complete ass of myself."

"No, no, never," he said and then he made another choice. "Here. Please." He patted the side of his bed and scooted over. It was half an invitation. A full invitation would have been throwing back the covers for her, allowing her to slide in next to him, but this way, the half invitation, allowed her the option to just sit on the bed so they could talk.

She moved quickly to the bed and reached for the covers. "May I?"

"Of course."

She pulled the covers back, slid into the bed, twisted her torso to turn off the lamp, then pulled the covers back over herself

258

and seemed to do it in all in one smooth motion. Her delightful coconut vanilla aroma arrived a moment later.

"You think I'm some kind of pathetic, needy crazy woman, don't you?"

"No, that's not what I think at all." Garland lifted himself on one elbow to look at her. Polly's face was turned away from him. "When I kissed your head, I did think how nice your hair smelled. And then I thought how much I wanted to kiss you again."

She turned to face him. "Why didn't you?"

"How many reasons do you want?"

"None."

Garland reached for Polly as she was already wriggling toward him. Their eyes kissed first, deep and long, then their mouths followed, tentatively at first, as they took measure of each other's willingness and commitment to the moment. Lips brushed lips. Heartbeats rose. Again they sought each other's mouths, arms and hands now encircling one another, pulling their bodies closer and tighter. Their kisses alternated between barely touching to what felt like unquenchable desire. Time was suspended and in one second they kissed forever.

Polly's delicate hands slid beneath the waistband of Garland's Façonnable boxers, gripped the taut warmth of his buttocks and pulled his hips even tighter against her. His hands were not so bold, but his erection surely was. Even for his six-one stature, Garland's penis was of the more generous variety – a mortifying embarrassment in his youth, a prized trophy in college, a household appliance for Daisy – and now there was no hiding its impertinence.

Garland lifted his face from Polly's and said, "we can stop."

Polly's hand moved around his hip and firmly grasped his impertinence.

"Or not," Garland agreed.

She released him long enough to wriggle her nightshirt above her waist. Garland lowered his own shorts. Despite her copious wetness, Garland entered her with difficulty and Polly slowly, incrementally, guided him in. She made soft, primal sounds that fueled his eagerness, hushed cries and whimpers, and when he was fully sheathed she wrapped her legs tightly around him.

"Don't move, don't move, don't move," she breathed over and over, "don't move."

Garland complied and she still held him tightly, squeezing him with her arms and legs as she buried her face against his shoulder.

"Just like this," she whispered, "just like this, don't move, don't move..."

They stayed motionless, he locked in her, for a very long time. And now as he felt the flush of her face against his body and could feel her crying, he knew it wasn't about sex at all, it was about closeness. Touching and being touched. Giving and receiving. Comfort. Kindness. Sharing warmth. Rekindling some measure of self-esteem and banishing the suffocation of loneliness.

Garland certainly didn't mind. He needed – missed – yearned for the same comforts as she.

When she felt his muscles begin to quiver, Polly said, "Relax. Let go."

"I'm too heavy for you."

"No. You're not. Please. I want to feel you, your weight."

He slowly lowered himself on top of her and Polly relaxed her arms and legs. She stroked his damp back and whispered, "You feel so good."

Garland's lips found hers again and when they kissed this time her hips began to move in a slow but deliberate rhythm. Garland released an unintentional squeaky groan and said, "If you keep doing that, I cannot be responsible for my actions."

Polly smiled. "Good. Turn over."

Without separating, Garland pulled her over on top of him. He noticed that as tall as she was, Polly was remarkably light. Still straddling him, she pushed herself upright and placed her hands flat on his chest. She was still wearing her nightshirt that now completely covered her and their union. Garland didn't mind that, either. Closing her eyes, she began to rotate her hips in slow, tight circles. Garland thrust his hips up, pushing deeper into her and Polly hushed, "No, lie still, let me drive." And drive she did, accelerating smoothly, taking the bumps and curves fast and fearlessly. When they finally approached their destination, Garland got off first. Polly got off at the next stop. Both experienced extraordinary journeys. And then she collapsed on top of him.

They lay that way for a very long time, still joined where it mattered and barely moving in order to remain that way. Sweating – not politely perspiring – breathing hard and hearts still racing, neither of them spoke. Garland held her against his body with one arm while his other hand stroked her hair.

It was Polly who spoke first. She said, "What are you thinking?"

"Měi lì hēi tóu-fà," he smiled, meaning 'beautiful black hair'.

"That's it? That's all?"

"For now."

They remained quiet for a few more minutes and then Polly said, "How smart was this?"

"Who said anything about smart?"

As he showered afterward, Garland thought about her. Out from under the demanding thumb of Jason Beck, away from the dangers and fears of the loathsome husband that preyed upon her, the real Dr. Polly Collier was emerging as a different woman. He was already very aware of her sharp mind and saw her precise surgical skills first hand, but this Polly Collier also had a wonderfully dry sense of humor. His kind of humor, the sense of which he had lost the day his ladies died. Polly Collier made him smile again. She was inherently sexy. He considered her breathtaking, exotic looks, her stature, her proud bearing. And then, for good measure, there was her intense, penetrating sexuality.

Garland used a hand towel to wipe the thick damp fog from the vanity mirror to shave. He leaned in to his clouded reflection, turning his head left to right. He looked at himself. Looked into his eyes. Looked into his thoughts and said to himself aloud, "Don't be a schmuck. You don't need this now. Let her go."

Choices. Life is all about choices.

58

While Polly finished packing, Garland checked his email and sorted through them to find the two he was expecting. The first was from Arleta Farleigh advising Garland that she had set up a meeting for him with Sgt. Larry Dugan of the U.S. Fish and Wildlife Service for late that afternoon. Dugan would meet them at what the locals called the Sweetwater 'Y', a small delta on Bull Shoals where Sweetwater Creek and the Little Bull River branched off toward the east. The second was from BIA Administrative Services with confirmation of room reservations near Bull Shoals at *Al 'N' Sal's Come On Inn*.

"Are you kidding me?" Garland said to the screen. "What does 'Al 'N' Sal's Come On Inn' sound like to you?"

Polly smiled.

There is no easy way to drive from Fayetteville to Bull Shoals, but the route does cross the amazing Ozark Plateau and is one of the most beautiful and scenic drives in the entire country. The 130-mile trip usually takes about three hours and Garland decided not to push it too hard.

########

Norman Starke followed them at a safe distance. He had stayed overnight after visiting his unpleasantness on Erno Pniak, and was surprised to learn that while he was dealing with Pniak, Garland, and the woman were already on the ground in Fayetteville, already at the VA asking questions.

The situation had become untenable. Starke had warned them when he was told to bring Sarah Levine to The 610 instead of killing her. Warned them again when Levine and that blind girl escaped into Hugger Wood. They didn't listen. Then he was told that Nathaniel Garland was a rank amateur as an investigator, that he was inept as well as inexperienced and it would take him weeks, if ever, to track his way to Bull Shoals. Now, just five days later, Garland and the woman were already heading east, just a few hours drive from the Shoals and The 610.

He should have killed Garland in Fed-Med when he had his chance. The girl, he learned, would have died anyway without his intervention. The Director should have known that. He should have targeted Garland instead of the girl and killed him. And he will. But now was not the time, this was not the place. And besides, unlike Pniak's Jeep, his nimble Chevy Caprice was still no match for the nearly three tons of rolling Expedition.

Starke settled back into the red vinyl and leatherette seat and kept the Expedition in sight. He had planned his exit strategy months ago and put it into motion when the two women escaped and he knew he would have to bail. It wasn't at all like him to cut and run. That bothered him greatly. He admired and respected loyalty, both giving and receiving. To Starke there was no virtue higher than fealty. Semper Fi. Didn't The Director restore his sight? Didn't he owe him everything just for that? Goddamn, he wished they had listened to him, heeded his warnings, dispersed the "clients" and destroyed all traces of The 610. Now it was too late. The best he could do now was buy The Director a little more time – not much, but hopefully enough to save his ass. To do that, he would have to derail Garland and the woman.

Garland would make mistakes. He knew that. And one of those mistakes would be Garland's last.

59

For the first hour of the drive Garland and Polly spoke very little. Polly knew it wasn't as if Garland was being intentionally uncommunicative, it was that he had retreated into himself and she was having a hard time discerning exactly where he was.

Polly had learned early how to read the subtle shifting sands of male moods. She could vaguely remember the capricious, often violent moods of her father before he abandoned her and her mother somewhere near Shijiazhuang. When she and her mother finally made their way to Beijing, she remembered the men her mother would take in like strays, pay her a few Yuan to spend a night or two and then vanish in the early morning mist, each stealing crumbs of their dwindling pride until there were no crumbs left to steal. Through the parted curtains of her wooden, shelf-like sleeping loft, Pu Li watched the men inflict their cruelties and humiliations on her mother and she quickly learned to interpret their unspoken signs and signals of bad intentions.

When Pu Li was six, an elderly, wealthy machine tool salesman from Tianjin brought them to měi-gúo – America – and Pu Li remembered how she loved the sound of the name měi-gúo, which almost rhymed with America, and how it translated, literally, to 'beautiful country'. But the old machine tool salesman, who insisted Pu Li call him gung-gung, an affectionate term for grandfather, was far more interested in Pu Li's prepubescent sexual development than her mother's sexual maturity. After several months of gung-gung's fondling, Pu Li told her mother about his strange games under her skirt and her mother chased the old man from their house with an eight-inch dāo-zō – kitchen knife.

On their own, life was extremely difficult, and slowly her mother regained some of her family's lost pride. Even in a city as metropolitan and as Chinese as San Francisco, the Mandarin majority still considered Tzhang Pu Li and her mother low class outcasts. The intense blueness of their eyes – impossible to hide – spoke of the significant early Roman influence in their Heilongjiang Chinese ethnicity, a minority not embraced by the Han. She was ostracized in grade school, further eroding her self-esteem. In high school she tried to buy acceptance with sex, but the trade off was decidedly one sided.

Polly's Heilongjiang heritage, however, also brought with it her super-model height and bearing, her exotic beauty and, most important, her superior intellect. When, with ironic synchronicity, all of these traits blossomed in college, she found that she frightened off the good men and attracted only the predators. She began to believe that a bad relationship, even an abusive one, was better than none at all.

Her life's instruction taught her how to read the cracks and fissures in the emotional terrain of most men. She believed she could handle any man and any situation. She met her match in Brendan Collier. He played by an entirely different set of rules. He dominated and controlled her completely – physically, sexually, emotionally, financially and, to her complete dismay, reproductively.

Now she found herself driving on a rural highway across northern Arkansas with a wonderfully decent man whom she sensed was withdrawing from her. She replayed their most recent conversations in her head for insight. She revisited their beautiful sexual encounter the night before for some inadvertent transgression she may have committed. True, she didn't know him that well, but she was sure she had read him correctly. So why was he pulling back? Maybe, she thought, it wasn't something she did or didn't do – maybe the reason was completely within him and had nothing to do with her at all.

She stole a long glance at him as he drove. He looked back, questioning, and she said, "Are you worried?"

"No. More like concerned."

"About what?"

"Nothing. Everything. Sarah. You. Finding Starke. Finding Corinne's brother if he's here. Stuff. Just stuff."

Garland turned his attention back to the road. A few seconds later he said, "Polly, look, I don't want to mislead you."

Ah, here it comes, she thought. "Mislead me about what?"

"What I mean is, I just don't want this to get too personal."

Polly looked away and smiled that little ironic smile to herself and shook her head. "Sure. No problem. Nothing personal."

"Please, believe me, it's not anything about you."

Ah, the 'it's not you, it's me' speech. How many times had she heard that one? "Like I said, Nathaniel, not a problem. We're adults, we're smart, we're professionals. Let's keep it professional."

Several silent miles passed beneath the Expedition and then Polly looked at him said, "So why the tzo mei toe?"

"Me? Tzo mei toe?"

"Yes."

"I have some serious issues I'm trying to work through."

"You mean like the insulin you keep in your refrigerator?"

Garland watched the road as he spoke. "Sometimes I miss my family so much it overwhelms me. It feels like I'm being crushed. Like it's physical. The void they left in my life is sometimes so excruciating, I just want to," he paused, searching for the right words. "That's when I consider the alternatives."

"You've never tried? Never attempted?"

267

"No. Thought about it. But never tried. Not that I'm afraid of it." Garland shrugged. "As I said, I have some issues to work through."

"We all do, Nathaniel. God knows I've got mine."

"So you understand why we, no, I'll speak for myself, why I can't make this personal?"

"Sure. I totally understand. I just want to know one thing, I mean, speaking of 'personal' – what do you call what happened last night?"

Garland paused a long time and exhaled slowly. "I call it one of the most beautiful nights of my life."

Not the answer Polly was expecting. She was suddenly speechless. "Really," she finally said as flatly as she could.

"Yeah," he confirmed. "Really."

60

As Garland filled the Expedition's bottomless tank at the solitary Amaco station in Ripton, he gazed out at a crooked finger of Bull Shoals Lake gesturing to him from just down the hill.

The travel brochures they picked up at the hotel described Bull Shoals Lake as having over a thousand miles of shoreline, but that statistic now seemed like a gross understatement. The lake surface itself extended over two states, six counties, and covered well over 71,000 acres. Surrounding the lake were a myriad of lazy one-road towns, villages and enclaves cut out of old forests and balanced precariously in the Ozark foothills. Hundreds of rickety resorts and small boat docks toed the endless shoreline. Out of sight and off the beaten paths, thousands of remote cabins and cottages lurked in the woods and gullies and hollows. If someone was determined to hide there, they would never be found.

Polly came out of the ladies' room and joined Garland as he squeegeed the rear window. She looked down at the lake as she pulled some paper towels out of the dispenser and handed them to him.

"Lake is way bigger than I imagined. I don't know how you're going to find what you don't even know what you're looking for."

"It's the amebiasis. If the Fish & Wildlife guy can help us find the source of the outbreak and then track its spread through the snake population, maybe we'll find everything else. And without being too obvious, look over my right shoulder and see if that big guy with the beard in the red pickup is still watching us."

Polly tensed, then glanced over his shoulder as casually as her nerves would allow. "Yes."

"Thought so. Okay. Plan B."

"What's Plan B?"

"I don't know yet. I was hoping to stick with Plan A all the way."

They got back into the Expedition and Garland pulled out of the station. He looked in the rearview and saw the red pickup, a beautifully restored 1958 Chevy Apache, pull away from the curb and make a U-turn to follow them. Polly looked over her shoulder, out the back window.

"He's following."

Garland gripped the wheel. "Big beard, bright classic truck, subtle, isn't he? Don't worry about him. Worry about the guys we don't see."

They drove the thirty miles to Bolton without incident and had no trouble finding a parking space in the center of town. The red Chevy Apache squirted past them and continued on when the bearded driver realized they had parked in front of the sheriff substation.

Bolton was a charming Ozark summer vacation town consisting of a quaint main street with maybe three traffic lights from end to end, a row of whitewashed shops, a diner, a 7-Eleven, a Tastee-Freeze, a Conoco gas station and a smattering of bait, antique and souvenir shops.

"Welcome to Mayberry," Garland said.

With Bolton as their center point and using Arleta Farliegh's hastily prepared list as a guide, Garland and Polly spent the remainder of the day checking out every hospital, convalescent home, hospice, women's health center and every other health care facility within a twenty-five mile radius. They showed photos of Corinne and Sarah at every venue and, in the hospitals and urgent care centers they visited, they also showed photographs and a swatch of Corinne's unique hospital gown. None of the people they spoke with recognized either Sarah or Corinne and none of the facilities ever used that particular gown.

Frustrated and disappointed, Garland held the door for Polly as they exited the Mountain Home Medical Center. Polly finally said, "You think all those people were lying?"

"No. That would mean there's a conspiracy of silence here and there's far too many people involved. Whatever happened to Corinne, wherever Sarah is, it's just below the radar."

As they walked past Courthouse Square, out of the corner of his eye, Garland thought he spotted the red Apache through the trees on the other side of the square, but he wasn't sure. He did, however, have the very distinct sense that they were being watched.

And then he saw it. Not the red Apache. The hearse. It had made a right turn past Courthouse Square onto Washington. Polly turned to Garland's gaze. She immediately saw the license plates, too: the distinctive black and yellow Calvert and Crossland flag colors between the embossed numerals on the hearse – Maryland plates.

Afraid that he would lose the hearse in the time it would take for Polly and him to get back to the Expedition, Garland took off at a full run after it. He jumped the low black iron link fence like a cross-country equestrian and cut diagonally across the square, churning through the freshly bedded Autumn Joy Sedum and Dragonwing Begonias – to the absolute horror of the assembled court watchers. The hearse driver did not notice Garland chasing him as it lumbered lazily up the street.

At the far end of the square, two young mothers were pushing toddlers in sleek three-wheeled strollers. Garland cut right to jump the far iron link fence, but the mothers had stopped to retrieve something one of the toddlers had heaved from the stroller. Garland was forced to abort his leap, and instead slid across the grass and pinwheeled like a Canada Goose lawn ornament to keep himself from falling. It didn't help. He took the fence short, caught his foot and tumbled over it, rolling to his left across the rough cement sidewalk to avoid hitting the strollers. The young moms couldn't react fast enough as Garland scrambled to his feet and, limping now, ran into the street.

A flock of senior mom-and-pop Harley riders, complete with matching stars-and-stripes helmets, had turned right on Courthouse and had to zig-zag maniacally to avoid hitting Garland or each other. They swerved around him, swearing loudly and giving him one-finger salutes. He had to wait for an opening between them before darting across the street. But he still had his eyes on the hearse. He tore after it, ignoring the throbbing pain in his left knee and watched it pull into a wide driveway halfway down the block.

Breathing hard, Garland reached the driveway on a full run just as the hearse driver was getting out. The driveway was a parking lot entrance. The building sign read "Furnham & Breech Mortuary - Since 1946" – and then, in much smaller letters, Garland saw the magic words: "A Turner/Eterna Company".

The hearse driver, a tall, blondish man in his mid-twenties was startled to see Garland racing toward him. He retreated back into the car, but before he could close the door, Garland had wedged himself against it and grabbed the young man by the coat.

"Get out. Get out of the car," Garland yelled, now breathing even harder as the first wave of adrenalin kicked in.

"Nyet, nyet." The man, obviously frightened, and just as obviously Russian, clung tenaciously to the steering wheel."

Garland pulled his badge from his jacket pocket with one hand while he still tugged at the man's coat.

"Did you hear me? Get out of the car."

"Я не говорить по-английски," the young man yelled back over and over, meaning, 'I don't speak English.'

"But you understand English?" Despite his excitement and breathiness, Garland modulated his voice.

The young man shook his head violently. "Nyet, nyet."

Behind them, the siren of the sheriff's patrol car came in short warning bursts as it slid into the driveway and braked just a few yards short of the hearse. Garland released his grip on the hearse driver's coat, stepped back, but kept the door wedged open. He tucked his badge case into jacket pocket to display the gold shield and opened his jacket just enough to reveal his holstered sidearm. A crowd began to gather. Polly stepped her way through, as Lyle Krauss, the deputy sheriff, approached Garland.

The young deputy's forest green pants and tan uniform shirt were pressed as stiff as lumber. His shoes were shined to a mirror finish and his blondish hair was buzzed flat as a table. Garland immediately noticed the huge caliber sidearm holstered at his hip. Military all the way, Garland thought, probably trained as an MP.

"Problem, sir?" He said to Garland.

Krauss, who was probably thirty-two, had very little in the way of an Arkansas accent. Garland guessed that he wasn't a native.

"Thank you, officer..." Garland read the engraved nametag pinned to the deputy's shirt, "...Krauss. Special Agent Garland, BIA." He signaled to Polly who came forward. "This is Dr. Collier. We want to take a look inside the casket this man is transporting."

"Sir?"

"The casket, officer, let's pull it out."

The mortuary door flew open and Howard Furnham, the mortuary's director, charged out into the parking lot. Despite his advanced senior status, his crest of linen white hair and his well cut dark charcoal pinstripe suit, Furnham made clear that he was not one to be easily intimated.

"What the hell is going on here?"

Lyle Krauss spoke before Garland could respond. "Howard, this is Federal Agent Garland. He's got a concern about the casket in your hearse here. Agent Garland, Howard Furnham, owner of the company."

"What concern about the casket? What do you want?"

"Part of an ongoing Federal investigation, Mr. Furnham. I just want to look at the body in the casket and then inside your mortuary, if you don't mind."

"Mind? Damn right I mind. What kind of bullshit is this?"

"Mr. Furnham, I'm investigating nine homicides and the abduction of a Federal officer. These occurred in Maryland. Your hearse has Maryland plates. A similar hearse ran down seven..."

"Right, I got it, Simmonds place on Burning Tree. It's been all over the company. I know all about it. What's that got to do with us here?"

"Hopefully nothing. But your funeral home is part of the Turner/Eterna chain and I'm curious as to why a mortuary vehicle in Arkansas has Maryland plates?"

"Yeah? Well take your goddamned curiosity to my lawyer."

Garland glanced over his shoulder toward the courthouse. "Mr. Furnham, in ten minutes I can have a warrant to take your place apart brick by brick. In an hour, I can have more Federal officers here than you can count. All I'm asking for is a little cooperation."

"You get your goddamned warrant and I'll get my lawyer and we'll talk about probable cause and..."

"Howard, Howard…" Krauss interrupted, raising his hands like a referee. "Just a minute. Now hold on. You have nothing to hide here, right? Huh? Am I right? Do you have anything to hide?" He spoke slowly and distinctly.

"That's not the point Lyle. There are significant privacy issues here."

"And we are all aware of those issues. But do you really want to raise everyone's dander with warrants and FBI agents and such? Huh? Am I right? So how about we accommodate Mr. Garland here, he gets his look-see and moves on, no harm, no foul. Huh?"

It took less than ten minutes for mortuary attendants to wheel out a chrome gurney, retrieve the casket from the hearse and bring it downstairs to the prep rooms. Polly and Lyle Krauss stood back as Furnham opened the casket for Garland. They all leaned forward as the top half of the lid opened like a shiny convertible.

The occupant of the casket, one Mr. William Huckabee, 71, a retired railroad worker from nearby Cochrane, had apparently died of natural causes. Garland and Polly scrutinized his face and upper body and found nothing extraordinary.

"Satisfied?" Howard Furnham said.

"Let's see the others," Garland said.

They then all moved into the prep room to examine Furnham's other reposed clients. He had two: a middle aged male jogger who was struck by a tour bus and an older, not elderly, woman who apparently died of a myocardial infarction. Both clients were resting on stainless steel embalming tables, uncovered and uncaring, but only the male jogger exhibited the breast to belly thoracic "Y" incision of a recent autopsy.

As Garland examined the deceased man, Polly scrutinized the woman. An incision on the left side of the woman's head, just below her ear, caught Polly's attention. She touched the incision with her gloved hand and felt a sticky, putty like substance.

275

"Mr. Furnham, could you please tell me why there's an incision here?"

Garland moved with Furnham to examine the woman's head. Lyle Krauss held back at the door.

Furnham glanced at the putty filled wound and shook his head. "You'll have to ask my cosmetician when she gets back. My best guess is the client must have struck her head when she fell, gashed her skull, it's very common."

"But she wasn't autopsied," Garland said.

"Apparently not."

"If she struck her head..."

"You'll have to ask the M.E. about it." Furnham picked up the clip chart hanging from the foot of the embalming table. "This woman was an itinerant. There's no history. Ask the M.E."

"Are you through here, Dr. Garland?" It was clear that Furnham was definitely annoyed and had had enough.

"For now." Garland slowly peeled off his gloves, further annoying Furnham, then said, "Tell me again why the hearse has Maryland plates."

"I didn't tell you once. You never asked. Just intimidated my driver."

"Well I'm asking now."

"The home office rotates rolling stock where needed, simple as that."

"But you have five other hearses in your parking lot. Seems like a lot of 'rolling stock' for such a small population."

"It's a dying town, doctor."

"Yeah."

"If that's all, I have a business to take care of. So if you don't mind…?"

"Thank you for your cooperation, Mr. Furnham, "we'll find our way out."

"Please do." Furnham said. Then he turned to the attendant and jutted his chin and added, "Theo, please escort our guests out of the building."

Furnham waited until he heard the upstairs door close and moved out of the prep room with Krauss. Both men were tense.

"You think they knew?" Furnham asked. "I mean, where Charlene took off that extra ear."

"Yeah, they knew. Where did you put the other stiffs?"

"Under the stock room. And I've asked you countless times not to refer to them as 'stiffs'. Now I've got to get them out of there or I'll never get the odor out."

"Then do it."

"This isn't what I sold the company for. You tell Starke I'm not taking any more of these clients. No more. You tell him."

Krauss unclipped his cell phone from his belt. "Here." He handed the phone to Furnham. "Tell him yourself."

61

As he walked around Courthouse Square, back to the Expedition, Polly asked, "You think they were lying?"

"Bet the farm on it."

"What do you think that incision was on the cadaver?"

"I don't know. It was deep. Something was definitely excised above the maxilla below her ear. Could have been anything. Or nothing." Garland stopped. "What would you guess the population of this town is?"

"I don't know. I'm so bad about these kinds of things. Ten to twelve thousand, maybe, I don't know."

"I'd guess about the same. So then let me ask you this – why would a town this size need a national mortuary chain?"

"I don't know. Why would they need three Starbucks?" They began walking again and Polly asked, "How's the knee?"

"Hurts like hell."

"You're not very good at this, are you?"

"No, but I am getting better."

The drive from Mountain Home to the lake was much closer than they had anticipated and, with Polly navigating and Garland driving, they made it back to Bolton within a half hour. They continued north, through town, approximately eleven miles, then west on Poplar Creek Road to Fass Landing, a town much smaller than Bolton, but which boasted a new concrete boat ramp. Garland pulled off the rural county road onto the graveled parking area of Wee Willy's Fish 'n' Fowl, the sole bait and tackle shop in town.

Garland bought boots and waders for both of them and some warm Pendleton shirts and jeans for Polly. And then they were back on the so-called road.

Although Garland continually checked his mirrors, there was no sighting of the red Apache or its bearded driver.

Within a mile, the already narrow county road constricted to little more than a half paved logging road, certainly not wide enough for two large vehicles to easily pass one another, yet they were surprised when at least a half-dozen cars passed them coming from the opposite direction. The road was riddled with potholes the size of wading pools and the red mud shoulder was dangerously soft. Garland engaged the Expedition's four-wheel drive as they continued to wend through a vibrant forest of magnificently twisted sycamores and towering cottonwoods, beautiful old alders, dogwoods and redbud trees.

As Garland concentrated on the difficult driving conditions, Polly took in the magnificent scenery and heady fragrance of the woods. They were about five or six miles in when she first spotted the coiled razor wire on a modest hill to their right and pointed it out to Garland. As they got closer, they could see that the wire was part of a very tall security fence that stretched into the woods and disappeared into the heavy growth. Within a few minutes, several old and very dilapidated low buildings – barracks, really – appeared on a soft rise behind the fence. From what they could see from the road, the windows on all of the structures in view were boarded up and their brown and tan paint had long ago surrendered to the ravages of sun and rain. As they drove on, the razor wire fencing and the old structures trapped behind it seemed to stretch for at least another mile and a half, maybe two.

"What do you suppose that was?" Polly asked.

"Looks like an old fort, an abandoned military base of some kind."

"All the way out here in the middle of nowhere? I mean, how far are we from anything even resembling a real road?"

"It's probably one of those old POW camps."

"What are you talking about?"

"During World War II, the War Department built hundreds of POW camps in the U.S., almost all of them are inland, hundreds of miles from any coast, for obvious reasons. They're all over the south, midwest, southwest. I think they built six or seven hundred camps here."

"I suppose if you had to be a POW, this was not such a bad place to be."

"Maybe that's why so many prisoners didn't go home after the war. They stayed, married locals, raised their kids here, blended right in. Hey, yesterday's immigrant is tomorrow's Governor."

Polly smiled. "*Měi-gúo*," she said. "You gotta love this place."

Larry Dugan was waiting for them, kneeling on the delta at the mouth of Sweetwater Creek, taking water samples and storing the test tubes in a plastic box. He was no more than a hundred yards from the road, but it was the longest hundred yards Garland and Polly could have imagined. Their new knee-high boots didn't make the slog through the thick, gummy mud any easier. Dugan barely looked up as Garland and Polly approached.

"You folks are late," he said by way of greeting.

'*And hello to you, too*,' Garland thought to himself, but instead said without apology, "It was a little trickier navigating here than we anticipated."

Dugan took another water sample and then slowly stood up — and kept standing up until he reached his full six-six height. And with his regulation U.S. Fish and Wildlife Service Ranger Rick hat perched high on his head, the entire package topped out at nearly seven feet. He would have been intimidating except for the fact that he was as thin as the pussy willows lining the creek bank and probably weighed as much.

Without making eye contact, Dugan said, "Well, there's nothing you can learn out here that I didn't already tell your forensics specialist in D.C."

"Sometimes it helps to come right to the source. You get a better perspective on things. Like you showing us where you found the initial amebiasis infestation. Where were the infected snakes?"

"Over there," Dugan said, waving vaguely toward the mouth of the creek.

"Mr. Dugan, would you mind showing us exactly where."

Larry Dugan sighed loudly. He moved down the shore and stood at the point where the tendrils of the two creeks meandered out from the body of the lake. He pointed at the 'Y'. "Right here. Looked like a die-off. Hundreds of 'em. Had your Copperheads, Cottonmouths, Corals, then your non-venomous milks and kings…they were dying all over, scaring the anglers and tourists."

"Anywhere else around the lake?"

"No place else. Just right here."

"And you're sure it was an amebiasis infestation?"

"It's my job to know. Collected the parasites myself. Yeah. I'm sure."

"Mr. Dugan," Garland said, "before this, when was the last snake die-off around the lake?"

"Few years back."

"And did you trace the source?"

"Infected Leopard Frogs from up north – Missouri shore."

"But it didn't get this far south."

"That's what I just said."

"Then where do you suppose this localized infestation came from?"

"How the hell should I know? We don't have budget or manpower to investigate every die-off like we used to."

Garland could feel his body tense. Polly could see it, too. It was the same tense stance she had witnessed in the restaurant parking lot when Garland nearly beat the life out of her husband. She quickly moved to him and lightly touched his arm.

"I think we've got it, Dr. Garland."

"Good. So if you're all finished here..." Dugan said as he snapped his sampling kit closed, "I'm leaving."

"Hang on a minute. Where does the creek go?"

Larry Dugan spoke as if it was a supreme effort. "Nowhere. It wanders past the camp, through Hugger Wood and dies just out past Route 15, 'cept in the rain. You got it? You mind I go now?"

"Yes. I do." Garland spoke softly and evenly, keeping a strangulation grip on his rising temper. "Is that the camp we passed driving in?"

Dugan nodded. "Camp Henry Hugger."

"POW camp?"

"What do you think?"

Garland took a step forward toward Dugan. Dugan took two steps back.

"Mr. Dugan, I'm trying to be very civil here and I expect the same of you. I don't know what your problem is, but if you answer me one more time like that, I'm going to rip your fucking head off and shove it so far up your ass you'll have to breathe through your dick. Is that clear enough for you?"

Garland took another step forward and again Dugan took two steps back, planting himself ankle deep in the lake.

"Nathaniel. Don't. Please."

Dugan was visibly frightened, but gathered his bravado and took one last shot at Garland. "Why don't you folks just ask your lying friends back in Washington? Thieving it out from us and then coming down here and acting all dumb and all."

"Excuse me? And while you're at it, get out of the lake."

Dugan stepped forward. "You know damn well what I'm saying. All the camp land, all Hugger Wood, the creek...you know damn well what I mean."

"No. I don't. Tell me."

"Trying to make the fool of me again."

"Mr. Dugan, I haven't a clue what you're talking about."

"You're telling me straight-faced you don't know the DOD was handing all this land to Interior. Everything here's Army. The Corps of Engineers run the lake, the dam and manage all seventeen parks. You don't know that?"

"No. So what you're saying is the Army was going to cede the old POW camp and the surrounding forest to the Department of Interior."

"Damn right. We worked our tails off nearly three years on plans to make it into a showcase campground. Then DOD reneged and gave it somewhere else."

"Who'd they give it to?"

"Don't know. Didn't say. We had a deal. All sixty acres of the camp, the woods, the two creeks…like you didn't know."

"Mr. Dugan, I can honestly say I didn't know.

"Well, sir, then you are way out of the loop because you're the only one who don't."

62

Bull Shoals Lake had already begun to settle in for the night as Garland and Polly slogged through the gummy red muck back to the road. His frustration was palpable as he tried repeatedly to get a signal on his cell phone.

Garland tossed the cell down. "I need a landline."

"I don't think you're going to find too many out here. And please slow down. I can't keep up."

Garland did, offering his hand to help her through the deeper patches of mud. At the SUV, Garland turned and jutted his chin toward the shore. "She was here. Corinne. Forensic evidence proved that she was in the creek." Garland peeled off his muddy boots and threw them into the hatch door then helped Polly out of hers.

They climbed in the Expedition and Garland had to make a difficult mud-sucking U-turn to get back on the road. Darkness came quickly.

"I've got to get some resources down here," he continued, "comb every inch of the creek, the camp, the forest…"

"Do you see how big this lake is? It's enormous. And how many thousands of square miles surround it? Corinne could have come from anywhere and ended up here. She could have walked. Could have come along the shoreline or even crossed the lake in a rowboat, for godsakes."

"C'mon, it's a duck."

"What's a duck?"

"A duck. If it looks like a duck, walks like a duck and quacks like a duck, it's a duck. Didn't you learn that in med school?"

"No. We used horse. If it looks like a horse, gallops like a horse, yadda yadda. Where did you go?"

"UCLA. You?"

"Baylor."

"Well it figures Baylor would use a horse. Every other place it's a duck."

Garland had to slow for some potholes. Even with the SUV's high beams on now, it was still difficult to gauge the depth of some of the holes. As he drove, Klieg-like headlights suddenly sliced across the Expedition's windshield and both Garland and Polly had to avert their eyes. The headlights swung in a tight arc, cutting across the road, so that a few seconds later the offending car's lights were illuminating the road ahead in the same direction as the Expedition.

"Where'd he come from?" Polly squeezed her eyes momentarily.

"Over there. There's a road cutting up the hill there. See it? It runs diagonally toward the lake. That's why we didn't see it coming in, the entry faces the opposite direction."

Garland slowed to a crawl, scrutinizing the opposite side of the road until he spotted the diagonal road entry. He stopped the Expedition and stared at it.

"Jeez," Polly said, "no signs, no markings, not even a reflector."

"I have to see what's up there," he said quietly. "Look, I can't leave you here. I can't leave you alone in our cottage or whatever it is."

"Nathaniel. I know. I'm fine. Really."

286

"I could take you to Bolton…"

"No. That's ridiculous."

"What did you do with the gun I put on your nightstand in Fayetteville?"

"It's in my purse."

"Get it. Please."

She rummaged through her purse and gingerly withdrew the rubber gripped .38 P Special. She placed it in Garland's outstretched hand.

"Look. This is the safety," he said, demonstrating the slide. "Before the gun can be fired you have to ease this back. It won't fire unless you do. Okay?"

Garland turned it and offered the grip back to Polly. She didn't accept it.

"Do you know how much I hate guns?"

"Yeah. Me, too. Until you need one." He nudged it toward her. "Please. Take it. Hate it if you want, but respect it."

Polly reluctantly took the gun from him and put it on her lap. She then watched as Garland opened his badge case and fold it into his jacket pocket to display the badge as if it was pinned to his breast. He opened his jacket and unsnapped the restraining strap across the holster of his sidearm, securing his jacket so that his gun was displayed as well as the badge. As Polly watched him prepare, a frisson of fear shuddered through her body and embarrassed her. Even if Garland saw it, she knew he wouldn't mention it.

"I'm sorry I'm such a pain. I shouldn't have come, I should have stayed."

"There was no way I was going to leave you alone in D.C." He put the SUV in gear. "Keep your eyes open and watch my six."

"What?"

Garland grinned. "Watch my back. My pé gu," meaning, 'my ass'.

He wheeled the Expedition across the road and up the gently sloped path that ran diagonally to the lower road. The path, which was not much more than wide rutted tire tracks with weeds and scrub grass flourishing between them, quickly curved back to a perpendicular direction. Within fifty yards, the path flattened out and ran parallel to a high iron fence crowned in coiled razor wire. The shiny, rust free razor wire reflected the Expeditions headlights, indicating to Garland that it was relatively new. A few seconds later, it opened on to a large flat dirt pad, the size of several baseball diamonds. At the far end of the pad was a high electrified iron gate mounted on a steel track.

Garland pulled up to the gate and stopped. He leaned forward, pressing his chest against the steering wheel as he surveyed the gate and its attendant security features. There was a numeric touch pad and ID sensor at driver height on the left side. Two remote servo cameras were mounted on the twin iron pillars that supported the gate. Beyond the fence and gate, illuminated by the Expedition's bright headlights, was an old cracked paved road that wound under an ancient wooden arch across which was burnished the weathered, barely legible inscription: "Camp Henry Hugger". The road continued through a thin stand of alders, oaks and sycamores. There were several low buildings behind the trees, but they appeared dilapidated and boarded up. From inside the SUV, Garland could not discern any lights or illumination from any of the structures beyond the gate, but that, he told himself, didn't mean nobody was home.

The Expedition idled smoothly as Garland reached for the door handle. "When I get out, scoot over behind the wheel and lock the doors."

Polly nodded and clenched the gun in her lap.

Outside the confines of the SUV, Garland was greeted by a loud symphonic cacophony of nature's night music: owls, crickets, frogs, wild pigs and gangs of small mammals arguing over water rights. He accustomed himself to the rich sounds, the intoxicating woodsy fragrances and the rural darkness and then walked slowly toward the gate, careful not to put himself directly in front of the Expedition's headlights. Why make himself an easier target, he thought.

As he walked, he slid his eyes from security camera to camera, but neither camera acknowledged his movement. The servos were definitely asleep. When he reached the gate he peered through the black iron tines, but could see nothing beyond the throw of the Expedition's headlights. He instinctively tried to pull the gate open, but it didn't give an inch, as he knew it wouldn't. Then he bent down to the guide track and ran his finger over several links of the gate's drive chain; from the feel alone he knew it was recently lubricated. There was no doubt this was a working gate. This was a working facility.

On the security monitors, from the comfort of his home, Norman Starke watched Garland examine the gate. He knew that the agent would eventually find The 610, but he didn't expect him to find it this fast. He needed a few more days to dispose of the remaining clients, but Furnham's mortuary was hot now – impractical and unusable – and a parade of hearses out of The 610 would bring an army of Feds to their doorstep. He knew Garland would be back very soon.

So did Garland.

63

As they bumped along the ruts, Garland tried his cell again. He still couldn't get a decent signal and jammed the phone into his pocket.

Polly touched his arm. "We'll be at the motel or whatever in a few minutes. I'm sure they have phones," then added, "I don't mean to be a kvetch, but I am really hungry."

"Kvetch?" Garland allowed an amused smile. "Where did you get 'kvetch'?"

"Well if you can speak Chinese, I can speak Yiddish."

"Why, you think I'm Jewish?"

"I'm sorry, is there someone on this planet who thinks you're not?"

For the first time since they had met, Garland laughed out loud. It wasn't a big belly laugh, but enough to incite Polly to smile with him.

She waited a long beat, then asked, "Was Daisy Jewish?"

"No, a recovering Catholic." He shrugged. "Perfect match, right? Jewish guilt and Catholic shame?"

"I'm sure you were a perfect match."

They reached the paved county road and Garland headed south, back toward Bolton. "Keep your eyes peeled for anything resembling a restaurant. And while you're at it, look for Al 'N' Sal's Come On Inn."

Completely shrouded from the county road behind a thick stand of old growth woods, Al 'N' Sal's was practically impossible to find in the dark. It was an old-fashioned family style resort with thirty or so cabins and whitewashed clapboard cottages sprinkled at odd angles throughout the pleasant grounds. To the north was a "kiddie beach" comprised of fine white sand hauled in from the gulf coast. To the south was an old, long, skinny wooden pier that seemed to be giving the lake the finger.

A hand-painted sign off the main road guided them along the twisting service path to the resort office where a small handwritten card in the window instructed them to ring the office doorbell to summon an attendant. Curiously, neither Polly nor Garland could tell if it was Al or Sal who registered them. Polly thought it was Sal because she thought there was a hint of breasts beneath the thick plaid shirt, but Garland guessed it was Al, based on little more evidence than the trace of an Adam's apple. Garland registered for two nights on the off chance they would require a second day at Bull Shoals – and he paid in cash. This gesture bought him the pick of the litter and Al, or Sal, offered them an upgrade to the deluxe lakeside cottage – two bedrooms and a kitchenette. As for food, Al, or Sal, suggested the all-night IHOP or, since the cottage did have a kitchenette, they could go down the road a half-mile to the Ozark Foods Market and get fixings to cook their own dinner.

As Al or Sal was unlocking the cabin for them, Garland asked, "You know anyone around here who drives a cherry Chevy Apache pickup?"

Al or Sal said, "Would it happen to have a driver with a big red beard?"

"That would be it."

"Then that would be Enos Hostettler, our resident conspiracy theorist. One of those Area 54 kooks. Your vehicle have any government markings on it?"

"Government plates and a CDC insignia decal in the back window."

"Well that's probably how Enos zeroed in on you."

"What particular conspiracy is Mr. Hostettler's cause?"

"Aliens conducting experiments on people they capture."

"Really."

"Says he was captured in Fayetteville once but escaped. Like I said, sir, he's harmless, just wearing his hat too tight."

The cottage was surprisingly clean and spacious. While Polly examined the kitchenette to determine what they'll need to cook, Garland found the phone and called Eugene Kessler. He deftly finessed through the small talk and got right to the point – he needed Kessler's help to find out everything he could about Camp Henry Hugger.

"What t'hell is Camp Henry Hugger?"

"An old POW camp in the Arkansas boonies."

"And DOD is ceding it to another department?"

"That's what Ranger Rick tells me. Get me everything you can, Gene. Everything."

"How soon?"

"You might have to wake up a few friends. I'm going in there tomorrow morning and I really have to know what I'm walking into."

"I'm on it, cowboy. Keep your shorts on and I'll get back to you posthaste."

Finding the supermarket was easy. Deciding on dinner was more difficult. Garland wanted something light, Polly could eat a truck. They compromised. Garland would have eggs, toast and a banana, Polly would have a salad and pasta with blackened chicken. They also bought juice, cereal, milk, tea and coffee for the morning.

They were almost back to the cottage when Garland thought he spotted it. He kept glancing at the mirrors, a gesture not lost on Polly.

"Look out the back window," he told her, keeping his voice casual. "You see anything behind us?"

Polly turned in her seat and stared out the large rear window. "Nothing but night," she reported.

"Keep watching."

Garland took his foot off the accelerator to slow but didn't touch the brakes. Then they saw it almost simultaneously.

"What is that?" Polly was frightened now.

"Brake lights on a road reflector – and they're not mine. Somebody's stupid, drunk or following us with their headlights off. They forgot about their brake lights." He gripped the wheel tighter and said, "Buckle up."

Garland floored the accelerator and the boxy SUV shot forward as if it was stung in the ass. He kept it floored for a few seconds and then yelled at Polly to hang on. He took a few more seconds to orient himself, then snapped off the Expedition's headlights and suddenly swerved to the opposite side of the road, resisting his urge to hit the brake pedal. Driving now with only the moon for light, he let the tires find the loose rough shoulder of the pavement and just steered as straight as he could. Low hanging branches and prickly bushes along the narrow shoulder insulted the right side of the Expedition as they gouged chunks of paint from the rear door and quarter panel. The SUV bounced and shuddered wildly across the dips and Polly couldn't help but swear loudly. Garland stood on the parking brake pedal, firmly applying more leg to slow the Expedition. As he did, bright headlights from the vehicle that was behind them snapped on like flashbulbs and ripped past them in a loud 'whoosh'. The driver had turned on his lights too late to see them. But they saw him. Enos Hostettler's Chevy Apache.

For several long minutes, Garland and Polly sat in the darkness accompanied by the songs of insects and owls and their own pounding hearts. When he found his voice, Garland said, "Are you still hungry?"

"Are your jokes supposed to make me feel better?"

"Did it work?"

"No." Polly swallowed and took a breath. "Do you think he'll come back as soon as he figures out what you did?"

"Yeah."

Another silence ensued and then she said, "What do you think he wants?"

"I haven't a clue," Garland said. "Tell me the truth, no false bravado, okay? I have to know that you're okay with what we're doing here."

"I know." She turned now to look at him, even though he was just a faint shadow in the dark. "I'd be lying if I said I wasn't scared."

"I'd be lying, too, if I said I wasn't scared. But this is something I have to do. For Sarah. For Corinne. You don't. We can find a safe place for you. Get you on a plane somewhere. Something, I don't know, I haven't thought it through. We can drive to Little Rock or Memphis right now, they're just a few hours away."

"And do what, Nathaniel? Go where from there?"

"I don't know. We'll figure it out."

Garland flicked on the Expedition's headlights and drove directly back to Al 'N' Sal's Come On Inn. But instead of parking at the front door of their cottage as he had when they checked in, he drove around to the back, parked nearer the lake, but he kept the engine running. It was only when he opened the SUV's door and the dome lights came on that he saw how truly frightened Polly looked.

He reached up and turned off the dome lights. He didn't want the interior lights coming on again when the vehicle doors were opened.

"When I get out, same drill as before. Get behind the wheel, lock the doors and keep the engine running. Hopefully, I'll be right back.

64

"Leave the key in the ignition, doors unlocked," Garland said when he returned. He scooped up his laptop from the backseat and looked up at her. "Which bag has your essentials and stuff?"

"That one," she said, indicating the small carryon. "What about our suitcases?"

"Leave the luggage. Take the groceries."

"The Godfather."

"What?"

"The movie. The Godfather. Remember? After Clemenza and the young thug killed Paulie, you know, the guy who fingered Marlon Brando at the fruit stand, Clemenza says, 'leave the gun, take the cannoli'."

Garland stared at her and then just shook his head in mock disbelief.

"But I need clothes and stuff in my suitcase."

"Take what you need. We're just going to eat. We're not staying here."

Once inside the cottage, they prepared dinner together. The conversation was easy and remarkably comfortable for both of them. After dinner they did the dishes together. Then, allowing that the water was hot and plentiful, Polly announced she was going to take a quick shower. Heading toward the bathroom, she stopped and looked back at him.

"Can I ask you an off-the-wall question?"

"Of course."

"I'm curious, after you — what's the word? — dismantled - Jensen-Dillard Pharmaceuticals, before Herbert Jensen went to jail, how did you get him to give up every penny of his personal stake in the company? I mean, all his pensions and perks and bonuses and hidden stuff? He gave you every penny, didn't he?"

"You've been talking to Grove, haven't you?" Garland said.

"He told me most of it. But he said he didn't know how you got to Jensen or how you convinced him."

"That's because I never told him."

"I thought he was your best friend?"

"Which is exactly why I never told him."

Polly nodded her understanding and moved off to the shower. Garland went to the wobbly wooden desk, opened his laptop and snapped in a USB 4G modem. Once online, he Googled the Turner/Eterna holding company. It took him less than ten minutes to find the pattern he knew was there. When Polly emerged from the bathroom, smelling sweetly of coconut and vanilla, Garland waved her over. She was dressed, but barefoot, and blotting her hair with one of Al 'N' Sal's thin cotton towels.

"Take a look at this."

She moved to the desk and scrunched over his shoulder. On the screen was the Google Earth map of the mid-Atlantic and southeastern U.S. There was a crescent of blue dots designating cities from Baltimore to St. Louis.

Polly straightened up. "You showed me this yesterday."

"No, no." Garland Alt-Tabbed the keyboard to reveal another map, almost identical, except it had red dots over the same cities instead of blue dots. "I showed you *this* map yesterday."

"Okay, one has red dots and one has blue dots. So?"

Garland Alt-Tabbed again and a third map came up, this one superimposing the red dots over the blue dots. "Red are the medical and bio-tech facilities associated with the Evinco Vixi papers. The blue dots are locations of Turner/Eterna mortuaries."

"They're practically the same. There's a Turner mortuary in every one of those cities."

"You know that old adage, 'doctors bury their mistakes'?"

"Corrine Burch?"

"And you have to know she's not the only one." Garland logged off, shut down his laptop and got up. "Now tell me why Furnham had five hearses in his lot?"

Polly looked at him, the reasoning was clear. But before she could respond, the first firebomb exploded through the front window, blowing them both to the floor.

65

They heard the second Molotov burst across the split cedar roof and Garland immediately lunged for Polly. The third cocktail smashed into the cottage through the side casement and the blue ethanol flames spread like juicy gossip across the tinder dry wooden floor. Some of the accelerant splashed on Garland's left arm and ignited his shirt. He leapt up from the floor.

"Get out. Get out," he yelled at Polly as he furiously flapped his arm, trying to shake the tenacious flames feasting on his shirtsleeve.

Within seconds, the fire had swept across the small room like a tidal wave. It climbed the walls and cascaded in an arc back across the ceiling.

Polly rushed at Garland, snapping open her hair towel. They collided and fell to the floor again. Now on top of him, she smothered the flames on his arm in the wet towel and the two of them rolled across the floor toward the kitchenette.

Suffocating toxic smoke was now flooding every corner of the small room; the light bulbs in the room exploded in a strange drumbeat.

In the kitchenette, Garland spun to his feet, pulling Polly up with him.

"Gas line," she yelled.

The flames circled closer, jabbing at them. Garland ripped the towel from his arm, turned on the faucet and soaked it. Then, holding it up like a shield in front of them, he pulled Polly through the hungry flames toward the front door. The molten doorknob seared Garland's hand, igniting a surge of electrifying pain up his arm that rattled his teeth, but it wasn't enough to stop him. Using the wet towel, he twisted the knob and threw the door open.

A shotgun blast from outside splintered the door just inches from Garland's head. He would have slammed the door closed if there was any door left to slam. Another blast tore through the window frame just to their right. The next shot would have leveled them.

"Back," Garland yelled."

"I can't...breathe."

"Grab my waist."

Again, using the towel as a shield, Garland pulled Polly through the inferno toward what he hoped would be the bathroom. He didn't know, he couldn't see it. He could feel his hair singe and his clothes about to ignite. Ten feet or die – he counted the steps. Nine feet or die --

Directly behind Polly, the roof joists collapsed and the excited flames, gorging on the dry timber, crackled in approval.

Two more steps and somehow, miraculously, they made it to the bathroom. Both Polly and Garland immediately sucked at the miniscule amount of oxygen remaining in the room. In seconds, the fire would devour the rest.

Garland leapt to the window and Polly frantically turned on the shower. The cool spray momentarily kept the flames at bay, but they were relentless in their advance, already tasting the flimsy walls in the tiny room. Garland tried the window. It was warped shut. He whirled around, grabbed the heavy porcelain lid off the toilet tank and used it to shatter the window and frame. The glass burst outward and the sudden rush of air only incited the flames to consume the tiny bathroom.

Garland ripped down the shower curtain and laid it over the jagged window frame. "Towels!" He pointed, unable to breathe, much less speak.

As he heaped a wet towel over the broken glass, a rifle blast ripped into frame, showering them in splintered wood and spears of glass. The shooters were waiting for them front and back. They were trapped. Wild flames were now voraciously consuming the ceiling above them.

A second shot rang out, echoing over the growl of the advancing flames. And another shot – this one definitely from a shotgun.

A man yelped in pain.

From the window, Garland could barely make out the muzzle flash.

"I – can't – breathe." Polly was gasping.

A second shotgun blast rattled them, but wasn't aimed in their direction. A man yelped again, but this time he kept screaming in pain.

Garland pulled his Glock from its nylon holster and blasted wildly out the window toward the sound of the screaming man.

"Now. Out. Get out." He could barely choke the words to her.

He grabbed Polly around her thighs, lifted and shoved her head first out the jagged window. When she was halfway out, he fired randomly to lay down cover. There was no return fire. And as the flames licked his back, Garland dove out the window after her.

66

Garland heard the unmistakable rumble of the Chevy Apache as it fishtailed away across the beach and disappeared into the woods. He couldn't be sure if the bearded driver was their attacker or savior, but that was unimportant now. They were alive, that's what mattered.

Trying to hold Polly with one hand and his gun in the other, Garland half-crawled, half-scrambled toward the relative safety of the Expedition. Flames lapped from the cottage, searing their backs, but lighting their way. His lungs ached as he struggled for breath and assumed Polly was in the same condition; she was coughing almost uncontrollably.

"Easy, slow down, deep breaths, come on, deep," Garland said. He looped his arm around her waist, helping her to the SUV.

They heard a flat, grunt-like noise to their left and Garland swung his gun in the direction of the sound. A tall man, apparently the man who was shot, was hopping, limping in the opposite direction from the Apache. He was too far away for either Garland or Polly to recognize, but he was obviously hurt and, to their relief, retreating.

And then Starke appeared. Coming around the corner of the burning cottage, he was just as startled to see Garland and Polly as they were startled to see him. He had fully expected to find the limping man on this side of the cottage.

The undulating flames of the dying cottage played across Starke's goggles giving him an eerie, bug like appearance. He held his hand up to his face, shielding his eyes from the intense firelight. Even the smoked lenses of the goggles had limits. Consequently, to shield

302

his eyes, he was forced to carry his shotgun one-handed in the crook of his elbow, giving Garland a distinct advantage. Garland immediately swung his Glock around and fired first. A marksman he wasn't and he missed Starke completely, but it was enough to send Starke reeling backwards.

Garland immediately pulled Polly up. "In the car, get in the car."

They ran, stumbling, to the opposite side of the Expedition, away from where Starke had appeared. Using the huge SUV as cover, Garland opened the passenger door and helped Polly scramble in. From this vantage he could see Starke running across the resort grounds towards a very large Dodge Hemi 4X4 pickup with a camper shell parked near the woods. Catching his breath, Garland moved around the SUV to the driver's side and climbed in behind the wheel.

Polly was still coughing and shaking. Soot covered her face and her clothes were scorched, but not burned through. Garland imagined he looked the same.

"He may be coming back for us," Garland said, choking on his words.

Polly nodded. Then, horrified, said, "My god, your arm."

Garland glanced down. A four inch swath of his left forearm was burned raw, 2nd and 3rd degree burns up to his elbow. They knew they couldn't do anything about it now – their one and only job was to just get the hell out of there. Garland glanced up and saw the slash of bright headlights in his mirror. Starke.

He put the Expedition into 4-wheel mode and took off, pulling a hard U-turn and then churned wildly along the lakefront behind the other cottages. The Expedition's fat tires grabbed the sand and sent an arcing rooster-tail spray into the air behind them. "Where's the gun?"

"Here, I've got it."

"Hang on to it. Take the safety off."

"Me?"

"I'm a little busy."

Bright headlights appeared behind them, blinding him in the mirrors, but he was driving too fast and too frantically to adjust them. Polly held on to the dash and overhead handle.

The headlights were gaining. Garland pressed harder. In the side mirror he saw the barrel of the shotgun poke out from Starke's Dodge. Too late. The shot shattered the rear window of the Expedition and a fusillade of lethal shot pellets fanned across the roof above their heads shredding the upholstery.

"Oh, god," Polly screamed.

"Hold on."

Garland twisted the wheel hard, turning the SUV away from the lake and into the hopeful cover of the woods. Forced to drive one handed, Starke couldn't navigate the turn as fast and the Dodge slid past them, giving Garland a slight but precious lead.

Polly was ashen. "Oh my god, he's trying to kill us."

"You think?" He glanced at her. "Hang on again, this won't be pretty."

Garland killed the Expedition's headlights and turned onto what he hoped was a dirt road. It was actually nothing more than a heavily rutted caretaker path. The Expedition bounced wildly and Garland was forced to slow down. At narrow points along the path, the SUV traded paint for bark with several large trees while heavy, grabby limbs scraped and clawed eerily along the roof and side windows. But he was sure the path would take them to the main road. Moments later it proved to be the right guess. They stopped at the road.

Polly twisted in her seat and looked out the shattered rear window. "I don't think he's behind us."

"He knows the area. He's going to come at us from a different direction."

"Which way?"

"I have no idea."

"That was Starke, wasn't it?" She said.

"Yeah. We met before." Garland scanned the road in both directions. "How's his night vision?"

"Sucks. I'm guessing his day vision is marginal, night vision would be mostly shapes."

"Could he find us in the dark?"

"With his headlights, yes, of course."

"We can't stay here."

"There," she pointed right.

A flicker of headlights behind a distant curve in the woods signaled Starke's advance to the road.

"Get out."

"What?"

"Quick. Get out."

"What are you..."

"He's my only link to Sarah. I've got to stop him, I've got to talk to him."

"No. I'm staying with you."

With the headlights now two hundred yards away, Garland had no choice. He stomped the pedal and the Expedition leapt out

305

onto the road. With no lights on, Garland straddled the center yellow line, taking ownership of both sides of the road, accelerating wildly toward the oncoming headlights.

"No, no, what are you doing?"

"Brace."

One hundred yards. Seventy-five yards. Fifty. Forty. At thirty yards, Garland ignited the Expedition's high-beam lights as he swerved the SUV to the right shoulder.

The sudden explosion of the lights blinded Starke. He did exactly what Garland had hoped, also swerving right – but Starke's right was a much softer shoulder and the skidding Dodge unexpectedly caught big air over the roadside gully. It went airborne, twisting as gracefully as an Olympic diver ten feet off the ground. The camper shell blew off on the first twist. On the second twist the 4X4 impaled itself into an unyielding alder.

67

Starke was not wearing a seat belt.

The sturdy ancient alder may have stopped the Dodge 4X4, but not its driver. Starke speared through the windshield, crushing his skull in the process and filleting his face. His reverse bodily impact into a second alder completely shattered his spine, grinding five vertebrae into bone dust, but it was painless. He was dead before he hit the tree.

Between the spreading fire at Al 'N' Sal's and Starke's horrific wreck, all of the volunteer firefighters and emergency personnel from both Bolton and Ridgeline were pressed into service. The Baxter County Sheriff, Andy Waddell, and Chief Medical Examiner, Dr. B. Reilly Boone, arrived forty minutes later from Mountain Home.

Polly helped the local EMS team extricate Starke from the tree, but when it was apparent he was beyond any medical help, she moved back to the road where Garland was watching the proceedings with numb detachment.

"We've got to get you to a hospital," Polly said, "those burns on your arm are ripe for infection and your hand..."

"He was my last fucking link to Sarah. My last one. And Corinne."

"I know. I'm sorry."

"I had no intentions of killing him."

"You didn't."

"Well he's dead, isn't he? How'd he get that way?"

"Nathaniel, he and that other guy tried to kill us. They tried to burn us alive. What you did was – you saved our lives, that's what you did. Mr. Starke had a choice, you didn't. He made the wrong one. You didn't."

"Mr. Garland, I'd like to take your statement." Sheriff Waddell approached with the M.E. Boone at his side. Dr. B. Reilly Boone appeared to be in his sixties, a small mountain bear, big, bushy grey bearded face and eyebrows, deep brown eyes, solid gut. Waddell was half again as big as Boone but two-thirds his age, and had a commanding, if polite, authority.

"*Doctor* Garland," Polly corrected, "and I've got to get him to a hospital first."

Garland pulled his badge and flipped it open. "BIA," was all he said.

"Oh," Waddell said, "good. That'll be helpful sorting through this mess."

"Hospital, Sheriff?" Polly said.

"You're way better off having me treat your burns, doctor," Boone said. "Do it back at my place, I've got a small clinic, everything we need."

"You're a burn expert?" Polly asked, unable to hide the skepticism in her voice.

"Two tours in 'Iraq, ma'am, I doctored more burns you can imagine."

"Nathaniel?"

"Yeah. Sure. Your clinic, Dr. Boone." Then to Waddell he said, "Did you know this man, Sheriff?"

"Everybody 'round here knows Col. Norman Starke, doctor, man's a local legend."

"*Colonel* Starke?"

"U.S. Army. Retired. Well, guess you could say very retired now. Question is, what the hell was he doing driving one of my deputy's pickups?"

"Would that deputy happen to be Lyle Krauss?"

"Yes it would."

"Then I would check the local hospitals, Sheriff; he's probably having a load of buckshot plucked out of his ass right now."

As they walked away, Garland said, "Sheriff, do you think it's possible to find Starke's cell phone in that mess?"

"If he owned one, we'll find it for you, doctor. Any particular calls you interested in?"

Garland knew the Sheriff was probing, but that was his job. "Yes," Garland said, "calls to the VA in Fayetteville and calls to CFS in Florida."

68

Polly watched Dr. Reilly Boone minister to Garland's burns. He was fast and efficient and knew what he was doing. His clinic was tiny, but well equipped. It was situated on the ground floor of a beautifully restored antebellum mansion very near the center of Mountain Home. Somewhat incongruously, several small, strange, lizard-like creatures floated in formalin in jars on the shelf across from the examination table.

As he worked on Garland, Boone explained that the home was once the town's funeral parlor and belonged to the Howard Furnham family. When the national chain bought out the Furnham & Breech Mortuary three years earlier, Furnham donated the house to the county — an act of civic generosity — that also had very serious tax advantages for the Furnham family. Now Boone and his wife, Esme, live upstairs, he keeps his clinic on the ground floor and houses the County morgue downstairs in the old embalming rooms.

"Dr. Boone," Polly said, "are you going to autopsy Starke?"

"It's required by law in this county. Probably do it tonight since I don't see any sleep in my immediate future."

"Would you mind if I stand in? I'm an ophthalmologist and I'm really intrigued about his eyes."

"Is that what this is about? That what brings you medical investigators down to our cozy little hamlet? The Colonel's eyes? Hell, let me tell you folks something, those rumors are all bogus."

"Which rumors?"

"Starke being blind. Losing his sight to a flash-bang in Iraq and then, supposedly, some quack at the Fayetteville V.A. restored his vision. Hell, I never bought that rubbish for a minute."

"How do you explain his unusual glasses?" Polly asked.

"That's his thing, you know? His symbol, trademark, you know, like Garth Brooks' hat. He used those goggles to intimidate, scare the b'jesus out of the townies, that's all."

"He live around here?" Garland hopped off the exam table and moved toward the shelf of pickled lizards.

"No. Up at the compound."

"Henry Hugger?"

"Yes, that's right, how'd you know? He was head of security there."

"What is that compound? What goes on in there that requires security?"

"And here I was hoping you could tell me. Used to be Army. Don't know whose it is now. But you ask anyone around here, they'll tell you, it's the famous 'undisclosed location'. Lots of secret government booga-booga going on in there. Personally, what I get from talking to people who say they've been up there, it's a rehab facility of some kind for big government honchos and such. Probably psychiatric."

"So you've never been?"

"Nope."

"Sheriff?"

"Nope."

"What happens when there's a death at the facility? Sheriff doesn't investigate? You don't perform the autopsy?"

311

"Uh-uh. It's across the line. Beaumont County. Outside our jurisdiction."

"That's convenient," Garland said.

There was a gentle knock on the clinic door. It opened and Esme Boone poked her head in. She was a sweet, pleasant looking, tiny woman, half Reilly Boone's size.

"Y'all must be starvin' by now. I fixed some tea and snacks in the dinin' room when y'all about ready."

"That's so kind, Mrs. Boone," Polly said, "thank you."

"Be right up, darlin'," her husband smiled.

"Dr. Boone, what are these lizards? I can't place them."

"First off, call me Reilly, second, you can't place 'em because they're not lizards. They're snakes. Pythons to be exact."

Garland smiled at the joke. He knew when he was being had. "Yeah, right."

"Pythons. Swear t'god," Boone said. "Caught 'em myself. They're hatchlings."

"Come on," Polly shook her head, "snakes with legs?"

"Damndest thing, ain't it? I've had my share of encounters with plenty of constrictors in m'travels, but you wouldn't expect 'em to be right here, I know."

"Legs. Reilly?"

"Kind of startled me, too. But check it out, constrictor family snakes, like pythons, boas, anacondas…was a time all of 'em had legs. Now all they have left are primitive claws. Vestiges. Through a couple hundred million years of evolution, many reptiles, like lizards, 'gators, turtles, what have you, they kept their legs, not constrictors, tough, they lost theirs. Luck of the evolutionary draw, I guess. Could just as easily gone the other way. They still use those claws for sex, but that's all."

"Where did you find them?"

"About a week ago, Sweetwater Creek, right where it flows out of Hugger Wood, up near the camp you were asking about."

"Larry Dugan said there was a snake die off in Sweetwater."

"Snakes, fish, rabbits, razorbacks – huge die off of most of the wildlife in those woods. Nobody knows why. That's how I stumbled on these babies. They were already dying on the bank. I was hoping I could find the mom – you know pythons incubate hatchlings for a spell, but she never showed. I suspect she's died off, too. What do you say we go upstairs?"

In addition to baking croissants, Esme Boone had also fried some fresh beignet and the wonderful aroma of the pastry filled the dining room with her New Orleans childhood.

As she poured tea for Polly, Esme said, "The children are gone and we have plenty of room here for you if you'd like."

"That is so generous. Thank you."

Sheriff Andy Waddell called up from the foyer and then, following his nose, joined them upstairs.

"Esme, tell me you didn't fry up some beignet now, did you?"

"Of course I did it just for you."

Waddell pulled up a chair, reached for the pastry, and said to Garland, "Had a real nice chat with your boss, doc. Nice fella."

"You called my boss? At this hour?"

"I like to think of it as due diligence. Actually, I called your boss's boss."

"You called Haynes?"

"You know he played ball for Bear Bryant? Same team as Joe Namath."

"That a fact," Boone said.

"Long and short is, he tells me you're the real deal and would I extend my full cooperation, which, of course, I will." Waddell paused to dump a load of sugar in his tea. "Now, about that little girl, the one with the deformity – well, I checked with my colleagues in the five surrounding counties and none of us has an open missing child case."

"The young girl in question, Sheriff, we think was kidnapped with her brother by Starke from a foster home in Florida. Names are Corinne and Calvin Burch. You wouldn't have a record here. We have every reason to believe the brother may still be alive. And I have to know if there are others and where they are. We know the girl was in Sweetwater Creek, we know she was in the woods here…"

Polly got up. "We have photos in the car. I'll get them."

"The only Jane Doe we've had in the last month was an older woman some boys found when they were playing under the bridge."

Garland sat upright. "What woman?"

"Like I said, older. No I.D., naked as a jay. Beat up real bad, looked like a hit-and-run."

"When you say older, how old do you mean?"

"Hard to say," Waddell said. "Hair was all white, but her features didn't look that old."

"That's where I found the snakes," Boone cut in. "Woman's left leg was chewed off. Looked like a snake bite, but we don't have any that big around here. And looked like the other animals got to her, she was chewed up pretty bad."

Polly ran up the stairs with Garland's Tumi bag. He quickly found the file folder and the photos of Corinne inside and fanned them out on the table.

"This is the girl."

"Not at all familiar. Never seen her around here. Reilly?"

"Nope."

Garland reached back into the folder and pulled out several photos of Sarah Levine. Both Waddell and Boone leaned in for a closer look.

"Damn," Waddell said, "if she don't look like that woman. How old is this one?"

"This was taken on her thirty-sixth birthday." Garland said. "Forget the hair. Look at her face."

Reilly Boone slid Sarah's photo closer. He flattened his beefy hands over her hair, masking it and then looked up at Waddell. "Sure as hell does look like her."

"Sure as hell does," the Sheriff said.

Garland struggled to rein in his churning excitement. He would have to see Sarah for himself, make a positive ID on her body before he would allow himself to release the emotions welling in his gut. Stuart flashed though his mind. What would he tell Stuart? Polly read his face and could not control the empathetic tears gathering in the corners of her eyes.

"Reilly," Garland said, "is she here? Is the body downstairs?"

"No, of course not," Boone said. "The woman, if this is her, hell, she was still alive when the boys found her. We got her to our hospital, stabilized her and Life-Flighted her to University Hospital in Little Rock."

"Last I heard," Waddell added, "she was still there."

69

It took three calls and ten minutes for Andy Waddell to arrange their transportation to Little Rock. It took another ten minutes for Waddell to drive them to Baxter County Regional Airport. Phil Busbee's Bell 206B-3 helicopter was already warming up on the tarmac when they arrived. Three minutes later, Garland and Polly were airborne.

The direct flight from Baxter to Little Rock's University Hospital is 115 miles. They made it there in one hour flat and received permission to land on the hospital's helipad.

Garland's heart was racing as he flew down the stairs from the roof to intensive care. Polly, somehow, was able to keep up stride for stride. They had called ahead and the Chief Resident, Dr. Prasad Sinha, was waiting for them at the central I.C. nurses' station. Introductions were exchanged and Garland opened his file and handed Dr. Sinha the photos of Sarah Levine.

Good chief residents are the same everywhere. Smart. Political. Medically astute. No nonsense get to the point give me the facts and get out of my way. Sinha was no exception. They talked on the move, no wasted time, disinfecting from the bottles of sanitizer placed strategically in the corridors.

"No question there's a similarity," Sinha said, "facial features, not her hair, but close enough. Eyeball her yourself, I'd love to be able to put a name on the chart."

They stopped briefly at a supply rack for Garland and Polly to pick up masks and paper gowns and they dressed on the move.

Sinha ran down the woman's condition for them as they hustled toward her I.C. bay. "Talk about an horrenda, this one had everything, one bitch of a pathology under another. The septicemia alone should have killed her. She was so hypothermic we couldn't even get a BP. WBC off the scale. Then add the massive hemorrhagic lesions…"

"Was she in an accident?" Garland asked.

"No. Animals got to her."

"What kind of animals?"

"Hell if I know. Big ones. Never saw bite marks like that before. I've got some biologists next door trying to identify them."

Animals. Ark.

The thought flashed through Garland's mind. The notation Sarah had made in the notes he and Carolyn Eccevarria found. *Animals. Ark.* It wasn't Biblical, as Dunbarton suggested. It was literal. Animals. Arkansas. Garland's excitement grew.

"Her left leg was pretty much gone when we got her. Gangrenous. We had to take it," Sinha said.

"How high?" Polly asked.

"Well above the knee."

They stopped at the I.C. bay. Garland hesitated.

"Another thing," Sinha said, "even if she's your missing woman, she's TGA – doctor speak for transient global amnesia – probably won't know you."

Garland nodded, still hesitating at the door.

"It's either her or not," Polly said. She meant it to be comforting, but it didn't come out that way. "Do you want me to go in with you?"

Garland shook his head. And stepped into the bay alone.

He recognized Sarah immediately. Despite the oxygen mask that covered much of her face, despite her halo of paper white hair, despite the dim lighting and tangle of tubes and wires, the woman in the bed was, without question, Sarah Levine.

Watching from the bay door, Polly saw Garland take the woman's hand and she knew that he had found her. Alive.

70

"Stu, we found her. She's alive."

There was a long silence. Garland thought his cell had dropped the connection.

"*Stu...?*"

"Don't shit me, Nate."

"I'm not. I'm with her now."

"Holy fucking Christ, you're serious."

"Stu, she's critical."

"I'm on my way, man, keep her alive, Nate, please, do what you have to. Keep her alive, I can be there in...where the fuck did you say you are?"

"University Hospital, Little Rock, Arkansas."

"Three hours...I can be there in..."

"Stu. She's not the same. She lost a leg."

"She's alive, man, that's all I care about."

Garland clicked off and slid his cell into his pocket.

Dr. Prasad Sinha had generously let them use his office in the basement of the hospital complex and while Garland spoke to Stuart, Polly reviewed Sarah's chart with him.

"This is really bizarre," Polly said. "Nathaniel, take a look at this. Her septicemia was a product of tularemia."

"Tularemia? Rabbit fever?"

"Not just tularemia, industrial strength tularemia," Sinha said. "I sent blood and tissue to Atlanta and your people at CDC tell me it's the most virulent strain they've ever encountered. Your guys won't confirm it, but to me, that's weapons grade." Sinha hesitated, then said, "Off the record, I had my own lab run it."

"Did they find the strain?"

"Yeah. Francisella tularensis."

"Jesus."

"I'm not familiar with that – what is it?" Polly asked.

"The tularemia bacterium is restructured and atomized so it can be released as an aerosol."

"Oh my god, so it is a bioweapon."

"Not many other uses for it," Garland said. "Dr. Sinha, did you have the amebiasis analyzed as well?"

"How'd you know about that? It's not even on her chart."

"I had a patient at Fed-Med and she and Sarah Levine were obviously exposed to it in the same creek."

"Yeah, we found very robust amebiasis, but that was the least of her problems." Sinha looked at Garland and Polly dubiously. "So what's really going on? You guys conducting some kind of CBW experiments up at Bull Shoals?"

"No. None that I know of."

"Then it's a hell of a way to thin the rabbit population. Kill every one of them with that strain."

Garland's cell warbled in his pocket. He checked the caller I.D. and said, "*Gene, what did you find?*" He grabbed a pen and Sinha offered him a pad to write on.

"You are not going to believe this one, cowboy,." Gene Kessler said.

"Try me."

"It's ours."

"What's ours?"

"That old POW camp. Henry Hugger. The DOD ceded it to HHS a couple years ago."

"You're kidding me. What agency, Gene? Who in the department took it over?"

"That was the real head slapper, Nate. No one. We own it, but we don't. It's off the books, under the radar, behind the curtain. No official department record that we paid for it, took possession or even operate it. It's like a ghost site, man, it doesn't exist."

"Gene, I've got to know who's running it and what it's used for."

"I'm still working it, buddy-boy, but it's all smoke and mirrors. I was being stonewalled everywhere so I had to call in a big marker with a friend at GAO. Took her forever, but get this, Nate, it's being administered as a non-department facility out of the Secretary's office, but GAO can't find the dollars, so they don't know how it's being financed."

"Forget the how. Tell me the what – what's being financed?"

"GAO has no docs on it. All they have is the name."

"Whose name?"

"Not who – it – the compound, the facility. It's called The 610. I don't know what the hell that means, either does GAO. "

Michael Braverman

Garland scribbled 610 on the pad. Polly looked over his shoulder as he wrote it. Then directly under that he wrote 'Sarah', 'Corinne', 'tularemia', 'ambiases'.

"Gene, this is fantastic, thanks. Hey, have you told anyone else about it, I mean, at the agency? Did you tell anyone?"

"No, I don't think so."

"Don't. Not a soul, Gene, don't even mention it, okay?"

"You got it, cowboy."

"I hate to do this to you, but I need one more thing."

"Shoot."

"It's a big one. I need the log files from Con-Con 5 for the last couple months."

"Con 5? Oh, shit, man, c'mon, give me a fucking break. That's a day down and a day up"

"I know it's a lot to ask. I'll make it up to you. But I really need those logs."

"Yeah, yeah, fucking logs, I'll get 'em for you. So Nate, anything new on Sarah? You guys getting any closer?"

"No, Gene," Garland lied, "not yet."

322

71

Sinha was called away. Polly and Garland were alone in his office. He stared at the notepad and shook his head. The head shake covered a multitude of emotions. It was simultaneous disbelief, relief, self-reproach and, above all, the feeling of abject stupidity knowing that he had completely and totally missed the obvious.

"Shén-me shì? Shén-me cuò?" What is it? What's wrong? Polly said in Mandarin.

He slid the notepad across to her, circled 'The 610', drew an equal sign and looked at her.

"If it's what we were talking about yesterday," Polly said, "then 610 equals CVDV."

"Right." Garland said. He scrawled in CVDV and then drew a line from that equation to the words 'francisella tularensis' and 'amebiasis'.

Polly's hand flew to her mouth. "Oh my god."

Garland got up and wadded the note paper into his pocket. "I've got to get back there."

As they climbed the stairs to the helipad on the roof, Garland said, "Beck never mentioned him to you?"

"No. The first time I ever heard his name mentioned was the morning Jason and I met you in the foyer at Fed-Med."

"Chris…" Garland thought to himself. Beck had the audacity – *the balls* – to call him *'Chris'*. CVDV – Christian van der Veldt – Dr. Biodeath himself. How did he not see it, not recognize it?

"I really thought he was dead," Polly said.

"No. His job is to make other people dead."

Polly grabbed his arm and stopped him on the landing between floors. She had to see his face, look in his eyes as they spoke about this.

"And you really believe we were financed through him?

"Yeah. Probably. You didn't operate on N.I.H. grants, did you? My guess is, through that bogus Evinco Vixi shell, van der Veldt supplied Beck and every one of his associates with everything they needed. And when they published, they credited van der Veldt with that bullshit Evinco Vixi 'defeating death' CVDV appellation.

"But from what I saw, Jason and every one of the researchers – including and myself – we're all honest, honorable, ethical…"

"You, yes, but not Beck. He made his deal with the devil, he just didn't know what the deal was."

"No. And neither do I. What is he doing?"

"I can only guess…"

"Okay. Guess. Tell me – don't parse – tell me what you *guess* he's doing."

Garland realized, too late, that what he had already said and what he was about to conjecture could easily be interpreted by Polly as the nullification of her work. As the primary research assistant to Jason Beck, she was an unwitting party to a criminal conspiracy of astounding proportions, a criminal conspiracy that no doubt included the murder of Corinne Burch and the probability of many others.

"Polly, I don't know if it's van der Veldt or not. It's just a ridiculous wild guess. And even if it is him, I have no idea what he's really doing."

"Oh, god, Nathaniel, it's a duck. And you are such a lousy liar."

There are monumental events in every life that strike with such absolute certitude that they are forever and inextricably woven into the fabric of that life. They are seminal events, great and small, subtle and magnificent which, years later, a person could look back at that precise moment in time and re-inhabit the experience. Such was this moment for Garland. This was the moment he *knew* he loved her.

"Will you wait here for Stuart?" Garland said.

"You're not going in there alone, are you?"

"I'm just going to poke around. See what's going on."

"Calvin Burch?"

"Yes."

"Get a warrant. Bring in the troops."

"It's a Federal installation. There's no way I can get a warrant on a gut feeling. I have no US Attorney here, no proof, no probable cause — no time."

"You've got a building full of lawyers at Fed-Med."

"The last time I got a warrant through Fed-Med, Carolyn Eccevarria ended up dead." His eyes washed the intense blueness of hers, locking on her trust. "I'll be fine," he said, "don't worry."

"I'm coming with you."

72

Phil Busbee's Bell 206B-3 helicopter was summoned back to the helipad and arrived within ten minutes. On the short flight back to Mountain Home, Polly articulated what Garland already knew. Christian van der Veldt's enterprise was absolutely brilliant in its simplicity. Under the auspices of Evinco Vixi, he carefully identified, recruited and helped finance the finest minds in cross platform genetic research. Each worked independently – probably not even aware of the others – and van der Veldt, a brilliant scientist in his own right, wove the disparate threads of their research into singular, mind-boggling scientific breakthroughs.

"That's why Jason found some our work, in Corinne's eyes," Polly said.

"Yeah. If we're right about van der Veldt."

"I thought your Department was supposed to be the genetic research 'clearinghouse', isn't that the job of the N.I.H.?"

"It would be if they weren't so ham-strung by politicians and policies warped by medieval superstitions."

"So, if I'm reading this right, The 610 is a shadow agency, somehow operating under the aegis of your Department, doing what your Department should be doing in the open if it wasn't so cowed by right wing extremists and religious fanatics."

Garland marveled at this woman's clarity. "Yeah," he said, "except for the fact that once you remove the restraints of law and oversight, you risk…Corinne Burch."

Both Reilly Boone and Sheriff Andy Waddell were waiting at Baxter Regional for Phil's chopper to arrive. On the drive in, Garland felt comfortable enough to share the local aspects of his investigation with them. He finished as they arrived at Boone's mansion.

"I'm really sorry about your deputy, Sheriff,." Garland said.

"He burned down your cabin and tried to kill you, you've got nothing to be sorry about, son."

"Man." Reilly Boone said. He must have said 'man' a hundred times as he listened to Garland, then finally added, "So this is why Furnham has all those hearses. You're right, man, he's burying their mistakes and I don't autopsy a single one of them."

As they got out of the car at the house, Garland said something he never in his life could have imagined himself to say: "Sheriff, could I impose upon you to borrow a shotgun and a couple clips of nines?"

"You ever hunt, doc?"

"Not once in my life," Garland said.

"It's pig season," Waddell said, "and I wouldn't mind taking a couple razorbacks with you this afternoon. All we need is a huntin' license from Larry over at Fish and Wildlife and we can take ourselves anywhere in them woods we want."

"Mind if I join you?" Boone said. "Man, I have not hunted in years."

"I'll need bolt and wire cutters," Garland said.

"Of course, who goes huntin' without 'em."

73

Garland had no trouble finding the unpaved road that led out to the delta and he just as easily found the rutted switchback that ran diagonally up to the camp. He pulled into the wide dirt pad that porched Camp Henry Hugger and stopped near the fence. As he expected, the heavy steel electric gate was closed.

They got out of the SUV and surveyed the camp through the fencing. It looked a lot different in the daylight. Dirtier, shabbier, more ominous.

Garland tried pulling the gate open manually. It didn't budge. "I can probably ram through it," he said.

Waddell said. "Your truck is beat up bad enough. There's another way in."

They swung around and came in from the east, very near the bridge over Sweetwater where the young boys found Sarah. Reilly Boone pointed to the exact spot. They then followed a path through the dense woods that was originally carved by migrating pigs.

Garland wore his badge on his jacket pocket, Waddell did not. They were no longer in his county. Without jurisdiction, he and Boone were just civilian hunters. Except for Polly, they all carried pump action shotguns in the crooks of their elbows.

"Camp looked a whole lot different from the last time I saw it," Waddell said as they now hiked west along the creek. "Used to go fishing down to the delta with my daddy. That iron fence wasn't there. Neither the razor wire. Camp entrance was that wooden arch with the name on it. There was still some German prisoners in there,

328

didn't want to go home after the war so the Army let 'em live in the barracks 'til they got themselves settled into the community."

"There're a lot of snakes in these woods, aren't there?" Polly said. It was a random comment, but signaled her aversion to having snakes crawl over her shoes.

"You bet your sweet – yes, ma'am," Reilly Boone said. "But I don't see 'em."

"You can see them?"

"Usually. And that's what's troublin' me. I don't see any. Not a one."

"It's the amebiasis," Garland said. "It's a particularly virulent strain. I wouldn't be surprised if all the snakes and lizards died off in the last few days."

"Excuse my ignorance, man," Boone said, "but from the little I actually remember from my parasitology class, amebiasis is just a little one-celled amoeba. How the hell can it be virulent?"

"One cell or a billion, it contains DNA. You mess with the DNA, pump it with little amoeba steroids and you've got yourself one mother of a parasite."

And that's when Andy Waddell stopped. Stared. He could neither process nor believe what he was seeing. "Sweet son-of-a – what the hell is that?" The others locked in on his gaze.

"Man," Boone said, "Man, look at that sucker, will you? Goddamn, has to be the mother..."

When Polly saw it, she instinctively grabbed Garland's arm.

The twenty foot long reticulated python was writhing on the soft bank, half in and half out of the creek. She was on her side and three of her eight fully formed legs were helplessly clawing the air in a pathetic attempt to escape. Thousands of fire ants were swarming over the python's head, feasting on her tasty eyes and mouth. She was too sick and too weak to fight her way back to the creek where she could shed her attackers. She was being consumed alive.

"Damn." Waddell said.

He pumped a shell in his shotgun and looked at Garland. Garland nodded and Waddell stepped closer to the dying snake and ended her misery. The sound of the shotgun blast reverberated through the woods. Hundreds of birds screamed as they fled in protest, their shrill calls quickly fading in the distance. Reilly Boone stood still, listening to the dying echo of the shot, then turned to listen behind them.

"What is it?" Polly asked. She realized she was still clinging to Garland's arm and self-consciously released it.

"No leaves rustling, no twigs snapping, no grunts, no animal chatter. Not a good sign."

"Let's get into that camp," Garland said.

They picked up their pace along the bank. Within minutes the animals began appearing. Dead.

"There," Polly pointed. "And over there."

They were looking at a destroyed warren of dead rabbits — rabbits that Sarah Levine knew all too well — rabbits the size of Rottweilers. Garland and Boone approached the carcasses, Waddell held back. Polly crept close enough to see their deformities.

"You bring gloves?" Garland asked.

"Nah, didn't think of it," Boone said.

"Polly?"

"No."

"It's the tularemia," Garland said. "This strain is lethal. Don't touch them."

"Sweet mother, they're...the eyes are...human. Look at that one, the mouth, got human teeth and everything. Oh, man...what is that?"

"Unformed ears," Polly said. "Cochlea's on the outside."

"There're more here." Waddell called to them from ten feet further up the path.

He had found a dozen more carcasses, mostly rabbits, but also some huge white lab rats, almost as big as the rabbits. And almost all of the white rats had two heads – the second head more human in shape and features than rodentia.

"I'm not like a bible thumper or nothing," Waddell said, "but this is the closest I've ever seen to the devil's work."

"No, believe me, it's man's work." Garland stood. "Let's get in that camp."

Their pace grew faster and they were practically trotting as they moved closer to the camp boundary.

It was Polly who first spotted the movement. It was subtle, silent, away from the creek, behind a cloaking stand of Hawthorne and basswood trees. "There's something there," she said quietly, "behind those trees."

Almost in unison, Garland, Waddell and Boone chambered shells. They approached cautiously, fanning out slightly, each man slowly raising his weapon. What they expected, hidden behind the trees, was one or more sick or wounded animals; what they found went beyond rational belief. They lowered their shotguns.

"Polly." Garland called.

She came immediately. And saw the horrifying display in the clearing. Two elderly women and a broken man, all completely disoriented, we're walking into the trees, stumbling into each other, falling and picking themselves up. The man was sobbing, crying tears but no sound, tragedy incarnate etched on his disfigured face. All three were wearing remnants of hospital gowns of the same style and fabric Corinne Burch was found wearing. The man's gown was open in front revealing his deformed body. One woman's gown was off her shoulders and tied around her waist. Extending down from her armpits and scapula were half-dozen vestigial appendages, mostly twisted fingers and arms, but under her natural left arm was a half-formed leg. The other woman was the least disfigured. She had a lipless mouth carved into her neck just below her chin. The mouth had an array of teeth that bit into her flesh as she gasped for every breath she drew.

Polly didn't hesitate. She pushed past Waddell and immediately moved into the clearing. She knelt next to the crying man and, taking him by the shoulders, tried to comfort him as she would a small child. Garland and Boone were a half step behind her, running to the aid of the women.

On the other side of the clearing, trees swayed and twigs snapped as more human test creatures appeared, each grotesquely disfigured. One woman, naked and in shock, had two withered human heads hanging from her neck. Another man's arms were lined with rows of boneless fingers. A third person, Garland guessed it was a young boy, had three empty orbits where his eyes once existed, his mouth was permanently open and toungeless.

Waddell already had his cell phone out. "I can't get a signal, I'm going back for help."

Garland rose from the clearing floor and looked toward the camp. His stomach was in a knot and he wanted to vomit – not in disgust, but in rage. He started walking across the clearing. His pace quickened and his walk became a trot, his trot became a jog and his jog became a run.

Holding the shotgun at his side in his bandaged left hand, Garland ran single-mindedly toward the fence. Two, three, five, a dozen horribly deformed human subjects streamed past him seeking safety in the woods. All were naked or partially cloaked in tattered hospital gowns. He dodged them like a running back, leaping over fallen trees and branches, side-stepping and ducking hanging limbs and every other obstacle that tried to impede him.

He stopped when he reached the fence. And vomited.

74

A dozen more of the pitiable mutants pushed through the breech in the fence to get to the woods. Many were barefoot and bleeding as they shuffled across the downed razor wire. They were beyond pain and beyond repair.

"Please go back," Garland said, keeping his voice steady, non-threatening, "there's nothing in the woods for you, there's nothing out there. Stay here. Help is coming. Go back. Please, go back."

A hairless woman with too many eyes turned to him. "Food. No food."

"Food is coming. Please, please go back."

She turned away from Garland and continued moving with the others in their slow, desperate escape march.

Garland quickly picked his way through the victims to get to the breech. When he found it, he crossed the lethal concertina wire and stepped into hell.

What he encountered was a mind-warping nightmare of unending Boschian anguish and unyielding torment. There were hundreds of them. Men, women, children. Damaged. Deformed. Grotesque. Some still clutched the ragged remnants of their gowns, others were naked, most were wandering aimlessly. There were several people on the ground, some were sitting and crying, others were dead. What lay before him was incomprehensible. A quote from Stalin flashed through his mind: 'One death is a tragedy, a million deaths is a statistic'. Joe was wrong. This was both a tragedy and a statistic.

As he continued through the camp, Garland realized that there was no one in authority present, no supervision of any kind, no medical personnel, no sign of any human concern. These victims of the most horrid cruelty were abandoned to their own devices, discarded to be forever victimized by an existence they neither sought nor deserved.

Once more he felt the bile rise in his gut as he fought to contain his rage. He began running again, shotgun clutched in his hand, frightening only those who were aware enough to be frightened.

Garland ran into the largest of the barrack type buildings. It smelled of piss and antiseptic and had the accoutrement of an antiquated back-alley abortion mill. A faint odor of rotted flesh permeated the dank air. Many of the victims' doors were opened and their rooms abandoned. Others were still locked from the outside. Garland tried one door. It wouldn't give. He banged on a second locked door and heard a loud moan from inside.

A man stepped out of a door halfway down the corridor. He walked erect, had a steady gait and wore scrubs.

"Hey." Garland said it loudly, moving purposefully toward the man.

The short, balding man turned to look at Garland, then tuned again and began running from him. His stride was slow and awkward.

"Hey." Garland yelled again. "The keys. Where are the keys?"

The man continued running. Garland pumped the shotgun and fired over his head. The sound was deafening. Splintered wood and chunks of plaster rained down on the man who covered his head with his arms, but he kept running. People behind the locked doors began wailing. Garland sprinted after the man, easily gaining on him. Panicked, the man twisted around and threw a clutch of keys on the floor. As Garland stopped to scoop up the keys, the man fled out the front door of the barracks.

Garland followed. Not to apprehend him, but to find someone – anyone – with some measure of authority or responsibility. Garland knew that Starke's violent death, the shooting of Deputy Lyle Krauss and the imminent arrival of Federal law enforcement officers sent everyone packing.

As he stepped out into the sunlight Garland recognized where he was – the other side of the camp's old wooden entrance. The barracks he exited was blocked from view by several of the larger abandoned buildings and he knew that was by clever design.

To his right, three Furnham & Breech Mortuary hearses were bellied up at the low barracks across the median, the maws of their rear hatches gaped open to receive. Several teams of mortuary assistants were wheeling chrome gurneys from the barracks to the waiting hearses. The bodies they were wheeling were wrapped in sheets, not even body bags. The tall blond Russian driver, whom Garland had encountered earlier at Furnham's mortuary in Mountain Home, immediately recognized Garland. Yelling something in Russian to the others, he took off on a dead run toward the main gate and the others followed on his heels, abandoning their gurneys.

Garland knew what he would find beneath the sheets on the gurneys: more of the biologically mutilated. He lifted each of the sheets and confirmed his suspicions. He was, however, surprised to find that all three decedents had toe tags. The center gurney held the body of a teenage boy. Garland read the toe tag. It was as if he was expecting exactly what he found when he read the boy's name – Calvin Burch. He knew he would find Calvin in the camp, he just didn't want to find him this way.

"Fuck," he said. "Fuck. Fuck. Fuck."

75

A green and white helicopter swooped down low from the west. Garland didn't even hear it coming. When he looked up, he saw it circling back at the far side of the camp. He watched it hover as it turned into the light wind and began to settle into a cloud of soft swirling dirt behind a slight rise until it disappeared from his sight. Garland didn't see any particular law enforcement insignias on the helicopter. It wasn't a Life-Flight chopper or the help he expected from any law enforcement agency. It was, he realized, a private chopper, not unlike the Bell he had hired from Phil Busbee.

He knew why it had come.

He knew who it came for.

He also knew he wouldn't make it in time.

Garland leapt into the closest hearse. Stomping on the gas, the stretch Cadillac fishtailed wildly in a full donut before Garland was able to wrestle control of it. He flew over the soft dirt, scouring the grounds for some type of road or path, but he couldn't find one. The rear hatch door banged angrily against the frame several times before the latch caught. He knew he was driving way too fast – what if one of the victims wandered out in front of him? But he had to get to the chopper while it was on the ground.

The hearse went airborne over a steep rise, but when it touched down and its belly scraped along the ground, Garland saw them, directly in front him.

Christian van der Veldt.

With the aid of a carved wood cane in one hand, and carrying an old fashioned lawyer type briefcase in the other, he was walking toward the waiting helicopter. Directly behind him were two women, one younger, one closer to van der Veldt's age. The women were carrying cardboard file boxes. They all turned simultaneously and looked at the roaring hearse bearing down on them.

Garland fishtailed the hearse directly into the skids of the helicopter, smashing the chopper's undercarriage and effectively disabling it. He opened the driver's door before the Cadillac even stopped rocking. Then, clutching the shotgun, Garland ran through the thick choke of dust raised by both the car and the chopper. The pilot immediately feathered the engine.

"Van der Veldt." Garland had to scream over the dying jet whine. "Christian van der Veldt, you are under arrest."

Van der Veldt and his party stared at him blankly.

"Put the briefcase down. You, too," he said to the two ladies, "boxes down, get on the ground, all of you."

Van der Veldt continued to stare at him. Garland noticed the hint of a smirk on his face, the same smirk that greeted him every single day from the portrait in the Con-Con lobby.

"Put the briefcase and boxes down. Now. On the ground. All of you. On the ground. Hands out in front of you."

"You cannot be at all serious." van der Veldt said, "Who do you think you're talking to?"

They are a type – Christian van der Veldt, Jason Beck, Herbert Harrison Jensen – men so imbued with a warped egotistical and inflated sense of entitlement that they truly believe the rules of law and society do not apply to them. Van der Veldt was exercising his well practiced entitlement. But he had miscalculated.

Garland's rage was blinding. For a fraction of a second his vision went black. It returned when he heard another Nathaniel Garland, a disassociated Nathaniel Garland, pump the shotgun.

"You. Asshole. I'm talking to you," he heard the other Garland scream. "Get on the ground, get on the fucking ground now. Now. NOW."

And then he heard the shotgun fire. He barely felt the recoil. The shot pellets burrowed into the ground just inches from van der Veldt's cane. Even as van der Veldt and the two women were falling to the ground, Garland pumped another shell. He fired again. Into the ground very close to their feet. Several pellets ricocheted into the file boxes.

Patricia Preston, the younger of the two women, screamed.

Drawing deep breaths, Garland walked around himself in a tight circle, trying to reclaim his reason and judgment, then moved to where van der Veldt was lying face down in the dirt.

"This is outrage…"

"Shut up. Hands behind your back."

Van der Veldt slowly and reluctantly complied. Garland knelt down, intentionally pressing his knee hard into the small of van der Veldt's back. He reached into his jacket pocket for a plastic hand restraint. He didn't have one.

"You have no idea who you are…"

"I told you to shutup." Garland stood. "Get up. All of you. Get up."

"Make up your mind," van der Veldt said.

Patricia Preston, apparently his chief lab assistant, scrambled to her feet. The older woman got up on her knees and then helped van der Veldt to his feet.

"He's a sick man," the older woman said. "He cannot be treated this way."

"Christian van der Veldt, you are under arrest. You have the right to remain silent. You have the right to an…"

"For godsakes, spare me."

"Do you understand all of your rights?"

"And do you understand who and what you are…" van der Veldt's eyes flicked over Garland's gold badge. "You are tragically over your head, agent."

"Let's go. That way. Move."

"Go? Go where? I'm not going anywhere with you."

"Let's get something straight, *Chris*, I don't care who or what you think you are, we're going down the hill. You can walk or I can drag you, but one way or another you're going down."

Van der Veldt took measure of Garland, then shook his head and reached down for his briefcase.

"Leave it. Let's go. You, too, leave the boxes."

"My notes. My work is in here."

"Your work is over. Let's go."

"I'm not leaving my work, my papers…"

Garland whirled and fired the shotgun. Van der Veldt's old leather briefcase was blown into the air and was all but obliterated by the blast. Shredded paper and leather fragments, caught by the breeze, created a funnel with the dirt and then slowly dissipated across the ground.

"My work."

"You want to see your work? Look. Look there. And there. And there. You see your work you arrogant, egotistical bastard. How many did you kill at work today? How many did you disfigure and maim and destroy at work today? Look. There. There's your work."

"You cannot possibly imagine – you can't even begin to comprehend the advancements I have achieved here. Kill them? Destroy them? I gave them worth and value, you imbecile. I gave meaning and purpose to their wasted, useless lives. They are historic now, they will be remembered and memorialized forever. Will you? What have you contributed to the advancement of humanity? I have given sight to the blind, I have given hands to the limbless, I have given hope to the hopeless, a longer healthier life to the living. I have brought humanity to the precipice of immortality. You, sir, you and your friends and family, you will someday need a new heart or a liver or eyes or limbs and then you will understand, you and everyone you know or may come to know, all will be beneficiaries of my work here. So spare me your righteous indignation. Given the intellect and opportunity, you would have done the same as I."

Garland stood speechless. Appalled. Sickened and disgusted by this man's rant. How could he possibly respond to such madness?

A vehicle appeared on the crest of the rise behind van der Veldt, then turned and drove toward them. Garland lowered his shotgun and waved to the vehicle. The pickup truck emerged from the dust a few seconds later.

It was a 1958 candy apple red Chevy Apache.

Garland tensed. He had expected Waddell. He reached into his pocket for more shells. He was out. His hand went to his holstered Glock and unsnapped the restraining strap, then he lifted the shotgun for show.

The Chevy stopped twenty feet away from them. The door opened and Enos Hostettler got out. Garland saw there was nothing in his hands.

"Stop right there, Enos."

I kinda knew when I saw you an' that lady you'd find him for me." Hostettler kept walking toward them. "Just wanna make sure it's him."

"That's close enough. Stop. Now. Right there."

Hostettler kept advancing.

Garland pumped the shotgun, but there was no sound of a cartridge chambering.

"It's empty, doc." And Hostettler reached behind his waist.

Garland dove at van der Veldt, not Hostettler, knocking the older man to the ground as he reached for his Glock. He tried to cover him, shield him, but he was a second too late. Hostettler's hand came up with a monster of a handgun – and fired. The first bullet caught van der Veldt in the neck. His severed artery sprayed blood in the air like a fire hose. Hostettler's second shot tore off the top of van der Veldt's head. Garland's hand was caught under van der Veldt's dead weight. He managed to pull it out from under, but, again, it was too late.

Hostettler had saved the third shot for himself. Without hesitation, he swallowed the .45's blistering hot barrel, squeezed the trigger and removed the entire back of his skull. Intentionally or not, he left intact the second set of eyes high on his forehead hidden beneath his shaggy hair.

76

Carter Haynes toured the camp, the delta and Hugger Wood by air. Garland and Andy Waddell flew with him, pointing out the geography and dispersion of the victims, the bridge over Sweetwater Creek where Sarah was found and the possible crossing point for Corinne. Haynes was appalled. Quiet. Pale. If he was faking his horror, Garland thought, he deserved fistfuls of Hollywood awards. Polly and Reilly Boone remained on the ground to treat as many of the victims as they could, but they found that The 610 stores and pharmacies were woefully lacking in antibiotics, bandages and painkillers. Alleviating suffering was not its mission.

Haynes had arrived mere hours after Garland had notified him of his discovery. He was originally going to stop in Little Rock to visit Sarah, but since Stuart was already there, he didn't want to interfere or intrude on their reunion, so he went directly to the camp. And although he ostensibly cooperated with local law enforcement, Haynes, bolstered by a phalanx of BIA agents, assumed complete control of the scene and the media. The victims of Christian van der Veldt's inhumanity were all found and returned to the camp. Haynes organized a massive triage, bringing in the finest civilian and military medical teams from the surrounding five state area.

Along the outer boundaries of the property were the cameras. The TV networks, cable news channels, print media, world press, magazine reporters, television and print tabloids, bloggers and gossip mongers all descended on Bull Shoals like flies to manure. It's called a media circus because of all the tents erected by news organizations and the attendant lunatic side shows drawn out of their slime holes by the glow of the cameras.

Michael Braverman

Throngs of religious zealots and charlatans set up camp on the wide flat pad outside the steel gate. Tall makeshift crosses and candles and prayer vigils erupted, but the "faithful" were unsure of what they were protesting against or praying for until a slick of televangelists and "family values" hucksters arrived to show them the way. Two images of Christ appeared: the first on the sun-shaded windshield of a fire truck, the second on the bark of a sycamore – candles and prayer groups immediately sprang up at both venues.

Of the thousands who flocked to the scene, not one individual and not one of the many organized groups voicing their enraged indignation – not one offered any substantive aid or comfort to the victims.

As evil as history may ultimately judge them, the deaths of Starke and van der Veldt hung oppressively heavy on Garland. Enos Hostettler's suicide was the bonus that pushed him to his ultimate despair. Filthy, and with the stench of van der Veldt's blood still on his clothes, he sat on the shady steps of the administration barracks and nursed a bottle of water.

"Neither one was your fault," Polly said.

"A better agent would have handled it differently," Garland said.

"Or be killed by them. Did you forget that part?"

"Calvin Burch. I should have been able to save him."

"How? You didn't know where he was or if he was even alive." Sitting next to him, Polly gently, affectionately rubbed his knee. "It's your exhaustion, Nathaniel, you need some rest."

"I know. You're right. But they're still dead."

Haynes approached and stood over them. From their sitting position he seemed fifty feet tall.

"You missed your press conference. Seems a might rude to be a no-show at your own tea party."

"You filled in beautifully, Carter."

"That's not the point, Nathaniel. What you've done here, son, is kick start our credibility and fine reputation despite our tarnished beginnings. Now you go put in some quality face time with the press and I assure you they'll give us a free pass on our stumble out the gate on Burning Tree."

Garland slowly stood up. Standing on the barrack's step, he was now an inch taller than Haynes. "Not going to happen, Carter," he said. "Not this time."

Despite Haynes' cajoling and full court press, Garland didn't cave.

After stopping at the Expedition to pick up their luggage, he and Polly left the camp in Phil Busbee's chopper and flew directly to Little Rock. The teams of medical personnel streaming in to treat van der Veldt's victims were more than qualified to handle the disaster and neither Garland's nor Polly's skills would be missed.

But Garland also had another reason that drove him to Little Rock – a need to reconnect with Stuart and Sarah Levine.

There was still some unfinished business.

77

Garland and Polly took a suite at the Hilton Little Rock Metro Center. After the events of the last several days, the pretense of separate rooms was no longer an issue – death is far more intimate than life can ever hope to be.

After showering, changing and nibbling some room service food, they took a five minute cab ride to University Hospital.

When they arrived at Sarah's bay, Stuart was sitting next to her bed holding her hand. He looked up, then placed Sarah's hand gently at her side and came out. He tried to speak, but choked up and instead he grabbed Garland and pulled him into a smothering bear hug, repeatedly slapping his back. Garland slapped back.

When he found his voice, Stuart said, "She's going to make it, Nate. It's going to be a long fucking recovery, but, goddamn, how the hell do I thank you?"

Garland dismissed even the mention of it with a head shake.

"I saw the news, man. That fuckhead van der Veldt's dead, and I say good riddance, he should rot in hell. You put him there, man, you guys put him there." He stopped as he read Garland's face. "What's wrong, man? You guys are fucking heroes, you should be bouncing off walls."

"Just tired. It's been crazy, you know."

"I know you too fucking well, Nate. Something else. Come on. What? Let me help you."

"Let's talk tomorrow."

"Okay. Tomorrow." Stuart impulsively bear hugged Garland again. "Sinha said I can bring her home. Not home home, I mean, you know, local hospital."

"We'll need an air ambulance. I'll make the arrangements."

"Thanks. I owe you, Nate. I owe you big time."

"Go, Stu, your wife needs you."

Polly and Garland walked back to the hotel. A block past the hospital, Polly tentatively took his hand and Garland clung to her all the way back to the hotel, through the lobby, up the elevator and into their suite. They ordered a nice '97 Saintsbury Carneros Pinot Noir and some cheese and fruit from room service and drank the wine in the bathroom as Polly changed the dressings on his burns.

They went to bed, but didn't make love. Instead, Polly melted into the contours of his body and draped her arm over his chest. It felt as natural as air to both of them. They slept for nine hours.

When they woke, Garland turned on the news. The talking heads on the cable news networks were chattering excitedly about the discovery of a "Dr. Frankenstein lab" in Arkansas. An undisclosed source, close to the investigation, had leaked information that The 610 was somehow administered through the office of the Secretary of the Department of Health and Human Services. Within days, and despite her vehement denials, the Secretary would lose the support of her patron benefactors in the White House and she would be forced to resign.

Carter Haynes was appointed interim Secretary.

"Well, what do you know," Garland said. "He did it. Carter got his goddamned cabinet post."

78

The air ambulance they hired was a state of the art critical care Lear-35A twin jet. Stuart would have nothing less. He flew home to Washington with Sarah, never once letting go of her hand.

Garland and Polly flew commercial. He could have prevailed on Carter Haynes for a company jet, but he didn't want to incur any more personal debt. The earliest flight they could get out of Little Rock was non-stop to Reagan. They took it.

As the jet circled the airport into its final approach, Polly gazed out the window at the Washington Monument in the distance. She was beginning to realize that she was leaving the surreal and reentering the reality of the life she had left days earlier. Garland had no trouble reading her face.

"You mentioned you have friends, family."

"Not here. Not close. My two best friends work at the University of Chicago, the other one's in Denver. My mother's still in San Francisco. But, no way would that work."

"What do you want to do with your husband?"

"What do you mean 'do'?"

"I mean — now that you've been away from him for a few days, had time to think, reflect…"

"Like do you mean reconcile with him?"

Garland shrugged.

"No. No way."

"I have some good friends who can help you. When you're ready. Lawyers. Security guys. Don't worry about a job or a home right now. You can stay with me."

"Thank you, but I couldn't possibly impose."

"Impose? Are you kidding? What's the opposite of impose?"

"Nathaniel, I don't know how long this, whatever the this is, I don't have a clue how long it will take."

"It'll take what it takes."

The plane slowed noticeably when the flaps were lowered and then it jolted when the wheels came down and locked into place.

"Nathaniel, I have to ask you this."

"What?"

"It didn't occur to me until just now."

"What?"

"Are you – how do I put this? What I mean is, are you seeing anyone?"

"Seeing? You mean as in dating? A relationship. Sleeping with – ah, I see, so you'd be in the guest room catching up on Tolstoy and I'd be in the bedroom schtupping Trixie? Is that what you're asking?"

"Not as crudely as that, but…okay, yes."

Garland grinned his killer grin. Polly actually blushed and turned her head away in the most charming embarrassment. Garland leaned into her.

"Polly, when we made love in Fayetteville, you were the first and only woman since Daisy." Without looking at him, Polly took his hand. And as Garland settled back into his seat, he wondered how many people sitting around him heard what he said.

349

They cabbed directly to the hospital from the airport. Stuart and Sarah had arrived hours earlier and she was already ensconced in one of the executive "at-home" suites. Garland consulted with her attending physician and reported to Stuart that she was getting the best care possible and, because of the drugs, would probably sleep for the next twelve to fourteen hours.

They stepped out into the corridor and Stuart said, "This Dr. Giamelli, she knows her stuff, right, knows what she's doing?"

"Giamelli's an incredible trauma doc, Stu, do what she says."

"Ok. You say." Stuart cocked his head. "You still got that look, Nate. What is it, man?"

"Just, you know, I've got some stuff on my mind, that's all. Maybe you can help me out. You want to take a walk?"

"Yeah, sure. Grab some coffee downstairs."

"I'll stay with her," Polly said, "go ahead."

Stuart ordered a double espresso, of course, Garland a decaf cappuccino. They found a small table outside on the patio, away from the noise and the chatter.

"I'm still having some trouble putting the whole Evinco Vixi business model together." Garland took a thoughtful sip of his coffee. "You know me and business."

"You're the worst, Nate, no question."

"Yeah, I know. You didn't see the camp."

"No. Course not."

"It was a huge, complex operation. Personnel, equipment, utilities, food, medical. And that's only Evinco Vixi's home base. Van der Veldt called it The 610."

"Why that?"

350

"610 - his initials in Roman numerals – CVDV. His ego required personal attachment and recognition. Guys like him always do. But The 610 was only a small part of it. Van der Veldt was hooked into at least eighteen major universities and listed biotech companies and other institutions. I mean, he even had his tentacles into the Beck Institute where Polly worked. Not only that, Evinco Vixi owns the Turner/Eterna mortuary chain, you know, sort of an in-house waste management service."

"Big fucking operation."

"Yeah. Huge. The Army was initially involved, but much earlier, working out of VA hospitals. That's where Starke and Ronald Polachek and probably more than a few others had their surgeries and gene therapies."

"Who the fuck is Ronald Polachek?" Stuart asked.

"Army sniper. The one who killed Carolyn Eccevarria and Rudolf Capiloff – the one who tried to kill me at Pinot, remember?"

"Yeah."

"So help me out here: how does an unlisted under-the-radar entity like Evinco Vixi get financed? Who pays the electric bill? Who pays the salaries, who pays for all the sophisticated equipment?"

"The news said you guys did. HHS."

"But there's no paper trail. No, my guess is HHS found a way to secretly finance the camp when they got it from the Army. But I think somehow van der Veldt was able to finance the research on his own. How would he be able to do it, that's what I can't figure out.

Stuart leaned back and drained his espresso. Garland could practically hear the wheels grind in his head.

"Well, I'm just venturing a guess here, but maybe van der Veldt put together a syndicate."

"What's that?"

"A group of outside investors. Venture capitalists."

"What would they be investing in?"

"The future, Nate, the future. I told you, biotech is huge."

"So, you're saying, if van der Veldt makes a breakthrough discovery, perfects a genetic therapy, grows eyes in a jar..."

"Jesus, Nate, a privately held company like Evinco Vixi, the patents would be worth a fucking fortune."

"And the investors and venture capitalists in the syndicate?"

"You kidding me, right? Billionaires. One significant patent? Through the roof."

"So is that why you did it? For the money?

"What the fuck are you talking about?"

"I'm talking about you setting up your own wife, for godsake, setting up Sarah."

"You're fucking out of your mind."

"I'm talking about you fingering Capiloff. What was Carolyn Eccevarria? Collateral damage? I'm talking about me. Me, Stu, me. The sniper on the roof at Pinot, what was that – a coincidence? Only two people knew we were meeting there for dinner. Two. Me and you. And I didn't tell a soul."

Stuart sprung up. "Man, you are out of your fucking skull."

"Sit down."

"Fuck you."

"Sit down."

Garland waited for Stuart to sit. His face was Christmas red, the veins in his neck were pulsating.

"Why are you doing this to me, Nate? You know you're talking out of your ass, you know..."

"We've got Starke's cell phone, Stu. We've got your calls to him. You're going to tell me that's another coincidence? You called him the night Sarah disappeared. You called him after I told you – *I told you* – we were going to bust Capiloff at the mortuary. I told you everything we were doing to find Sarah. Everything. That's why you wanted me – needed me – to stay with the investigation, so you'd know exactly where we were. You want to kill me, I own a badge, it's a risk I take, but Sarah? Sarah, Stu?"

The two men sat across from each other in silence. Too long a silence.

"It was you or her, Nate." Stuart finally said. "I didn't have a choice. They had my nuts in a grinder. I couldn't let anything happen to her."

"Me or Sarah? What the hell is that supposed to mean?"

"That asshole, Capiloff, he was a fucking loose cannon. He and this drunken Russian surgeon guy, they were cutting up the dead bodies and Capiloff was driving around in his fucking hearse selling off the parts. When Sarah started investigating Capiloff, the whole van der Veldt thing was going to unravel. Nate, I swear to God, swear on anything you want, they were just supposed to detain Sarah. That's what they promised me. Detain her. In a nice suburban house. They promised me nothing would happen to her, not a hair on her head. They'd move the operation out of Arkansas, take care of Capiloff and Sarah'd come home. That was it. I swear."

"Starke blackmailed you with Sarah's safety? Traded her life for information."

"They were going to kill her. I had to tell them where the investigation was going."

"That's why you needed me to stick with it."

353

"Yeah."

"You were in on Corinne Burch, too?"

"Who the fuck is Corinne Burch now?"

"The little girl Starke tried to kill at Fed-Med."

Stuart paused. "Yeah. Starke needed the security information. Checkpoints, surveillance cameras. I've been in there so many times with Sarah – look, no one were supposed to get hurt. No one."

"Except Capiloff, Corinne Burch. Me. And what about all those people in the camp? What the hell did you think was happening to them?"

"I didn't know a thing about them. I know as much about science and genetics as you know about business and finance. Nothing. Nada. Zip. Zero. So what're going to do? Arrest me?

"I don't know what I'm going to do." Garland got up so abruptly, he knocked his chair over. "Right now I'm so sick I…"

"Look, Sarah's back, she's going to recover. Starke is dead, van der Veldt's dead. It's over, Nate, it's all over. And we got the money."

"What money?"

"The money you fucking owed me."

Garland stared him blankly. He was lost. "I didn't know I owed you anything."

"Bullshit. You have any idea how much I lost when you fucking put Jensen-Dillard out of business? You went in there like some fucking caped crusader and I lost my fucking shirt. You cost me millions, man, millions, you're goddamned right you owe me."

"You are so warped. I should throw your ass in jail right now." Fight or flee. Garland had to get Stuart out of his sight.

354

"Yeah? Fucking arrest me? Yeah. Go ahead. Try it."

Garland turned and walked away. Stuart yelled after him.

"Try it, Nate. Where do you think your money comes from, asshole? All those checks I give you? You're an investor, man. Yeah. Think about. That's right. You own a huge fucking piece of Evinco Vixi – a huge piece. You're invested up to your neck. So go fucking arrest yourself."

79

Polly and Garland finished their dinner wine in the kitchen.

She took a sip and said, "I don't remember Waddell finding Starke's cell phone."

"He didn't."

Polly looked at him curiously. Garland shrugged it off.

"There was only one possible explanation for the sniper showing up at Pinot. Stuart. He was the only one who knew we were meeting there. Garland considered opening another bottle, decided against it. He was trying hard not to be lured into a depression. "I lost another friend. A good friend. And good friends are hard to come by."

"You've got a strange sense of loyalty. He tried to have you killed. In my experience, good friends don't usually do that. You are going to arrest him."

"When it's time, I'll turn it all over to the Fibbis."

"When it's time for what?"

"There had to be a much stronger hand at work than van der Veldt to allow an enterprise this sophisticated to flourish undetected for so long. Okay, at one point, DOD gives the Army its blessings to experiment with transgenic engineering. For whatever reason, the Army bails on the research and turns the whole thing over to HHS. Then van der Veldt somehow comes on board. Who's calling the shots on this one?"

Polly looked at his face: drawn, pale, sad, the ragged cut on his cheek healing, but still red with anger at the edges. And she could see the depression darkening his eyes, rising on a tide of despair.

"Let's go upstairs," she said.

Garland set the security alarms and they walked upstairs hand in hand. At the top of the stairs, Polly briefly hesitated and, as she expected, Garland gently nudged her into the master bedroom. They got undressed and brushed their teeth and got ready for bed as casually and natural as any Mr. and Mrs. America. She redressed his burns and applied an antibacterial ointment to his arm, his hand and his cheek.

"God, you're a mess," she said.

"You should see the other guy."

He forced the joke, but Polly could see thorough his pain. She folded back the bed coverings. "You didn't know anything about Stuart investing your money in Evinco Vixi. It was done without your knowledge."

"So you think my ignorance should excuse me? You think any of van der Veldt's victims will let me off the hook?"

They got into bed. Polly pulled the covers over them and laid her head on his chest. The fresh sheets had a mild, relaxing lemon scent.

"Nathaniel, you saved them. You liberated them."

"He gave me papers to sign all the time. I'm sure I signed a bunch of documents acknowledging the investments, never bothered reading them."

"He was your best friend. You trusted him, so you signed."

"So I signed. How dumb is that?"

Polly was not about to state the obvious. Instead she craned up and kissed him.

They made love. This time Garland drove and found Polly to be an exceptional passenger. They fell asleep with his arm around her damp back and her head on his chest, rising and falling with the rhythms of his troubled dreams.

The front doorbell chimed at 6:00 am.

Garland sat upright and fumbled for the clock. Polly pulled her covers up tighter and looked at him with a tinge of concern. He slid out of bed, groped around on the floor for his shorts, then padded to the security monitor mounted next to the bedroom door.

The door chimed again. Garland flipped on the monitor and pushed the intercom button. "Yeah," was all he said.

A sharp image appeared on the security monitor. Two men were on Garland's front stoop leaning in to the camera and intercom. Dressed in what appeared to be hunters' vests, the men looked totally out of place in the fashionable Georgetown landscape.

"Dr. Nathan Garlan'?"

"Close enough. What is it?"

"Hope we din't come by too early for ya, Dr. Garlan'. My name's Warren Clementine, this is my brother Darren."

"Hello, there," Darren felt obligated to say.

"Lookit, we come up from that mess goin' on down t'Camp Hugger. Like t'talk t'ya a quick spell. Have some information you'll be wantin'."

"How'd you find me?"

"Well, sir, thas' our job," the brothers "uh-huh'ed" together.

"Give me a minute."

Garland threw some sweats on, pressed a fresh clip into his Glock and carried it in plain sight at his side downstairs to open the door. He instructed Polly to lock the bedroom door after him.

He pressed the security code numbers on the pad next to the front door, flicked the safety off the Glock and opened the door for the Clementine brothers.

"What can I do for you, gentlemen?"

"Well, sir," Warren said, "first off, we don' think you'll be needin' that sidearm, but if it makes ya comfortable. We jus' come by to give ya this." Darren handed Garland a folded piece of paper.

Garland unfolded it and saw a neatly hand printed name and address.

"Russell Elston Louder?"

"Yessir. Mr. Louder operates a big rig out a Richmond, uh-huh," Darren said.

"He's the one what brought that young'un – Corinne Burch – up here from Bolton. Brought 'er up in his rig." Warren said.

Garland looked up from the note to the Clementine brothers' faces. "You gentlemen had your coffee yet?"

80

As Garland showered, Polly, wearing her chenille "guest" robe, sat on the bathtub and peppered him with questions.

"What do you know about these men? Why would you trust them?"

"I think 'trust' is pushing it. Look, they certainly knew the area, knew Starke, knew about Corinne and Sarah, the animals in the woods. All I'm saying is they seem pretty credible."

Garland stepped out of the shower, toweled off and told Polly what the Clementine brothers had told him: Warren and Darren tracked Sarah and Corinne through Hugger Wood. They saw where Sarah was pursued by what they suspected was a huge lizard of some kind, not having seen the python. It was Starke who insisted they find Corinne, since she was the one who got away. They easily tracked her to a truck stop in Bolton. That's where Louder picked her up. According to the Clementines, Louder and four other men raped and tortured Corinne in the back of the truck stop, after which she was forced into Louder's rig.

Garland started to shave. Polly took the razor from his hand and carefully maneuvered the blade around the cut on his cheek. As she scrutinized his wound, she said, "If they were a day behind Corinne, how did they know it was Louder who abducted her?"

"Apparently these guys are pretty well respected in their neck of the woods, and I mean that literally. They had no trouble getting that information from the locals."

"But he could have driven anywhere, taken any highway in any direction, how did they find his truck?"

"The locals knew Louder, knew his run, and knew where he operated from – this one's not tough."

"So as he got close to home he just abandoned her?"

"You saw her injuries. I think 'abandon' is being kind."

"You mean like he could have thrown her out of the truck?"

"After raping her again."

Garland was dressed now and Polly helped him untangle the straps of his nylon shoulder holster.

"I'm sorry. Call me cynical, but I don't like this. Out of the blue these two guys show up at your door with this incredible story, hand you the supposed perpetrator's name and address and you believe them, just like that, you don't question their motives?"

"They seemed like decent men. Not criminals. They made it clear to me how guilty they felt about their unwitting participation in Corinne's death."

"And you believed them."

"It doesn't matter what I believe. They knew Corinne was in Fairfax Hospital, they followed us to Fed-Med, these guys didn't have to admit any of that to me. They did. It was an act of conscience."

Garland slipped into his jacket and they walked downstairs.

"Pu," Garland said, using an affectionate diminutive of her Chinese name, "this one's a duck. If Louder's the guy, we've got gallons of his DNA from Corinne and we can put him away for the rest of his life. It's worth a look, isn't it?

Before pulling out of his garage he gave Polly all the alarm codes and told her to set the doors as soon as he left. He also said that after Richmond, he was planning to meet Grover Wheeler and

Eugene Kessler at the hospital to look in on Sarah. He would swing by the house and pick her up.

The drive from Georgetown to Richmond is a two hour shot straight down Interstate 95. When Garland finally shook loose of the Beltway traffic and was able to nudge the Jaguar up to cruising speed on the road, he called Fitch and Hollister. He filled them in on the amazing events of the last few days and then asked if they would run a quick check on Russell Elston Louder for him. If the truck and driver checked out, he would arrest Louder for probable cause and haul him into Hoover. He'd know within a few minutes if Louder was his man.

########

The house in Richmond was easy to find, tucked away in the woodsy end of a cul-de-sac. It was a low, well maintained unassuming bungalow in a neat and tidy working class neighborhood. Garland didn't need the address – Louder's tractor was parked across the street on the wide curve of the cul-de-sac. It was a massive black Kenworth W900 with Louder's name and DOT registration number prominently painted on the door in gold cursive.

Garland parked behind the tractor and hopped out of his car to inspect it. He slid his cell out of his pocket and called Fitch and Hollister again. Fitch answered – obviously on his cell and just as obviously in traffic.

"Dude, where are you?"

"Richmond," Garland said, "I'm at Louder's house. His truck's here. I'm just calling you with his DOT number."

"We've got it already. This guy looks good for that girl's abduction. We're on our way down."

"What? No. Hey, this one's mine – this one is personal."

"The collar is yours, doc, we're just heading down to watch your six."

"Don't worry, I'll have him plucked and ready for you."

Garland clicked off. He moved to the huge tractor and climbed up to the passenger side door. As he expected, it was locked. He tried, in vain, to get a look into the sleeper section behind the cab. That's where his evidence would be found. That's where the stains would be found that would put Louder away for the rest of his life.

Garland hopped down, folded his badge over his jacket pocket, pulled the safety strap on his Glock and headed to Louder's front door. The lawn was freshly mowed. Kids' toys littered the yard and driveway. Garland counted three tricycles. Did that mean he had three little kids?

######

The front door chime in Garland's home startled Polly. She was already showered and dressed and in the process of making the bed. As Garland had done earlier, she went to the intercom monitor and turned it on. The image on the screen made her lose her breath. The door chimed again.

"Come, luv, I know you're in there. Time we had a wee chat." Brendan Collier looked directly into the camera as he spoke.

Polly involuntarily stepped back from the security monitor. Brendan was smiling into the lens. Her finger hovered over the intercom button. She had to work up her nerve to press it.

"What do you want, Brendan?"

"You, of course, luv, what more could a man want?"

"We have nothing to discuss. Please, go away."

"To the contrary, my little Pu Li. We have much to discuss. For example, we can discuss the future health of your Dr. Garland."

"What's that supposed to mean?"

363

Michael Braverman

"Am I to stand out front here, hat in hand, and discuss this over a security camera? I was hoping you'd have the courtesy to invite me in. Well, I don't know if this will function properly or not, but let us give it a go, right?"

Collier held a smart phone up to the security camera lens. On the screen was a TV image – motion – houses – cars.

Polly could vaguely make out the image on the screen.

"Colin, you there?" Brendan said to the cell.

The image on the screen swished around and Colin MacDonough's face filled the screen. "That I am, Mr. Collier."

"Colin, would you mind showing my skeptical wife where you are."

The screen swished again and now the image on the screen was Garland, standing at Louder's front door. The door was open. Russell Louder was standing behind his screen door. The image was far too small and fuzzy for Polly to make out any details.

"Can you see it, luv?" Brendan said. "You remember Colin and Bobby, don't you now? Do you know where they are? Richmond, Virginia. What an astounding coincidence. And that tiny figure at the door of that dreadful little house? Why, none other than your fine doctor friend."

"What do you want, Brendan?" Polly felt her chest tighten.

"I told you. You. I believe we can take a fresh go at it, luv, don't you?"

"No...no, I – let me - I need time to..."

"Oh stop your stammering, twit, you know how much I despise that in you. I am offering you a trade, as they say here. Your doctor's life, for you and me. You can choose to stay locked in this fortress and young doctor Garland dies where he now stands or you come home with me this moment and he lives. He lives, he dies, your

364

decision. A very clear cut choice, would you not agree? You have one minute to decide."

"Brendan, please, I'm begging you, don't do something like this. Please, Brendan, you can't...you..."

"Fifty seconds, the clock is ticking. Bobby?"

"Waitin' on your signal, Mr. Collier."

"You hear that, pet? Forty-five seconds. Colin?"

"Aye. Ready, sir."

"No, wait, please, Brendan. Look. I'm turning off the alarms. You can come in, we can talk, we can..."

"Thirty seconds, luv."

"Alright, alright, I'm coming down, I'll go with you, whatever you want, please, call them off, please, Brendan."

Polly fumbled with the number key pad and somehow managed to disengage the alarm on her first try. She knew that pressing the so-called panic button on the alarm would serve no purpose. Neither the police nor the security company could prevent Brendan from uttering whatever their prearranged signal was. The red "armed" light on the alarm snapped to green.

"Good. Now that's my clever girl. I will give you thirty seconds to come out. Leave no note and do not try to call him. If the lads see him reach for his mobile, they have their instructions."

#######

It was 63-degrees in Richmond and Russell Elston Louder was sweating. The screen door separating him from Garland was locked and he wasn't about to open it. Louder was much smaller than Garland anticipated, almost frail looking.

"No, I'm sorry, I won't. Not unless you tell me what this is about. Officer."

365

"Please step outside with the keys to your truck, Mr. Louder."

"I want you to tell me what this is about. You have a warrant of some kind?"

"Do I need a warrant? Just to talk?"

"I watch TV. I know my rights. You just can't come barging into somebody's house and…"

"Mr. Louder, you open this door right now." Garland turned his head to look at the truck. "Forget it. I'm just going to open that truck my way. I'll try to keep the damage to a minimum. Then I'll have my lab tow it out of here."

Garland turned to walk away. The screen door snapped open and Louder came pouring out.

"No, wait, I'll do it, I'll open it."

Garland spun on his heel and caught Louder plunging forward. In a second he had Louder face down on the ground, his knee grinding into the rapist's back. As he was pulling Louder's arms behind his back to cuff him, Garland began to recite his rights.

"I swear, it wasn't me, you…I wasn't…no…you got the wrong…"

"Shut the fuck up." Garland didn't intend to scream. In a horrid flash, he saw this puny little man, this sadist, this coward tormenting the girl. Laughing with his buddies as they ripped Corinne apart. He pulled Louder to his feet, hoping he would dislocate the man's shoulder in the process. He didn't.

A stifled cry pulled Garland's attention to the screen door. Three children were huddled there, eyes like saucers, watching their father and the big man who was hurting him. Three children, the oldest maybe five or six.

"Who else is home?" Garland asked

"Nobody. I'm babysittin'.'"

Garland grabbed his elbow and pushed Louder in front of him down the walk.

#######

Polly came out the front door of Garland's home. She was shaking, but resolute. Brendan took her elbow and guided her to his waiting limo.

"Now there, that wasn't too difficult, was it, luv?"

"You're not going to hurt him. You promised. You're not."

"Of course not. We did a deal." He opened the limo door for her and then spoke into the Blackberry. "That does it, lads, pack up and come home." Turning back to Polly, he said, "There. A deal's a deal."

#######

The automatic rifle fire ripped into Louder first, serrating his midsection. He was shielding Garland and had to go down for Frick and Frack to get a clear shot at their target. Several more rounds passed through Louder's torso and one struck Garland on his side, drilling into his flesh. The bay windows of the house imploded. The children screamed. With all of his strength, Garland struggled to keep Louder upright, keep him in front. Another burst of fire caught Garland on his exposed shoulder. His arm went limp and he lost his grip on Louder. The dead man slid down Garland's body, trailing a wide swath of blood down his shirt. The next round caught Garland in the ribs, shattering two of them and blowing him backwards across the freshly mowed lawn. Another round caught him in the upper thigh. And another scorched into his gut. That's when the artery erupted.

That's when he knew he was dying.

81

Garland was in surgery for seven hours. He coded on the table, but not long enough to inflict brain damage.

Fitch and Hollister stood vigil at the doors of the surgical unit as they had for Carolyn Eccevarria. By the time Garland was wheeled into post-op, Grover Wheeler had already consulted with the trauma surgeon and came out to report to the two Fibbis.

"He's in a whole world of hurt," Grover Wheeler said. "Listed critical so the next twenty-four to forty-eight – I'm staying with him, I'll keep you guys in the loop." Grover took a breath. "I heard you had to kill the assassins."

"They went macho on us," Hollister said.

"They were in a goddamned cul-de-sac," Fitch said, "where the hell did they think they were going to go?"

"Why did they have to shoot him? I just can't understand it."

"Was just a domestic dispute, doc, pure and simple. These were the same two shitbags who tried to take him out at the mall on Little Patuxent."

"Have you located Dr. Collier yet?"

"We're working on it."

"No idea where she went, where she may be?"

"Like Gil said, we're working on it."

It took three days for Garland to stabilize. He was brought into surgery again to repair the blood supply to his right kidney. He would need more surgeries, when he was strong enough, to repair and graft new bones into place.

On the fifth day, Garland stablized enough to be transported back to Georgetown, to the same hospital in which Sarah Levine was recuperating. Grover rode in the back of the ambulance with him. His wife, Wendy, drove his Jaguar home.

Grover helped settle him into his room, checked Garland's vitals and sorted the tubes and I.V.'s that pumped life and massive doses of pain relief into him.

"Thanks," Garland said. It took an effort to speak.

"Save the chatter, pal. Hey, Sarah's up. They got her standing with a walker. She's going to come down and pay you a house call."

Garland flickered a smile, "Good." Then he said, "Polly?"

"Haven't seen her."

"Don't mess with me, Grove. Is she okay?"

He paused a long time. "Yeah. We think so."

"Think so?"

"Rest, man, we'll talk about it tomorrow."

"It is tomorrow. Where is she? Why didn't she come?"

Grover took a breath, didn't answer. He hoped the pain drip would make Garland lose his train of thought, as it often did.

"Grove? Where is she?"

"London. They located her in London. Nate, look, apparently she reconciled with her husband. She went back to England with him. Fitch pulled their diplomatic passport records."

Garland let the information filter in. "When did she go?"

"The day you were shot."

Garland closed his eyes. His breaths grew deeper. Grover thought he was asleep.

"I have to talk to Haynes." Garland said without opening his eyes.

"He's been in to see you a couple times already. You don't remember."

"No."

"Gene Kessler. Dunbarton, too. And so has Arleta Farleigh, can you believe that? Oh, Gene had an envelope for you. Said you'd know what it is. I left it in the drawer here."

"Yeah." And a few seconds later, Garland slipped back into a most welcoming, pain free drugged sleep.

######

At Garland's request, Carter Haynes came to visit him the day before he was scheduled to be discharged. They walked the length of the hall, then turned around and went back into Garland's room.

"I've been following your Senate committee confirmation hearings," Garland said. "You looked great on C-Span. Maybe TV's your true calling."

"No, son, my true calling is sittin' three chairs down from my President."

"Confirmation looks pretty good, huh?"

"That's what the nose-counters tell me."

Garland opened the drawer of the bedside cabinet and pulled out a large envelope, the envelope Kessler had delivered days earlier. He handed it to Haynes.

"Carter, I know how much that Cabinet position means to you. But you're going to have to withdraw your name for Secretary. Step away. Resign. And I promise you, it stops here. Right here. Right now."

Haynes suspected what was in the envelope, but didn't open it. "I've worked my ass off my entire career for this appointment. I have sucked hind tit for near on thirty years gettin' here."

"I know. Goddamit, you think this is something I want to do?

"You don't have to."

Garland felt weak and it reflected in his voice. "Please, Carter, don't make me do this. Withdraw and I burn the envelope. Nobody has to know."

"You wouldn't blow me out of the water now, Nathaniel, not when I'm this close. I know you too well, son, and we've raised too many glasses together. I'm asking you to flow with the conventional wisdom here. Christopher van der Veldt ran that house of horror with the Secretary's full knowledge and protection. It was her doin'. Nobody knew, includin' us. Run with that, boy, ever'one else is."

"I can't do it. It's killing me, but I can't do it. I'm begging you, walk away. I know why you did it. But you're a good man, a decent man. You just got caught up in this Washington thing. You saw a cabinet post with your name on it. It's seductive, so you made one bad choice and then you tried to undo it and it was too late."

"You are talking out of your ass."

"That's why you handed me this case isn't it? You gave it to Sarah first, which was really the right thing to do. I mean, she's smarter than both of us put together. But you didn't count on Stuart's greed. You couldn't possibly have imagined he would have put his own wife in such incredible jeopardy. So you gave it to me. You knew from our experience with Jensen-Dillard there was no way I'd give up. Ever. That's why you skipped over the other agents on call that night and sent me to Fairfax when Corinne Burch was brought there. That's why you insisted Jason Beck come in on the consult. You knew he was on van der Veldt's payroll – your payroll – you orchestrated the whole thing, kept steering me to The 610. When I took a wrong turn, you steered me back."

"Just tell me why the hell would I do something like that?"

"Deniability," Garland said. "You couldn't go to the media, you would have been eaten up and completely discredited by the Washington machine, drummed out of your job, disgraced, humiliated, for Christ's sake, Carter, you know the game. You needed Evinco Vixi to be uncovered – exposed – and having it uncovered by us, your own agency, was just icing on the cake."

"You've got a hell of a wild imagination, Nathaniel."

"No, Carter, I've got the money trail."

"In a pig's eye."

"I warned you the FBI was investigating you."

"They didn't find a damn thing."

"They did. Stuart Levine gave it all up. The syndicate. The offshore money. The Secretary funded millions of dollars of phantom offshore research projects. Your job was to wash that money into the syndicate. Her deniability is that she funded those offshore projects in good faith, had no idea you were stealing it to fund van der Veldt."

"You've got a tough sell there, boy. Why on God's green earth would she do that in the first place?"

"You know why. She was instructed to do it."

"By who?"

"I don't know who, yet, but it came from the White House. Publicly they took go slow position with new embryonic stem cell research. Privately they knew they we were falling years behind the rest of the world. They gave it to the Army first, but they couldn't get their shit together, so they gave it to HHS. That's why the Camp was ceded to us. And that was your deal with the Secretary. You get appointed Director of the BIA, she gets the research that was demanded of her. She's got the fox guarding the hen house. You just turned it around on her, that's all." Garland jutted his chin to the envelope. "It's all in there."

Haynes issued a touch of a smile, tossed the envelope on the bed and shook his head. He got up and moved to the door. "I wish you a speedy recovery, Nathaniel. We'll stay in touch."

"Carter. Please."

"The way it works in this life, son — you scrub my back, I scrub yours. I gave you Jensen-Dillard. You give me my post."

Haynes left and Garland already felt an overwhelming sense of loss. He waited, then said, "He's gone. Pull the stuff out."

A few seconds later, Fitch and Hollister appeared. They were obviously very close. They began removing the cameras and bugs planted in the room.

"You alright, doc?"

"That man saved my life. Put his head on the block for me."

"We know all about. Jensen-Dillard," Fitch said. "So what's in the envelope?"

"Enough. The end of Carter Haynes' career. The end of our friendship."

Hollister reached for the envelope on the bed and opened it.

"These look like security photos and log entries of Haynes and — and who's the woman?

"Patricia Preston, van de Veldt's lab assistant. She'll give him up for the right deal."

"These were taken at your place, right?"

"Con-Con 5. I had Kessler go down and get them for me."

"Help me out, here, it's all biomedical stuff."

"Con-Con 5 is where we store all the really bad, nasty bugs."

"CBW shit?" Fitch asked.

"Yeah. The worst of the worst. You can see by the date stamp, Haynes and Preston made a withdrawal from the germ vault: weapons grade francisella tularensis and amebiasis. DNA has a unique fingerprint. These germs were created by Christian van der Veldt, so he knew where they were stored. When they were scrambling to kill off all the test animals in the creek and in the woods, van der Veldt sent his assistant to Fed-Med and she and Haynes went down to the storage vault and got these particular microorganisms for him."

"So they were working together."

"No. I think they were both trying to save their own skins. Haynes couldn't turn him down because he knew van der Veldt could drop the dime on him."

"Look, doc, we know this really sucks, but you're doing the right thing here."

"Am I? This is D.C. There is no right thing."

"What if Haynes told you he'd withdraw his name? What would you have done with these logs and pics?"

Garland looked at them for a long beat, and shrugged. "You mind if I hang on to this stuff for a while?"

Fitch said, "We can't make our case without it."

"I know," Garland said.

Fitch looked to his partner. Hollister shrugged.

"Sure, doc," Hollister said, "no prob, hang on to it."

Epilogue

Velella velella is a hydroid – a unique jellyfish about two inches in size shaped like a flat ovalish disk. Velella velella are transparent, save for a bluish iridescent hue that on the ocean surface make them appear like an oil slick. Washed up on a beach, Velella velella look identical to discarded condoms. What distinguishes Velella velella from all other jellyfish is its sail – a tissue-thin but rigid inch-high wedge-shaped transparent fin set diagonally at a 45° angle across its flat body. Velella velella's common name is "By-the-wind Sailor" because the wind in its sail is its only means of propulsion and movement. As it's pushed along, skimming the ocean surface, its transparent tentacles grab what nutrients they can from the sea's endless buffet of microscopic organisms. It eats well. It survives. It multiplies. But the Velella velella is totally at the mercy of the ocean's fickle winds. With no breeze, it drifts aimlessly, without time or purpose or concern. Wherever the wind blows, so goes the Velella velella. No mind of its own. No will. No ambitions. And when the wind tires of its tiny blue-tinged sailors, it blows them ashore where they die quickly and mindlessly on lonely beaches.

And that was precisely how Nathaniel Garland felt as he floated along his life's current. He went through the motions. Barely. Took some comfort in Sarah's recovery, but his depression was profound and his sense of loss unrelenting.

Corinne and Calvin Burch were laid to rest next to Daisy Lyonne Bryant Garland and Margaret Gwendolyn Breezy Garland. As burials go, it was a very nice service. Non-religious, of course; if Garland was anything, he was not a hypocrite. He was, however, surprised that the cemetery workers used a loud diesel backhoe to lower the vault into the ground, but then he never really thought about it before. He had hired a string quartet and they played the selected Bach and Beatles pieces that he requested. At the conclusion, Garland tipped them all very generously.

Grover and Wendy Wheeler and Sarah Levine waited for him on the cemetery service road. Sarah was still trying to get used to her prosthetic leg and was relying heavily on her walker. Garland was still using a cane, but he looked at it philosophically – at least his cheek had healed.

At the road, Grover Wheeler said to Garland, "Carter was indicted today."

"I know."

"They say this is going all the way up to the White House."

"It will."

"Do you want to come with us, get something to eat?"

"No, thanks, Grove. I think I'll just go home."

#######

A few days later, Fitch and Hollister came to Garland's home with an interesting offer. With BIA in chaos, its director on trial and its future in doubt, their boss at Hoover would like Garland to move across town and join their little bureau. Same pay grade, slightly more bureaucracy. Garland was flattered and told them he'd consider it after what he hoped would be his final surgery.

In the ensuing weeks, during the final stages of his recovery, Garland learned something very interesting about himself. He liked being alone, but despised the loneliness.

He drank far too much wine.

He ate far too much takeout.

He desperately missed – yearned for – all those so precious to him who vanished from his life, as if plucked away, one by one, by the hand of a laughing fate.

On a night when he was feeling particularly peevish, while putting his leftover pasta in the refrigerator, Garland's eyes drifted to the little white insulin box at the back of the shelf. It had been months since he had last checked it and knew that it was well passed its expiration date. He plucked it off the shelf to read the embossed "use by" date on the bottom of the box. That's where he saw the writing and heard the rattle inside.

The writing was in Chinese. Of the words hastily scrawled on the bottom of the box, he only recognized one character: *wǒ ahnee* – I love you. He opened the box to see what was causing the rattle. Inside he found Polly's simple gold band encircling the neck of the glass insulin bottle.

Tomorrow Garland will have someone read the Chinese note to him. But for tonight he now knew she did not vanish without a word.

About the author

EMMY© Award nominee Michael Braverman is a noted television writer, producer and director who had been instrumental in guiding such primetime television series as *Chicago Hope, Beverly Hills 90210, Quincy,* and *Higher Ground.* He was also the creator and Executive Producer of the ABC television series, "Life Goes On". Michael was nominated twice for the prestigious Writers Guild of America award. He has taught writing and directing at the extensions of Columbia College of Chicago, UCLA, and Academy of Art University, San Francisco. He and his wife currently live in the San Francisco Bay area where he is completing his second novel.